Praise for Whatever Life Throws at You

"I loved this book so hard. It was perfect, fun, and swoony!"
—Katrina Tinnon of Bookish Things & More

"Julie Cross's writing is so addictive that you will be instantly hooked. I fell in love with Jason Brody!"
—Amanda Pedulla of Stuck in YA Books

"A delicious mix of baseball and romance, WHATEVER LIFE THROWS AT YOU is a book I was reluctant to put down. I absolutely loved it!"
—Jessica of Stuck in Books

"An irresistible story about family, first love, and following your heart."
—Jen of Jenuine Cupcakes

"Julie Cross once again delivers with this swoon-worthy, laugh-out-loud romance between a sexy rookie baseball player and the new coach's daughter."
—Yara Santos of Once Upon a Twilight

"WHATEVER LIFE THROWS AT YOU is a perfect story about growing up and the hardships you'll uncover no matter what profession you choose. It's filled with laughs, heartbreaks, tears, suspense, and plenty of romance."
—Jessica Reigle of Step Into Fiction

whatever LIFE throws AT YOU

JULIE CROSS

Entangled Publishing, LLC
2614 South Timberline Road
Suite 109
Fort Collins, CO 80525

Visit our website at www.entangledpublishing.com.

Edited by Liz Pelletier
Cover design by Heather Howland
Interior design by Jeremy Howland

Print ISBN 978-1-62266-404-7
Ebook ISBN 978-1-62266-299-9

Manufactured in the United States of America

First Edition October 2014

10 9 8 7 6 5

spring
TRAINING

chapter 1

I'm afraid that the second I allow Frank Steadman, the new general manager for the Kansas City Royals, to enter our small Arizona townhouse, my mother will be right on his heels. Whenever major league baseball makes its way back into Dad's life, Mom likes to make a surprise appearance, screwing with Dad's head all over again.

Last time she showed up was Christmas two months ago when an old teammate of Dad's was in town and wanted to have dinner. I don't know how she found out about it. She stayed for exactly forty-eight hours, and it took a month to get Dad out of his post-Mom funk.

I can't deal with that again.

I've got track starting next week, and someone has to take care of Grams. God knows we can't have another incident of her shuffling outside in her old lady underwear at noon telling all the neighbors that the air-conditioning is broken.

Frank Steadman is grinning at me from the other side of the screen door. I can't make myself return the smile. He's a very nice guy, don't get me wrong—one of the few baseball people who regard my dad with some amount of respect instead of pity. I've just had my guard up since two hours ago when Dad told me Frank was stopping by for dinner. The good thing is that two hours' notice probably isn't long enough for Mom to get here from whatever dream she's chasing at the moment.

"Little Annie Lucas," Frank says, pulling open the screen and letting himself in. "You're practically a lady now, aren't you? Bet your dad is scared shitless."

I hear the familiar uneven thud of Dad's steps, his metal non-leg banging against the wood floors. He can insist on wearing pants 24/7, but his part-robot status is still obvious. "You got that right. I think it's about time I locked her in her bedroom for five or so years."

"Jimmy" — Frank looks over my shoulder — "How are you?"

Frank Steadman and Mom are the only people I've ever heard call my dad Jimmy instead of Jim.

They give each other the one-armed man-friendly hug before Dad ushers him into our small kitchen where my lasagna is now ready to be removed from the oven.

"Congrats on the new job, Frank," I say, sliding on green oven mitts. "They must have been really desperate for wins if they're turning Yankees recruiters into general managers."

Both Dad and Frank laugh. "Yep," Frank says. "That, and I came cheap. Anything to get away from New York. Been there too long."

"How's spring training going?" I hear Dad ask after I've set dinner on the table and started down the hall to wake Grams.

"All right." Frank sighs. "Got a couple rookies with potential. It's the veterans that are driving me batshit crazy. We don't have enough room on the field for all their egos."

The rest of the dinner conversation switches to non-baseball topics, like Dad's barely above a minimum wage job at the glass factory in town, and then onto his non-leg.

"Everything good with the leg, Jimmy?"

I watch Dad's face carefully while holding a fork out for Grams. Her wrinkled hand drifts in front of me, blocking my view.

"Same as last time." Dad swallows a bite of pasta, chewing slowly. "I'll have another scan in two months."

My heart speeds up. I hate the scans. I'm a head case for three or four months before and then relieved as hell after for only a few months before it starts all over again. I miss being too young to keep track of these things. To not understand the term *oncologist*.

It isn't until an hour after Frank's arrival, while we're in the living room and I'm curled up on the love seat beside Grams reading to her from my physics textbook, that Frank finally gets to the point of this visit.

"I got a kid I want you to look at," he says to Dad.

"Huygens' principle states that each point on a wave front…" I read quietly to Grams while watching Frank remove his laptop from its case.

"A wave front," Grams mumbles beside me. "Isn't that what took out the *Titanic*, Ginny?"

I grind my teeth together. She can't help it. I know she can't. But I hate with a passion being called my mother's name. "That was an iceberg, Grams."

Frank must have caught what Grams said because he looks up from his laptop resting on the coffee table. "You look just like her, kid. It's amazing."

My expression probably represents anything but happiness, and Frank bows his head quickly. "Sorry."

Unlike the other baseball-related "old friends," I've always had the impression that Frank is aware of the real woman Dad is married to. Either he's observed enough, or Dad has confided in him.

He and Dad lean their heads together as they sit at the edge of the couch waiting for the video to download. I close my textbook and turn on the TV.

"Look Grams, *Wheel of Fortune*."

She turns her gaze to the television across the room. "Thanks, Ginny, sweetheart."

"Annie," I whisper in her ear before standing up. "I'm Annie."

I walk behind the couch and lean on my elbows. Dad reaches behind him and pats my hand, glancing over his shoulder for a split second. "It's just a phase."

I shrug, like it doesn't bother me, and nod toward Frank's laptop. There's a guy on the screen now, standing on the pitcher's mound. He's young. Really young. Sweat glistens on his forehead, dripping down from the edge of his dark hair. He's Italian or something that gives a person beautiful tan skin, dark hair, and chocolate brown eyes. Features much better suited for Arizona sun than my pale blue eyes and white-blond hair. I cart SPF 70 around like a diabetic with their insulin.

"He's hot," I say, winning an over-the-shoulder glare from Dad. "What's his name?"

"Why is that important?" Dad says, though he knows we have different priorities in this situation.

I shrug again, looking all innocent while ogling the computer pitcher.

"Jason Brody," Frank says. "He's only nineteen. Spent half a season with our farm team in Texas."

We all watch as Jason Brody winds up and throws his first

pitch. Even with the *click, click, click* of Pat Sajak's wheel spinning on the television, I hear the smack of the ball against the catcher's glove, loud and clear.

"Holy shit," I murmur, leaning over Dad and seeing his unreadable expression. Frank is silent while Dad watches Jason Brody throw about thirty more pitches. Finally the video ends.

"Well, what do you think?" Frank prompts.

Dad leans back against my arms, carefully evaluating his answer. That's how he is with everything—quiet and calculated. Frank's hinted on previous visits that Dad was quite the hotshot in his own pitching days. His BC days. Before Cancer. I was too young to remember any of that.

"The fastball's great, obviously," Dad says. "What's he throwing? Ninety-five, ninety-eight?" Frank nods. "Have you given him any coaching? There's potential for a decent slider with his arm, but not without some work, some good instruction."

Frank grins. "I was hoping you'd say that."

"It's jelly donut, goddammit!" Grams shouts at the TV.

Frank is temporarily distracted but returns his focus after Grams throws the newspaper at the television.

"She's got an arm, too." He chuckles and then tucks his laptop away. "Johnson, the Royals' new owner, isn't too keen on signing a nineteen-year-old rookie to close this season. Plus, Brody's got a few *indiscretions* on his record, for lack of a better word. No high school diploma, not much family contact that I know of... Could be a problem player, especially given his age."

Now Dad's eyebrows lift—even though he had no reaction while he watched the guy throw ninety-eight-mile-an-hour pitches.

"Right," I say. "'Cause a hot nineteen-year-old bad-boy pitcher won't help get some asses in the seats this season. Guess the owner is fine relying on giving out bobble-heads and seat cushions every night."

Frank laughs again but Dad just rolls his eyes. "Annie. Dishes. Now."

"Why? Because I'm a girl?" But I'm already walking away toward the kitchen. I let the water run at only half speed so I can eavesdrop.

"She's got a point," Frank says. "This kid will sell tickets. Maybe even help us win a few games."

"If it were my decision, I wouldn't give a damn about his record," Dad says. "He's got potential, he's hungry. I can see that from the footage. And really, what the hell do you have to lose? It's not like you're coming off a World Series win or anything."

"So if it were you in my position, you'd coach this kid? You'd sign him?" Frank asks.

"In a heartbeat," Dad says matter-of-factly. And Frank probably knows as well as I do that Dad doesn't bullshit anyone. Frank has known my dad since before I was born. He's the one who discovered Dad, who recruited him for the Yankees before he even finished college.

"Which is why I'm really here. I need a new pitching coach, Jimmy," Frank says. "And I think you're the best man for the job."

The soapy plate slips through my fingers and crashes onto the kitchen floor, snapping into a dozen pieces.

Dad is up so fast, his non-leg thudding into the floor until he's standing in the doorway of the kitchen. "You okay, Ann?"

"Leave the dishes and come in here, Annie," Frank calls from the living room. Dad and I walk back together, standing behind the couch, waiting to hear Frank's punch line. "What do you think about moving to Kansas City? What do you think about your daddy coaching big league ballplayers?"

The first thought to drift through the shock of Frank's proposal is *Mom*. She'd love this. She'd be all over this. All she's ever wanted was to be Dad's trophy wife and to dress me up like her personal Barbie doll, but accept none of the responsibility that comes with marriage and kids.

Dad responds before I get a chance to. "I can't pull Annie out of school in the middle of the semester. She's got track season coming up."

Frank lifts an eyebrow, shifting his gaze to me. "Another athlete in the family, huh? Can't say I'm surprised."

"She runs a mile in four fifty-five." Dad grins at me. "Her coach thinks she'll get offered a scholarship to Arizona State."

"Damn, kid, that's quite a time. But there're schools in Kansas City. Good schools with great track teams." He turns to Dad again. "The pay's not great. They'll probably let me start you out at one fifty a year."

I gape at Frank. "One hundred fifty thousand a year?"

Dad's eyes drop to the floor for a sec. "You don't have to do this, Frank. You don't owe me anything."

A silent exchange of words and memories seems to pass between the two of them. Things that happened years ago, most likely. Before I was old enough to understand.

"It's not that," Frank says firmly. "I want that Brody kid, and I need someone on my side. Someone to back me up and honestly, I need a real technician on my pitching staff, not a goddamn washed-up player who's been promised way too many perks. You know this stuff as well as anyone in the league, if not better than most of them."

Does he? I've never seen Dad coach baseball or even play. But we've watched hundreds of games together, and I've heard him mumbling things under his breath, shaking his head when he's not happy with a pitch. I've seen the intense way he studies players' movements, leaning forward on his elbows like he's willing the TV to move closer. It's definitely different from the typical shouting and cheering in the sports bar kind of behavior. He's the opposite of a rowdy, temperamental fan. And when I ask questions, he has very technical, logical answers. So maybe Frank is right?

Dad glances at Grams and shakes his head. "I can't leave Evelyn."

"Bring her," Frank booms, throwing his hands up in the air. "Bring whoever the hell you want to bring. We'll take care of everything for you."

"I don't know…" His voice trails off, his eyes meeting mine.

Suddenly I understand his resistance. It's crystal clear. He thinks Grams is the way to keep Mom coming around. He thinks if he keeps her mother close and takes care of her, that Mom will change her mind and come live with us again.

Fuck that. We're getting the hell out of here.

"Kansas City, that's like in Kansas, right?" I ask.

"Missouri," Frank and Dad both correct.

I clap my hands together. "I'm dying to go to Missouri. Let's do it, Dad."

His forehead wrinkles. "You want to leave your school, your friends, your boyfriend?"

You mean my boyfriend who just dumped me for Jesus and other boys? Yep, let's get the hell out of here. "Yeah, about that boyfriend… It's kinda over."

Dad looks relieved but tries to hide it. "Since when?"

I just shake my head. "Think about it, Dad. Grams can visit her sister in St. Louis. She'd love that."

I have no idea if she'd love it. Honestly, I could probably grab some random old lady in the supermarket and tell Grams it's her sister, and she'd believe me. But like me, Dad adores Grams, and he'd do just about anything if he thought she'd enjoy it.

"Why don't you take Grams for a drive, Ann?" Dad says.

I groan like I'm super annoyed with being shooed out of the grown-up conversation like a toddler before hauling Grams toward the front door. Hopefully, Frank has some persuasive skills.

"This would be a great opportunity for your daughter, Jimmy," I hear Frank say as we step outside.

"I'd be away all the time…on the road," Dad says, but I hear the tiny hint of concession in his voice.

"Where should we go, Grams?" I help her into the old beat-up Ford Taurus that Dad and I share, and then make my way toward the driver's side. "Ice cream?"

"Florence!" Grams shouts, punching her fist into the air.

I laugh and back out of our assigned parking space. "We went to Italy yesterday. How about Hawaii this time?"

"I love a good pig roast, Ginny."

The sigh escapes despite the fact that I don't blame Grams. "Do you remember Dad playing baseball?" I glance sideways at her. She's waving her hand over the air-conditioning vent, no hint of a response coming anytime soon. Her lucid moments have become very rare lately. I try a different tactic more out of boredom than actual curiosity. "Remember Jimmy playing ball, Mom?"

She looks directly at me. "Don't you worry about those women all over him, dear. He loves you."

"I know he does," I whisper.

"He can be an arrogant cad, but he's smitten with you. One of these days, that boy's gonna get pelted in the head with a fastball and the rest of the world will be standing over him, laughing their heads off. No one likes a showboat. You be sure and tell him that, Ginny."

I laugh under my breath. My dad is so not a showboat. What's the opposite of a showboat? Because that's the label I'd give him. He's worked the same dead end, low-paying job for five years, and I doubt a single one of those guys in the glass factory have any idea about Dad's baseball days. If it weren't for guys like Frank, I probably wouldn't have a clue either.

I get both me and Grams each a two-scoop hot fudge sundae and then drive around until she falls asleep. When I get home, Dad comes outside and helps me get Grams into the house. Frank is gone and the kitchen is spotless.

"So…?" I say after he's closed Grams' bedroom door. "Are we moving to Kansas?"

"Missouri," he corrects me again.

"So we're going?" I fold my arms across my chest, tapping my foot against the wood floors in the hallway.

Dad rubs his hand over his face, looking completely tormented. "I don't know, Annie."

"Why not?" He's walked away, so I follow behind him. "This is a huge opportunity for you, Dad."

"Your mom—" he starts to say, but I cut him off.

"Don't even go there," I groan. "Seriously, Dad? What the fuck?"

"We're still married." He's using the firm Dad voice that only comes out when I've really pissed him off. "I can't just take her mother across the country."

"Yeah, you're such an asshole." I step in front of him, not backing down. "How dare you take care of your negligent, flighty wife's mother and keep the state of Arizona from locking her up in an old people's home. I can't even believe people like you are allowed to exist in society."

He cracks a smile and leans forward, planting a kiss on the top of my head. "I love you, honey."

"We're going," I say, adopting his firm tone. "Or I'll start partying all the time and become one of those girls who makes sex tapes and posts them on the internet."

He flinches even though he knows I'm kidding. He hates that I'm not a little girl anymore. But then I hear that sigh again. The one that means he's giving in. I bite my lip to keep from grinning.

"Okay." He releases a breath. "I'll take the job."

"And you won't tell Mom where we went? Please, Dad? I need you to promise." I didn't even realize how much I wanted *this* part more than anything. It would be worth the new city, the new school, the new everything if I could just know for sure she wouldn't come knocking on the door, ready to break him into pieces all over again.

Dad's eyes meet mine. He's still handsome, even at thirty-six years old. He could have someone else. Someone who won't leave him or fuck with his head. Someone who will love how he obsesses over any guy who calls or texts me, and the way he sits with Grams for hours, telling her stories that might trigger her memories even knowing she's only going to get worse, not better. Maybe that's what I can do in Kansas. *No, Missouri.* Whatever. I can find Dad a new woman. Get him some of those baseball pants and a blue Royals hat and the ladies won't be able to resist.

There's pain in his eyes, but he still gives me the answer I want—and Dad's word is the most reliable thing I've ever known. "All right, Ann, I won't try to contact her…*for now.*"

I'll take it. It's a step in the right direction.

"Do you think Frank's really going to sign that Brody guy?" I ask. "He seems pretty young."

"The Royals have an injured pitcher, so if Brody does well during spring training games," Dad explains, "then we'll probably try him out Opening Day, give him a two-way contract so he's not a big leaguer yet. We can use him once or twice, and then send him back to Triple-A."

"See? You're already saying, 'we' like you're part of the family," I point out.

Dad rolls his eyes, but I can see the grin he's trying to hide.

preseason

chapter 2

Annie Lucas: *Goodbye Arizona, you have been wonderful to me. Facebook, you are my only friend now*
20 hours ago, near Gallup, NM

Annie Lucas: *States I've visited in the last 2 days — Arizona (hot, dry, familiar), New Mexico (why not call it Arizona? What's the point of separation?), Texas (slept through it), Oklahoma (hot cowboys at rest stops that hold doors open and call me ma'am, MORE PLEASE!), Kansas (Toto, we're totally not in Arizona anymore)*
6 hours ago, near Wichita, KS

Annie Lucas: *Does anyone else find it ironic that I have to leave Kansas to get to Kansas City? Why do humans insist on making life more complicated than it needs to be?*
2 hours ago, near Topeka, KS

Annie Lucas: *One question — who is Lee and what is he summiting?*
1 hour ago, near Kansas City, MO

Annie Lucas: *Apparently Kansas City is the barbecue capital of the world. Wtf? Is it also land of the frozen*

zombie people? How do they barbecue in this weather?
30 minutes ago, near Topeka, Kansas

'm freezing my ass off.

Dad's standing on the pitcher's mound, mesmerized by the empty stadium. "Get over here, Annie!"

I jog over to him and stare at home plate. "Looks great. Now can we please go look at your office? Frank's ready to give us the inside tour."

"How many people get to say they've seen home plate from the pitcher's mound?"

"Thousands." I tug his arm. My hands are numb and my nose is running. "Isn't March supposed to be springtime? Where's the spring?"

"All right, all right, let's go inside." Dad laughs and throws an arm around my shoulders. "I never knew you were such a cold-weather wimp."

I give him a shove. "Whose fault is that? You've never dragged me anywhere cold before. It's dangerous. We could die out here."

He laughs even harder, and we finally catch up to Frank, who is standing in the dugout with Grams. I hadn't been as impressed with the stadium as Dad. I'd been to the Diamondbacks' stadium in Arizona, and the Rangers' stadium in Texas, but walking from the dugout to the locker room, I've completely changed my attitude.

Seeing the inside of the athletic training facility, the place where they sit before a game, the place where they get good news and bad news, is so cool. The locker room is huge and the office Dad's now going to occupy is off to the right of the players' lockers. There's a couch across from Dad's desk where Grams and I take a seat. Grams walked a lot already today and it looks like she's about to nod off any second. I reluctantly remove my coat even though I'm wearing appropriate cold weather clothing—skinny jeans, furry boots, and a sweater. It doesn't seem warm enough, even inside.

"Annie and Evelyn can wait here while I introduce you to the rest of the coaching staff," Frank tells Dad.

"Ann?" Dad asks.

I give him a nod even though I'm starving and tired from the long drive and also pretty curious about this house we're supposed to live in that I still haven't seen yet. It's not like I could really say no and demand a snack and a nap. I'm seventeen, not five.

"What do you think, Grams?" I say after the thud of Dad's non-leg has stopped and he and Frank are in some conference room.

"Holiday Inn is so much better than that Marriott place," Grams says. "I saw bugs in the shower."

"We're staying in our new house tonight, Grammsie."

"Well, good." She leans her head back against the couch. "Wake me up when we get there."

I roll my eyes. "Sure thing." There's a stack of spiral notebooks on the desk, and all of them have the blue and white Kansas City logo in the center. I pick one up, grab a pen, and start doodling until fifteen minutes pass on the clock behind Dad's desk. My stomach growls loudly.

Grams is snoring now, so I decide to go in search of food—there must be a vending machine around here somewhere. I reach the doorway of Dad's office and stop.

Jason Brody and all his dark hair and dark eyes and muscles is standing in front of a locker whistling to himself.

Wearing only a towel.

I can't decide if I should dive back into the office or make him aware of my presence. I doubt Dad would have left me in this office if he'd anticipated naked baseball players roaming around.

A blaring rock song from his phone sends my heart all the way up to my throat. I'm still frozen in the doorway when Jason Brody answers his cell.

"Hey, how's it going?" he says, then pauses to listen to the person on the other end. "Yeah, you're assuming I actually know where anything is in this town." Another pause. "Live music, beer, and easy women? I think I can handle that."

I roll my eyes in disgust. What a pig.

"Um, yeah, I've got the ID thing covered. No worries."

Now I really don't want to be caught like a deer in headlights when he drops that towel and puts on his clothes. And if Jason Brody finds out I was lurking in the doorway like a high school girl trying to get a glimpse of a naked major league baseball player, I will literally die of humiliation.

He'd probably get off on that, too, and I'd rather not give him that option. Which leaves me only one choice—dive back into the office and hide out until he's gone. I turn partway around and the notebook slips from my hand, the metal rings on the side clanking against the floor. My arm crosses the doorway barrier when I reach down to snatch up the notebook.

He jumps a mile when he spots me. "Jesus!"

Okay, now I've really only got one choice. I stride out into the open, preparing to introduce myself. My gaze drifts down to the towel dangerously close to slipping off his waist.

He grabs the ends, holding it together with one hand. "Sorry, I thought I was alone."

My heart takes off in a sprint. I can't do it. I can't just say I'm Annie, a seventeen-year-old high school girl. "Um yeah...

I'm…" He stares at me waiting for my big reveal. The notebook and pen in my hand catch my attention, giving me an idea. I swallow back the fear and lie. "I'm interviewing players for an article. You're Jason Brody, right?"

He eyes me skeptically. "What kind of article?"

"It's for *Sports Illustrated*," I say without hesitation and then quickly realize that I don't look nearly old enough to be a real reporter for a huge publication. "I'm an intern," I add.

The skepticism falls from his face and he looks nervous, which gives me a boost of confidence. I walk closer and pull out the chair in front of the locker beside his, propping my feet up on the bench across from me. "Frank Steadman said you'd be willing to answer a few questions."

His mouth falls open, and he looks down at his towel and then back at me. Water drips from his hair and off his dark shoulders. "Um…okay," he says. "Mind if I get dressed first?"

I wave off his concerns, my face heating up, blowing my confident cover. But him getting dressed might allow enough time for Dad to return, and I'd rather not have to deal with that. I duck my head down, letting my hair hide my cheeks and flip open the first page of the notebook. "This will just take a minute… So, you're nineteen? And you're from Texas?"

"Chicago," he corrects.

I have no idea where he was from but figure it sounded better if I pretended to know. I write down this information and then search my brain for some more questions. "Does the wind in Chicago affect your curveball? Do you throw into it or against it?"

He gives me a funny look. "I…well…I just throw toward home plate."

My face gets even hotter. "Right, kidding. What's your favorite color?"

"Orange."

I take my time writing *orange* in really big loopy cursive while I think of my next question. "What are your opinions on sushi?"

His forehead wrinkles like I've just asked him to publicly declare a political party. "Raw fish and seaweed? I think it's best eaten while stranded on a desert island with no other options."

"Very diplomatic." I scribble down his answer. "How many strikes have you thrown in your career?"

"Don't know," he says. "Do people actually count that stuff? Before the majors?"

"Some of them do," I say, though I have no idea. "If you could be any magical creature in the Harry Potter series, which would you choose?"

"You said this is for *Sports Illustrated*, right?"

"Yeees, But it's the…kids' edition."

"Oh, right." He scratches the back of his head. "I guess maybe one of those elves."

"A house elf? Seriously? They're slaves." I shake my head. "Why would you want to be an enslaved elf? They can't even wear clothes."

He grips his towel tighter and releases a frustrated breath. "Fine, I'll choose an owl. That's what I'd want to be."

I snort back a laugh and drop my eyes to the page again.

"What? What the hell's wrong with being an owl? They're smart, they know geography and shit like that."

"Owls in real life are actually pretty stupid. But no big deal, I'll just relay that message on to the children of America. Jason Brody, temporary Royals pitcher, wants to be an owl when he grows up because *they know geography and shit like that*."

Okay, I'm getting way too into this fake reporter role.

"Who says this is temporary?" he snaps.

"Your two-way contract." Isn't that how Dad explained it? He plays a few games then goes back to Triple-A, all without signing a real major league contract.

He yanks a pair of jeans from his locker and then grabs a bundled up orange T-shirt. "Well, I plan on kicking some ass on Opening Day and making this a permanent gig."

"I think you need a reality check," I say. "One game isn't going to be enough—"

"Annie, what the hell are you doing?"

I leap off the bench and turn around to face Dad and Frank standing about five feet from me. "Introducing myself to your new pitcher."

"Brody, what are you doing here, son?" Frank asks. "We're off today."

"Just getting in some cardio and weights." His gaze darts from me to Dad to Frank. "I was just finishing up this interview for *Sports Illustrated*. The kids' edition."

"Well, we won't keep you from getting your clothes back on, then," Frank says, like he's trying not to laugh. "And just for future reference, all interviews will go through the team's publicity department so no one will be wandering in here, surprising you. Savannah will meet with you tomorrow to discuss publicity."

Dad moves forward and extends a hand to Jason Brody. "Jim Lucas, nice to meet you, son. I've seen your spring training videos. You've got some real talent. I'm looking forward to working with you."

Brody shakes Dad's hand, his eyes still on me.

"And this is my daughter Annie," Dad adds.

Brody glares at me. "Let me guess—you don't work for *Sports Illustrated*?"

I turn quickly and head toward the office again. "I'm starving. Can we get dinner?"

Franks laughs and Dad groans like I've embarrassed him. He's probably regretting leaving me alone in the first place.

By the time we're ready to leave the stadium, Jason Brody is fully dressed, winter jacket zipped up, and following us out of the building.

He grabs my arm and holds me back, allowing some distance to form between us and Dad, Grams, and Frank. "Well played, Annie Lucas."

I shrug and flash him a smile. "Thanks."

"You're gonna write that interview for me," he says, winking at me with a knowing smile.

I keep my eyes forward. "I'm not writing anything for you."

"Fine, then I'll just have to explain to your dad some of the concerns I have for his daughter's well-being," he says.

I grab his coat sleeve. "What concerns?"

His eyes dance with amusement. "Touching naked guys inappropriately…"

"I did not touch you!" I let out a breath and lower my voice. "Besides, he's not going to believe you."

"Maybe not," he says, all casual. "But I do think your lying problem and your lack of respect for other people's privacy could be masking a bigger psychological issue. You might find therapy helpful."

"Whatever." I fold my arms across my chest and continue walking. "Don't you have beer and women waiting for you? Better hurry so you're not late."

Of course Dad wouldn't really send me to therapy, but my

behavior was a bit extreme and Brody looked really uncomfortable when they walked in. Better not take any chances.

"Can't wait to read my interview," he says before rounding the corner and heading in a different direction.

I stand there for a minute scowling at his back and then jog to catch up with Dad, wondering what Brody would say next time I saw him without that interview.

It's hard to complain about the weather after seeing the large four bedroom ranch home Frank rented for us. My room even has a bathroom. I've been sharing one with Dad for as long as I can remember. Dad's also got a brand-new silver SUV, which gives me full driving privileges to our very old, yet still running family car.

So yeah, I'm liking Kansas City so far. Even after the Jason Brody incident.

The movers have already arrived with our stuff and piled the boxes in various rooms. The house is furnished, so we only brought clothes and other non-furniture items. All I want to do is flop on my new queen-sized bed and play around on my laptop, but Frank is still here standing in the living room with us, waiting for some woman named Savannah to arrive.

I'm trying to figure out how to work the TV for Grams when a twenty-something red-headed woman walks through the front door carrying clothes on hangers with dry cleaner plastic in one arm and a stack of folders in the other arm. She's wearing heels, a black pencil skirt, and a matching black blazer. She looks the opposite of a baseball-associated person.

"Savannah, you're under there somewhere, aren't you?" Frank

jokes, reaching out to take the dry cleaning order from her arms, setting the clothes across the back of the couch.

The woman reaches out to shake Dad's hand. We've both been doing a lot of hand shaking today. "Nice to finally meet you in person after all the emailing over the last month."

"I'm gonna take off. Call me if you need anything," Frank says, heading toward the door. He turns to me before leaving. "And stay out of trouble, kid, all right? Jason Brody's going to turn interview shy if you spend any more time around him."

Somehow I doubt I'll ever be able to fool him again.

I stand up perfectly straight and give Frank a salute. "Yes, sir."

Savannah immediately launches into a major info dumping session with Dad, pulling out various papers from folders for him to sign. She's going through the hours Grams' babysitter will be here to keep an eye on her when I finally get a good look at the clothes across the back of the couch.

I pick up the first hanger and hold it out. "Dad, have you taken up bagpipes as a hobby?"

Savannah laughs. "Those are your school uniforms."

"Uniforms?"

Savannah looks from Dad to me. "For St. Teresa's Academy." It's obvious to Savannah that Dad has made some plans without informing me. She looks worried. "Oh boy…your dad said to find the best track program in the area and this school has the best girls' track-and-field coach in the state. They won last year."

I lift the hanger up to get a good look at the red plaid skirt. "Well, this is different. That's for sure. Do they care that I'm not Catholic?"

"Not really," Savannah says. "But I can give you a crash course if you'd like?"

I let out a breath. I don't want Dad to know I'm nervous since I've conveyed nothing but confidence regarding this whole move north. That's probably why I subconsciously avoided drilling him with questions about school and the house before arriving in Kansas. No, Missouri. "Yeah, we should do that."

Savannah helps me carry all the clothes to my room. I sit on the bed and watch her peel off the plastic covers and place the five skirts, seven white polo shirts, and two V-neck sweaters into the closet. "The school's about twenty minutes from here. It's right downtown near the stadium."

"I don't think I've ever worn a skirt to school in my entire life," I admit.

She gives me a sympathetic smile. "The good thing about uniforms is that you'll look like everyone else."

"The boys wear skirts, too?"

She stops in the middle of smoothing pleats. "No boys."

I stare incredulously at her. "An all-girls school?"

"Is that bad?"

"I don't know." We've moved a lot and with taking care of Grams, outside of the ex-boyfriend, I haven't really had many close friends that are girls. My ex's friends were my friends, which means by default, we all sort of broke up when he and I split. "Girls can be a pain in the ass sometimes but then again, much of that revolves around boys and fighting over boys so maybe…" I look at Savannah. "What do you think?"

She takes a seat in the desk chair. "I went to visit last week and it seemed very relaxed, no one really wore much makeup, lots of ponytails and headbands. I think the lack of boys allows everyone to sleep in a little later in the morning."

I shrug. "Guess I can live with that." I wouldn't say I ever really primped for boys at school but I'm sure even I was influenced by their presence at least a little. "So the track team is good? Have they already started practices?"

Savannah looks relieved that I'm not throwing a teenage tantrum and goes back to hanging uniforms. "Yes, they have, but the coach is really looking forward to having you. Your dad emailed your times and events from last year to her. Also, I haven't picked any courses for you or anything. You'll meet with the counselor tomorrow morning and take care of all that."

I'm not used to having people hang up clothes for me. I've been doing mine, Dad's, and Grams' laundry for years. Sitting and watching her work for me is uncomfortable so I grab a box from the floor, toss it onto the bed, and start removing items. "Thanks for…you know…visiting the school and all that. I'm sure the last thing you wanted to have to deal with is registering someone's kid for high school."

"I don't mind at all," she says. "I've wanted to visit St. Teresa's for a while now. I'd love for my daughter to go there."

I drop my running shoes onto the bed. "You have a daughter?"

"Lily." She gives me a sheepish grin. "She's only six, but I can't help planning ahead. Not sure if I'll be able to afford the tuition at St. Teresa's though. We'll see."

"Is it expensive?" Can Dad afford it? I'd been too caught up in the Catholic, uniform, all-girls school details so private school equals expensive hadn't crossed my mind.

"It's five times more money than the neighborhood Catholic elementary school around here," she admits. "That's where Lily goes now. She's a first grader."

"You live in this neighborhood?" I'm surprised because it's kind of fancy and she just expressed concern with school tuition.

"We live in the apartment complex a few blocks away." She's

finished hanging all my school clothes, but instead of leaving, she picks up a box of clothes from home and begins unpacking that next. "Jake London's daughter goes to St. Teresa's, too. They live right down the street."

I'm carrying a stack of books from the bed to the shelf beside the dresser. "Jake London?"

"First baseman," she says.

"Oh, right." I shake my head. I tend to reference players by their position rather than names. Probably because I've never really had to address one personally. Until Jason Brody. Ugh. "What exactly is your job?" I ask Savannah.

"For your dad, I'll handle scheduling, interviews, and travel arrangements, and I work with two of the other coaches as well. I'm also the publicity liaison for the all the Royals pitchers. I go between the press and the agents and get everything scheduled and keep everyone happy." She quickly steers the conversation back to me. "Sounds like you got to meet Jason Brody today?"

I laugh. "I guess you could call it that."

Savannah turns around to face me. "Do tell?"

"Yes, Annie, do tell." I look up and see Dad leaning on the doorframe. "What exactly was your goal earlier? The fake interview and all?"

I walk over to the doorway and shove him back. "Sorry, Dad, this is girl talk. I gotta practice, right? Since I'm being sent to an all-girls school."

He has the decency to look embarrassed for keeping this important detail from me. "Best track program in the state, Ann."

"Oh, I'm sure that was your main focus." I succeed in shoving him the rest of the way out of the room and close and lock the door before turning back to Savannah. "Okay, so, Jason Brody…killer abs, let me tell you. He wears a towel very well."

She covers her face with her hands, laughing. "Your dad's going to ban you from the locker room now, isn't he?"

"Oh yeah, no doubt." I flop onto the bed again, already bored with unpacking. "The track is like inside and heated, right? It's gotta be against the law to make kids run in the cold."

She shakes her head. "I'm pretty sure they practice outside."

I groan. "Great."

I may have survived my first Jason Brody encounter, but it's quite possible I'll die trying to run outside tomorrow.

RIP, Annie Lucas. The girl who may have been the fastest runner in the state. Now we'll never know…

chapter 3

Annie Lucas: *Can someone PLEASE tell me why Jesus is hanging on the cross? I just need the condensed SparkNotes version, like in the next 5 minutes. Oh! And what's up with the Holy Ghost thing? Google isn't explaining it very well.*
4 hours ago

Annie Lucas: *Disregard my earlier question. Apparently I just need to say, "Holy Ghost." I don't need to know what it is.*
20 minutes ago

"I've got two classes with you and lunch," Lenny London tells me after we've been introduced by the school counselor and I've shared my schedule with her. Only minutes of observation, and it's obvious that Lenny has the air of being the daughter of a major league baseball player. She doesn't seem spoiled or anything, just important. Her tall, dark-skinned, thin, and gorgeous figure stands out among the crowd of red plaid. She makes the uniform skirt look trendy, and somehow the polo enhances her boob size. She's got at least two cups on my almost-*Bs* that seem to look more *A-* in this school-issued top. "What do you think so far?"

"Well, you don't have boys," I say. "And I can't decide if that's good or bad."

"Honestly, I'm all about the boys, but not at school," Lenny says. "I like them at the weekend parties, but here it's nice to just focus on schoolwork and clubs."

"I went to public school in Arizona, so this is a bit different."

She leads me down a hallway toward the cafeteria. "Well, I've never been to public school, so I can't compare. And there's always some catty fighting going on between various girls, but everyone here is at least capable of being nice even if they don't choose to do so all the time."

"Good to know." I tug at my skirt, trying to keep the waistband from twisting.

"And next year, we'll be seniors together, and that's even more fun. Junior year is rough."

"No kidding," I say. "I've only been to three classes so far, and I can already tell my school was way behind St. Teresa's."

"Yeah, don't let the Catholic label fool you." Lenny opens the door to the cafeteria. "They are hard-core about academics here. That's why there're tons of kids that aren't religious."

"Me included." I'm relieved not to be the only one. I freaked out a little in homeroom when everyone started reciting prayers from memory. "So do you, like, go to all the games and stuff? The Royals' games, I mean."

She shrugs, heading toward the hot-lunch line. "Mostly. If I feel like it. Sometimes we have to do these lame family promos for people who want pictures of wealthy athletes who go to church and spend time at home. My brother Carl and I...we're apparently perfect teen role models—well, Carl is twenty-one so not a teen anymore." She rolls her eyes. "It's all bullshit, but whatever. It's paying for my college and funding my parties and nightlife." Her face lights up. "Speaking of nightlife, I've appointed myself head of the Annie Lucas welcoming committee, and we are totally going out tonight. And you're totally coming to my party next weekend. You should be in boy withdrawal by then."

"Cool." Will I be in boy withdrawal? I'm not really sure.

"And I bet you won't have to be subjected to the cheesy family promos since your dad's not the only pitching coach." She spins to face me. "Oh! Guess who is staying in our guesthouse?"

I'm still trying to process the fact that Dad's not the only pitching coach, so it takes me a few seconds to respond to Lenny. "Who?"

"Jason Brody," she says. "He's the new—"

"I know who he is." I could totally do some bragging about seeing the guy in a towel, but I decide spilling this to Savannah was probably enough. I'd hate for Jason Brody to think I spent all my time daydreaming about him in a towel. "My dad's talked about him a lot."

"He's going to be hanging out in my guesthouse at least until Opening Day, probably overflowing the place with easy women," she says. "Then I imagine he'll get shipped back to Triple-A. I don't know enough about it to guess, but he's so young, right?"

I just shrug because the only thing I know is that both Dad and Frank want Jason Brody on the Royals' roster, but that probably means dumping another player who's been on the team for years. Either the other guy's injury needs to get worse, or Brody needs to do something amazing in that first game. I glance around the cafeteria. "So who's my track competition?"

"What's your event?" Lenny asks.

"The mile."

She scans the room and points to a tall, dark-haired girl. "Jackie Stonington. She's a senior. Placed at state in your event the last two years."

I placed at state last year, too, but that was Arizona, and Missouri might be more competitive. I already know this team is more competitive than my old school. "Are you on the team, too?"

"Oh no," she says right away. "I don't do sports at all. That would please my dad and I just can't have that, can I?"

Since I don't have a response to that obviously rhetorical question, I allow my brain to catch up on this conversation. "Wait...Did you say something about going out tonight?"

Lenny grins. "Yep. I'll come by your house around eight. We'll be back by eleven. School night and all that. There's this band playing at a bar downtown, and I'm obsessed with the lead singer. And the bouncer is obsessed with me, so we won't have any trouble getting in."

Trouble getting in?

Lenny's gaze moves over me. "Just don't wear your uniform."

Obviously.

Annie Lucas: *Under Armour? Why am I picturing thongs made of steel and bras that double as bulletproof vests? Also, it's not actually possible for lungs to freeze while you're still alive, is it? Never mind. Don't answer that.*
2 hours ago

Annie Lucas *is now friends with Lenny London and 14 other people*

B y the time track practice comes around, I've got a pounding headache thanks to St. Teresa's academic excellence. A girl in the locker room before practice is nice enough to loan me some tights, a long-sleeve running shirt, and an ear band with the school logo embroidered on it. I stick close to Jackie Stonington during the four warm-up laps and then after stretching, Coach Kessler pulls me aside.

"Lucas, we're really happy to have you on the team this year," she says. "As you've probably heard, St. Teresa's is currently number one in the state."

I'm rubbing my chest. Is it supposed to hurt when I run? It's only thirty-two degrees, maybe my lungs froze? "State champions, that's awesome."

"Here's how I do things on my team," Coach Kessler says. "It's very simple, and I don't deviate for any reason. The best times in the practice before the meet are in the event. No excuses, no questions. If you're annoying and lazy, we'll glare at you and imagine you falling on your face in front of hundreds of watching eyes, but if you're the best, then you're in. No favoritism, no politics, no parents persuading me, just time, distance, height—got it?"

I sigh with relief. I'd been worried that coming in junior year might not allow me to take someone else's spot, but according to Coach Kessler's plan, all I have to do is run faster than the other girls. "I think I can handle that."

She claps me on the back a little too hard. "We'll have our first time trials next week."

Coach Kessler sends all the girls who run the 800 or longer distance out on a five-mile run, led by Jackie Stonington. I make sure to stay about two stride lengths behind her the whole time and when we get back to the school, I'm hating the cold temperature about 50 percent less than I had at the start of practice.

"Lucas!" Coach Kessler shouts after dismissing everyone to the locker room.

"Yeah?"

"You ever run the two mile?" she asks.

"Just once as a freshman. My mile time has always been better, and it was too much to do both in the same meet."

Coach Kessler snorts back a laugh. "Says who?" She doesn't wait for my answer. She pulls a sheet of paper from her clipboard and hands it to me. "All my long-distance runners do additional workouts. I'm here every morning before school, and you run on your own on the weekends."

"Oh…" I glance at the paper and start calculating the additional miles for each week. "I didn't realize there was extra—"

"I can't require it, Annie," she explains. "But I'm telling you now, if you follow my program, you'll not only be competing both the mile and the two mile, you'll win, okay?"

"Okay."

"And remember to check out my training diet on the website," she calls after me. "Very important that you load up on carbs."

Annie Lucas: *If I knew how to say overwhelmed in Spanish that's what I'd type for my status update. But then again, if I knew I might not be overwhelmed enough to need this update.*
5 minutes ago

Lenny London: *Boys come and boys go, but learning to swear at them in multiple languages is a skill you can keep forever. Exactly why studying is a priority for me.*
2 minutes ago

'm standing outside the Royals' locker room trying to decide if I want to take the chance of getting in trouble for walking into Dad's office when Frank comes up behind me.

"Frank, take me to my father." I slap a hand over my eyes and stick my other arm out for him.

"Oh Lord, this is gonna get real old," he grumbles, dragging me along. He stops after only a short distance. "It's all clear, kid."

I uncover my eyes and follow Frank into the training room where Dad is working with the starting pitcher, going over video footage. He smiles when he sees me, tosses a PowerBar in my direction, and goes back to work

Dad wanted to drive me to school this morning, so I'm stuck waiting for him to be done. I hop up on one of the tables and spread my books out. It's been a couple hours since my last academic headache, and I figure it's time for another. I give half my attention to my history book and the other half to Dad's coaching session. I can't hear everything he's saying, but from what I do pick up, Mr. Starting Pitcher, who has apparently been hot stuff around here for an entire decade, isn't too keen on Dad's advice. It's like he's half out of his seat already.

"Well, this just gets more and more interesting every day." I glance over my shoulder and see Jason Brody, standing near one of the treadmills in workout clothes. His eyes travel up and down, taking in my school uniform. "Got my interview written up yet?"

I smirk at him and then retrieve a sheet of paper from my bag. "As a matter of fact, I do."

He eyes me skeptically and walks over, plucking the paper from my hand. "*Jason Abraham Brody—*" He stops reading and looks up at me. "That's not my middle name."

"We didn't get to finish the interview, so I improvised."

He rolls his eyes. "*Stands five foot ten inches...*wrong again, I'm six feet. *His favorite food isn't sushi. His best pitching advice for kids wanting to follow in his footsteps is to always throw toward home plate.*"

"Cute." He shakes his head and folds the paper, tucking it into his gym shorts pocket. "Real cute."

My homework speed gets cut in half watching Brody on the treadmill. He's all muscle and hotness but at the same time I can't help studying his stride and analyzing his technique. "You should really relax your shoulders more. You look better with a neck."

He starts laughing, stumbles a little, and almost falls off the treadmill. Dad shoots a glare in my direction, and I decide to zip my lips and spend the next hour listening to the pounding feet against the treadmill while lying on my back and catching up on my American Lit class by reading *The Great Gatsby*. Finally, Dad leans over me and kisses my forehead. "I'm all done."

"Good because I'm going to throw a childish tantrum if I don't get an entire large pizza all to myself in the next twenty minutes." Pizza. That's carbs, right? Coach Kessler told me to load up on carbs. I sit up again and begin tossing my books into my overflowing backpack.

"Nice work today, Brody," Dad says, before turning back to me. "I hear the showers running. Better stay here for a minute, Ann."

"Twenty minutes, Dad. Then it's tantrum time."

"I know, I know." He walks off with his non-leg tapping against the floor.

Brody stops the treadmill and rolls off the end, bending over to catch his breath before grabbing a towel to wipe the sweat off his face. His T-shirt is soaked, front and back. He walks over and picks up my algebra book. "So you're in high school?"

"Did the outfit give me away?"

He lifts his eyes to meet mine. "The outfit is…well…yeah, it gave you away."

I'm trying not to laugh because he was totally about to say something else and then got all embarrassed. I might be bold, but I'm not quite bold enough to truly flirt with a guy like Jason Brody, so I quickly change the subject. "Please tell me you didn't act all high and mighty and petulant, like Mr. Starting Pitcher during my dad's coaching session?"

"No way," he says. "I'm on trial so no boats will be rocked. Besides, I like your dad." He hesitates and then asks, "What's the deal with his leg?"

"His leg or his non-leg?" I can't help being snappy and defensive about Dad. After years of questions from friends and random kids that I played with at the park, it gets old.

Brody keeps his eyes on my textbook and eventually he starts flipping through the pages. "His non-leg."

"Have you ever heard of osteosarcoma?" Brody shakes his head. "It's bone cancer."

"Cancer?"

I nod. This is the hardest part for me to deal with, too, because his leg is gone, but the cancer can still come back. "Yep. When you get a tumor in your bone, they sometimes can't remove it without taking the whole bone off."

"But he was pitching already, right?"

I hold up my right index finger, imitating Frank's response when I asked him this same question nearly ten years ago. I'd been curious, but too afraid to ask Dad. "One regular season game with the Yankees."

"And then it was over?"

"Yep."

"I wouldn't have done it," he says firmly. "I wouldn't have stopped pitching. Wouldn't have let them take my leg."

I snatch the algebra book from under his hand and stuff it in my bag. "Well, you don't have a wife and a baby, so maybe that makes your perspective a lot more selfish."

After jumping off the table and grabbing my school stuff, I can feel him watching me. He probably thinks I'm some crazy girl, but he hit a sore spot just now. Truth is, I'm not sure me or my mom were the reason Dad chose losing his leg over pitching a little longer and taking the risk of the cancer getting too aggressive to fight. I know he thinks of me first now, but I have patches of faded memories that involve a very different man from the one I know today. Which is why I'd always wait for Frank's visits to ask for specifics about Dad's baseball years.

I have a feeling this new place, more importantly, this new job of Dad's is gonna bring up all the cobweb-covered past that we've been avoiding almost my entire life.

chapter 4

DAD: *Not too late, Ann. And be careful. I heard you can get lost for hours in the Londons' house.*

After reading the text, I shove my phone into my coat pocket along with the guilt that forms as a result of lying to Dad. I'm sure he's right. I could get lost in the London house. Assuming I was there. Which I'm not.

Cold wind whips us in the face as Lenny strides toward the entrance to a lively downtown bar, her high-heeled boots clanking against the sidewalk. She's a superior vision to me in her tight pants and silver sparkly sweater. Though I did ditch the uniform, like she suggested, my brown sweater, jeans, and flat boots are bland in comparison.

Before reaching the door, I take in the line of people outside, and more importantly, the huge dude with massive biceps examining IDs of said people outside.

I grab Lenny's sleeve. "I don't, like, have a fake ID or anything…"

She turns to face me, displaying her perfect makeup job. Concern flickers across her face for a second and then she shrugs.

"It won't matter. Bean is working tonight."

Bean?

I stumble behind Lenny, watching her flip her hair over one shoulder and strut right up to the front of the line. "Hey, Bean."

The dude with massive biceps lifts his eyes from the ID he's currently inspecting. A broad grin spreads over his features, making him look 50 percent nicer. And younger. "Lenny London, come on in!"

He hops off his stool and ushers us both in after Lenny reaches for my hand and brings me with her. The music inside is loud but not unbearable, and the scent of barbecue ribs is also not unbearable. The mix of patrons varies in age but definitely no one in high school like us. My stomach twists with nerves. I'm not one to play the straight arrow or anything. I like a party as much as any kid my age. But seriously, how long have I been in Kansas City? Forty-eight hours? And I'm already breaking laws and lying to my dad.

Oh wait…maybe impersonating a *Sports Illustrated* writer is a felony? If that's true, then I lasted less than an hour. I know I said I wanted a brand-new start here, but good daughter to raging criminal isn't exactly what I had in mind.

After making flirty eyes at the way-too-old-for-her lead singer, Lenny rushes off to the bar and returns with a bottle of beer in each hand. I stand awkwardly, leaning against a table while Lenny flits around the bar greeting people and, like me, not actually drinking her beer.

Over the next twenty minutes, I check my phone about a thousand times. It's not even ten yet. Finally, she returns to my side and says, "You're not having fun, are you?"

I shrug. What am I supposed to say?

"I'm sorry." She releases a breath. "My parents are doing this stupid dinner party tonight, and I needed an excuse to get out of it." She strokes her cheeks with her thumb and fingertips. "My face is still sore from holding the fake smile at the last party."

This one small mention of her family brings the high school girl out again in Lenny's features. "So hanging out at a downtown bar was your excuse for missing the dinner party?"

"Yeah, totally." Lenny laughs. "Actually, you're my excuse. My mom has elected herself head of the Royals' welcoming committee. Meaning any new players or staff and families get to learn the lay of the land from my family."

My eyebrows shoot up. "That's…diplomatic of her."

Lenny snorts. "Right. Diplomatic. More like she wants to scope out the wife and children of the competition and make sure everyone knows that my dad is the highest paid player on the team, and they plan on keeping it that way."

"Wow." I shake my head. "Keep your enemies close…"

Lenny's eyes widen, and she rests a hand firmly on my arm. "Not me, Annie. Seriously. I don't play their games."

"Except to get out of dinner parties."

She shrugs. "If I didn't want to hang out with you, I wouldn't. I've blown off more than a few Royals' kids."

There is no question that she's telling the truth. Lenny London is going to be an enigma to figure out, but at the same time, she seems to be exactly as she says.

"What the hell are you doing here?" a deep voice growls from behind me.

I spin around and come face-to-face with Jason Brody. And yeah, I panic for a second thinking about how he saw me in my pleated skirt earlier today. As in my *high school* uniform. Then there's that whole threat to tell my dad so I get sent to therapy lingering from a few days ago. But then I lift the beer bottle to my lips and take a sip, trying my best not to make a face. "Hey, Brody. Great music, huh?"

He glares so hard at me I'm sure his forehead is gonna stay permanently wrinkled. "What the hell are you doing?" He snatches the bottle from my hands and slides it across the table until it taps the wall.

A tall brunette with a twenty-inch waist approaches him from behind and rests a hand on his shoulder. I take a second to glance at Lenny, who rests a hand on her hip and says to the girl, "I think you left your panties by my pool the other night. Right beside loverboy's boxer briefs. I've collected them both for safekeeping. In case you were wondering."

A bewildered look crosses the girl's face and then Lenny fakes shock, covering her mouth with one hand. "Oh. Maybe that wasn't you. Now that I think about it, I'm pretty sure that girl was a redhead, but it's hard to tell in the dark, especially with all the flailing around."

The girl gives Lenny a tight-lipped smile, spins in a half circle, and walks away. Brody drops his head, pinching the bridge of his nose with one hand. "Nice. Real nice, Lenny."

My gaze bounces between the two of them. I don't know whether to laugh or be disgusted. Brody lifts his head and I look right at him, holding his gaze. "Go easy on him, Lenny. He's just taking advantage of his major league status while it lasts. Can you blame him?"

Brody cocks one eyebrow, challenge dancing all over his features. "While it lasts? Let's get one thing straight—"

He stops cold when all three of us take in the older man approaching our table. A man I met only briefly when we toured the stadium the other day. Johnson. The new Royals' owner. Brody swears under his breath. Johnson's walking toward us with such purpose that I know he recognizes us. Or hopefully he only recognizes Brody. I mean the guy probably meets kids of Royals' staff all the time. How likely is it that he memorizes faces?

He stops abruptly in front of us, adjusting his tie. If I hadn't just noticed the suit-wearing clan at the table he emerged from, I'd say his attire was out of place here. I glance at Lenny, who looks cool as a cucumber, but she does set down her beer bottle.

Johnson addresses Lenny first, eyes narrowed. "I take it you were being hospitable, giving our substitute relief pitcher a sample of the town's best barbecue."

It's obviously not a question. And if I know this, Lenny definitely does. The cheek-numbing fake smile spreads across her face. "How'd you know?"

And substitute relief pitcher? That's a bit redundant. Relief already indicates substitution.

"Lucky guess," Johnson says, returning the fake smile. "How about you go and get that car warmed up."

I start to follow Lenny out, thinking that maybe I got away with not being recognized or assumed to be one of Lenny London's insignificant friends. But Johnson touches my arm and says in a low voice, "Not so fast, young lady."

Lenny takes in the situation and looks at me. "Meet you outside in five, Annie?"

I nod, not knowing what else to do. My heart thuds, the sound blocking out the music, and Brody shifts beside me.

Johnson leans in closer, still wearing the fake smile. To an outsider, this could almost look like a friendly conversation. But I know better. Especially with all this tension rolling around between us.

"I don't know what you're playing at, going after ballplayers. But this is not the image I want my Royals' families portraying,"

Johnson says. "I won't tolerate bad PR. Not from your daddy and certainly not from you. That's one strike, young lady."

Heat rushes to my face. My mouth falls open, but I can't form any words. What the hell kind of cult did we get ourselves into?

Johnson turns to Brody. "And you came into this gig two strikes in the hole, son. Consider yourself at two and a half. Dragging innocent children into a bar late at night..." *Oh, so now I'm an innocent child? What happened to me going after ballplayers? Or maybe Lenny is the innocent child?* "I heard you'd done some pretty bad things, but this is way outside of my comfort zone."

"He didn't—" I start to say. Why the hell am I defending Jason Brody—but Brody pushes me from behind toward the exit.

"Don't worry," he says to Johnson, his voice tight and re-strained. "It won't happen again. Trust me."

"That's the problem," Johnson says, all smooth and old-man-business like. "I don't trust you. I doubt anyone in their right mind trusts an ex-convict."

Ex-convict? Jesus Christ. Are we going to have to ride home together?

When I don't walk fast enough for Brody, our bodies collide. The hardness of him presses against me, and then I inhale his aftershave. My thoughts fog up. This is probably how he lured the redhead to the London's pool house the other night. And how he almost repeated the performance with the brunette now sulking in the corner. Good thing for Lenny London and her panty-snatching skills.

"Please tell me you have your own car," I mumble when we reach the door.

"Right," Brody snaps. "Because that's entirely possible on my minor league salary. And important when I'm on the road with the team over two hundred days a year."

"So no, then?"

He groans and shoves the door open, pushing his way around me and heading straight for Lenny's brand-new beamer. It's a two door, so Brody's forced to allow me a second to crawl into the backseat before dropping in beside Lenny.

Lenny laughs when she sees both of us, obviously pissed off. "Fun night, huh? We should do this again sometime soon."

"Not a chance in hell," Brody grumbles. He slides down in the seat, like he's hiding from being seen in Lenny's car even though it's dark and probably no one is paying attention or even cares.

Lenny blasts the music, sensing that we're not up for small talk. I recognize the first song as one the band in the bar had played. I guess she really is a fan. When we turn onto our street, Lenny glances over her shoulder at me. "Should I drop you at your house?"

"Uh-uh." Brody shakes his head. "Johnson's already got ideas. I'm not having Jim think I spend my free time clubbing with high school girls."

I roll my eyes. "Right. 'Cause your nineteen-year-old self is so much older and wiser than us seventeen-year-olds."

"I'm sixteen," Lenny corrects. "Summer birthday."

"Older and wiser is not the issue. More like legal." Brody points to his chest. "And not legal." He waves a finger between both me and Lenny.

According to Johnson, he's had no problem doing the illegal things in the past.

"He likes his women leggy and independent," Lenny says, while avoiding my house, taking us around the block and eventually pulling into the pool house driveway. She looks at Brody pointedly, waiting for him to exit the car. "I can drop you off now, Annie."

I tap my fist against Brody's seat, hinting for him to get out. "I'll walk." I need to get my head on straight before facing Dad, who unfortunately is relentless when it comes to waiting up for me.

Lenny turns to me. "You sure?"

Brody finally opens the door and gets out. I tumble after him, answering Lenny's question.

"See you at school tomorrow, Annie," she calls, heading around the back. "Thanks for being my cover tonight."

I'm prepared to stalk quickly away from the infuriating pitcher ruining all my fun, but he grabs my purse, holding me in place.

"Johnson was right, you know?" he says.

Nerves flutter in my stomach. I don't want to like the way his long-sleeve shirt forms over his muscled body or the perfect way his worn-out jeans hang from his waist. "What? About the ex-convict thing? I've already heard all of those details."

Okay, so I haven't heard any actual details. Only Frank's reference to Brody's "indiscretions." Is that polite talk for *ex-convict*? "Can you really be an ex-convict at nineteen? Convict, yeah, but ex…must not have been much of a crime if you're already in and out of the slammer."

"God, you're such a brat." He sighs. "Your stupidity is bad enough to ruin my playing chances."

"You didn't have to come up to me and Lenny in the bar. That was your screwup."

He shakes his head, jaw tensing. "Word of advice—if you want to stick around here, don't give Johnson a reason to cut your dad."

I yank out of his grip and take a step back down the driveway. "Why the hell do you care what happens to me or my dad?"

Brody's expression clouds over, but he doesn't answer.

I grin, knowing I've found a crack in his exterior. "Oh. Right. Because my dad and Frank seem to be the only ones who think you can pitch."

Brody laughs awkwardly and looks away. "I *can* pitch."

"Guess we'll see, huh?" I turn around and take off in a jog, hoping he doesn't follow me. When I complete the half-mile journey home and walk through the front door, Dad is sitting in the living room watching TV. No surprise there.

"Hey, Ann," he says, smiling over his shoulder at me. "Did you have fun tonight?"

Good. Johnson hasn't called him to tattle. Yet. I borrow Lenny's fake smile. "Uh, yeah…it was fun."

Dad frowns. He knows me too well to be fooled by fake smiles. "You okay?"

I sigh and flop down on the love seat beside him. "Yeah, I'm fine. It's just exhausting. Meeting new people, learning a new city…"

Concern fills his face. "Good exhausting or bad exhausting?"

I give him a much more genuine and hopefully reassuring smile. "I'm feeling a little of both."

"Me too, honey. Me too." He sets the remote in my lap and pulls himself off the couch, hobbling a little on his way to the kitchen. "You find a show. I'll make us a snack."

Okay, I officially solemnly swear never to lie to my dad again. Well, at least not the big lies.

I sink further into the cushions, trying to relax, but it's hard to do after the evenings' events. Could I really cause Johnson to fire my dad? Is this major league family image really that important? And while I'm solemnly swearing, I need to vow not to have any more inappropriate thoughts about Jason Brody, the pitcher from the wrong side of tracks. If only I hadn't seen him wet and wearing just a towel. That's not an easy image to erase from memory.

From now on, I'm going to avoid Jason Brody. He's Dad's project, not mine. Maybe I should swear on a Bible or something? It feels like a rule intended to be broken.

chapter 5

Annie Lucas: *I've witnessed a miracle! Where is the Pope? Where are the Cardinal dudes that come and verify it? Yesterday it was 32 degrees and currently the outside temperature is 71 degrees. *lights candle* *lights 2 candles* is 2 really better than 1? Says Doublemint gum...*
17 minutes ago

Lenny London: *Just to set the record straight, being proud of white women who accomplish great things and overcome obstacles does NOT mean that I'm not proud of my African American heritage. Can't I just be inspired by inspiring people regardless of race? And yes, the purpose of this status update is to justify my obsession with foreign cars. Sorry, America.*
30 seconds ago

'm running outside in shorts. What the hell is up with this bipolar weather?

Dad and I mapped a two-mile route around the neighborhood so I could complete my weekend running per Coach Kessler's "non-required" extra workouts. What a relief it is to not have to worry about death by frozen lungs. If this were my team in Arizona, I probably would have ignored the extra workouts. But after a week of St. Teresa's academic excellence, my brain is so fried all I want to do is run. Amazing how lazy substandard education can make you.

Savannah came by to go over meeting schedules with Dad the other day, and she drove me around the neighborhood, pointing out her apartment complex. A quarter mile down my street is where the houses start getting really big, and Lenny's is like a mansion.

I round the corner, kicking hard, focusing on the mailbox in front of my house. My lungs are ready to burst.

"Come on, Ann!" Dad shouts.

Finally, I hit the finish line, gasping for air. My hands lock behind my head, and I walk in circles until I can talk again. "Time?"

He looks at his stopwatch. "Five-oh-five, not bad?"

I shrug. It's not the time I want for the first trials, that's for sure. I strip off my T-shirt and wipe the sweat from my face. The second I lower my shirt, Jason Brody comes into view. He's opening the screen door, a bottle of water in one hand.

I suppress a groan. We haven't spoken since the other night at the bar, but he's stopped by here three days in a row to work with Dad on his technique. Seriously, how much technique is there to be learned? Especially for him. Throw straight and fast. It's not rocket science. But I guess maybe the picking up women and panty-discarding activities are reserved for evenings and he's got nothing to do all day.

Grams is sitting on the porch swing. I divert my eyes from Mr. Nosy Pitcher and plop down next to her.

She hands me my water bottle. "You should slow down, child. You'll fall on your face."

"Thanks, Grams, I'll do that."

Dad and Brody both have gloves and Dad's got a practice stand set up in the yard. I try not to look pissed off, but really, it'd be nice if he could warn me before inviting hot guys over. That way maybe I wouldn't be sweaty and I'd be wearing something cuter than a hot-pink sports bra and lime green running shorts. I don't even match. Not that I care what Jason Brody thinks. Actually, I already know what he thinks—that I'm a brat. And too young.

"The slider is all in the way you plant your front foot," Dad says.

He takes a stance a measured distance from the practice stand, a baseball in his right hand. If I focus on Dad's upper body, the way he licks his fingers before rotating the ball in his hand, eyes narrowed at the target, I can almost see the major league pitcher in him. The biggest problem for him is putting all that weight on his left non-leg. He's doing it halfway right now just to demonstrate the motions, and it's obvious he's already in pain. But pain isn't the main issue. It's balance and not having a foot to turn outward. I wonder if it'd be different if he'd lost his right leg instead or if he were left-handed.

Dad moves aside to let Brody take his spot. He rubs the top of his non-leg absentmindedly. I know better than to ask him if he's okay in front of one of the players, so I make a mental note to bug him later. He's a coach, not a player. He shouldn't have to be hurting.

Brody's got rituals of his own, and I'm ashamed to say I've already begun to memorize them. The way he looks at that target, it's straight out of a romance novel where the hero is in a room full of beautiful women and he can only truly see one of them—his soul mate, the woman of his dreams. In this case,

Jason Brody's soul mate is a makeshift strike zone planted in my front yard.

The smack of the ball against the stand still shocks me. It's amazing—the force, the speed. He'd take out the most durable luxury vehicle window if he got a little wild.

"You're still over-turning your hips," Dad says, calm and quiet.

Brody nods and, even though I thought the last pitch was perfect, I can see with my own eyes the change that one tiny adjustment makes. Since none of the other pitchers have made visits to our front yard for practice sessions, I have to assume that their loyalty lies with the other pitching coach. Or else they don't have any desire to improve or change. But Brody's way younger than all of them. What's that saying? *Can't teach an old dog new tricks.* Maybe that's it. But what's Dad going to do when the injured pitcher recovers and Brody goes back to his Triple-A team? Maybe they're a package deal? I swallow back the returning anxiety from the other night. Johnson's not-so-nice words still ring in my head along with Brody's warning—*if you want to stick around here, don't give Johnson a reason to cut your dad*—when I'm not busy distracting myself with other things.

Maybe I should just tell Dad what happened at the bar the other night and see what he thinks?

Or not.

I take one last swig of water and pull myself to my feet again. "Dad, I'm doing my two-mile run now."

"What's your strategy?" He's already clearing his stopwatch even though he's been a bit unsure about Coach Kessler's plan for me to run both races.

"Run fast." I bound down the porch steps and stretch my calves.

Dad's forehead wrinkles. "Come on, Ann, you need a plan. You can't just push it full-out. Your right hamstring's tight."

"Is not."

"Yes it is," he says firmly. "I could see it on your last mile. You're not extending all the way in your stride with the right leg."

I make a deliberate show of sitting on the grass and stretching my hamstring, making sure not to give away even a hint of discomfort on my face. "There. I'm ready now."

Dad stands there with his arms crossed, then he turns to Brody. "Watch her run and tell me if you don't see what I'm seeing. Apparently, my word weighs too heavily on the concerned Dad side and not enough on the expert side."

"Whatever." I take my stance in front of the mailbox again, then draw in a deep breath before starting. Unfortunately, there's some truth to Dad's concern about my lack of plan for this two-mile race. I have my mile race timed so perfectly—when to hold back, when to kick—and with this new distance, I've got kinks to work out.

All the more reason to get started now.

"Ginny, you fool! Slow down!" Grams shouts after I take off.

I can't help but use my mile technique on the first half of the run. My muscles know exactly when I hit each quarter mark of the mile and there's just no fooling my legs yet. By the time I get three-quarters of the way done, my entire body is screaming at me. I pull back a little, shortening my stride. Then I see Jason Brody, all hot muscles and tight jeans, standing in my yard with his arms crossed just like Dad and I find an extra surge of energy to push through to the end.

I'm walking in circles again, trying not to puke up the water

I drank only minutes ago when I notice Dad staring at his stopwatch.

"What?"

"Eleven ten," he says. "Pretty damn good, Annie."

When I can breathe and speak again, I head back up to the porch to retrieve my T-shirt and water. "But both times are shy of placing at state. So, I either have to run faster or ditch one event."

"Or do a decent job with both this year and focus on placing at state next year," Dad says.

After a few painful steps to get off the porch, I plop down on the grass. "No way. I'm not half-assing it."

Dad shakes his head like I'm crazy, but I know my natural competitive edge pleases him.

"When's the chocolate pudding gonna be ready?" Grams shouts from the porch swing. "And lobster, aren't we having lobster?"

I lay back in the grass and let out a breath. "I'm coming, Grams. Count to twenty."

"I'll get her lunch," Dad says. "Stretch, Ann. And Jason, keep working on turning your hips more."

The second Dad is out of sight, Brody leans over me. "He's right, you know? Your hamstring *is* tight."

I hold his gaze. "I really don't think it's appropriate for you to check out my legs. What with that big *giant* age gap and all."

I expect some snarky reply from him, but he just shakes his head and turns back to the pitcher's stand. "Whatever. It's not like it matters to me."

Right. Because you have phone calls that include you using the plural *women*. And brunettes and redheads with panties attractive enough to leave lying around for anyone to see. My legs are of no real interest to Brody.

"So," I say. "Tell me about the slammer? What's it like in there?"

He fires the ball at the stand with an exaggerated amount of force. "I really don't think it's appropriate for you to ask that question."

After pulling myself off the grass, I'm expecting him to add on to his snappy retort but he just leaves me hanging for an entire minute, ignoring me completely. Since it's my house, I head up the steps without a word, giving him equal silent treatment.

But once I'm out of Brody's sight, my frustration overflows. I stomp into the house, breezing past Dad. "You weren't like that when you played baseball, were you?" I nod out the front window toward Brody.

Dad laughs but keeps his back to me as he piles cold cuts onto bread for Grams' lunch—definitely not lobster. "No, honey. I was nothing like Jason Brody."

My mouth falls open, and I want to ask him, *Is it because you had me? Is it because of Mom? Did that make you less self-centered?* But I can't bring myself to ask those questions aloud. I'm afraid of the answer.

After an extra-long shower, I take my time blow-drying my hair and getting dressed again, hoping Jason Brody will be long gone by then. No such luck. He and Dad are sitting in the kitchen eating sandwiches. Yep, my dad and the alleged ex-convict—hot, alleged ex-convict—hanging like old pals. Great.

The only thing left for me to do is make my own lunch. Coach Kessler's diet includes lots of big, healthy-sounding words, so I've made some minor adjustments to make it work in my favor. I trade the whole grain bread for a giant kaiser roll and pile it with cheese, turkey, roast beef, lettuce, tomato, mayo, spicy brown mustard, and banana peppers. I reach for the Doritos, but self-control wins and I decide on an apple and yogurt to accompany my mess of a sandwich.

"Yeah, I don't know," Brody says, continuing whatever conversation they'd been discussing before I walked into the kitchen. "School and me…we just aren't compatible."

School? Why are they talking about school?

"I'm not talking about school," Dad says. "Just the GED. You can even get a tutor to help you prepare. All you have to do is take the test."

"You mean *pass* the test," Brody corrects. "All I have to do is pass the test."

Dad leans back in his chair, appearing surprised by this response. "Look, I think you have a great baseball career ahead of you, all I'm saying is that having a plan B is not a bad idea."

I head toward my room with my lunch, but Dad stops me. "Sit, Annie."

With a loud sigh, I take the chair beside Dad and across from Brody. "Don't you think I'm old enough to eat in my room? There's not as many bugs here as in Arizona."

Dad slides a book in my direction. *Complete Guide to GED Preparation* is written across the front. "Do you know any of this stuff?"

"Probably not well enough, considering I haven't graduated high school." I lift the sandwich to my mouth. It's almost too big for me to take a bite.

Brody watches with interest. "That's quite a sandwich."

"I'm carb loading," I say with my mouth full. For Dad's benefit, I flip open the book, leafing through the math section. I swallow the big bite before speaking this time. "It looks like pre-algebra, some basic geometry, maybe a little of algebra I."

Dad claps his hands together, looking pleased. "Great! You can help Jason study."

My eyes widen. What happened to the tutor plan? Or maybe I am the tutor?

The amusement that came with watching me eat my sandwich drops from Brody's face, and he stands up, pushing his chair back and taking the book out from underneath me. "That's all right. I'll figure it out." He turns to Dad. "Thanks for the books and the extra practice."

Dad looks like he wants to say something but after glancing at me, changes his mind. "No problem. Come by again tomorrow if you want."

After Brody is out the door, Dad angles his chair to face me, staring hard. "That was rude, Ann."

"I didn't say anything," I protest, filling my mouth with more bread and meat to avoid this confrontation.

"That's the problem."

"Get real, Dad. He doesn't want some high school kid teaching him equations. That'd totally bruise his ego."

"It wouldn't if you were nice about it." He stands up and shoves his chair back into the table and hobbles over to the sink to load the dishwasher. "Not everyone is lucky enough to have a parent who forces them to go to school and actually do well. Some kids get into trouble and have no one to help them out of it."

Is that what happened to Brody? He didn't have anyone to answer to? My stomach sinks. The bread in my mouth goes down in one dry lump. There's really no worse feeling than getting called out on your wrongdoings by your dad. He doesn't toss up criticism lightly. In other words, he's almost always right and it absolutely infuriates me. But today I feel a lot more guilty than angry.

"Imagine if I didn't have my high school diploma, Ann." He lifts his non-leg as if I need a reminder. "The best I could do before this coaching gig was a fifteen dollar an hour job. Without that diploma, it would have been so much worse. Give the kid a break, would you?"

My face heats up. When did I become so judgmental? "I'm sorry. I'll apologize or something, okay?"

He looks at me then turns back to the sink, shaking his head. "Forget it, Ann. I'll get someone else to help him. Maybe Savannah."

I don't know why, but the idea of Savannah and her much kinder disposition huddled close to Brody while discussing verb tenses bugs me. I reach for Dad's phone on the table, find Brody's number, and while his back is turned to me, I program Jason Brody's into my phone.

It takes me the rest of my sandwich and half the apple before I figure out what to text.

ME: Just so you know, I'm barely pulling Cs in my class. Haven't exactly been honest with my dad about this. So I'm probably not the best tutor—Annie Lucas

I wait only three minutes for his one word—two letter—reply.

BRODY: OK

A little while later, I'm in the kitchen scarfing down the Doritos that I resisted earlier, when I spot, through the kitchen window, a blue convertible rolling down the street. A blond leggy (okay, I can't see her legs, but I know they're super long) girl probably five years older than me is behind the wheel. And in the passenger seat, one arm tossed across the girl's seat, is

Jason Brody.

I roll my eyes, disgusted. That's what I get for apologizing. I should probably warn Lenny about the potential for random undergarments turning up by her pool tonight.

And I actually felt sorry for him about an hour ago.

Vow to avoid substitute relief pitchers officially reinstated.

opening
DAY

chapter 6

Lenny London: *Why not just skip ahead to the World Series? Why all the foreplay? I smell a conspiracy within the hot dog industry.*
4 hours ago

Annie Lucas: *What is the statistical probability of throwing a strike? I mean, I know it's harder than shooting fish in a barrel, but how much harder? And what really defines a strike? Throwing it within the strike zone or getting the batter to swing and miss? These seem like two very different skills.*
3 hours ago

'm sitting in Dad's office a couple hours before the game starts. I'm trying to get my weekend homework done so I can let loose at Lenny's party tonight. I've been running and reading and running and reading…words and mile paces are starting to ooze out my ears and I need some pure teenage fun. And I can only assume a private party at Lenny's will be free of Larry Johnson's judgmental, strike-issuing self.

The phone on Dad's desk rings, pulling me away from *Gatsby*. I can't tell who he's talking to, but I don't think it's Frank. His posture is too formal for a Frank call. After a minute or two, the vein on the side of his neck bulges, his forehead wrinkling. "I'm really not sure this is the best plan… Yes, I understand… What about Halloway…?"

Halloway? Right. Another pitcher.

"I see," Dad says. "We can't get two or three innings out of him? I realize I said he had the arm to be a starter, but I was referring to the future—preferably the distant future, and I'm sure that you know that."

He's gotten snippier with each word, but I have no idea what's going on.

Dad slams the phone down and drops his head in his hands. "Fuck."

"What? What happened? They aren't going to use Brody?" That last part is a wild guess. Brody is the player Dad is most invested in and therefore most likely to get this upset over.

"They're using him." He's up on his feet, piling up papers onto his clipboard. "He's starting."

"That's good, right?"

"No, Ann, it's not good." He sighs, stops moving, and looks at me. "I need you to go up to the seats wherever you're supposed to meet Lenny, all right?"

I pile my books into my bag quickly, but I press him for answers before leaving the office. "Dad, what's going on?"

He closes the door, leaning his back against it. "Johnson doesn't like the idea of Brody replacing a seasoned player, he never has. But he also knows that he has to give Frank room to do his job. In addition, I've gotten the sense that Johnson isn't too keen on having two pitching coaches."

It's exactly what Brody said. Damn.

From what I've heard, Johnson expects Frank to sign some hotshot free agents from other teams for a tenth of their former salary. Yeah, right. Frank might be from the Yankees where twenty million dollar contracts are regular occurrences, but he's realistic about the Royals much smaller budget and commitment to developing younger players. Like Brody. I'm not a baseball expert, but this seems like a great strategy to me. Too bad Johnson doesn't agree. Or maybe his real issue is the ex-convict thing.

My stomach twists into knots. The problem is clear now. And if I'm feeling sick, I can't imagine what Dad's feeling. "Johnson wants you and Brody both to screw up so he has an excuse to dump you?"

God, I hate that Brody was right. I hate that Johnson saw me in the bar. That I've added an unnecessary strike to my family's record.

"Something like that," Dad says. "I'm temporary, too, Ann. I haven't signed a full contract yet."

I sink back into the chair. "Shit…"

Dad bends down and rests his hands on my shoulders. "This is exactly why I didn't want to tell you. I need to focus on getting Brody ready to start and not worrying about you worrying, okay?"

God, I have to tell him about the night at the bar. He has to know everything that's behind Johnson's motivation to ditch Dad and Brody. "Dad, me and Lenny were at this—"

"Annie, please," Dad says. "Later, okay? We'll talk later. I need to focus."

"But, Dad—" I protest and then stop after rationalizing that this information won't help him help Brody. It will only make the objective seem that much more difficult. Like they're standing in a bigger hole than they originally thought. "Okay, I'll…I'll see you later. Good luck."

Lenny is waiting for me in the suites reserved for players and families. It's a fancy room with all kinds of food. As much as I love to eat, I can't even look at any of it. I'm too nervous. Lenny introduces me to her mom and some of the other players' wives and kids.

"I'm so excited for this party tonight," Lenny says. "It makes suffering through the game worth it."

"Yep, I'm totally suffering through this game." I stare out the windows, watching the team warm up. An hour passes and I don't see Brody at all, but Dad's in the dugout. He looks really good in his uniform. I'm going to be so pissed off if he doesn't get to wear it again.

We've only been in Kansas City for a couple weeks, but I already like it here. Dad is happier than I've ever seen him, and Mom has no idea where we are. Grams seems to be calm and content with her new caretaker, Caroline. Lenny is turning out to be a pretty awesome friend for a spoiled rich girl who has Daddy issues.

I don't want this to be over.

Johnson passes through our suite to get to the owner's box, greeting various family members. He catches my eye, and I swear he glares, silently passing a word of warning through that glare. I turn away from him quickly—*God, we're screwed.*

When Dad disappears through the dugout, I'm too antsy to sit here any longer. "Hey, Lenny? I left something in my dad's office, save a seat for me?"

I'm not even sure what I need to tell him, just that I need to say something. Some kind of magic words that will make everything work out. I managed to do it when I convinced him to take this job and move to Kansas City. Maybe there's something that will work magic today. But unfortunately, Dad's not in his office and I can't exactly go into the dugout to have a father/ daughter chat. Even if I could get past the security guards, he'd be pissed at me.

Before I can form a new plan, I hear the loud echo of some-one vomiting in the bathroom stalls. *Oh no.* "Dad?" I say, my voice bouncing off the empty locker room walls. "Are you in here?"

The stall door opens, but it's not Dad who steps out. It's Jason Brody.

I try to turn around and hide, but he sees me right away, closes his eyes, and sighs before leaning over the sink, splashing water on his face, rinsing his mouth out. "Great…just great," he mumbles to himself.

I should leave, but I'm frozen in place. The pressure, the stress he must feel right now, it's right here in the air between us. And the fact that he's handling it all alone, that he's probably aware, like Dad, that the team owner is trying get rid of him, softens my attitude toward Brody. A little.

"You okay?" I ask finally.

He keeps his eyes on the mirror, grabs a bottle of Listerine resting on the counter, chugs it, swishes, and spits. "I'm wonderful." I wait while he grabs a towel, drying off his face. He finally looks right at me. "Your dad's out on the field."

"Right. Sorry." I turn around and head for the exit. Brody breezes past me, wringing his hands together in front of him. We get all the way to hall that leads to the Royals' dugout before, on impulse, I reach out and grab his arm. *Magic words.* He needs them just as much as Dad. Despite my feelings toward Brody, their futures here are tied together.

He turns to face me. "What?"

"I…um…" I take a deep breath and keep my eyes on his. "Before Frank Steadman offered this job to my dad, we watched videos of you pitching. Frank asked my dad if he would sign you and you know what he said?"

The anxiety drops from his face. "What?"

"He said, *in a heartbeat*. He knows you can totally kill it today, he's only worried because it's a lot of pressure."

He laughs bitterly. "That's an understatement."

"Pressure is just that—pressure. It's all in your head. It has nothing to do with what you can or can't do." My face is flaming. I've totally overstepped my boundaries and this is all getting a little too *Chicken Soup for the Soul*.

I wait anxiously as he takes a deep breath, nods, steps closer to me, and squeezes my arm, just above my elbow. "Keep this between us, okay?"

He walks away, and I release all the air in my lungs and fall back against the wall. If I'm feeling the pressure, he must have five hundred tons more resting on his shoulders. I take the long route back up to the seats and instead of going inside the suite, I stand outside, leaning against the rail, listening to them introduce the players for both teams. I'm right behind home plate when Brody stands on the pitcher's mound, his white and blue Royals' uniform spotless and tight in all the right places. But it kind of sucks, playing your first major league game without the support of your team's owner.

I'm holding my breath while Brody throws a few warm-up pitches. The speed registers between ninety-six and ninety-eight, but they're wild pitches. Not even close to strikes. Dad is statue-like in the dugout, his arms folded over his chest, his gaze locked on Jason Brody. My hands turn white from gripping the railing so hard. I let go and lean my stomach against it instead.

Another wild pitch is thrown, forcing the catcher to dive sideways.

Come on, Brody…focus.

My heart pounds when the first batter steps into the box.

They can't dump him for one out, right? He's going to get at least an inning?

The first pitch is way outside. Fast but outside. I manage a breath and see that Dad hasn't moved an inch. He's not breathing either. Brody's first pitch replays over and over again on the giant stadium screens. He shakes out his arms and takes his stance a second time, and I swear to God, he looks up at me. For a brief moment, I'm sure he sees me. Then his focus narrows, his expression identical to the one I've seen many times when he's staring down the pitching stand in our front yard.

The second pitch goes right down the center.

Strike.

Thank God.

I'm so relieved I have to lean over and rest my head on my hands for a minute.

Brody throws another ball, followed by another strike.

2-2 count.

It takes one more strike and the first out for the Royals' new season for Dad to finally move some part of his body. He should be screaming and cheering, but in typical Dad fashion, he just gives a tiny nod.

While the next batter steps into the box, Brody shakes off the excess weight he'd carted out here. I can see him sweating a little, taking normal breaths, looking around at the other players and the stadium.

Good. Now do it again.

I turn around and finally head back into the suite to take my seat beside Lenny for the rest of the game.

Brody manages to pitch six innings, letting only a single runner on base. He's taken out after the sixth inning and replaced by a relief pitcher. The relief pitcher lets a double and then a home run sneak by, causing the Royals to lose 2–0.

But six solid innings in his first major league game ever has to be enough to keep him around a little longer. I hope. Or at least to absolve some of the bad from the night at the bar. I don't want to be sent back to Arizona, but even more, I don't want it to be my fault.

After the game, I head down toward the locker room to see Dad, but can't even get through the long hall leading there because it's jam-packed with media people—players standing in the middle of the storm talking into tape recorders, lights flashing everywhere. Dad is nowhere in sight, but I see Brody come through the doors, Savannah at his side.

A man in a blue suit shoves a microphone at Brody and drills him with questions. "How does it feel to play in the big leagues, son?"

Brody's grin is so big I can see it from all the way down the hall. "Awesome. Seriously."

Those two words from the team's current youngest player earn the attention of half a dozen other reporters, causing them to abandon the player they were interviewing and focus on Brody instead.

"Think Johnson will let you stick around?" one reporter dude throws out casually, like my own life doesn't depend on this answer.

"I hope so."

They shout a few more questions at him, and Brody answers each with a grin.

My phone buzzes in my pocket, and I pull it out to read a text from Dad.

DAD: It's a zoo in here. Hiding out in my office. You're getting a ride with Lenny, right? I'll call you in a few minutes.

I spin around and head away from the zoo before replying to Dad.

ME: Yep, talk to you soon.

I meet Lenny back in the suites, and she drives us to her house in her silver beamer.

"That was the most amazing game ever," I yell over Lenny's blaring music.

She turns the volume down. "Were we at the same game? Losing isn't usually a cause for celebration."

I almost spill about today's drama, but it's nobody's business. And Lenny hasn't asked me what Johnson said that night in the bar, meaning she probably doesn't want to get involved. "It's just cool to see everything up close."

Lenny rolls her eyes but smiles at me. "I forgot you're still new to this. It'll get old real fast."

Dad calls when we're halfway to Lenny's and my heart speeds up a bit before I answer it. "Dad, how is everything? I mean…" I shoot a sideways glance at Lenny and wait for him to fill me in on our fate.

"Good, Annie," he says with real enthusiasm in his voice. "They've decided to let Harper have that surgery he needs on his shoulder."

Harper. One of the starting pitchers.

"So that means…?"

"Brody's getting a three month contract," he says like we've just won a big prize. I think we have. "If all goes well, he'll sign for the rest of the season, at least as a relief pitcher. That will mean bumping someone off the roster. But if he kills it like he did today, there's at least four guys we could lose with Brody's stats."

"Have I told you I love you or that you're a super super

awesome coach yet today?" I spit out, so relieved I can hardly sit still in this car. This is clearly the work of guilt.

Dad laughs. "No, you haven't and thanks, Ann. Today was rough. I just need a little more time to get Brody to take off and hopefully get some of the other guys on my side."

"Well, they're stupid boys if they don't want to listen to you."

Lenny's watching me carefully, a curious expression on her face that makes me hurry up and end my call with Dad.

"So you're cool to stay all night?" she asks once I'm off the phone.

"Yep." I raise the duffel bag at my feet. "Your parents really don't care if you throw a big party?"

"Let's just say they turn a blind eye," Lenny says. "But we're gonna use the guesthouse. I imagine they've got their own wild party happening in the main house."

"But Brody's staying in your guesthouse?" And surely he has a better much cooler party to go to. What with his years of maturity and non-family appropriate plans for the night.

Lenny pulls into her huge driveway, raising up the garage door. "Don't worry, I talked to him. If he doesn't end up out on the town with some loose bimbo, he'll stay in one of the guest rooms in the main house. He's got the garage code already."

I try not to focus on the image of some Royals' groupie with bouncy size-D boobs putting her hands all over Jason Brody.

I open the car door and lift my bag out. "That could be a problem…"

Lenny stops and turns to face me. "Why?"

"Well, Brody is really tight with my dad, and my dad knows I'm staying here tonight. He might tell him about the high school party that got in his way."

"And your dad would have issues with this…?"

I can't believe she's so confused and surprised by this fact. "Yes, my dad would have major issues with me being at a party with an open bar and horny boys."

There are already tons of cars parked near the house and loud music coming from the guesthouse. Lenny's older brother Carl got things started, apparently.

"Don't worry," Lenny says, "He's not going to rat you out to your dad. He didn't tell your dad when he saw us in the bar that one time, right? Besides, just say you thought we were having a girls' night and Carl decided to throw a party."

Maybe that would work?

Let's hope so 'cause I don't want to imagine Dad's reaction if he found out about this party.

chapter 7

Annie Lucas: *The definition of a perfect game in baseball means not letting anyone get on base. So my question is—why is only the pitcher credited? Does the pitcher shoulder all the responsibility for this feat?*
20 minutes ago

Lenny London: *PARTY!! Don't judge me. I'm still gonna be brilliant even minus a couple brain cells. And what will you be? Exactly.*
10 seconds ago

Lenny's brother Carl is a complete asshole. He's also completely brainless. The polar opposite of his National Honor Society sister. He's supposed to be in college, but I highly doubt he's willing to take a break from his pot smoking, binge drinking schedule to actually attend class. After three hours of loud music, beer, and not nearly enough food, I'm strung out on the celebrating plan.

"Annie! Make sure I don't sleep with that guy." Lenny points without even attempting subtlety at a tall, lanky blond dude. "Yes, you! We are so not sleeping together."

The guy looks at her from across the room, and it's clear he's confused.

"He's a Scorpio," Lenny explains. "I can't be with a Scorpio, we're not compatible."

"I'll pry you apart if it comes to that," I say, patting her on the back. I stand up from my spot on the couch and stretch out. Through the guesthouse windows, a very different party comes into view. I walk closer, and the view inside Lenny's house lays out clearly for me to see. Everyone is dressed for the Oscars and holding champagne glasses. There are even waiters in crisp white shirts and black dress pants wandering around with trays of things like stuffed mushrooms. Jake London is the highest paid player on the team—though he makes half of what the highest paid in the league makes—and he can probably afford a party like this after every home game.

I spot Brody, the only person wearing jeans to the grown-up party, walking toward a group of his teammates. Even with this window-to-window, pool-between-us view, it's obvious the four guys stop talking when Brody enters their space. Brody offers a hand to one of the pitchers, like he's congratulating him or something. But the guy doesn't move a finger in Brody's direction. All four faces tighten and then seconds later, they've turned their backs and headed in different directions.

My neck heats up. I don't have any reason to feel humiliated, but I do. For Brody's sake. Maybe for the fact that I saw something I hadn't been invited to see. But then Mrs. London—sporting the best fake smile I've ever seen—stalks in Brody's direction, steering him to a plate of mushrooms, a glass of champagne, and a few twenty-something women in tight black dresses.

I drop my gaze to my own boring attire—jeans and a sweater. Again. Brody does that eye roaming, boob gawking game that guys do, and in an instant his deflated shoulders rise and he's Mr. Charming all over again.

I shake my head and turn my attention back to the party. But less than twenty minutes later, my phone buzzes in my pocket. I remove it, glancing quickly at the text I just got.

BRODY: Have you seen the pool yet?

I haven't but obviously I'm about to because my legs have decided to stand up on their own and I'm already heading for the guesthouse door, leading out to the pool.

The sky is clear outside and moonlight is bouncing off the water in the pool. Brody is now seated by the edge, his jeans rolled up and his feet dangling in. For barely a second, I debate going out there. He's bound to piss me off and ruin my fun. That seems to be our norm. But then I remember the way he looked at me in the tunnel to the dugout right before the game and that feeling I got, that maybe I'd been the only one to tell him he belonged here.

Be polite, Annie. But also cool. "How's the water? Any icebergs in there?"

Brody looks up at me and grins. "It's warm. They probably spent a shit-ton of money heating this giant mass."

I nod toward the house. "Looks like one hell of a bash. Wouldn't you have more fun inside than out here?"

"They tried to feed me mushrooms and fish eggs. I had no choice but to bail."

I slip off my shoes and roll up the bottom of my jeans, taking a seat next to Brody. The water *is* warm. Probably eighty-something degrees. "Then you should be out celebrating. Finding some groupie girls that work at Hooters to hook up with."

"Hooters, huh? Chicken wings do sound good right now."

He laughs. "How's *your* party?"

Wow. Civil conversation with Jason Brody. Alert the media. And the *Guinness Book of World Records*. We need an official timer for this event.

"It's fine." Through the tall living room windows, I spot two blondes in short black dresses with their noses practically pressed to the glass, eyeing Brody. They look like models. Like they should be lying across the hood of a sports car. Maybe a blue convertible that they're willing to drive Brody around in. I tear my gaze from the house and swing my feet back and forth in the water, watching it ripple outward. "Lenny's brother is an ass and Lenny's IQ drops about a hundred points when she's drunk."

"Doesn't everyone's?"

"I guess."

We sit for a few minutes in a comfortable silence, listening to the sounds of two very different parties meshing together until Brody speaks up again. "Jim seems pretty excited about sticking around here for a while longer. How about you?"

"Totally," I say, feeling that relief all over again. But I'm waiting for him to bring up the fact that he'd been right about our position. And maybe he wasn't just thinking of himself when he gave me that warning about Johnson. *Polite small talk, Annie.* "I bet your family's pretty stoked. Did anyone come to the game?" He's from Chicago, which isn't that far away, so maybe his family came to watch.

Brody's face clouds over. "No one came."

"Well, did you at least talk to them after it was over?"

He shakes his head but doesn't say anything more.

And then I remember what Dad said a few weeks ago: *"Not everyone is lucky enough to have a parent who forces them to go to school and actually do well. Some kids get into trouble and have no one to help them out of it."*

Shit. My stomach flutters with nerves and regret, my mouth falling open to utter an apology, but Brody quickly moves on to something else.

"Thanks for what you said earlier…before the game."

His eyes meet mine and my heart quickens. Guess they *were* magic words after all. "You were amazing. Seriously," I blurt out despite all my previous harassments regarding Brody's questionable pitching talent.

"I was a wreck." His eyebrows lift, a silent reminder of his time spent in the bathroom stall before the game.

"I barfed like three times before state last year," I admit. "I didn't tell anyone else, not even Dad. We can keep each other's secret."

"Deal." He stares down at his feet in the water. "And I'm sorry for what I said last week about your dad."

Right. The part where he declared that he would never let anyone cut off his leg.

"You didn't really say anything about him, you just said what you'd do if you *were* him." I pull my hair up off my neck and secure it with the hair tie around my wrist. "It gets old sometimes, explaining his non-leg to people. No excuse to snap at you though. I could chalk it up to PMS if that helps?"

This being-nice-to-Brody direction is easier than I thought, but I still have this feeling things will turn awkward any second now. I mean seriously, what do we even have in common?

He laughs again. "A little. And that's the thing, I'm not him, so it's not my place to say what should have been. He's a great coach. It obviously worked out fine for him."

Did it work out fine? I don't really know any different, I

guess. Actually, I don't even know this baseball coach version of Dad much better than the baseball player version of him. But I know he deserves to be this person.

"I was so nervous for both of you today." I cover my face and groan. "God, that was awful. And your warm-up pitches were so wild I thought you might knock someone out."

He gives me a tiny shove in the shoulder. "Thanks for the vote of confidence."

"Seriously, the game was amazing. I couldn't care less that we lost." I hesitate for a minute and then plunge into a question I'd only be able to ask after drinking two beers. "You didn't happen to see me, did you? Like in the stands during the game?"

"Yeah, I did." The smile fades from his face. "That's kind of what got me to focus and not suck." He laughs. "Not you exactly, but seeing you reminded me of what you said before. How Jim only got to play one game. I hadn't let myself think about that possible scenario. But today, I told myself this would be it, and I had to make it count."

"What are you going to tell yourself next game?"

He exhales. "Fuck if I know."

I laugh. "You'll think of something."

Some random guy stumbles out of the guesthouse and shouts at us. "Hey, baby! Can I get your number?"

"My number or yours?" I ask Brody.

"Looks like a real winner," Brody whispers, leaning close to my ear, sending a shiver down my spine—*I swear he did that on purpose.* "Don't get up too fast."

"You look like my little sister's Barbie doll!" the guy shouts at me.

"Hey, buddy," Brody says, fighting laughter. "Fuck off."

The guy turns around and pukes into the bushes. I wrinkle

my nose and twist my body to face Brody and not the puking guy. "Disgusting."

"I bet London pays someone to clean up after them," he says.

"How did you end up staying here?"

He levels me with a look. "Jake London's wife insisted on it."

At first it makes sense, given what Lenny said about her mom being the self-elected "welcoming committee" leader, but the way Brody says it sends my thoughts in a very different direction...

"Please tell me you haven't..."

"God no." He drags his hand through the pool and then flicks water in my face. "I just turned nineteen last month. You've got me hooking up with forty-something-year-old married women who have had way too much cosmetic surgery. Where do you get these ideas, anyway?"

"Don't know. Guess I'm stereotyping and being judgmental." I shrug. "You don't have a girlfriend, then?"

"No. I need to focus on making this chance count." He glances at the guesthouse. "What about you? Did you leave some guy crying back in Arizona?"

"Not even close. I *had* a boyfriend for almost a year. We broke up before I moved."

Why am I telling him this? He'll use it later to make fun of me or call me a child.

"He couldn't handle the long-distance relationship?"

"It ended even before I knew I was moving." I release a breath, and I'm surprised by the fact that the wound doesn't feel as fresh as it had a month or two ago.

"So what happened?" Brody presses.

"You really want to know? Like for real, not to tease me about it later?" I ask and Brody nods. "He started going to church all the time and then one day he told me he didn't want to sin anymore so we couldn't like, you know…*do stuff*. And believe me, Kenny is not the type to go all Jesus freak, so I had a feeling something else was up. I did a little investigating and found out it wasn't so much church, as a boy at church."

"Oh," Brody says, eyes widening. "Bummer. So did you call him out on it?"

"Nah. I mean, I told him that I knew his secret but he didn't want people to know. I kind of let him tell everyone that I wanted to leave Arizona unattached once I knew about the move." Another reason why I'm not jumping at every opportunity to stay in contact with the remains of my past life.

Brody gives me a half smile. "You'll find someone else. Someone better."

"Where?" The models are still ogling him from the window, and it's making me uncomfortable. I stand up and unroll my jeans. "At my all-girls school?"

"Are you leaving me?" His dark eyes lock with mine, and for a moment, he's that guy again—the one with the sunken shoulders, watching his teammates refuse his handshake and turn their backs on him.

"I was thinking maybe I'll go home and sleep in my own bed tonight." I look over my shoulder at the wild guesthouse. "I've got a workout to do in the morning and that requires some sleep."

"What's the plan tomorrow?" he asks. "Another two-mile sprint?"

"Nope, just five miles, easy."

He stands up and slips his flip-flops back on. "Want some company?"

Wait…what? I nearly trip over my own shoe. "Company?"

"Tomorrow. Running," he clarifies.

"Right. Running." That makes way more sense. "Sure…I mean if you think you can keep up."

Brody grins. "I'd like to try."

"My house. Eight o'clock." I catch myself smiling when he turns around and walks toward the house, but the second he lets the blond models invade his personal space, the smile easily fades. I make a quick exit, so I don't have to witness any more fan-girling. I can't decide if I should be honored or insulted by the fact that he can sit and have such a relaxed personal conversation with me and then seconds later, turn into this playboy with models on both his arms. Does he hook up with two at the same time?

I shake that image from my head and continue the half mile walk home. I'll feel better tomorrow when I kick his ass, running.

Annie Lucas: *Okay, I lied. Winning isn't everything. So sue me.*
15 seconds ago

Annie Lucas *is now friends with* **Carl London** *and 22 others*

Annie Lucas *likes the page* **Jason Brody Royals Pitcher**

True to his word, Brody appears in my front yard at five minutes before eight. He's wearing a red hoodie and track pants, his hair disheveled into a beautiful bedhead mess. My foot freezes mid-step when I see him.

"You look surprised." He leans against the lamppost in the yard.

I shrug like it's not a big deal. "You're the one who claimed you wouldn't ever be caught hanging out with high school kids again."

"This is not hanging out." He reaches into his pocket and pulls out a baseball cap, yanking it low over his eyes. "This is working out. And working out with you is not something Johnson would ever be concerned with. Or anyone for that matter."

I busy myself retying my running shoes. "Is that why you're in disguise, trying to hide your face?" I lift a finger, pointing at his hat.

"I did pitch pretty damn well yesterday. A mob of fans could be lurking around the neighborhood." He mocks, darting his eyes around, and then presses his back against the only tree in my yard. "Can you check for paparazzi? How does my hair look in case they do get a photo?"

I laugh and roll my eyes. "Are we running or what? It feels like your stalling?" I take off in a jog and Brody catches up with me right away. The swish of his track pants rubbing together creates a rhythm we can both move to without talking.

"So what's your definition of an easy five miles?" Brody asks after mile one. He sounds a tad winded, but it could be my imagination.

"I don't ever watch the clock when I run. Only after. But maybe seven and a half minute miles... Sometimes it's probably closer to eight minutes."

He pulls his hat up just enough for me to see his eyes. "Can I request an eight minute day?"

"Wimp." I grin at him and then my eyes betray me, roaming over the length of his body. So much for solemnly swearing not to do that. To cover my slipup, I start tossing technical corrections at him. "Maybe if your shoulders weren't all hunched up you could conserve some energy for your legs and lungs."

He grunts out a few choice words, but I see his shoulders drop.

"You look good with a neck," I say again and then regret the statement immediately. My face flames, and my gaze drops to the road in front of us.

"If you say so." Brody grins and falls into step with me, much less winded now. He's probably one of those runners who needs a lot of warm-up to get comfortable. "You're pretty into this running thing, aren't you?"

"Not like you and baseball," I say.

He's quiet for several seconds then finally replies. "I think it's exactly like me and baseball. Except maybe more like playing for my Triple-A team."

"Lower caliber, like I said."

He shakes his head. "That's not what I meant. It's just with Triple-A…my teammates were…"

Nicer? Willing to shake your hand? "Were what?" I ask, afraid to admit to what I saw through the windows last night.

"It's hard baseball without the show," he concludes, steering away from mentions of teammates. "Well, actually they do all kinds of weird crap for fans at minor league games, but our number one job is to play baseball."

"Isn't that your job here?"

"I don't know," he says, staring straight ahead, his expression shifting to what I know as the focused athlete face. "I'm just not sure anymore."

The awkward silence has finally arrived in time for the beginning of our third mile around the neighborhood. I concentrate on our steps and the sound of Brody's swishing pants. Pretty soon sweat is dripping down my face, and I'm lifting my T-shirt to wipe it away. From the corner of my eye, I'm nearly positive I catch Brody checking out my stomach, but he looks away so fast I can't be sure. And I'm not sure I'm ready to know that answer. I kick harder and increase the pace, despite it being an easy day. "Come on, superstar, let's see if you can really keep up."

His response is instant, his steps matching mine. And for a little while, we stop being Annie, the coach's daughter, and Brody, the new Royals pitcher. We have the same ability to leave our damaged outer shells behind and float through the streets as nothing more than two athletes.

In less than thirty minutes, the pressure, the doubts and fears, the guilt of built-up lies and past mistakes will return full force, but for now, that weight is off.

pre-all-star
BREAK

chapter 8

Lenny London: *Good luck to my St. T gal pals—Annie Lucas and Jackie Stonington—who are running at sectionals today. In case you're wondering, running is like driving only there's more sweating and less sitting. I don't recommend trying it if you haven't already.*
2 hours ago

"My dad's not coming," I say to Coach Kessler after tucking away my cell phone. "His flight got delayed in New York."

Coach K pats me on the shoulder. "It's all right. You'll have your best run ever today and qualify for state, and he'll be there for that race."

I can't do anything about it, so I nod and keep warming up.

Today's the first meet that I'm doing the mile and the two mile full-out. I've done both in two other meets, but Coach K had me run one race hard and the other event easy and then flip-flopped them at the next meet. Now I need to hit both with my best times so I can qualify for state.

I squint up at the bleachers and spot Savannah and her daughter Lily walking across the first row of seats.

A smile spreads across my face, and I run over to the fence to greet them. "What are you guys doing here?"

"Your dad called and told us you needed a cheerleader or two," Savannah says.

I high-five Lily, who doesn't like to talk much. She sometimes likes riding her bike alongside me while I run in our neighborhood.

"Thanks for coming," I say to both of them. A bullhorn sounds, and I hop down from the fence. "Gotta go."

"Good luck!" Savannah calls after me.

When it's time for the one-mile race, butterflies are going batshit crazy in my stomach, but I turn my focus to the track in front of me and up until that last lap, I'm following my routine perfectly. The only person ahead of me is Jackie Stonington. The logical part of me knows she's taller than me, her stride is longer, and most importantly, I don't *have* to beat her to qualify for state, but as we round the last curve, I can't think about anything but winning. My legs kick harder, my arms swing faster, and suddenly my step overtakes hers and I cross the finish line a full three strides in the lead.

Coach Kessler is going nuts, jumping up and down because St. Teresa's has just claimed the top two spots at sectionals for the one mile. My teammates are screaming like crazy, which is why I don't feel the muscles tensing in my right leg until I break away from the group and retrieve a Gatorade from my bag. Savannah gives me a thumbs-up from the bleachers and motions to her phone pressed against her ear, indicating that she's already calling Dad to tell him the news.

I finally see my time up on the scoreboard: *4:47.*

Not only is it my personal record, but also damn close to the state record. I start to head toward the bleachers again to sit with Savannah, but a guy leaning against the fence behind me catches my attention. I squint into the setting sun and try to identify the person with the *Chicago Blackhawks'* hat pulled way down over his face. He's in disguise.

Is it bad that I've memorized the outline of his body even without seeing his face?

I glance back at Savannah once more. She's turned around chatting with Lenny and some of the other junior girls who aren't on the track team. I check to see if anyone else is watching me and then slowly, I make my way over to the guy on the other side of the fence.

"I thought you were stuck in Chicago?"

Brody pulls the hat further over his face. "Nah. I wasn't on that flight. Your dad and Frank had to go to some meeting, I guess. My flight missed the storm by an hour."

I lift my tank top up to wipe sweat from my forehead. I bet the blond models never sweat. They probably smell like roses all the time. "But what are you doing *here*?" At a high school track meet. More specifically at *my* track meet.

He shrugs. "I was in the neighborhood. Didn't you hear? I got an apartment a block away from here."

I knew this would happen eventually. He's got a contract for half the season now and tons of money to spend on a place of his own. No need to borrow the London's guesthouse anymore.

I work really hard to hide the disappointment from my face. As much as I enjoy Lily's one-speed bike clicking beside me, I like running with Brody around the neighborhood even more. "So you've got your own man cave. I don't even want to know what will go on behind those doors."

Brody doesn't deny anything. *Figures*. But whatever. His free time, his life. I get it.

"Did you…um…see the race?" I ask, not knowing if he really was just wandering the block, or if he came to watch, and when he doesn't answer right away, I glance sideways at Brody. He's looking at the times on the board, like he's thinking hard.

"Your hamstring hurts," he says.

If it were Dad asking, I'd deny it. Instead, I nod.

"You shouldn't have pushed it so hard. You didn't need to win today."

So he did watch the race. "I know."

"What's the qualifying time for the two mile?"

"Eleven twenty-seven," I say right away.

"That's a cakewalk for you, right?" he asks.

"I wouldn't call it a cakewalk, but it's not full-out for me."

He points toward the running clock at one end of the track. "I know it's against your rituals of not checking your time during the race, but you can see the clock every time you hit the last straightaway. Just run the race against the clock, qualify, and then figure out your strategy for state later."

He remembers my race rituals? I mentioned it on our very first Sunday afternoon jog around the neighborhood, but that was weeks ago. "That could work."

"You can't get all *I'm the best* at the end and start trucking over people or you won't be able to walk tomorrow," he warns.

I bite my lip and look away from him. "That's gonna be hard."

He laughs and then both of us glance up to see a group of five girls in purple uniforms heading over this way.

"You're Jason Brody, aren't you?" one of the girls squeals.

"Guilty." Brody removes his hat and the serious expression is replaced by the playboy smirk I've seen on the cover of way too many newspapers and websites since Opening Day. "I was hoping to snag a hot dog from the concession stand, but this girl spotted me, begging for an autograph." He nods toward me, and I roll my eyes.

"We, like, *love* you," the girl who spoke first says, practically shoving me out of the way.

"Seriously," another girl adds.

"Can we get a picture?"

Savannah and Lily appear out of nowhere. She must be trained to spot this kind of commotion from a mile away. She holds out her hand for the girl's phone. "Let me take it for you."

The girls race around to the other side of the fence and Savannah narrows her eyes at Brody. "No more high school girls after this, understood?"

"Yeah, yeah," Brody says. "Women. Lots of women. Never girls. I know the drill."

Ugh. Talk about major TMI. I'd rather eat raw oysters than stick around to see this event.

My escape goes unnoticed because Brody's crowd never thins out for the rest of the meet. He's officially reached celebrity status. This is something that weighs heavily on my mind through most of my next race. Is he going to get too busy to hang out with me? Is he already hooking up with new girls every night? With the new downtown bachelor pad, why would he ever need my company?

And why do I even have to care? Why can't I go back to hating him?

During the race, I follow his plan exactly and keep my eyes on the clock. It literally kills me to not push it at the end, but I hold back and hit the finish line just under eleven minutes and twenty-seven seconds.

And I manage to do this without ever looking over at Brody and his parade of fans. Bonus points for me.

The doorbell rings at ten thirty at night. I've just showered and put on my pjs so I'm totally not expecting Brody at my front door. I glance outside into the driveway and spot what looks like a brand-new SUV. "Did you get an apartment *and* a car?"

"Yep," he nods. "Like it?"

He's holding a small black box and a pile of wires. The object he's brought over distracts me from answering the car question. "Are you cloning me or something?"

"Two Annies? Not sure I could handle that." He walks through the front door and locks it behind him. "Electrical stimulation."

"That sounds R-rated."

His forehead wrinkles, and he stops in the hallway. "Can't be R-rated since your dad told me to bring it over. Where is he? Not back from New York yet?"

"He will be in a few hours," I say. "Is this gonna hurt?"

"Not much. You're tough, you'll be fine. Last door on the left, right?" He steers me into my bedroom before I even answer him and flips on the light. "Lay down on your stomach."

I hesitate for a second, my brain scrambling to guess what this procedure will involve. Eventually, I flop onto the bed, grab a pillow, and pull it under my head. He sits on the other side of me and places several stickers attached to wires onto the back of my thigh. Goose bumps form all around the places where his fingers brush against my bare skin. My pulse shifts and it's now much closer to what it had been during sectionals today. My face heats up, too, and the reaction catches me off guard. I haven't felt these awkward guy/girl feelings around Brody since the day we met, when I interviewed him in his post-shower state.

That day, my embarrassment revolved around being in over

my head, not to mention potentially getting in trouble, but today is different. The goose bumps, the heat from his touch—I don't have to be a scientist to understand this reaction.

Forget it, Annie. Just forget it.

I use my athlete focus to block out this revelation, at least for right now. Brody turns on the black box and his hands finally leave my skin, giving me the chance to clear my head. I do feel a shock running through my leg from the machine, but it's not exactly painful.

"One hour of this three times a day until state, okay?"

I'm afraid he's going to leave, and I really don't want him to—for no reason I'm willing to admit. "So, did you get rid of all the girls eventually?"

He groans. "I took like a thousand pictures. There's no way I can go to your state meet."

Had he planned on going? Maybe Dad invited him. If Dad asked, Brody would probably want to say yes, though not for me exactly.

"Yeah, no one will be watching me run, it'll be all about you," I joke, pushing the questions aside.

"You were such an idiot tonight." He grins at me, before leaning back against my favorite pillows. *Okay, so he's not leaving.* "But watching you pass up that tall girl with six foot long legs, that was fucking awesome."

"And now I'm getting electrocuted for it."

Neither of us have a response to that because it's true. I got impulsive and stupid and yet it still felt awesome to win. And there's no way to know right now if it was worth it. Not until after state.

"Can I ask you something?" he says. I nod and, before speaking again, Brody plucks the book off my nightstand and starts flipping through it. "Why does your dad wear a wedding ring?"

I adjust my head on the pillow so I'm looking at his side, instead of his face. It's less intimidating this way. I mean, Jason Brody is stretched out across my bed, that's like every teenage girl in Kansas City's dream right now. "My parents are technically still married. I think my dad takes that saying, 'If you love someone let them go' a little too seriously."

"But where is she?"

I close my eyes and let out a breath. "I don't know. We saw her in December and she was in the middle of touring with some folk band."

"She's a musician?"

"Musician, singer, actress…adult film actress." I press my face into the pillow briefly, not wanting to take a chance of seeing his reaction to that last thing.

"Wow," Brody says. "How long has this been going on?"

"The running away or the porn films?" Okay, they aren't exactly porn, but really really close to it.

"The running away." His calm voice relaxes me, and I roll over onto my side to face him finally.

"Forever, I think. When Dad's baseball career didn't work out, she wanted to find her own spotlight. I can't remember much from when I was really little, but I remember Dad taking me to school on my first day of kindergarten." And I remember the teacher going all wide-eyed at my mismatched clothes and messy hair. My mom never has a hair out of place. "She wasn't around then. He'd just tell me she was working. I figured it out eventually."

"But you had Grams?" He idly flips through the pages of my book again.

"We moved from Texas to Arizona right before middle school so Grams could live with us. She was already having problems, early Alzheimer's, and my mom's brother, my uncle, wanted to put her in one of those homes run by the state, but Dad wouldn't let him."

I miss those days when Grams was lucid more than not. Now it's like she sleeps too much, and she doesn't ever have a grasp on reality. I don't tell Brody this, but I really want a few hours with the real Grams. Even though I'm happy Mom's out of the picture, I want to ask Grams about her before she started running from us. Like when she was my age. What was she like? I could have asked Mom on her last visit, but she's not a reliable source. And I'd ask Dad, but I'm a little bit afraid that she was a better person back then and if he remembers that, he'll never be able to let go.

"Grams is your mom's mom?" Brody's face fills with surprise. "She's not related to Jim?"

"Correct." I pick at the fuzzy material of my comforter, keeping my eyes down again. "He still loves her. I don't get it. It's like he thinks he can't do better. Sometimes I think he wants to stop having those feelings, but then she shows up again."

His brows rise. "So they're like, *together* when she visits…?"

"Oh yeah," I say. "And then when she leaves, he's a mess."

"That's fucked up. Especially with his leg and everything. I can't believe she screws around with him like that."

I nod my agreement. "Literally and emotionally."

"Sorry," he says quickly and returns to picking at the book again. "It's none of my business."

Truth is, I don't mind telling him these things. A few weeks ago, I would have been annoyed, considering how we loathed each other, but I know he's just curious and he's not going to judge Dad. Besides, it feels good to talk about it, especially because lately so many things that confused me about my life and my parents are starting to make sense.

Brody pulls himself upright and leans his head against the headboard. "Okay, ask me something and I'll answer it, it's only fair."

We both know what I want to ask him — *ex-convict, ex-convict, ex-convict* — but I chicken out and go for an easier question. "Are you Italian?"

He laughs and shakes his head. "Why would you think that?"

"You're dark," I say.

"My mom's Hispanic and my dad…" He pauses, biting his lower lip and glancing over at me. "Well, I've never met him but my guess is he's as white as you are."

"Do you think he knows that you're playing baseball?" And yes, I'm dying to ask if he's in jail, but ever since that night when we dangled our feet in the London's pool and I offhandedly asked him if his family had come to the game, I've wanted to find out those details even more than the *indiscretions*. Okay, maybe not more, but equally.

"No idea."

"What about your mom?"

"I don't think she knows either. She gave up on me when I was sixteen."

My eyes widen. "She gave up on you? Were you like homeless or what?"

"Let's just say, I caused her a lot of problems. She probably did the best she could." He shakes his head, like he doesn't know what to believe. "I wasn't homeless. I got a job, dropped out of school, and crashed at friends' places." He picks up a strand of my hair and twirls it around his finger. I can't feel his touch but just this small gesture makes me realize how much I'd like for his hand to be on my skin in some situation that doesn't involve hooking me up to electrical wires. "I know Jim has issues with your mom but he's a good guy. You're lucky, Annie."

Hearing him explain his past this way, it kind of makes the ex-convict thing seem both understandable and also behind him. I mean, look at him… He's a professional athlete, not that professional athletes haven't been known to commit horrible crimes now that I think about it…

But I don't want to think about that Jason Brody. I want to focus on the guy seated on my bed, here late at night with nothing on his agenda outside of helping me run at state.

My gaze travels to his finger holding my hair, and he drops it immediately.

"I know I'm lucky. In fact, we should do something special for my dad," I suggest.

"Like what?"

"Let me help you study for that GED test," I spit out fast before I can take it back. I know this would make Dad very happy. He's talked about it a bunch with Brody when I've been around, and I've overheard him and Savannah discussing the subject.

Brody chews on his bottom lip again—he's thinking. "I want to, I really do…"

"Okay, then it's settled. I'll help you study and whatever I don't know, we'll find someone who does. It can be like a summer project for both of us."

"I'm not going to pass that test, Annie," he says with some hesitancy. Finally, he lets out a breath. "I feel like that guy in *Shawshank Redemption* saying, '*I don't read so good.*'"

I stare at him openmouthed. "You can't read?"

He rolls his eyes. "Of course I can read. I'm dyslexic. It's not a big secret or anything, though I'm not looking for a big PSA campaign for learning disabilities with my name attached. Even if I can learn the material, taking the test in a timed setting... It would be almost impossible to pass. It's like asking your dad to hop on his right leg."

I'm quiet for a long moment, my brain reeling with ideas. "Don't give up on it yet. I bet there's some alternate test or an oral exam."

He looks nervous already. "I'm sure there's something, but it would have to be completely confidential. I know it may seem mean and self-centered, but I'm not ready to be a public advocate for dyslexia."

"Your secret's safe with me." I do the sign of the cross that I've picked up from Catholic school.

Brody drifts into several seconds of deep thinking, maybe about the GED test, maybe about his parents or mine. I can't do anything but stare at him while he stares at my book, pretending to flip through the pages. I didn't think it was possible to find someone you can relax around and yet they still get your heart racing.

I don't know when this happened, but I know for sure tonight I've developed a big fat crush on Jason Brody, and unfortunately there's a club forming and membership is growing with every inning he pitches.

And this isn't like my previous boyfriend Kenny or any other relationship I've been in. Those were more like experiments in learning how to make out and pretend you love someone. With Brody, I want to slice him open and see everything inside. I want to stand by the railing at Kauffman Stadium, all the way in the stands, and feel his eyes meet mine. No, I want to see his eyes *search* for mine. To pick me out of a crowd of thousands.

But I'm not stupid. I get that this is nearly impossible, and

I'm not planning on stepping in that direction ever. I'm just a high school girl (high school girls are off-limits according to Savannah), and he's a hot rookie pitcher whose life is currently in the process of taking a one-eighty turn. My dad has been his mentor, his biggest supporter, of course he's going to connect with me. Of course we're going to share in our respect for my dad, but I can't imagine him ever wanting more from me. It doesn't fit.

"You can unhook now," Brody says, nodding toward the machine. He yawns and then adds, "I should get going. Jim will be back soon, right?"

I tug the wires from my leg and sigh. "Yeah, any minute now."

He pats me on the head like a little sister. "I'll see you later, Annie. Lock the door behind me, okay?"

After he's gone and I've locked the door, I go into Grams' room, crawl into bed beside her, and spill all the details of my secret unrequited crush on Jason Brody. Maybe if I say it aloud I'll be able to get rid of it sooner. I'm worried about the inevitable rejection that may come from these feelings, but even more than that, I'm worried about falling hard for someone — not just Brody, anyone — and not being able to let go. I've seen what that's done to Dad's life. He's ruined by it. I'd rather be alone than be head over heels in love. It's like being drunk. Your IQ drops a hundred points and you make stupid choices.

By the time I finished telling Grams everything, I'd made up my mind — crushing on Brody had to stop, for both our sakes.

chapter 9

Lenny London: *I will eat my words only when they come in 5 different fruit flavors.*
23 hours ago

Jason Brody Royals Pitcher: *"Kids should practice autographing baseballs. This is a skill that's often overlooked in Little League." — Tug McGraw*
22 hours ago

Annie Lucas: *What's the deal with overshoes? So you put them over your shoes? Why do I need a whole poem about this mundane, old-fashioned task? My brain isn't wired to understand poetry. Can I please be excused?*
3 hours ago

Carl London: *Watch me on ESPN tonight with my sis, the amazing Lenny London! 7pm ET.*
1 hour ago

Major League Baseball's Hottest Rookie Pitcher Proves to Be Quite the Lady's Man... *Nineteen-year-old rookie pitcher Jason Brody, recently signed for half the season with the Royals, hasn't wasted any time*

showing fans that fast isn't exclusive to his pitches. A
source counted four different women entering and exiting
the player's hotel room during the team's three night stay
in Atlanta this week.

I stare at the photos of three different bimbos putting their
lips on Brody's lips. *God I hope he's getting daily testing done.*

Disgusted, I toss the magazine aside in the dugout and turn
my attention back to practice. I've only got a week until state
and my hamstring's feeling way better. I can't let my mind get
bogged down with obsessing over Brody's "groupies."

After an easy four-mile run around downtown, I'm eating
an apple and relaxing in the dugout. Frank is standing right
outside, making pages of notes on his clipboard. I get up and
move beside him, crunching my apple. "You know what your
designated hitters were eating before practice today?"

"What?" Franks asks. "Animal bi-products? Whales? Something else that will cause a team-related scandal?"

"Hot dogs," I say, and when he doesn't react, I repeat it, "Hot
dogs, Frank! If I ate a hot dog before track practice, even the
lightest workout, I'd be puking my guts out." I gesture toward
the players swinging bats around. "I'm not seeing any puking
out here."

He narrows his eyes at me. "What's your point, kid?"

"They're lazy." I throw my hands up like this is so obvious
because it totally is. "They can't run for shit and they're not all
hitting home runs every time they're at bat. Could be useful to
have a little speed for those doubles and triples?"

"They're big guys," he says. "They're not made to run fast."

"Okay," I correct. "How about *faster*? Think about it... five
seconds—hell, one second—can make the difference between

being safe and out. Add that up for an entire season, and I bet you'd get at least four or five more wins on the Royals' record."

He sets his clipboard down on an empty bench and turns to me, arms folded across his chest. "From my experience, designated hitters are the biggest prima donnas in baseball. They'll all throw a diva tantrum if I even so much as suggest a different workout. Plus, if we slim them down too much, they might not hit as well."

I shrug. "Whatever, you're the manager."

Frank lets out a frustrated sigh before walking out onto the first base line. "If I find any one of you eating hot dogs before practice, I'm fining you ten thousand dollars!"

I snort back a laugh and head toward where Dad is standing, but the sight of Lenny, Carl, their dad (aka First Base) and his wife walking this way stops me. Lenny's wearing a flowered skirt that falls past her knees and a light pink cardigan. She's traded her usual weekend red lipstick for a neutral gloss. Lenny's mom is wearing an outfit almost identical to her daughter's except in yellow. Carl and First Base are dressed for a golf game at the country club.

"Hey, Len," I say, pulling her aside. "What's going on?"

She points toward right field where a camera crew is setting up. "ESPN is doing a story on my dad, the family man. I'm gagging already."

I look her up and down. "That outfit is so not you."

She rolls her eyes. "No kidding."

Dad joins me just as Lenny is heading back to her perfect family. We both watch First Base put his arm around his daughter as he shakes hands with the ESPN interviewer guy. The second the guy turns around, Lenny shoves her dad, wiggling out of his hold, and stepping off to the side.

"Stuff like that makes me glad my baseball career didn't

work out," Dad says.

"She's not bad," I say.

"I know that." Dad tugs on my ponytail before walking back toward the pitcher's mound.

I stare after him, trying to figure out what he meant by that if he wasn't making the comment simply to note that Lenny is a brat. I mean, she sort of is, but rightfully so. And she's a straight shooter who knows how to keep a secret. I'm used to girls who want to do nothing but gossip. Lenny's probably heard enough gossip for two lifetimes.

The interview goes on for over an hour. I can't hear what anyone is saying from my spot outside the dugout, but I can clearly see smiles plastered on and then fading the second the camera turns off.

I turn my focus back to Brody on the pitcher's mound. Dad's behind the plate now with a catcher's mask, playing umpire. Not a single Royals batter has been able to hit off Brody today. I keep my satisfaction carefully hidden because I know the team needs people who can actually score some runs.

But practice is the best place to fantasize about Jason Brody without feeling like I'm giving in to the crush. He's focused on home plate and nothing more, and there's no line of girls, women, and kids in little league uniforms waiting to meet him or sleep with him. I can almost fool myself into thinking they don't exist. At least until I start envisioning this apartment of his—leather furniture, silver countertops and appliances, remote control curtains on all the windows, and a giant aquarium with blue lights that cast a sexy glow over the room, setting the mood for his nightly hookups. Of course, I've never been in this apartment of his, but I'm sure it looks something like that.

One of the overweight designated hitters actually manages to connect the bat with the ball and hits it right toward the pitcher's mound. Brody sprints to the side, then dives right, catching the ball in his glove before springing to his feet, easily making the throw to first base.

I hear laughter coming from the dugout behind me, but I don't turn around.

"Stupid kid," one of the other pitchers says. "He's gonna break his arm fielding a ball in practice."

"Nice play, Brody!" Dad shouts, and Frank claps along with him. The team's reaction is quite the opposite of Dad's and Frank's. Lots of eyes rolling behind Brody's back. One of the outfielders even flips him off. I grind my teeth together and lean on my hands so I don't end up returning the gesture.

"Don't worry, he'll choke eventually," another player says from the dugout. "They all do."

"Or he'll get arrested again and open up that roster spot permanently. I'm sick of this in and out routine."

"How about you both get your asses out there and practice," a different voice says. I glance over my shoulder and see Juan Julio, who plays third base, hitting the pitcher in the head with his glove before stepping out of the dugout. "Maybe that'll help you earn your spot back on the roster."

I like him.

After a few more minutes, Lenny joins me while the rest of her family does solo interviews.

"That boy is full of hotness," Lenny says, nodding toward Brody. "Why do they insist on practicing with their shirts on?"

My face heats up, and I look anywhere but the pitcher's mound. "I think I'd lose my lunch if all of them went skins."

"Good point. We'd need to be selective." Lenny finally peels her eyes away from Brody. "So, are you getting nervous about state next weekend? I promised Jackie I'd come watch her race."

"I didn't know you were friends with Jackie?"

Lenny pulls a compact from her purse and reapplies her lip gloss. "I've been tutoring her all year in physics and calculus. She's on a track scholarship at St. Teresa's, so she's got to maintain a B average."

I had no idea Jackie Stonington got financial aid to attend St. Teresa's. As much time as she and I spend running alongside each other, we've hardly talked. It isn't animosity exactly, just a silent tension that comes with me stealing her spotlight. Me, the new student who happens to be a year behind her. She did beat me in the two-mile run at sectionals but then again, I didn't really race, I just focused on hitting the qualifying time.

"You're her tutor? She's a senior and you're a junior?" I say.

Lenny shrugs. "What can I say? I'm brilliant."

"Where's Jackie going to run next year?"

"She hasn't gotten a scholarship yet," Lenny says. "She's hoping maybe at state there'll be some scouts in the stands."

This really surprises me and makes me just a bit sympathetic toward Jackie–and I totally don't want to be. Not until after state anyway. Before I'd left Arizona, I'd already met the track coach for Arizona State. "But she won the two mile at sectionals. Last year she placed at state. She should already have a scholarship."

"Yeah, but St. Teresa's is only Class II. The top colleges give offers to state champions and Class IV state qualifiers first and then they get to us after," Lenny explains. "That's what she's hoping will happen at state."

When I don't say anything, Lenny adds, "I'm sure it's gonna be a great meet. You guys will both do awesome."

I don't get a chance to respond because wailing sirens are going off all around us. "What the hell is that?"

Lenny looks annoyed but not freaked out like me. "Tornado sirens."

My head turns upward toward the sky, taking in the odd green color. But it's not even raining or storming or anything. "There's gonna be a tornado? Should we be out here?"

Frank is already ordering the players to head inside and take shelter. First Base argues with Frank and tries to leave, but I grab Lenny's arm in the hallway outside the locker room and hold on to it tightly. "You can't drive through a tornado!"

First Base laughs at me, but Frank lays down the law. "Locker room, everyone. No arguments. If you leave here while the sirens are going off, our insurance won't cover your untimely death. You can take off as soon as they lift the warning."

Many grown men grumble over these instructions. Seriously? Do they think being rich baseball players makes them immune to death by twister?

I search for Dad in the crowd of players, coaches, and ESPN people. I duck under arms and squeeze my way over to him. "Grams is at home—there's no basement."

He's already got the phone to his ear. "Caroline is there with her, and Savannah and Lily are on their way over. And our house is south of the storm's path. Savannah says they don't have sirens going off over there. They're fine. Just stay right here, okay, Ann?"

I nod and stuff my shaking hands in my pockets where he can't see them.

Dad escapes into his office with Frank and shuts the door. Lenny finds me again several minutes later while I'm standing in the middle of the locker room Googling tornado pictures. "Look at this! That's exactly what the sky is like right now."

Lenny barely glances at my phone and then shrugs. "I

haven't been in here for years."

"Really?" I'm surprised because, despite my failure at proving maturity my first time in the locker room, I still haven't exactly been banned.

"I mean, why would I come in here? To wish *Daddy* good luck before a game?" She laughs. "He'd think I was on drugs."

My tornado research is only reiterating the fact that it really seems like we're about to have one come spiraling through here. Logically, I know the walls are concrete or something that will hold up, and we're not going to end up buried alive under a pile of rubble but, logic is quickly losing the battle today.

I tug at the collar of my T-shirt. It feels tight. My stomach is cramping and I'm debating whether I can use the bathroom stalls in the locker room. Sweat trickles down the back of my neck. "Is it hot in here?" I ask Lenny.

She's flipping through Facebook status updates on her phone, but she shakes her head. "I'm fine."

I discreetly move toward the bathroom stalls and decide it might be safest to sit on the floor in case I suddenly need to go. I wipe more sweat from my forehead and breathe in jagged breaths, fighting off the nausea.

I'd be fine if those damn sirens would turn off.

Red cleats clatter across the floor and then stop in front of the stall I'm occupying. Brody opens the door and looks down at me, seated on the floor, my knees pulled to my chest, my face half buried, my back leaning against the wall. "Annie, what are you doing?"

"Bathrooms are one of the safest places to go during a tornado."

"Says who?"

"Google." I press my forehead against my knees, closing my

eyes to keep from feeling dizzy.

"You don't look so good," he says and squats down in front of me and then laughs. "Don't tell me you're scared of tornadoes?"

"How can I be scared of something I've never seen?" I argue. I detest this feeling of my subconscious mind taking over control of my body and causing these physical reactions. If something is going to make me sweaty and out of breath, I want a choice in the matter. This is exactly how I imagine falling in love—not that I've experienced it before, but I get the sense that your subconscious takes over and just like with fears, you have no control. No choice. And it sucks. Big time.

"I've never seen zombies before, and I'm scared to death of them," Brody says.

"We're not even in Kansas!" I protest. "This is Missouri. We're not supposed to have tornadoes in Missouri."

He sits all the way down and scoots beside me. "Actually, tornadoes are a Midwest thing."

I groan. "You're never going to let me live this down, are you?"

When I lift my head to look at him, the amusement falls from his face. "You really don't look good. Want me to get your dad?"

I grab his ankle, anchoring him to the bathroom floor. "No! He'll make fun of me forever. One of you is better than both of you."

His forehead wrinkles as he studies my face. "I think you're having one of those panic attack things. Don't people usually pass out from those or stop breathing or something?"

"I'm not having a panic attack!" I exhale and then bury my face again. Actually, I very well might be having a panic attack. "If I pass out or stop breathing *then* you can get my dad, okay?"

I feel heat from him leaning closer, the scent of his deodorant and the grass from the field seeps through my nose. He flips my ponytail to the side and then his fingers land lightly on the back of my neck. His skin is warm and rough. "Everybody's afraid of something, Annie."

"What are you afraid of?" I ask. "Besides zombies."

"Cops." He laughs darkly, reminding me of the conversation I heard earlier between the relief pitchers. "I'm kidding…mostly. I've had my share of being 'scared straight' by cops, I won't lie about that. I guess I'm afraid of addiction."

"Like alcohol?"

"Maybe," he says, thinking. "It's more of a general thing than something specific. I'm afraid of starting something that I can't make myself stop, you know?"

I lift my eyes to meet his. Boy, do I know. But I've never heard anyone word it that way. Not exactly. I think a lot of people look forward to being absorbed by something. Falling down that rabbit hole. "But you're addicted to baseball, to pitching. I can see that with my own eyes."

"Yeah and it scares the shit out of me sometimes," he admits. "And you're addicted to winning. I've seen that with my own eyes."

Is that true? Am I addicted to winning? I kind of proved that at sectionals when I sacrificed my hamstring unnecessarily in order to beat Jackie Stonington. "I think my addiction is not as severe as yours."

"Maybe what I'm really afraid of is having more than one addiction," he says. "That's when you really get screwed up in the head."

"I don't know," I say, bitterly thinking of Dad with Mom. "One addiction can totally screw you up."

This conversation distracted me for a good two minutes, but I can't block out the sirens any longer. I cover my ears with my hands. "I wish they would turn those off."

"You have no color left in your face." He leans in even more, his breath hitting my cheek and making the hair on the back of my neck stand up. His fingers massage my neck and I'm sure he must be able to feel the goose bumps he's given me. "You're all clammy now, too."

Great. Just what every girl wants to hear a hot guy tell her.

"Let's talk about something else," he says. "How about school? Is it going okay?"

I let out a short laugh. He's trying way too hard. I know he doesn't want to talk about academics. But whatever. I'll try anything. "I'm a millimeter away from a D in Spanish at the moment, which would make me ineligible to run at state next weekend."

"Spanish?" he says. "Like what? What are you struggling with?"

"Conjugating verbs."

"That does sound very…technical." His breath is still landing on my skin, and it's doing a good job of distracting me. "Give me an example?"

I breathe in and out, trying to relax over the wail of the sirens. "Like if I wanted to say, *I'm speaking*, then I have to know how to say *you're speaking* and *he's speaking* and *she's speaking*…and then I have to know the past tense of all of those. I just want to memorize the words and string them together to make sentences, but it's not that simple."

"It's easier than English, actually," he says, and before I can ask him how he knows I remember what he told me about his mom. And then Jason Brody, hot rookie pitcher, is whispering Spanish verbs into my ear. "*Estoy hablando, estás hablando, está hablando, están hablando.*"

Heat crawls from my belly up to my neck and eventually my cheeks. "You're going to be my tutor this week," I whisper. "What about working and running and playing and sleeping...? Actually, just make up anything and say it in Spanish."

He laughs softly and moves his hand lower, rubbing circles between my shoulder blades. He continues speaking into my ear, low and sexy, and it's such a turn-on, I close my eyes and get lost in it.

"Anoche soñé contigo y esta mañana no me quiero despertar... me haces feliz... Me gustaría poder decirte lo que siento... Quiero decirte todos mis secretos..."

After I don't know how long, Brody's tone changes, and he switches to English, jolting me out of my meditation/fantasy. "The sirens stopped. We should go check and see if the warning's been lifted."

I stand up on shaky legs and both of us exit the bathroom stall. "Thanks, Brody," I say while we're still alone.

He smiles at me. "No problem. Your secret phobia is safe with me."

I check to make sure no one else is nearby. "So...I looked into the GED stuff we talked about and..." I glance around again and then turn my gaze back to Brody. "You can get extended time and do some of the sections as an oral exam, and it's all completely confidential. I asked my school counselor, and she just said that you need proof of your diagnosis. Do you have that?"

Tension and anxiety fill his expression, but he nods. "It exists, I just don't have it myself."

"Probably in your school records," I suggest. "Was it school people who did your diagnostic testing?"

"Yeah." He exhales and then gives me a weary smile. "Guess I have no way out of this now."

"I'll help you," I remind him as we walk back into the main part of the locker room.

Lenny looks up from her phone and yells to everyone, "Kansas City is now under a Tornado Watch. We're free!"

Brody rests his hands on my shoulders and whispers, "You survived." He gives me a quick squeeze and then lets go.

After Dad and I get home, guilt eats at me because I told Brody I'd help him study and I know zilch about dyslexia. How the hell am I supposed to help him? Read everything to him? I set my Spanish grade concerns aside and Google dyslexia.

An hour goes by in no time and I'm still researching. From what I've learned, it sounds like having dyslexia means words can appear smashed together or spaced incorrectly. A sentence may appear more like this: Jason Brody isth e mostsex ypitchere ver. Also, people with dyslexia are often of above average intelligence and extremely hardworking.

I'm positive that last part is true specifically in Brody's case. He's the most hardworking athlete I've ever met.

My gaze drifts to the iPod lying on top of the stack of GED practice lessons my counselor gave me. I wonder if my voice humming in his ears for lengthy amounts of time will have the same effect on him as it did for me while he whispered sexy Spanish verbs into my ear today.

I set up my own little recording area at my desk, the first GED practice lesson resting in front of me, and hit record. Hopefully he won't laugh at my attempts to sound sexy reciting fraction and square root practice problems.

chapter 10

Annie Lucas: *Nothing beats hitting up the stadium concession stand for pregame/post Spanish cram session eats.*
10 minutes ago

"I'm not gonna be your damn history interview," Frank barks at me. "How old do you think I am?"

Ignoring his refusal to help with this history project that I need done ASAP, I set my hot dog, nachos, and Cherry Coke Icee on the edge of his desk. "You're old enough to remember the Yankees 1995 season…"

Frank stops shuffling papers, looks at me, and lifts an eyebrow. I smooth away the smirk threatening to spread over my face. *Thank you, Dad* for that one-line clincher. My history teacher is obsessed with the Yankees, so I know interviewing Frank could get me an A. And I really need an A.

"I got a game to manage tonight, kid," Frank says, then he sighs and nods toward the door. "Come on, walk on the field with me."

I smile down at the floor while scrambling to my feet, snatching the hot dog and my notebook and pen from Frank's desk.

"What do you know about '95? You weren't even born yet," Frank grumbles, sounding exactly like the old man he's trying not to be. I trail behind him, hoping that was a rhetorical question because all Dad told me was to mention 1995. "Everyone forgets about '95. You know why? We didn't make it to the World Series that year. But I'll tell you what, that September was some of the most amazing, crowd-pleasing baseball I've ever seen."

Frank and I make it out onto the field where fans are slowly trickling in. It's batting practice right now, so the stands won't fill for about an hour and a half. I stuff the hot dog into my mouth and leave it hanging there while I write as quickly as I can.

"Guess who had their rookie season that year?" Frank asks, and after seeing that I can't talk, he answers. "Derek Jeter."

The mention of the word *rookie* causes me to glance around, looking for signs of Brody. I spot him in the bullpen with Dad. *God, he looks hot in that Royals' uniform.* My heart sinks, seeing tangible evidence of this divide between us. Professional athlete and well…me. Just me. A nobody in comparison.

After I jot down plenty of notes from Frank's thorough explanation of the Yankees' "most underrated season," I walk over to the bullpen just as Brody is exiting, his glove tucked under his arm. The need to feel that comradery we've had lately is so strong, I can't resist approaching him.

I wave my remaining hot dog half in front of him. "I'm taunting you with forbidden fruit. Got ten thousand bucks to lose?"

He swats my hand away. "Cut that out."

"Come on, you know you want it." I bump my shoulder into his, trying to knock him off balance, but he's too quick. He grabs both my arms to steady me and then lets go like I've got leprosy or something.

"Oh, I get it," I say. "This is the focused athlete version of Brody. No celebrity date or fangirls to make out with…"

He takes a long stride into the dugout, and I hang back. But I don't miss the repeat of that night at the Londons' party, where several of Brody's teammates stopped talking the second he came near—today's it's four of the Royals pitchers. But this time, he's not attempting to shake hands or make conversation. His head is down, and he's aggressively taping his left wrist with a roll of white athletic tape.

"Why don't you let the trainer do that?" I say, following the retreating teammates with my eyes.

"Because I'm a big boy," he snaps. "I can tape my own damn wrist."

Whoa. Okay. Someone's grumpy today. I reach out and grab the back of his jersey, giving it a little tug. "Shake out of this. You're gonna play just fine, like every other game you've been in so far this season."

"Glad you're so sure." He rips off the tape with his teeth and then yanks his long-sleeve shirt over his wrist, covering it. "Can you please just go hang out with Lenny and eat free shrimp or whatever the hell you guys do during the game?"

The words hit like a punch in the gut, but I do my best to shake them off. "Yeah…sure. No problem."

I turn halfway around before I hear Brody say my name, so quiet I'm not sure if it really happened. But I glance over my shoulder anyway. He's leaning against the metal post framing the dugout now, his glove tucked under his arm again.

"Sorry," he says, the second I'm fully turned around.

My face is on fire. This humiliation wouldn't happen if I didn't harbor all these secret feelings. We'd both just care the same instead of me caring so much more. "It's fine."

He glances around and after it's clear no one is nearby, he shuts his eyes. "I had the worst meeting with Johnson and some of his *people* today."

Every time I hear Johnson's name, my heart speeds up, remembering that night in the bar and the way he looked at both of us like we were…like we were *dispensable*.

I take a step closer so Brody can lower his voice even more. "Yeah?"

Brody opens his eyes again, squinting into the setting sun. "Have you ever had one of those conversations with someone where they manage to tell you how great you are while simultaneously making you feel like you're worth nothing?"

"Like a backhanded compliment?" I suggest, my stomach already tying in knots. When will this instability end for him and for Dad? For all of us. "Like telling me I run fast…*for a girl*?"

"Kind of." He sighs. "I get hung up on such fucking stupid shit sometimes. It doesn't matter."

"You're right. It doesn't matter," I say, feeling that surge of confidence after landing on the right words. "Only the numbers matter. And your numbers are awesome right now."

He flashes me a halfhearted smile. "Remind me next time not to snap at the person who always has the answer."

My cheeks warm for a completely different reason than a minute ago. "I do have a perfect record so far, don't I?"

For a second, our eyes lock and it feels like one of us is about to spill something important. *Please let it be Brody and not me. Impulse control, Annie.* But then Brody taps a light punch to my shoulder, as if to say, *Thanks, pal* before walking away.

When he's out of sight, I collapse against the fence, close my eyes, and groan. This is getting totally out of control. He's Jason-freakin'-Brody. Twenty years from now, Dad will be old like Frank, telling some annoying teenager about Brody's rookie season, like Frank did when he mentioned Derek Jeter. And Brody will be rich, famous, and retired with a lifetime of athletic endorsements to sit on.

I bet even Derek Jeter had some friendly comradery with a batboy or something his rookie year. Someone who is far gone from his life now. That's what I'll be to Brody in twenty years— the forgotten batboy.

I should probably distance myself sooner rather than later. It will make things easier. Except we've got this whole Johnson-may-give-us-all-the-boot issue hanging over our heads and, for now, that requires me to help wherever and whenever I can.

Or maybe that's just my excuse.

Mostly to spite Brody and his asshole comment about eating free shrimp while watching the game, when the ball game starts, I decide to hang out in Dad's office and watch it on his TV. Brody goes in during the fourth inning, only lets one batter on base, pitches the rest of the game. Lenny's dad hits a home run, bringing in the batter on first. We beat the Oakland A's 2–0.

Hopefully I'm right. Hopefully the numbers are what matters.

chapter 11

Carl London: *I had class today? Oops.*
23 hours ago

Jason Brody Royals Pitcher: *"All pitchers are born pitchers." —Joe DiMaggio*
1 hour ago

Lenny London: *About to watch my friends—Annie Lucas and Jackie Stonington—run an entire mile. On purpose. Wtf is wrong with them? Whatever. Go team.*
5 minutes ago

Don't look at the clock. Don't look at the clock.

Instead, I focus all my attention on Jackie Stonington's back. Her stride is longer than mine, but after rounding the last straightaway on our third lap during the one-mile race, I can feel her panic. She knows I'm right on top of her. She knows I haven't made my move yet. She knows I'm about to.

I have no idea who's behind me. It's hard to believe we started in a group of twenty runners. I don't hear or feel anything but Jackie and her steps. We cross the start/finish line for the third time and the bell rings, signaling the last lap. Our teammates are lined up in various places on the inside of the track, cheering us on. Both our names were yelled during the first two laps but as we broke away from the pack and took the lead, they all became the Jackie Stonington fan club. Which I get, I totally do. She's been with these girls for four years. She's graduating and competing in her last high school track meet ever.

And the lack of "Go, Annie!" emerging from inside the track only drives me harder to win.

My toes get dangerously close to her heels before I finally step around and take a huge stride forward. My steps match perfectly with Jackie's, our elbows practically rubbing together. And I hear her breathing change, the gasp that comes with panic and losing the mental game. I can feel a grin begin to spread across my face, but I tuck it away quickly and focus on lengthening my stride, pulling ahead.

We hit the halfway mark on the track and blood pumps to my head and ears so hard I can't hear or feel Jackie's presence. The distance between us grows to several strides apart as I round the last straightaway. My heels kick harder and a tunnel forms around me, my eyes zooming in on the finish line.

I cross the line and take ten more strides before stopping abruptly, causing all the blood to shift toward my feet and my vision to temporarily blacken. I bend over and catch my breath. It takes a full ten seconds for Jackie to cross the finish line and by then, the ringing has died down in my ears and I can hear Coach Kessler congratulating both of us.

The announcer's voice fills the stadium, "*A new state record set in the sixteen hundred meter run by Annie Lucas, junior from St. Teresa's Academy.*"

By the time I stand up and glance around, accepting the bottle of water a meet volunteer has just handed me, Jackie is inside the track, sitting on the grass near the long-jump pit. I stand in the middle of the track, past the finish line as the eighteen other runners complete their race and watch Jackie, her head buried in her hands, crying so hard she's shaking while Coach Kessler squats beside her, offering comforting words. A completely new feeling settles itself in the pit of my stomach.

Jackie and I have a few hours to kill between races and of course engaging in small talk while hanging out in the locker room isn't gonna happen. So both of us busy ourselves following the rest of the world's every move via our smartphones. I'm ashamed to admit that I spend a good hour stalking the Twitter accounts of several of Brody's recent celebrity dates. When I pull up the Twitter page for a model/actress named Shannon Belmont, the first thing I see is a picture of her and Brody on a red carpet posted three hours ago.

@shannonBelmont: Hot date + premiere of my first movie Swimsuit Models of Sports Illustrated! #BestDayEver #JasonBrodyIsHot @JasonBrodyPitcher

I choke on the gulp of lemon Gatorade I've just swallowed. *Swimsuit Models of Sports Illustrated* is the title of a movie? And a movie worthy of a red carpet premiere in…I flip through @shannonBelmont's tweets and land on the answer: Chicago.

It's not like I expected Brody to be at my state meet. I totally didn't. But since he showed up at sectionals, I can't help but be disappointed hearing he's in Chicago watching swimsuit models parade around on the big screen.

When it's finally time for us to head back onto the track, I do a double take after seeing the guy—arms crossed, hat pulled low over his eyes—standing next to Dad. Both of them are leaning against the fence in front of the bleachers.

How the hell did Brody get from a movie premiere in Chicago

three hours ago back to Kansas City?

Dad waves at me, signaling me to come over there.

"Can I go say hi?" I ask Coach Kessler, nodding toward Dad. She hesitates so I add, "We've still got forty-five minutes."

Coach K grants me permission to talk to Dad but warns me to be in the warm-up area in no more than twenty minutes.

As soon as I get over to Dad, I drop my gym bag at my feet and accept a giant bear hug. "I'm so proud of you, honey. You were amazing!"

"We've been talking to college scouts for two hours straight," Brody says.

I step out of Dad's embrace and stare at both of them. "Seriously?"

Dad laughs. "Not for two hours straight, but we had a steady stream of them coming over to our seats to chat for a while after your first race."

Brody turns his back to me and points at random people placed in the stands, "Missouri State, University of Illinois, Northwestern, Cal Tech, Ohio State, Penn State…basically the entire Big 10 conference."

"Oh my God," I whisper under my breath. Of course, I've always wanted a scholarship. My old coach in Arizona had pretty much told me I'd get offered one from Arizona State, but hearing this many schools are interested, it's insane.

"We've been negotiating all kinds of perks," Brody says. "I figured while they're fighting over you, might as well ask for some extras—single dorm room, a golf cart to haul you from class to class, an honor student to do your homework for you, room service for all your meals. The basics."

Dad rolls his eyes. "Don't listen to him. We've only dipped a toe or two into an NCAA gray area."

"You should probably get an agent," Brody suggests.

I notice today he's wearing the St. Teresa's T-shirt I gave him and a Chicago Bulls cap pulled low over his eyes. This returns me to reality because, *hello*, what happened to the suit jacket and skinny tie he was just wearing at that premiere. *In Chicago*.

"Hey…" I say. "How did you get here from—"

"From where?" his eyes dance with amusement.

Damn, I think I've just been caught internet stalking Jason Brody.

"Nowhere." My face flushes. "Just…*you know*, figured you had somewhere else to be. Besides a high school track meet."

Brody opens his mouth, and I know he's about to tease me for the stalking, but Dad claps a hand on his shoulder and says, "I asked him to come. Figured you'd be excited to have more people cheering for you instead of Jackie." He glances around the bleachers. "Frank's here somewhere, too. Might be negotiating those perks with college coaches…And Savannah and Lily."

So Dad asked him to come. Makes sense. I release a sigh and attempt to hide my disappointment, but Brody leans in close, invading my personal space. "In case you were wondering, I watched about five minutes of that movie and then left."

I snort back a laugh. "Seriously?"

Before Brody can explain, Dad interrupts, pointing to my knee. "How's your leg? You gonna make it through this next race?"

I jump up and down a few times, then lift my knees one at a time, testing out my hamstring. "It honestly feels great. Better than ever."

Dad's eyes narrow like he's not sure whether to believe me. "I'm gonna get you a heating pad from the trainer." He hobbles away before I can stop him. But whatever. If he wants me to heat, I'll heat.

Since we're alone, I bend down and open my gym bag. "I've got something for you," I tell Brody, before standing up and handing him my old iPod. He stares at it, confused. "I made you some lessons for your GED studying. I figured you could listen to them while you're on the road."

"Lessons? Like you read the test prep book and recorded it?"

I nod. "The first three study guides for each section plus the first practice quizzes. It's like sixteen hours of material. You can write your answers down on paper and then grade them yourself."

He opens his mouth and then closes it again as he lifts his eyes to meet mine. "How long did this take you?"

I laugh trying to brush it off. Maybe my real intentions are too obvious. "About sixteen hours."

He squeezes the iPod in his hand. "Thanks, Annie. This is… really nice."

I divert my eyes to the bleachers. "Okay, so tell me again how awesome I am? Which colleges want me and who's going to beg the most and worship me the most? Because I totally have to be worshipped at all times."

"They all want you." He levels me with one of his famous Jason Brody intense athlete looks. "But they might not if you totally choke on this next race."

I stick my tongue out at him and accept the heating pad Dad hands me after returning. That's when I glance up, above Brody's and Dad's heads, and notice the crowd hanging on the railing of the bleachers, like we're at Kauffman Stadium and not a high school track meet.

"Uh-oh," I mumble, low enough for only Dad and Brody to hear. "Your disguise failed."

For a split second, I'm sure I catch something that resembles annoyance or exhaustion cross Brody's face. But then it's gone and he's wearing a huge grin, looking up over his shoulder at the gathering crowd of fans.

Savannah appears behind me. "So, we're going to have you do some autographs now," she says to Brody. "Nothing formal, just accept one request and the rest will start flowing."

Brody lifts an eyebrow at Savannah. "What happened to your no high school girls policy?"

Savannah grins like she's five steps ahead of him. She probably is. "There are three sororities volunteering here today. I've already invited them over to meet you. That should keep you busy for a while."

"College girls," Brody says with a nod. "All right then."

And I think that's my cue to leave. "Coach Kessler is going to have a breakdown if I don't get over to the warm-up area soon."

Dad leans forward and plants a kiss on top of my head. "Good luck, Ann."

I wave to Lenny on my way back out on the track. She's sitting in the fourth row from the bottom with several other girls I recognize from the junior class at St. Teresa's.

Jackie's already stretching, staring straight ahead, her face completely tense and focused. Coach Kessler is pacing in front of her. I toss the heating pad on the ground and then roll it under my right leg after sitting down.

Coach K bends down to talk to Jackie. "I don't want you thinking about the scouts or scholarships or the future. I only want you to think about the lap you're on and the next lap. Nothing else, understood?"

"Yeah," Jackie says. "I know."

"Lucas," Coach K says to me. "You've got to hold back a little longer on this one. I don't want you kicking at all until lap seven or you'll run out of gas or aggravate that hamstring again."

"Yeah," I say. "I know. Thanks."

We each down a cup of Gatorade and go through a series of warm-up jumps and drills in unison, neither of us speaking. The closer we get to race time, the more tense I get. About ten minutes before we start, I glance over at Dad and Brody, still in the same spot. Brody's now signing autographs for sorority girls with tan skin and all kinds of cleavage.

I do *not* need this distraction right now. I shift my eyes down to the track at my feet and take in ten slow, deep breaths, rolling out my shoulders and swinging my arms back and forth. When I look up again, he's got three other girls around him and one of them is handing over a Sharpie and lifting her shirt, pointing to her super flat stomach. I scowl to myself as he raises the marker and signs the girl's fucking stomach. Is she not planning on showering anytime soon? Seriously, what's the deal with getting body parts autographed? I don't get it. Not like you can sell it on eBay. Why don't they just ask, *Can you please touch me somewhere inappropriate in public?*

Dad watches Brody for a minute then shakes his head, moves over to keep from getting clobbered by girls, and returns his attention to the track. The race in front of ours finishes, and Jackie and I move to our starting lanes. She turns to face me before taking her stance. "Good luck, Annie."

"Thanks. You too," I murmur, watching as she glances up into the stands, swallows hard, and then faces forward again.

"Let's go one-two again, okay?" she adds. "For Coach Kessler."

"Sure." Somehow, this verbal commitment sends the butterflies loose in my stomach. My legs are shaking and my hands
tingling. I take one more glance over my shoulder at Dad and
Brody, who now has a five-girl entourage surrounding him. Now
I kind of wish he had stayed in Chicago watching that stupid-ass
movie.

Focus, Annie!

The gun goes off and I and nineteen other girls take off
running. For the entire first mile, I stick close to Jackie, toward
the front of the pack, but neither of us moves into the lead.
After lap six, Jackie and I both pull ahead, running side by side.
Her stride is so perfect, so precise, it's like she's decided to leave
everything here on the track for this race. I guess she doesn't
really have any other options. And instead of intimidating me,
her confidence gives me confidence, especially knowing I beat
her once already today.

We're so together it's like we've rehearsed this choreography.
The bell rings for the final lap and both of us simultaneously kick
harder, our heels raising. Our arms are swinging to an identical
rhythm. We're going to fight all the way to the finish line. But
then as we come around the final straightaway, I do something
that I've only ever done once in my life and that was during this
race at sectionals.

I look at the clock.

We're both on pace to break the state record. And only one
of us will get credit for it. My lungs and legs are screaming but I
feel that addiction Brody mentioned last week. I'm addicted to
breaking records, to seeing my foot cross that finish line first. I
break away from Jackie, getting half a stride ahead of her.

"Come on, Annie!" I hear Dad shout as if I'm running alone
around our neighborhood, Dad and Grams seated on the front

porch waiting for me to come around the corner.

With only fifty meters to go, my thoughts shift to Jackie crying after the last race, the way she glanced up in the stands at the scouts, the details Lenny inadvertently told me last weekend about her needing that scholarship.

Ninety percent of my brain is shouting, *Win, Win, WIN*. And the remainder is telling me something else.

Jackie's going to break the state two-mile record and no one will ever know.

I've already got my name down, and I can beat her time next year.

The decision is made.

Ten meters before the finish line, I pull back just enough to let her left foot cross the line before mine. My eyes zoom in on the clock again. Five hundredths of a second separates our times.

The announcer's voice booms over the loudspeaker once again. "*A new state record set in the thirty-two hundred meter run by Jackie Stonington, senior and four-time state qualifier from St. Teresa's Academy.*"

Jackie immediately falls to the ground in a heap, relief and pride spilling off of her. After we've both taken a minute to catch our breath, I bend over and reach out a hand to help her up. She grabs it and springs to her feet, wrapping me in a big hug. We're quickly joined by Coach Kessler who's crying and cheering at the same time.

After I finally break away from the two of them, I catch Brody's eye. He's leaning against the fence, arms crossed, forehead wrinkled. Does he know that I just let Jackie win? I can't decide if that's a bad thing or not.

The moment of us connecting from a distance is short-lived

because a couple more girls and two guys have approached Brody. One of them taps him on the shoulder, and he turns his back to me.

Lenny has hopped the fence and is heading over this way. She stops first to congratulate Jackie, giving her a big hug, and then she heads over to me. "You amaze me, Annie Lucas. I almost felt inspired to run a few laps beside you guys. *Almost.*"

I laugh, but I can't tear my eyes from Brody. Lenny's gaze travels to where he and Dad stand. "You're like a green-eyed monster right now."

"Am not," I protest. "Just sick and tired of people lifting up clothing to get autographs. I bet they don't even like baseball."

Lenny grabs my shoulders and twists me around to face her. "Annie, you seriously can*not* spend all your time and energy crushing on a Royals player. It's a pointless pursuit. Think about it. You're in high school. And he's on the road all the time, alone in hotel rooms with women who know exactly how to find players, get them to drop their pants, and they give some damn good blow jobs. Is that what you want to do? Get his attention by flashing your boobs and relenting to sexual favors? You're not that girl."

I've never really had close female friends before, ones who can point out the obvious. It's both aggravating and useful.

I sigh. "I know I'm not that girl, but how do you know it's really that wild on the road? They do have baseball games to play, right?"

Lenny snorts back a laugh. "Because my dad's been sleeping with other women for the last decade at least. It's like it's so easy for them it can't be wrong. And Jason Brody isn't even married, so he's totally got an all-access pass."

My stomach drops. "God, Len, I'm sorry."

She shrugs. "I'm used to it. The only thing that pisses me off is all the stupid happy family, happy marriage, good Catholic ballplayer bullshit that gets told about my family in articles and TV clips. Why can't the shit hit the fan at least once? Why can't he get some bimbo on the road pregnant and have her sue him for child support?"

It is surprising that First Base has never been caught considering how many photographs are printed or posted online of Brody with various women. Although maybe they don't send photographers alongside the married players, like they obviously do with Brody. Or at least they did today.

We walk toward the athlete hospitality area so I can grab some water. "You want that to happen?" I ask Lenny. "You want bad publicity?"

"Not really." She sighs. "I just want people to stop liking him for his fake personality. I want to believe at least to some extent that negative behavior has negative consequences, but obviously he's invincible."

She swipes a bottle of water for herself and another for me. "Let's not talk about my life anymore. We need to figure out what to do about your little problem."

"I don't have a problem," I lie. "I'm totally over it now that I've seen how disgustingly futile it is."

She levels me with a "yeah right" look and then digs through her purse, handing me what looks like a driver's license. My school ID photo is in the corner, but the name reads: Marie Conner and according to the birth date on the card, Marie Conner is twenty-two years old.

"You got me a fake ID?" I squeal.

Lenny claps a hand over my mouth, glancing around quickly. "Say that a little louder and your dad might get to hear it, too."

"Sorry," I whisper through her fingers.

She drops her hand and grins. "Carl and his frat brothers are going to this club downtown tonight, and I bribed him to take us and get us these very believable IDs."

"And you have to be twenty-one to get in?"

"Eighteen," Lenny clarifies. "But what's the fun of getting in if we can't buy drinks, right?"

I chew on my thumbnail feeling extremely conflicted. I hate lying to Dad. I still feel guilty from the last time, especially after running into Johnson. Then I glance over at Brody, who's been given a chair so that some sorority girl can plop down on his lap and wrap herself around him while her friend takes a picture that will mostly likely be a Facebook status update in the next twenty seconds. Is he going to sign her boobs, too?

And it's not like Johnson is going to be hanging out in downtown dance clubs. I doubt they serve barbecue.

"You know, I'm not one to coddle and talk about feelings," Lenny states. "So I'll just give this to you straight. You and Jason Brody are in a place that's even worse than the friend zone, Annie."

"What? Like enemies?"

She shakes her head. "That would be a step up. Enemies often have lots of pent-up sexual frustration. You're in the kid sister zone. I'm afraid that's about as hopeless as it gets."

I exhale, staying silent as we head toward Dad and Brody. She's right. And the way I see it, I have two options: 1) stop looking and acting like the kid sister and/or 2) find someone more obtainable to crush on. I'm pretty sure going to a grown-up club with Lenny tonight could potentially achieve both of those things.

"All right, I'm in. But what do I tell my dad?"

She smiles at me. "Let me take care of that."

I get another big hug from Dad when we reach him. "What happened at the end, Annie? Was it your leg?"

"Uh-huh," I lie. "It just seized up all of a sudden. I think I pushed it too hard."

"So, Coach Lucas," Lenny says, interrupting. "Mind if I steal your daughter for the night so we can celebrate her athletic achievement properly without adult supervision."

I glare at her and Dad leans back, folding his arms across his chest. "What do you two have planned?"

Lenny bats her dark eyelashes. "Well, your daughter's barely pulling a C in Spanish and finals are next week. She's obviously in need of Lenny London tutor extraordinaire. But I won't make her study all night. We'll be eating plenty of ice cream, candy, and pizza." She lifts up one of my hands and shakes her head in disgust. "Also some nail polishing…you know, the usual sleepover activities."

Brody chooses that moment to spin around and face us. "Really, Lenny? You're going to put nail polish on Annie Lucas? Alert the media."

Lenny's brows go up and she gives me a look that says, *See? Kid sister zone.*

"Be home for brunch with Grams tomorrow?" Dad says and after I nod he gives me another hug and a kiss on the forehead. "I'm sorry I doubted your ability to run both of those races. I was wrong. Next year, you can break Jackie's two-mile record, all right?"

I squeeze him back. "Deal."

After Dad lets me go, Brody holds up a hand to high-five me. I just stare at it, leaving him hanging and then glance at Lenny who's managed to look both sympathetic and satisfied that her assumptions regarding our relationship were completely accurate. I wrinkle my nose before finally tapping my hand against his.

Lenny and I walk toward the parking lot, and she hesitates then asks, "Is your dad always like that or was it just the 'I'm here for my daughter act'?"

I almost don't want to tell her the truth, but there's no point in lying because Lenny has an amazing talent for reading people. "It's not an act."

She shakes her head, bewildered. "So weird."

When we get to her car, I tell her that I need to stop at home to shower and get a change of clothes. She rolls her eyes before unlocking the doors. "Honey, nothing you own is going to be club friendly. I can guarantee that without even glancing in your closet."

I plop into the car with a frustrated sigh. "You really are going to paint my nails, aren't you?"

She slides her sunglasses into place and starts the engine. "We're going to do a hell of a lot more than that. You need to look twenty-two if you want to be Marie Conner."

"You know what?" I sit up straighter. "I think Marie Conner is going to be my much cooler, much more flirtatious, much more adventurous alter ego. So yeah, give me the full sexy woman makeover."

And if I'm Marie Conner then I won't feel as guilty about lying to Dad. Because I didn't lie. Marie did. She's badass like that.

chapter 12

Lenny London: *Can I still get credit for wearing cute shoes if I'm carrying them?*
30 minutes ago

Carl London: *I have friends and I have benefits therefore I see no problem in mixing the two.*
5 minutes ago

"**D**o I really look twenty-two?" I ask Lenny and Carl. "The guy didn't have an ounce of skepticism on his face."

"You look hot." Carl's dark-eyed gaze drifts up and down, taking in the formfitting, very short gold-sequined dress, tall black heels, and bright red lipstick Lenny dressed me in tonight. "Besides, he doesn't give a fuck if you're twenty-two as long as you provided him acceptable proof, his ass is covered."

"Now hush about the age thing," Lenny orders.

Walking into this club—music blaring, bodies smashed together, grown men buying girls drinks—I feel like a freshman at my first party with boys and beer. Wild high school parties are no longer an adventurous feat for me, but posing as Marie

Conner with a homemade fake ID has left me a bit shell-shocked. Lenny and Carl even made me drink two shots of rum before leaving the house so I wouldn't look like an uptight anxious seventeen-year-old and give myself away before getting in the door.

And now I've got an orange band around my wrist proving I'm old enough, not only to get in the door, but also to buy some real drinks. Not just that, but we went straight to the front of the line—the VIP entrance. The guys at the door know Carl and Lenny both, and of course they know First Base, so if they wanted to it wouldn't be all that hard to uncover Lenny's real age. Carl is actually twenty-one , so he doesn't even need a fake ID to buy drinks here.

Lenny and I stand near the bar, scoping out the people on the dance floor. "You need to find a hot guy to flirt with," she says. "Get over *you know who*."

"You know who?" Carl comes up behind us and hands us each a beer.

"Her ex," Lenny says right away. "From Arizona."

"He's gay." I take a gulp of my beer and try not to make a face. "I hate beer."

"Are we supposed to like it?" Lenny says, drinking from her own cup. "And remember, Annie, *you know who* is probably screwing one of those sorority chicks in his apartment right now. And he's probably got a wild party going on, while he's busy in the bedroom. I've overheard all kinds of stories about single players and their private parties. He's just been handed at least a quarter of a million dollars. His personal life, his personal space, is beyond anything you could ever grasp or even want to be involved with."

My heart sinks down to my stomach, but I force logic to

dominate like Lenny has. She's right. I want nothing to do with that star pro athlete life. I want Dad and his quiet ways and Grams and maybe a cute straight guy to make out with, but not fall in love with because that's almost more scary than the wild parties at Brody's bachelor pad.

The repetitive beat of the music is thumping inside my head and the pre-club alcohol I drank is taking effect, helping me keep my mind off being an awkward non-adult. People keep bumping into us and after downing my beer, I grab Lenny's hand. "Let's dance. Marie Conner loves to dance."

Lenny checks out the room like the scholar she is, then hands me an Altoid from her purse and takes another one, popping it into her mouth. "Just in case Mr. Perfect sweeps us away for a hot make-out session on the couches in the back of the club. You know Haley Hunter from school? She lost her virginity on one of those couches."

I wrinkle my nose. "Gross."

"I know, right?" Lenny nods.

We push our way toward the center of the dance floor. Pink and blue lights swirl around us. It's hard to see anything clearly and being this fake identity tonight allows me permission to let loose. There is something about high heels and a tight dress that gives you a certain level of confidence, like there's power in feeling sexy. I hadn't really anticipated that when I agreed to put on Lenny's clothes. Of course, I've dressed cute for the ex-boyfriend before but never did it include a dress quite this short. Or shiny. After a good thirty minutes of dancing, I'm starting to sweat, and I pull my hair up off my neck. Lenny shoots me a glare and swats at my hand. "Don't you dare mess up your hair! It looks amazing!"

Just to piss her off, I turn my head upside down and shake

out the long blond curls she carefully fixed for me. When I stand upright again, she grins. "Sexy."

Carl and his frat-boy friend, the same dude who'd drunkenly told me that I looked like his sister's Barbie doll before upchucking into the London family garden at the last party, shove their way out to us on the dance floor and pass us a shot glass filled with mysterious blue-ish liquid. We both stare at it briefly before downing the drink.

It's syrupy sweet, but I can feel the burn of alcohol trickling down my throat. Lenny passes me more Altoids mid-dance, and Carl's friend runs off to discard our glasses. Just as I'm getting back into dancing with Lenny, I spot a guy near the bar who's got at least three girls invading his personal space.

What the hell?

"Shit!" I pull Lenny closer and spin her around so she can see Brody, drinking his much more innocent bottle of water. "What's he doing here?"

She turns back to face me. Her arms are blissfully lifted in the air, her hips moving side to side. She bumps a hip into mine to get me moving again. "Quit worrying. He's not going to notice you and if he does, who cares?"

My heart slows back to normal. She's right. I know too many of Brody's secrets for him to go and rat me out to Dad.

Lenny turns around and reaches for the guy behind her. She pulls him by his tie, his eyes going wide, like he's about to live out one his of fantasies. Maybe he will? I laugh and grab Carl's friend. I can't remember his name but he's not a jerk wad like Carl, just really dumb, but I can't really fault him for that. I pull the guy closer, and he flashes me a grin with his perfectly white frat-boy teeth. Despite being an idiot, he's not a bad dance partner. He doesn't lay a hand on me, only grinds against me on occasion, and he does have some sense of rhythm. My phone vibrates several times through the beaded bag dangling in my hand. I almost pull it out to look at it, but Carl coming up behind me and laying a hand on my ass distracts me.

He shifts my hair over to one shoulder and leans closer, shouting into my ear, "You want another drink?"

My body stiffens and just as I turn my head to look at him, a hand tightens around Carl's wrist, yanking his fingers from my ass. My gaze travels upward, landing on Brody's intense brown eyes.

Lenny bumps her hip into mine again and says, "Busted!"

Brody keeps his eyes locked on mine while lifting both hands and shoving Carl and frat-boy friend in the chest, forcing some distance between me and them. Brody leans in and says, "Walk out the back exit, turn right, and meet me at the end of the block in the next two minutes."

I shake my head, but his serious expression stops me, and I remember my phone going off just seconds ago. Did he try to call? Did Dad call and then had to get ahold of Brody because I didn't answer? Did something happen? I turn around and tell Lenny, "I'm leaving."

She opens her mouth to protest, but I step around her before she has a chance to get a word in. It takes a good ninety seconds to shove my way toward the exit. The outside air feels fresh and cool against my sweaty neck.

Brody is already pacing in circles at the end of the block.

He grabs my hand the second I reach him and stalks across the street, dragging me along. "Keep your head down," he hisses.

"What—"

"You didn't notice the paparazzi inside that club?" he whispers.

There are various people mingling around the downtown

streets. My heart races, and I glance around completely panicked. "It's not a big deal, right? Why would people want to take
pictures of me?"

And why didn't Lenny or Carl notice this? They've been
dealing with being public profiles much longer than Brody and
I have.

"Keep your head down," Brody repeats.

I drop my gaze to the sidewalk and let my hair fall forward,
half covering my face. It's not until another two blocks that I
fully register the fact that I'm holding hands with Jason Brody.
Except it's more like I'm being dragged out of the carnival after
trying to sneak onto a roller coaster I'm not tall enough to ride.
I shake his hand from mine and my pace shifts to the heavy-
footed stalk he's already adopted.

"Where are we going?" I ask.

"I'm taking you home." He finally stops in front of a tall
apartment building and points to the garage. This must be his
building. Maybe he walks to that club every night and brings
a different girl back to his place? And I don't even get invited
inside for a drink.

He takes me straight to his new black SUV with tinted
windows. I slump into the passenger seat and slam the car door
shut with more force than is needed. Once we're both safely
inside the vehicle, Brody exhales. "I didn't want to talk outside
in case anyone heard us, but seriously? What were you doing in
there? How did you even get in?"

His gaze travels to the small beaded bag Lenny loaned me.
He swipes it before I can stop him and quickly finds my ID. "Let
me guess? Carl got this for you?"

I fold my arms across my chest, keeping silent.

"Twenty-two? Seriously? I'm surprised they fell for that.

You can get in at nineteen, you know." Brody starts laughing, his shoulders shaking. "I choked and spit water all over these two girls when I saw you in there." He unfastens the buttons on the sleeves of his blue dress shirt, rolling them up to his elbows before turning his gaze on me again, his eyes sliding up and down, taking me in, his laughter picking up even more. "What did you do to yourself, Annie?"

The words and laughing sting. He might as well have slapped me across the face. Dancing in the club, I felt sexy, older, *alive.* He's managed to suffocate all that in a matter of seconds. My eyes burn, but there's no way in hell I'm shedding a tear right now. I lean back against the chair and turn my head to look out the window. "Are you taking me home or not?"

He's still laughing to himself as he backs the car out, exits the garage, and hops onto the freeway. He tries to make conversation for the first couple minutes and then gives up after probably growing tired of my lack of eye contact and one-word answers.

When we get to my neighborhood, he parks his car half a block from my house, cuts the engine, and turns off the lights. Only a single streetlamp across the road illuminates the inside of his SUV.

"Look," he says, his gaze on the dashboard. "I think you should come clean with your dad right now and tell him where you really went tonight."

I turn to face him. "Why? Are you going to tell on me, Brody? Seriously?"

"I'm pretty sure your picture's going to end up in the paper or on the internet. Don't you think it's better if he's prepared and hears it from you first?" Brody finally looks at me and his serious expression fades, the corners of his mouth twitching, fighting a smile or more laughing at my expense.

Before I can get more pissed off at him, he leans in close, his mouth inching toward mine. I suck in a breath and then release it, disappointment washing over me as he reaches around, opening the glove compartment. "I can't take you seriously with that red lipstick on." He laughs again.

With a heavy sigh, I fall back against the seat, squeezing my eyes shut, turning my head away from him. "I left the club with you. I'm going to 'fess up to my dad. You're getting your way, so you can stop treating me like a child playing dress up."

"Annie—"

"I get it," I interrupt. "I'm just a high school kid, and you're a grown-up baseball player with money and crazy parties in your apartment and swimsuit models programmed in your phone. You don't need a fake ID to get into the cool clubs. And you are like my dad and feel some obligation to make sure his daughter doesn't screw up her life or his. It's fine."

Warm fingers land underneath my chin, and Brody gently steers my head, forcing me to look into his adorable brown eyes. He's so close I can feel our breaths mingling in the same air. He smells really good, too, like Irish Spring soap and some kind of aftershave. I stay perfectly still while he holds my face with one hand.

Using a napkin he must have gotten from the glove compartment, he gently wipes the lipstick from my mouth. A small part of me wants to hold on to this last sliver of dignity and swat his hand away, but the rest of me won't move a muscle. I'm lost in being this close to him, having his fingers on my face and touching my mouth with only a thin tissue between us.

Heat is slowly making its way toward my neck and face… and down lower. I've temporarily forgotten everything else that happened tonight.

"I've never treated you like a kid, Annie." Brody takes one last swipe across my bottom lip and then balls the tissue up in his hand.

And then because he doesn't drop his hand or move away immediately, and maybe because of the alcohol, I'm able to channel my alter ego, Marie Conner, again. Without giving him any warning, I close the gap between us and press my mouth against his.

chapter 13

Heat and longing cloud my thoughts. Brody's mouth is hot against mine and when my brain registers that he hasn't pulled away, I reach out and slide my hands across his cheeks, over his neck. Finally just as I'm touching the bottom of his dark hair, preparing to comb my fingers through it for hours, his fingers press more firmly against my cheeks. And then his lips part.

I sigh against his mouth, but before either of us can deepen the kiss, somewhere far in the back of my mind, I register him pushing my face away from his.

Reality slams into me. I jerk back, practically hitting my head against the window.

"Shit." Brody places his arms over the steering wheel then rests his forehead on them.

I blindly reach behind me, fumbling for the door handle. "I'm sorry. I didn't mean to—actually, it was just this thing Lenny and I were doing tonight. You know, kissing someone else, getting over your ex?" *Lies, lies, and more lies.* Seems to be my theme for the night.

He lifts his head and takes my hand, not allowing me to jump out of the car. "Listen to me, Annie. You are amazing. You don't need to make out with me or any guy like me to figure that out. Don't sell out because you're worried about *not* being someone's type."

How did he know?

Was he listening in on my conversation with Lenny at the track meet today? I know he wasn't but damn, he nailed all my concerns spot-on. I swallow back the lump in my throat. Lenny's right. I'm the kid sister, but now I can't even be pissed at him anymore, not after what he just said and the gentle tone of his voice.

I grasp the door handle, open it, and mutter, "You're right. Thanks for bringing me home."

He sighs and scrubs his hands over his face before flinging his own door open. "Let me go in with you. I'll help explain things to your dad. He's probably going to find out I was there anyway. I'd rather come clean with him now, too."

Sure. Anything to keep your relationship with my dad in perfect standing.

When I open the front door with my house key, Dad sits up from his spot on the couch. He's sleepy-eyed, the TV playing a late-night infomercial with the volume turned nearly all the way down, his non-leg propped up on the recliner beside the couch.

His forehead wrinkles more and more as he takes in my appearance and the fact that I'm home after telling him I'd be gone all night. For a study session sleep over. Though to Lenny's credit, she did make me study Spanish while she fixed my hair and makeup. She doesn't kid around when it comes to her tutoring reputation.

"What happened?" Dad says right away followed by, "Are

you all right?"

Guilt eats further into my stomach, forming an instant ulcer. Leave it to Dad to ask me if I'm okay after I've lied to him and potentially caused a family scandal. It's like he knows the worst way to get to me.

"Lenny and I went to this club downtown." I take in a deep breath and glance at Brody. He stuffs his hands in his pockets, looking just as guilty as I feel right now, which doesn't make any sense. "It's not exactly for high school kids…and…well…"

Brody scratches the back of his head, his gaze bouncing from me and then back to Dad. "I was there, too, but on my own, and I happened to see the girls. There were photographers around. I got Annie out of there as soon as I could, but I think there'll probably be some mention of this."

Dad's jaw muscle is already flexing, his mouth a perfect thin line. "And how did you get into this grown-up club?"

Brody looks at me, his face weary. "It's an eighteen and over kind of club."

Dad just raises an eyebrow. We both know I am *not* eighteen.

My stomach ties in knots. I hear the words that he doesn't say. *I might as well come clean about the ID, too.* I remove the Marie Conner license from the beaded purse and, with shaking hands, I hold it out for Dad to see. Brody's eyes are glued to Dad's non-leg as he reaches for it and straps it back into place, the shoe at the bottom standing out against his bare other foot. He raises himself off the couch and stands in front of me, swiping the ID from my hands.

He reads it quickly and then lifts his head again. His glare practically knocks the wind out of me. "Where did you get this?"

"Someone made it for me." I'm not going to sell Carl and Lenny out even though Dad will probably be able to guess like

Brody did.

Dad throws the ID onto the coffee table and then leans closer to me. "You've been drinking."

I nod wearily, not meeting his gaze. He shifts his glare to Brody. "Please tell me you weren't drinking, too, and then drove my daughter home?"

Brody holds his hands up, shaking his head. "No...no way, I wouldn't—"

And just like that, he's done interrogating his perfect star pitcher.

"What the hell is wrong with you, Annie?" he shouts, startling both me and Brody. "And what the hell are you wearing?"

I refuse to stand here and cry in front of Dad and Brody, so I let my inner teenage girl take over. "Why don't you ask the responsible, nondrinking teenager in the room? He can fill you in. I'm going to bed." I toss the beaded bag and both black heels onto the couch before stomping off to my room and slamming the door shut. Tears are already spilling down my cheeks as I shimmy out of Lenny's dress and grab a T-shirt and flannel pants from my laundry basket to throw on. After I'm dressed, I flop onto my bed and bury my face in my pillow so no one can hear me crying.

The whole Dad-is-disappointed-with-me thing can't even fully sink in yet because my mind is preoccupied with the fact that I kissed Brody and he turned me down—and now he probably knows exactly how I feel about him. I can't have those secret thoughts about him without wondering if he can tell, if I'm giving something away in my expression. Those were my feelings to guard and protect and keep for only me, and now I've been sliced open and exposed. As much as I fantasized about Brody liking me back, I'm not sure I was ever ready for him to see inside me like that.

Is anyone ever ready for that? Is that what it's like for Dad? Is it impossible to keep his feelings for Mom to himself even when hers are obviously not identical?

I groan. Why the fuck did I have to kiss him? Actually, why did Marie Conner have to kiss him? She's the one to blame for waving my secrets out for Brody to see. She's the villain.

I press my face harder into my pillow, rubbing tears and snot into the silky material. I hear the front door close and then shortly after my bedroom door opens. Dad comes in and sits beside me.

"Let me get this out of the way first," he says quietly. He's returned to Calm Dad at least. "You're grounded for a month. No going anywhere except school, workouts, and whatever else isn't fun, all right?"

I use my free hand to wipe the evidence of my sob fest from my eyes, but I still don't roll over to face him.

His hand lands in my hair, moving it aside so he can see my face. "I'm not stupid enough to believe you've never done any drinking or been to parties where there's drugs and alcohol. I didn't worry because I know you're too smart to do anything stupid. But using a fake ID and going into a public place where people might know who you are, Ann? That was pretty damn idiotic. You can't pull shit like that again. You could have gotten away with it just fine in Arizona, but not here in Kansas City, not with my job now."

"I'm sorry," I mumble into the pillow.

Dad rubs my back, using the same circular motion between my shoulder blades that Brody had used to calm me down during the tornado sirens. My heart gets jabbed all over again. Brody's always been kind to me, but not romantic. All of our interactions have evolved into so much more inside the confines of my imagination.

But not in real life. I'm just a girl he likes to keep an eye on. *A girl he shares his secrets with*, I can't help thinking.

"Are you having some kind of crisis that's causing you to go all wild and rebellious?" Dad asks.

I half laugh, half cry into my pillow. "You're such a dork."

"Seriously, Ann, talk to me." There's a plea in his voice, fear even. What is he afraid of? Me turning into an episode of *Girls Gone Wild*? I totally don't have the boobs for that.

"It was just a stupid idea, that's all." I finally roll onto my back and look up at him. "Did you ever want to be someone else so you could do something you wouldn't normally do? Maybe impress someone or—"

"Is this about a boy?" Dread fills his face, but he hides it quickly. "It is, isn't it?"

I let out a breath. "Yeah, pretty much, but you have nothing to worry about because this particular boy does not share my feelings. I'm not his type." I roll over on my side again.

"Boys are pretty stupid, Ann," he says. "Not to sound cliché, but you're smart and talented and often the young guys don't want someone who's going to make them think too hard or call them out on their own stupidity."

"I don't think that's the problem." I sigh and blink back more tears. It's the humiliation of kissing someone who pushes you away that brings on the biggest tears. I hate looking like a fool or like a girl with a crush. Even if that's exactly what I am. "I think we're just different."

The conversation is getting too awkward for Dad. I can practically feel him starting to squirm, and then he goes for his old-school fix-it Dad methods. He pats my leg and stands up.

"Come on, I'll make you an extra cheesy grilled cheese and a milk shake."

I sit up and roll off the side of the bed. My legs are sore from the meet earlier. "Can we wake up Grams, too? You know how she loves milk shakes."

He grins at me. "Sure, if you want."

The story breaks on Sunday morning.

After spending Saturday in my pjs, moping around the house, drowning in my humiliation while the Royals played another home game, I'm woken early Sunday by Savannah.

"Annie, your dad told me to get you up," she says, standing beside my bed.

The alarm clock on my nightstand reads 8:10 a.m.

"What's going on?" I toss the covers aside and sit up. "Is Grams okay?"

"Grams is fine," Savannah assures me before dropping the Sunday paper onto my lap.

The headline reads:

Royals Kids and Their Wild Ways: *VIP rooms at downtown clubs, drugs, and alcohol are just the beginnings of the wild and cash-filled world these kids live in. A world where rules don't apply, age isn't a factor, and being part of a major league ball club gets you unimaginable perks.*

Below the headline is a giant photo of me in Lenny's sleazy dress. I'm standing inappropriately close to frat-boy friend of Carl's. Lenny is off to the side in the picture, her lime-green dress and caramel skin standing out against my pale skin and gold sequins. She's got her hands wrapped around the tie of the guy she'd danced with Friday night, his mouth practically touching hers. Then there's Carl standing behind me, sandwiching me between two guys. I'm looking at Carl over my shoulder, our faces are unnaturally close.

And right in the center of the front page of the Sunday paper is Carl's hand planted on my ass. The caption underneath the photo reads: LOOK AT WHO IS HAVING A GOOD TIME WITH KANSAS CITY'S FAVORITE CELEBRITY KID, CARL LONDON. AND FRIEND.

Nausea sweeps over me, and I lift my gaze to meet Savannah's. "Oh my God."

Her face is both tense and weary. "The Royals' PR department wants to hold a press conference this afternoon. Frank called everyone this morning and told them to get over here right away so we can all sort through this and prepare a statement."

My hands are shaking. "This is bad, right? Really bad?"

"You should probably get dressed," she says, avoiding the question. "Mr. Johnson is coming by as well. He's pretty upset."

"The Royals' owner is coming here?" I gulp a heavy breath. "Oh shit, this is bad."

chapter 14

Ten minutes is all I get before people start tumbling into our front door. I quickly brushed my teeth, tossed my hair into a ponytail, but left my tank top and flannel pajama pants on because the doorbell rang.

First Base and his wife enter the house, followed by a sleepy Lenny who's also sporting some pajama pants and black-rimmed glasses instead of contacts. Carl has a clean-pressed polo shirt and khaki shorts on but his eyes are bloodshot. The smell of stale beer seems to have seeped through his pores as a result of whatever Saturday night adventure he engaged in.

Grams is watching TV, oblivious to the extra people and tension that have just invaded her *Jeopardy* marathon. "That Alex Trebek… He's such a smart-ass. Someone needs to give him a kick to the groin."

Dad is leaning against the fireplace, defensive stance holds him firm, his eyes zoomed in on Carl. I can't decide if he's more pissed off at me now that the photos are out or if he'd anticipated this already. Before I can ask him, Lenny nudges me down the hall toward my bedroom, shutting the door behind us.

"I swear I didn't tell anyone where I got the fake ID from," I say right away. Guilt has been eating at me all weekend. Dad went in search of a parent power trip yesterday and decided to take away my laptop, phone, and texting privileges for the weekend. He left me home alone with my phone (for emergencies only) during the game yesterday, so I totally could have cheated but I knew it would make him feel better if I was properly punished.

Lenny shakes her head. "Whatever. I could care less about that. This whole dragging everyone out of bed on Sunday morning is ridiculous. Carl and I have been in every tabloid in existence at one point or another, though this is our first time making the Kansas City paper, at least for something scandal-related." She pauses like she's thinking about whether or not that's a bad thing. "It's just Johnson and the big moral stick up his ass. We've been through four owners now since my dad's been playing, and they all have different *visions* for the team." She uses air quotes on the word *visions*. "He'll catch on soon enough and get used to backing off and letting us have our way. Now back to the important stuff... What happened with Brody on Friday night? He shocked the hell out of me, going all alpha male at the club, and then you were both gone."

My face heats up with embarrassment just thinking about the events that took place in his car. I glance at the mirror above my dresser and sure enough, my cheeks and neck are beet red. Lenny's eyebrows shoot up, but she doesn't say anything, just waits patiently for me to explain. I sink down onto the end of my bed. "You were so right about us, and I was such an idiot."

"Let me guess," Lenny says. "You crossed the kid-sister line, and it didn't go over well?"

I cover my face and with my hands and groan. "It went terrible. I think I wanted him to feel the same as me so much that for a few seconds I made myself believe he was kissing me back, and then he had to practically pry my mouth from his."

Lenny shakes her head. "Oh God. Not good. Not good at all."

"The worst part is that I can't even get pissed off at him or give him the silent treatment because he was infuriatingly polite about it, like he already knew his rejection would break me apart." I drop my hands and squeeze the wooden footboard underneath me. "I hate that. I hate having him know what's going on inside my head. It's the worst feeling ever, like I've given him control or something, you know?"

She nods and pats my shoulder. "I think in the future, we'll just stick to actually going through with the sleepover and the pizza and the ice cream because things get tragic whenever I take you out. No more dance clubs, shots of rum, and alter egos named Marie Conner, all right, young lady?"

I exhale. "Yeah. Good idea. And be sure to keep me from being alone in cars with hot boys who think of me as a kid sister."

"Done." She holds out a hand to help me up, just as Savannah is knocking on the door and calling us into the kitchen.

As Lenny and I walk back down the hall, we both take in six-year-old Lily seated on the couch with Grams, an episode of *Good Luck Charlie* now playing on the TV.

"Guess we have to be either unaware of reality or still writing letters to Santa to get out of this pre-press conference gathering, huh?" she whispers, nodding toward Lily and Grams.

I glance longingly in their direction, wanting nothing more than to curl up with Grams and watch hours of mind-numbing television and game shows even though I did that very same thing all day yesterday. "No kidding," I mumble.

Both of us stop in the foyer before heading into the kitchen when the front door swings open and Brody walks in. He's wearing gym shorts and a blue Royals T-shirt. He's rubbing his eyes and his hair is adorably disheveled. He freezes when he sees us and then reaches up to smooth down his thick dark hair—which doesn't do any good.

My face is hot again. My mouth falls open to speak, but no words come out. Lenny elbows me in the side and then says, "How did you get wrapped up in this scandal?"

He yawns and rubs his eyes again. "I'm not wrapped up in it. But Jim called me, thought it might help to tell my side of the story, so here I am."

"Lovely," Lenny says, rolling her eyes. "This is all a bunch of bullshit."

Brody shrugs, but the casual body language isn't completely hiding his anxiety. "Frank said Johnson is pretty set on taking some extreme action to *redeem our image*." He also uses air quotes on the words *redeem our image*.

The three of us walk into the kitchen and take in the seating arrangements. Lenny's three family members are taking up one side of the ten-person table. An empty chair lingers beside her mom. Her parents are completely stone-faced, hands carefully placed in their laps, neither of them touching the coffee mugs in front of them. Carl is between them, leaning on one elbow, like he might nod off any second.

Lenny stares at the open chair beside her mother, wrinkles her nose, and turns to me, "Guess I'll be sitting with my kind for this meeting."

Brody cracks a smile but tucks it away fast when Frank glares at him from his spot at the end of the table. Savannah is beside Frank. She's already scribbling notes on a yellow tablet.

Since Dad is seated at the other end near First Base, I have no choice but to sit beside Brody. I drop into the chair closest to Dad, and Brody slides in beside Savannah. He reaches across the table and snatches a glazed donut from the box in the center. Savannah's peace offering, I'm sure. Can't have a morning meeting without donuts and coffee. Lenny swipes her mom's untouched mug of coffee and takes a sip.

"Johnson decided not to come?" Brody asks Frank, sounding very hopeful.

"He'll be here soon. We wanted to get a head start," Savannah says, answering for Frank. She raises her head from her notes, opens her mouth to speak, but stops abruptly. We all watch as Carl removes a bottle of Visine from his pocket, tilts his head back, and squeezes two drops into each eye.

Frank rubs his temples, closing his eyes briefly. "Oh Lord, this is a nightmare."

"What is this crap?" Grams says from the other room. "Where the hell is Mickey Mouse?"

"He's at Disney World," Lily answers as if that was a completely valid question.

Frank is now rubbing his chest with one hand and wiping sweat from his brow with the other. I watch him carefully for more signs of distress. He *is* really old, like fifty or sixty, and he's got a big beer belly. Maybe we're giving him a heart attack with all our drama.

"Mr. Johnson asked me to mediate," Savannah says when everyone's attention is back on the task at hand again. "I'd like to create a list of facts related to Friday evening's indiscretions and from there we can decide what information, if any, we'll convey to the media during the press conference and what nonfactual embellishments we can add to the story without it coming back to bite us later."

"You mean lies?" Lenny asks. "What lies we can make up without getting caught?"

It's a pretty strong statement, but her tone is flat and she looks more bored than angry or even curious. Sometimes I can't tell what's real and what's an act with her.

I realize that Brody's presence beside me is affecting me more than I'd like. My back is perfectly straight, my hands twisting in my lap. Like subconsciously I'm afraid allowing even an elbow or a loose hair to fall out of my personal bubble and into Brody's will cause me to lose control and fling myself on top of him.

"It's not about lying," Savannah clarifies, "it's about presenting a united front and a streamlined seamless story for the public to ingest. But right here, right now, it's very important that I get the entire story with every detail so that we don't end up with any surprises after this press conference takes place."

"What I'd like to know," Dad says slowly, making an obvious effort to keep his tone even, "is whether or not Jake London is aware of the fact that his son provided my daughter, and probably his daughter, with fake IDs?"

I glare at him. "I never said where I got it."

"See?" Lenny's mom purses her lips. "You have no evidence."

Dad's arms are folded across his chest as he tips his chair onto the back legs. "That's right, she's not willing to rat out her source, but I have no doubt that your kid is behind this."

First Base shrugs, an arrogant smirk plastered across his face. "She didn't have to take it from him."

Dad keeps his eyes locked on First Base. "Annie knows that and she's been grounded for a month. She's not going to be hanging around clubs downtown for a long time. What I'm asking is, what are *you* going to do about *your* kids?"

First Base stretches and leaves his hands behind his head.

"I've already paid off the kid Carl gets the IDs from. He won't say a word."

Dad looks over at Frank. "Are you hearing this?"

"Look," First Base says, "we've never had any problems until you and your kid showed up. I don't know about your parenting skills, but I make sure to cover all my bases. Carl and Lenny are permanently on the VIP lists at all the downtown clubs and bars. They don't drive when they go out. We hire a car service. No drugs outside of the house or Carl's room at the frat house. Lenny knows not to stay overnight with any guys. She can bring them home, just can't go home with them."

Frank swears under his breath, shaking his head. Mrs. London is frozen like she's just had Botox injections and can't move her face. Hell, maybe she has. And First Base isn't completely informed: my first night out with Lenny, she drove her own car to that bar. But then again, she carted a beer around but never took a sip. And she was avoiding that dinner party.

"My family is the spokesfamily for good communication and high moral standards," First Base adds. "They communicate what they plan to do, and I have someone go behind them and cover the evidence. My kids know their limits and from the looks of this front page article, your daughter isn't exactly the picture of innocence. Juggling two guys at once? My guess is she's been around the block a few more times than you're aware of."

Oh. My. God.

Dad's chair tips over backward as he springs up, showing no sign of having only one real leg. In two seconds flat, he's pulled First Base from his chair, his fists clenching around the front of his shirt as he slams his back against the wall.

Oh boy. Not good.

chapter 15

My heart jumps up to my throat. Lenny's eyes go from bored to wide and alert. Carl falls back into his mom in an effort to stay out of the way. My eyes are glued to Dad's back, but I feel Brody stiffen beside me, like he's ready to spring into action, too.

Frank stands up and walks around the table. "Jimmy!"

"Don't ever say anything like that about Annie again," Dad says, still gripping First Base's designer shirt. His voice is low and calm, but his body is quite the opposite.

First Base looks startled for about a second and then the smirk returns. "Be careful there, Jimmy Lucas," he says. "Wouldn't want you to lose your other leg."

"Dad…" I plead, trying to break the spell.

But Savannah is the one who actually gets through to him. She pushes her chair back, stands between Dad and First Base, and says firmly, "My six-year-old is in the other room, and I swear to you, if I have to explain to her why a room full of adults can't have a civilized nonviolent discussion…"

Dad releases First Base and steps back. He points a finger at

Carl, his eyes narrowed. "Don't ever lay a hand on my daughter again. Unlike your dad, I have a lot less to lose if I commit murder."

My mouth falls open. "Dad, enough!"

Brody's hand drifts under the table and lands on my knee, squeezing it. I know he's only doing it to shut me up, but I can't help feeling the butterflies in my stomach, the heat in my face.

Frank flips Dad's chair back up again, and everyone returns to their seats. Carl has adopted his father's arrogant smirk.

And *oh my God* Brody's hand is still gripping my knee. Is anyone else seeing this? Am I imagining it? I take a deep breath and allow my gaze to travel up to his face. He's completely consumed with the task of glaring at Carl.

"Okay," Savannah continues as though we didn't almost have a kitchen brawl between a major league ballplayer and a pitching coach. "So I can assume the alleged fake ID accusation is accurate?" Lenny and I both nod. "And you bought drinks with these IDs?"

"We drank but didn't purchase," Lenny says.

Savannah scribbles more notes. "You used a car service to get to and from the club, correct?"

Lenny and Carl nod. "Brody drove me home," I say.

First Base snorts. "Oh, that's nice. Trading in one playboy for another. Where's that story? Coach's underage daughter and the rookie pitcher from the wrong side of the tracks. Sounds like a front-pager to me."

Brody tenses beside me and, sensing that he's about to do exactly what Dad did, both Savannah and I grip one of his arms. I release a breath. He really doesn't have any allies on his team. I mean, I've seen the behavior of some of the other players, but I never thought about how difficult that must be for him.

"No," she says firmly to Brody. "Don't even think about it."

"He was there on his own," I tell Savannah, being careful not to look at Lenny's family. "He's the one that saw the paparazzi. He made me leave, brought me home, and made me 'fess up to my dad about everything. That's the real story."

"I already know exactly why Brody was there," Savannah says, continuing her notes. "And why photographers were around. Which would have been fine had we not included the presence of two team-related high schoolers and the older brother who purchased alcohol for them."

Wait a second…does she mean they planned to have Brody photographed there?

The conversation ends right then because the Royals' owner strides through the front door without ringing or knocking first. His gray cowboy boots thump across the foyer and into the kitchen.

Savannah stands, offering him her chair. He shakes her off and points to her notebook. "Forget the story and the angle. We're not gonna dig for a way to spin this in our favor," he says, causing everyone to look surprised. His eyes rest on me and he gives me the same "you're dispensable" look that he gave me that night in the bar forever ago. "You kids want to act like screw heads, fine with me. That's exactly what angle we're playing today. You got yourselves to that club, wrangled the documentation you needed to get inside, you drank alcohol willingly without your parents' knowledge even though you've been told many times that it's wrong."

Screw heads?

"Sir, I don't think—" Savannah interrupts, but Mr. Johnson raises a hand to stop her.

"Our focus isn't going to be on what's been done, but on

what we're going to do about it. I want you out of town." He waves an index finger around, pointing right at Carl. "Purchasing for minors is not going to happen by you again. Not in this country anyway. That summer internship you asked for in South America? Done. You leave by Wednesday. In two weeks, we'll send a camera crew down to Rio." He turns to Savannah. "Write that down, Ms. Dawson. Find something humanitarian for him to do, like playing soccer with orphaned toddlers." His finger drifts to Lenny and then me. "And you two...you better find some sick kids to hug and some Habitat houses to build, got it? The ball club is assigning you one hundred hours of community service, and I want every single hour documented on camera. We'll make a little show out of this."

"Do you really think it's the ball club's job to punish them?" Dad says. "It's my responsibility to keep an eye on Annie, and my responsibility to issue appropriate punishment."

Mr. Johnson turns to Dad. "That's where you're wrong, Jim. Unless you keep her locked up, your daughter is my show now. And at Club Royal, we expect the children of players and coaches to be good role models, and when they fail to do so, they need to make up for it, understood?"

No one says anything, and Johnson shifts his attention to Brody. "I'm sick of this playboy rookie shit. It ends today."

"But, sir," Savannah says. "We've polled fans, and they're almost unanimously in favor of players under twenty-five being single and...um..." She clears her throat. "Sexually vibrant."

Dad closes his eyes and shakes his head. Lenny and I both burst out laughing but stifle it the second Frank's glare bounces between us.

"Don't care," Johnson says. "Get him a girlfriend and make sure she makes up for his lack of a perfect record. What about one of those Disney Channel girls? Squeaky clean and innocent. Assuming you can catch them before they shave their heads and start swinging naked on wrecking balls."

"What the fuck," Brody mumbles beside me.

"I know!" Johnson snaps his fingers together, the idea light switch flipping on. "That deaf girl that just released her first album in sign language, get ahold of her people," he orders Savannah. "See what kind of deal you can work out. We don't have nearly enough disabilities and terminal illness in this ball club."

If I'd been able to concentrate instead of being preoccupied with the bizarre idea of arranging some kind of courtship between Brody and a Disney Channel actress/singer, I may have pointed out that my grandmother has Alzheimer's and my dad is both an amputee and a cancer survivor.

"Detroit just signed a player with sickle cell," Johnson says, continuing his speech. "And the Cub's third baseman is dating a blind woman. A blind woman! She can't even watch him play, can you imagine that? Talk about a tear-jerking story for *Dateline*. And what have we got for *Dateline*?" He gestures between me and Lenny. "Royals' kids gone wild."

Frank and Dad are exchanging glances—both of them look on the verge of laughing.

"So if I can find a human interest story to pitch to *Dateline*, you'll consider the disability and terminal illness void to be filled?" Savannah says, her gaze shifting to Dad for a split second, and the amusement immediately falls from his face. He narrows his eyes, giving a tiny shake of his head.

Johnson seems to consider this offer for a few long seconds. "But I still want Brody and that Disney Channel girl."

"I didn't use a fake ID," Brody snaps. "Or buy drinks for minors like that idiot asshole." He points to Carl. "I'm not the one in trouble here. I just came to help with getting the facts straight. Nor am I letting you play matchmaker. You have a demand, you can bring it to my agent and we'll discuss the options. I'm here to play baseball, not put on your show."

"Yes, you're here to play ball. For two more months," Johnson reminds him before turning to Frank. "This is exactly what I warned you about, Frank. You take on these delinquent charity cases, and it causes nothing but trouble for everyone. Have you gotten it out of your system yet?"

Frank stands up, not quite as quickly as Dad had a while ago, but he's obviously pissed. He points at Brody. "That charity case is the only damn reason we've won any games this season."

"And whose fault is that? You're the fucking manager." Johnson nods toward Dad. "Still think we need two pitching coaches, Frank? Or do you have some other personal stake in this little project?"

Silence falls over the kitchen. It's not hard for me to figure out what's going on, and I'm almost as humiliated as I was after kissing Brody. Dad stands up slowly, his face calm. "I think I've had enough mediation for one day."

He grabs his car keys from the counter, and I immediately rise up from my chair to go after him, but Savannah reaches across Brody and touches my wrist. "Let him go."

She turns her attention back to Johnson. "About this Disney Channel girlfriend idea…I really don't think it's the best interest of ticket sales—"

"Fine," Johnson barks, waving the idea away with one hand like he hadn't practically demanded it happen moments ago. "But I want a sappy, positive human interest story to pitch to *Dateline*, and I want those kids showing remorse through community service."

"Are we through?" First Base asks, already standing up.

"Yes." And just like that, Johnson stalks out of the kitchen, out the front door, and into his car.

I'm the next to leave the table. I head outside and sit on the porch swing, watching for Dad to come home. First Base and his wife exit, not even giving a glance in my direction. They get into their car, and I realize that the four of them didn't even ride together—and their house is only half a mile away.

What a happy family.

When Lenny and Carl finally exit, I stand up to tell Lenny good-bye. Carl's got his arrogant smirk plastered on again and he comes right over to me, like he's going to hug me.

And then his hand is on my ass again, just like Friday night. Did he not take Dad's threat seriously? This time, I have a second to react, and I quickly grab his hand, bend his fingers back, and then twist his arm behind his back. He lets out a yelp of pain, but I hold his arm firmly in place and lean in closer. "You're lucky that you're heading out of the country."

Lenny is standing on the porch steps, taking this in and practically bending over with laughter. "Nice move, Annie!"

The screen door flies open, and Brody is suddenly ripping Carl from my grip. He shoves him toward the steps so hard, Carl stumbles to keep from falling. "Get the hell out of here, dude. My self-control is about gone."

Carl glares at both of us but he doesn't make a move to get closer. "Come on, Len," he yells at his sister, "get in the car."

Lenny stops in the grass, shaking her head. Brody hops down the steps and is at her side in seconds. "I can drop you off."

Lenny shakes her head and then her eyes find mine. "I'd rather walk. Talk to you later, Annie?"

"Yeah, okay."

Brody plays with his keys, obviously preparing to leave like everyone else, but he turns to me before getting in his car. "Johnson is the worst kind of asshole. Just remember that, okay?"

Yeah, but assholes are still capable of telling the truth.

After he's gone, I fall back onto the porch swing. I'm totally beat and it's not even lunchtime. After a few minutes, Frank comes outside and sits beside me, causing the swing to rock.

He keeps his eyes trained on the mailbox across the yard. "Johnson wasn't completely blowing smoke, Annie."

I sit perfectly still, not speaking a word. My thoughts drift back to our townhouse in Arizona and the last time Frank visited us there, his job offer and what Dad had said—and more importantly, what he hadn't said.

You don't have to do this, Frank. You don't owe me anything.

"Do you?" I ask, my stomach already tying itself in knots. I don't want me or Dad to be some charity case for Frank. Brody's proven himself already by throwing a shit-ton of strikes. But has Dad? "Do you owe him anything?"

Frank doesn't shift his gaze from the mailbox. "He wanted to wait. He didn't want the surgery right away, but I had everything lined up for him. Rehabilitation specialists, a Johns Hopkins team of med students and doctors who'd convinced me that they could get him pitching again, even with the prosthetic limb. They wanted to revolutionize what amputee athletes were able to achieve, and Jimmy was their guinea pig. Your dad was a phenomenal talent. One of the best pitchers I've ever seen. And remember, I spent thirty years recruiting for the Yankees. I've seen every brand of talent."

The significance of Frank's confession isn't quite clear. "Either way, waiting or not waiting, he still had cancer."

Frank nods slowly. "I suppose that's true, but a few more weeks of playing regular season, maybe a month or two, and he could have set some records, snagged more endorsements. He could have had a bigger nest egg for himself and for you."

The missing pieces snap into place. "That's why you kept visiting us every year, that's why you hired Dad, you feel guilty for telling him not to wait to have the surgery?"

And then I remember Brody's words that day in the training room. *I wouldn't have done it. I wouldn't have let them take my leg.*

"It's true that I've wondered many times if he should have waited, if the cancer would have spread as fast as the doctors anticipated," Frank says. "And maybe guilt would have been enough to bring him to Kansas City with me, but here's the other truth, kid… Jimmy was just as committed to finding a way back as all those doctors. And eventually, he became even more driven than anyone else. He studied pitching techniques, body mechanics, biology—anything that could potentially help him. He truly is one of the greatest baseball technicians I've ever seen. I'd even go as far as to call him a great athletic technician. His understanding of body mechanics isn't restricted to baseball."

I'm not sure why, but I'm overcome with emotions and grateful that Frank isn't looking at me right now. Maybe it's because I want so desperately to see Dad get back what he's lost and I know that won't ever happen. "So, what's the problem, then? Can't you just explain to Johnson that Dad knows what he's talking about? That he's the right person for the job?"

"Johnson tried to sign him back in the day when he was with the Angels. But Jimmy wanted million dollar contracts, and his name written in the sky. To Johnson, Jimmy is nothing but a could-have-been-great player who believes he's entitled to a coaching job just because. And on one hand, I get where Johnson is coming from. Your dad was worshipped and fawned over in his day, and I'm not gonna lie, it went to his head. But you're allowed that when you have the skills to back up the arrogance, and he damn sure had the skills. He's changed, though, Annie. He went through a bullheaded, I-can-fix-myself phase followed by some pretty scary depression, and then he emerged from it—humble, hardworking, and a damn good father—not that I'm an expert on the subject. But none of that matters." Frank lets out a frustrated sigh. "If I can't get one fucking pitcher to listen to him—except Brody who doesn't really count—I can't prove he's good. How the hell am I supposed to get Johnson to let me keep him around?"

Silence falls over us for several long minutes while I allow everything Frank's told me to sink in. Bits and pieces of the story I already knew or had found by myself on the internet, but the reasons behind everything weren't something that had been public knowledge.

Frank pats my leg and stands. "I'm sorry, kid, I didn't mean to unload on you. I just wanted you to know the truth."

I realize Frank never really answered my question. "So it *was* mostly guilt that kept you coming back to visit?"

Frank nods. "In the beginning, probably. I mean, Jimmy first entered major league radar when he was still in high school. He was this pain-in-the-ass little shit that I had to deal with. But when you stick around and watch someone grow up and go from a lost kid to becoming a good man, that's not a relationship you ever want to sever. That's what really kept your dad and me friends over all these years. I can get caught up in the show just like Johnson, but then I'd pay Jimmy and you a visit and remember what it's like to be human again. To be in the real world. That's something I'd hate for you to lose as well. So be careful who you make friends with," he warns.

"Are we going to be able to stay here after this season?" I ask.

He gives me a sad smile. "I don't know, kid. I just don't know. But I'll do everything I can to keep you and Jimmy around."

I swallow back unshed tears and watch Frank walk away and get into his red pickup truck. That's when I notice Savannah standing in the doorway, half hidden by the screen door. "I didn't mean to listen in," she says right away, coming out to sit in Frank's abandoned spot. Unlike Frank, her petite, slim figure barely moves the swing. "I just got off the phone with your dad. He's bringing Chinese home for lunch."

I laugh despite my depressed mood. "And I thought he was running away, leaving me to live with the London family and be Carl's new sister."

She laughs with me. "I don't think there's any chance of that happening. I thought I was going to have to break out a whistle or a Taser earlier."

I lay my head back against the swing. "I'm thinking of crawling into bed and waiting until tomorrow to wake up."

"Only one more week of school," Savannah points out. "What are your plans this summer?"

"Run and sleep," I say before adding, "and community service, of course."

"How would you like to be my intern for the summer? Help with PR and schedule events and interviews with the players, sift through fan mail…"

I roll my eyes. "Is this a ploy you and Dad came up with to keep me out of trouble?"

"Partly," she admits. "But I also think you'd be very good at this job. Especially now that you have a clear understanding of both wanted and unwanted media attention."

Brody comes to mind, and I know I can't just sit around all summer and wallow in my short-lived moment of rejection. I need something else to focus my attention on. Something safe.

"I'm in," I tell her. "But if Johnson changes his mind about Brody and the hearing-impaired Disney Channel girlfriend, I'm so not taking on that task. Besides, it has ridiculous written all over it. Like Brody would actually settle down with one girl."

She eyes me skeptically. "Well, you never know."

I shrug, not wanting to elaborate on how badly I'd like for that to happen.

Lenny London: *No comment.*
5 minutes ago

Annie Lucas: *No comment.*
2 minutes ago

Carl London: *Headed to Brazil in two days! All Brazilian women get Brazilian waxes, right? I think I've found my calling. Maybe I'll become a citizen?*
1 minute ago

post-all-star
BREAK

chapter 16

Lenny London: *Ok so maybe I don't hate physical labor. Just so long as it includes nail guns and Annie Lucas's homemade brownies.*
1 day ago

Jason Brody Royals Pitcher: *"Maybe I called it wrong, but it's official."* — *Tommy Connolly, umpire*
3 hours ago

Annie Lucas: *I always wondered what kind of people sent fan mail. Now I know.*
5 minutes ago

"*Well, there you go. Here comes Frank Steadman,*" the announcer says. "*It's about time. He can't afford to wait for young Jason Brody to walk three batters in a row before he pulls him out of the game.*"

"*Yes, he's clearly run out of gas,*" the other announcer says.

"*I'd say he ran out about two innings ago.*"

I throw a wad of paper at the television in Savannah's office. "Shut the hell up, douche bags."

Savannah laughs and then drops her eyes back to the papers

in front of her. "I really think Brody needs a bigger, more personal online presence to get those younger fans. What do you think, Annie?"

I wave a hand to stop her. "Don't jinx it! He still doesn't have a contract for the rest of the season." And neither does my dad.

And right now, Brody really does look tired. My stomach sinks, watching him in his blue uniform as he lifts his hat and wipes sweat from his forehead, his glove hanging limply in his left hand as Frank approaches the mound. This is Brody's fourth game in four days, and he's pitched at least three innings every day. And they've won two of the three games in the series. Winning today against the Twins would be huge.

Which is the only reason I'm obsessed with this game.

It has nothing to do with the fact that I've barely spoken to Brody since my idiot alter ego kissed him. Of course it doesn't. I mean, why should it? It was only the most humiliating, awkward moment of my entire life.

The camera shifts to the bullpen. Dad and the other pitching coach are speaking loud enough to see their mouths moving. The other coach is waving his arms around a lot.

"*I don't know what's happening over there, but this is why you don't have two equal pitching coaches for one ball club, right, Dave?*" the announcer says.

"*Exactly, John. Someone needs to be in charge. Looks like Jim Lucas wants to put in a number five pitcher instead of using the Royals ace. I don't think Larry Johnson is going to be happy with this move. He's the most hands-on owner I've ever seen.*"

"*But Frank Steadman does have the final say. And he's got to be worried about those loaded bases.*"

The camera switches back to the mound. Frank is walking

away, and Brody is still there.

"I'll be damned. He's not taking him out! What is going through Frank Steadman's head right now?"

I hold my breath as Brody gets in position again. Goose bumps raise all over my arms. He looks so good. Like a star. Nobody should take that from him. Brody focuses intensely on home plate and two minutes later, he's struck the batter out and the team is jogging into the dugout.

I flop onto my back beside the stack of papers and baseballs on the floor of Savannah's office. "I think I just had a heart attack."

"This is why I can't watch away games," Savannah says. "I'm only doing this for you. I'd much rather turn it off and hear the results after."

"But if they end up winning, and Brody's pitched most of the series, won't you be glad to have witnessed it live?"

"I can watch it from my DVR and pretend it's live just as easy. But Brody pitching all these extra innings... That's really gonna help from a PR standpoint. Gives me a little human interest meat to work with."

More than the fake girlfriend angle? I hope so. An idea suddenly forms in my head. "Have you ever done something like surprising a player by bringing their family to a game? Maybe reuniting them after a falling out...?"

Savannah's head snaps up, her gaze sharp on mine. "I would never do that unless a player expressed interest in having their family present. That's not an area you want to meddle in, understood?"

"Okay, okay," I say, trying to play it cool. "It was just an idea. You're the expert, I'm the intern."

She smiles. "It's a nice thought, Annie. But family drama can be very damaging to players and to the entire club."

I don't know if she has any clue about Brody's disconnect with his mom or if she was speaking in general terms, but I can't help but think his mom would be proud to know what her son's doing. Okay, maybe not the four girls in and out of his hotel room in three nights, but the pitching… Surely she'd be proud of that part.

The commercial break ends, and I turn my attention back to the game. The score is 2–0. Them. And after two outs, Frank does something that causes even me to side with the douche bag announcers.

Brody leaves the dugout with a batting helmet, a bat, and gloves.

"*I don't believe this,*" the announcer says. "*This is certainly not in the original game plan.*"

"*Well, we knew he'd have to bat against the Cardinals in two weeks when they play on National League territory,*" the other announcer says. "*Although no one seems to be talking about the fact that Jason Brody was originally recruited as a closer with no plans to bat on any territory. How many games has he played mid-relief in now?*"

"*Thirty-two games, Dave. Not to mention starting on opening day. The Royals have suffered from a lack of starters and mid-relief pitching depth these past few seasons. They really didn't need another closer. Not as badly as they needed starters and mid-game guys.*"

"Oh my God, Savannah." I hit my hand against the desk. "He's gonna bat. Does he even know how?"

"I have no idea." Savannah looks just as rattled as I feel. She gets up from her chair and perches herself at the end of the desk. We both lean in and watch Brody on deck, taking practice swings. "He did bat with the farm teams…For that whole half a season."

"I really hate to question Frank Steadman, but the Royals have a real shot at tying up this game in the sixth inning. Two runners on base and two outs."

"Exactly, Dave. I can't wrap my head around Steadman's strategy, putting in a cold hitter with a tired arm at such a key moment in the game…and a rookie who's never bat in the majors before! Things had been looking up for the Royals this season."

Had been.

We get a shot of the dugout and Dad—not Frank—is passing signals to Brody who sees him, nods, and then steps into the batter's box.

"Why does this feel like a really, really bad idea?" I say.

Savannah shakes her head, her hands wrapped around the edge of the desk, her knuckles white.

Brody swings at the first pitch. And misses. Strike one.

"Looks like Jim Lucas is sending twenty-one-year old, Campbell, the second year number five pitcher into the bullpen, leaving the Royals ace on the bench," the announcer says.

Brody looks so much smaller than the hot-dog-obsessed designated hitters who would normally take his place in the batting lineup.

"Talk about pressure. He's got to be shaking out there," the announcer says.

I've already chewed away all the skin around my thumbnail, so I sit on my hands just as the pitcher releases the ball. I squeeze my eyes shut, but that doesn't keep me from hearing the crack of the bat connecting with the ball. My eyes fly open, and I jump to my feet.

"A line drive out to right field!"

"Ohmigod," I say over and over. Brody takes off for first base. The ball gets scooped up in the outfield. The Twins right fielder throws home. Lenny's dad had been on third base and he easily beats the ball home. The runner on second slides into third and the camera shifts back to Brody running.

"Look at the speed on that kid!" the announcer says. *"He's going for second!"*

The Twins scramble to make the throw to second base to get Brody out, but he's much faster than they anticipated. Brody easily slides into second and the runner on third touches home base.

"What an unexpected play for the Royals!" the announcer shouts. *"Nineteen-year-old rookie pitcher Jason Brody just tied up this game in his first major league turn at bat. I bet the Twins never saw that one coming!"*

I'm jumping up and down, and Savannah's phone is ringing like crazy. She hurries around the desk, back to her chair, and starts fielding media calls. She's got the cool-we-totally-planned-this voice down so well, but her expression is ecstatic.

"One more run, guys," I say to myself. "Just one more."

Third Base is up next to bat, and he's one of our best hitters. He's had fifteen home runs this season already. The Twins shift around in the outfield, obviously anticipating a long hit.

But he doesn't go for the home run. He drives the ball right to a hole between shortstop and the outfield. And Brody's on the move long before the ball is picked up. He sprints toward third base and doesn't stop there.

"And Brody's heading home! Look at him go."

The throw to home plate is so fast I'm sure Brody's about to get tagged out, but he slides with perfect timing. The umpire leans in and waves his arms, shouting, *"Safe!"*

"Yes!" I scream.

Savannah covers the phone with one hand and waves at me to hush.

"And the Royals have just taken the lead in the sixth inning of this four-game series, thanks to the nineteen-year-old temporary pitcher from Chicago, Illinois."

"John, didn't we hear rumors that Jason Brody's contract with Kansas City is only three months?"

"I heard the same thing, Dave. Larry Johnson and Frank Steadman will have to do something about that very soon."

Shortstop bats next and strikes out and the Royals grab their gloves and jog out to the field again. Brody stays on the bench, finally getting a chance to rest.

"John, I don't know about this pitching decision... They've gained the lead and Jim Lucas is still dead set on taking another big risk with Campbell pitching. He's nearly as green as Brody."

"Well, they've had some luck already, maybe Frank Steadman is hoping it'll continue."

"Dave, you could be right, but remember? Jim Lucas has been out of this game for sixteen years. Does he really have the experience to choose a pitcher at a crucial time like this?"

I hold my breath on and off for the rest of the game, watching the other young relief pitcher get more time on the mound in one game than he got all last month. I only know this because the announcers say it like five hundred times. Campbell isn't as talented as Brody, but he holds his own and we end the game 3–2.

Five minutes after the game ends, Savannah is still on the phone setting up interviews and giving statements about both Dad and Brody. Suddenly, the announcers vanish and the shot goes back to the field where Brody and Third Base are standing beside a local Fox Sports reporter.

"Let me call you back," Savannah says, her eyes on the TV.

She hangs up the phone, turns the ringer off, and returns to her seat at the edge of the desk.

"What was going through your head standing in that batter's box?" the interviewer asks Brody.

Brody pulls his hat down further over his eyes and shakes his head. *"I was kinda hoping for a miracle or four bad pitches."*

The interviewer laughs and then sticks the mic out to Third Base. *"You've got fifteen home runs this season, but you didn't go for the homer tonight. What was the strategy in tonight's game-saving play?"*

"Winning is all about skill and strategy. With this move, we went with strategy and it worked," he explains simply.

Very diplomatic answer. *"And how about your arm, son?"* he says to Brody. *"Pitching four straight games isn't following the normal rotation."*

"Steadman and Coach Lucas gave me the choice to sit out one of the games, but I've learned that you gotta take all the chances you can get," he says. *"My arm felt good, some of the other guys are just coming from injuries, and I was happy to help the team take this series victory. It's something I only dreamt about as a kid playing little league ball."*

The interviewer is all smiles. *"So we can all assume that your game-saving play hasn't sunk in yet?"*

Brody laughs and shakes his head. *"Not at all. Maybe after I go home tonight and watch the replay about a dozen times."*

"What do you think? Everyone on Twitter is now claiming you're the fastest runner in the league?" the interviewer says. *"Are you?"*

Brody tilts his cap back, revealing more of his forehead before looking right into the camera. *"I have a very inspiring workout partner, and I've gotten a lot faster over the past couple months."*

My face heats up instantly. I can't look at Savannah. He's got to be talking about me. Who else? The treadmill in the training room? Even though he's got his own apartment, and I have Lily and her bike, Brody still found an excuse to run with me at least a couple times a week. Well, at least he did until the little incident in his car. Maybe this is his way of saying he wants to run with me again?

Don't read too much into this, Annie.

And it's true. He could mean a dozen different things, all involving me and none involving liking me like *that*. Or needing me to continue hanging out with him one-on-one. Maybe he'd hate to let a girl beat him or just that I gave him advice on his technique. Although he sprints and I'm more mid-distance.

I'm dying to grab my phone and text him, make some joke about his comment or him shaking in his boots while at bat, but I can't. Not like I used to.

Annie Lucas: *If you weren't just watching that freakin' amazing baseball game, I've officially disowned you. OK, I'll give you a chance to explain yourself, but there better be an awesome story involving three-headed people or Hollister models.*
20 seconds ago

Savannah walks across the office and shuts off the TV when the station goes back to the news desk and ends the post-game interviews. "See what I mean?" she says. "He's insanely charming and youthful on TV. We need that same feel for his social media outlets online."

I shake off my Jason Brody love haze and turn to face her. "Wait, you mean like his Facebook page? The one with all the song lyrics and famous baseball quotes?"

"Yes, exactly," Savannah says like I'm supposed to understand what she means. "I think fans want to know where he's having dinner or coffee or what clubs he's hanging out at. What he thinks before a game and what's he feeling walking into Wrigley Field or Yankee Stadium where players older than his great-grandfather made baseball history. The music references are great, but we need to know what he likes about that band or group. What's he watching on TV? This is how people get to know celebrities nowadays." She shakes her head and laughs. "Why am I even explaining this to you, you probably understand current social media better than I do. Everyone knows if you have a question about the internet, ask a teenager, right?"

"Maybe if you just gave him some pointers?" I suggest.

"I have," Savannah says. "A few times actually, and he tells me it sounds like a great idea and then nothing changes. Maybe he's just been too busy to keep up with it all. Lots of travel."

I shove the mail and baseballs aside and plop down on the floor again. I understand what she's trying to say perfectly, and I might know why he hasn't made any changes. It's not really my place to tell Savannah, but I trust her. "I think I know what the problem is…" Her eyebrows rise, waiting for me to continue. "He's probably copying and pasting quotes and lyrics…"

"Probably."

"He's dyslexic," I say. "He can read and everything, I've heard him read before. But the process of putting words from his head into a tweet or Facebook might be more difficult."

Savannah is already scrunching up her forehead, thinking it through. "But he'll text you, right? And he read something out loud to you?"

"It was just like two sentences." I'm quickly growing uncomfortable discussing this without him around. It feels like a betrayal. "And yeah he texts me, but I bet the real issue is the public aspect and representing the team… It seems very official and probably intimidating."

She nods. "Right. Totally get that. Since he's already talked about his learning disability with you, why don't we just keep it between the two of you? Mention my concerns and then suggest a plan. He can grant you access to the page, and he'll text you things to post and you can handle that for him."

I lean back against the wall and exhale. "That sounds like a perfect solution."

She grins at me. "It's not anything new. The really big players all have interns and publicists handling their online communication, and no one ever knows it's not really them."

"But it will be Brody, right? I'm just the messenger?"

"Correct." She turns the ringer back on the phone, and it goes off right away. "I better take care of these calls, but thanks, Annie. You've mastered my philosophy for publicity and that is that you do a much better job when you take the time to get to know your clients."

Right. That's exactly why I got to know Jason Brody so well. I'll run with that lie.

A few hours after the game, while Lenny and I are painting the living room at our Habitat building site, Brody sends me the first text either of us have sent to each other in weeks.

BRODY: What r u doing in 4 hrs?

ME: Why?

BRODY: Ur pop and I might need a ride hme from airprt

ME: your car is there right?

BRODY: hve good news. 2 things. Finished lessons and took my practice test. got 87%

ME: That's awesome! What's the other thing?

BRODY: I can drik mre scotch than your dad. Didn't think they were gonna let him on the plane

ME: You guys are drunk? That's why you need a ride?

BRODY: Yep. Did u see the game?

ME: Yes. Watched with Savannah. It was amazing. Glad you got to celebrate.

BRODY: wish you were here…

My heart takes off in a sprint. He just played the game of his life, got drunk with my dad in celebration, and instead of finding some bimbos to bang he's thinking about me? That he'd be happier if I were there, too?

God, what is wrong with me? I have to stop doing this. I have to stop taking these tiny windows that he leaves open and jumping through them into fantasy land.

"I was really hoping for six hours with the nail gun." Lenny bends down and dips her roller into the tray of light gray paint. "You didn't even bring chocolate today."

I'm still staring at the last text, my own roller hanging loose at my side, getting paint all over my jean shorts. "I told you I was in Savannah's office all day working and watching the game."

Lenny lifts her head and stops when she sees me engrossed in my phone. "What's going on?"

I stuff it back into my pocket and press the roller to my wall again. "Nothing really…it's just…well…"

"What?"

"Brody's last text," I say. "He said '*wish you were here.*' I'm trying not to read too much into that but—"

"Wish you were here," she repeats and then says it again using a slower more drawn-out tone. "Hmm... It could be completely innocent. But then again, he knows how you feel, and I think he'd be very hesitant to type something that could be misinterpreted as romantic with you."

"He and my dad are both drunk, so maybe he's not thinking clearly." But this tiny part of my brain is thinking about his teammates freezing him out, walking off whenever Brody approached them. And the fact that he has no contact with his family, and he's already with Dad. Who would he text tonight besides me? Who am I kidding? He's got an army of Jason Brody fangirls probably programmed in his phone already.

"In my experience, people are more honest while intoxicated," Lenny says, leaving me to ponder that and become five times more confused.

When I pull up to the airport, it's nearly eleven and Grams has been forced to stay up way past her bedtime. She's in the passenger seat beside me, drinking a chocolate milk shake.

"I asked for nuts, Ginny! Where's the nuts?"

"It's a shake, Grams." I scan the people standing at the curb with luggage, looking for signs of Brody or Dad. I'm driving Dad's SUV instead of my old clunker. "Want me to get you a sundae on the way home?"

"This looks like Vegas," she says.

Brody and Dad finally emerge, Brody's rolling both suitcases behind him and Dad's stumbling and looking pretty nauseous. They get loaded up into the backseat. Dad pulls his hat over his eyes and slumps down in his seat.

Grams looks over her shoulder at Brody. "Well, put your seat belt on, goddammit."

Brody seems way more sober than Dad. He laughs and buckles his seat belt. "How are you, Grams? How's the milk shake?"

"Terrible. They forgot the damn nuts again." She holds it out to him across the front seat. "You want it?"

My eyes meet his in the rearview mirror. "Um…sure," he says, taking the cup.

"Doing okay back there, Dad?"

He grunts but no actual words are spoken. Not any that I can comprehend.

Since my house is on the way, I decide it's best to drop Dad and Grams off first before he spews all over his new car.

Brody moves into the front seat and makes small talk all the way to his apartment—my job with Savannah, the Habitat project, my workouts over the last five days. By the time we get to his apartment, I realize we haven't talked about him at all. And today was a really big day for him.

I put the car in park and hop out to grab his luggage, even though I know he can do it himself. Once he sets the suitcase on the ground in front of the building, I lean forward and hug him around the waist.

I only meant for it to be a quick hug, but long enough for me to take notice of the fact that my head fits perfectly under his chin. "You were so good today. Not that you're not good every game, but today was extra amazing." I start to pull away, but his arms encircle me, pressing my cheek against his chest. I close my eyes and inhale, savoring every second.

And yeah, I can smell the alcohol on him. Not as much as Dad. He's still got that freshly showered scent lingering in the background, so I try to pretend he's completely sober.

"Thanks." He dips his head, and his nose touches the top of my hair.

My heart is sprinting all over again because this hug has gone about five seconds past the acceptable friend length. And just before he releases me, I feel his lips in my hair, kissing the top of my head.

Is that friendly? Do friends do that? I've never had a friend kiss my head before, but Dad has, so maybe if it's fatherly it's also brotherly. Ick.

He's probably going to head inside to his swanky, silver-applianced, black-leather-furnished bachelor pad and call one—or maybe even two—of the models or sorority girls programmed into his phone. If he wanted me, he'd invite me in.

"Good night, Annie." The sticky summer air sweeps in between us. Brody grips the handle of his suitcase and rolls it toward the door. "Thanks for the ride."

I climb back in the car and touch my hand to my head where he kissed it and the other hand feels my cheek where it pressed against his T-shirt. I lift my own shirt to my nose to see if it smells like him.

Oh my God, this is getting creepy and extremely unhealthy.

My hands quickly grip the steering wheel and I drive off, breathing through my mouth, not letting myself smell anything. *Weirdo, Annie. You're a weirdo.*

No, I'm a Jason Brody groupie. That's even worse than mentally unstable.

chapter 17

Annie Lucas: *Old people shouldn't be allowed to have hangovers.*
9 hours ago

Dad was such a mess this morning after his drunken celebration, I made sure to stop at the grocery store and pick up some Gatorade on the way home from eight hours of Saturday home building/community service. Johnson didn't stay completely true to his word about having cameras follow me and Lenny during all our community service hours. We've had three camera-free sessions. Today, unfortunately, wasn't one of those.

My senses should have been alert the second I spotted the beat-up blue truck parked just past our mailbox, but honestly, I hadn't thought about her for weeks. There just didn't seem to be any reason for Dad to try and get her to come here.

But sure enough, when I walk through the front door, Mom is sitting on the couch between Dad and Grams, looking all cozy.

My stomach drops and dread fills my insides. The sack full of thirty-two ounce Gatorade bottles falls from my hand onto the tile floor in the foyer. I take slow, careful steps into the living room.

Mom and her perfect body and straight shiny blond hair bounces to her feet, a grin on her face as she rushes over to me. "Oh, my baby!" she gushes, throwing her arms around me. "Look at you!"

I just stand there frozen, my arms hanging at my sides while she squeezes the life out of me. From over her shoulder, Dad's eyes meet mine—guilty and hopeful.

No, this isn't happening. It can't happen. He can't get sucked into her Mom spell and screw everything up. She'll leave, and he'll turn into zombie Dad again for an entire month. A month that the Royals will have to play fifteen or twenty games.

Mom pulls back and cups my face in her hands. "Where's that handsome boyfriend of yours? Back in Arizona crying over his broken heart?"

No, that would be Dad when you leave in a few days.

I'm too upset to filter. "What are you doing here?"

Her face tightens, and she pats my cheek before sitting down closer to Dad again. "I had a little audition today. Got a part in a show here in Kansas City. It runs for three months. Isn't that great news, honey? I'll be sticking around."

Yeah, I'm sure it's the show that brought you here, not Dad's major league job.

I'm already backing up toward the door. I need to get out of here. I need to be somewhere where I can scream at the top of my lungs and then maybe after I'll be able to think clearly. I can figure out what to do.

"Annie…" Dad says.

"I'm…I have to go," I say. "With Lenny. Community service."

"Let's talk first, okay?" He knows I just got back from community service. He knows I'm lying.

I shake my head, anger seeping out without permission. "You promised, Dad. You promised this wouldn't happen."

He tries to reply, but I don't give him or Mom a chance. I bolt out the front door and jump into my car. I drive past Lenny's house and debate knocking on the door, but I'm pretty sure she's getting ready for a date tonight and I don't want to deal with First Base or his Botox-addicted wife. Not to mention the fact that I've never told Lenny about my mom. I've only told one person in Kansas City. One person period.

And then I'm breaking my own rules, sending Brody a text. Making the first move.

ME: Are you home?

The second I knock on the door, I'm already regretting this move. It's too much. Too personal. And my regret thickens when Lenny's words come back to me, "*His personal life, his personal space, is beyond anything you could ever grasp or even want to be involved with.*"

My body is half turned around, ready to bolt, when the door opens. I slowly turn back around, and Brody's standing in front of me—shirtless and messy haired, wearing only a pair of gym shorts. He's positioned himself in the doorway, concealing any space and any glimpse inside I may have gotten otherwise.

His forehead wrinkles with concern. "What's wrong?"

"I'm not sure." I let out a heavy breath. Okay, I am sure. Mom is what's wrong. "I just need somewhere to hide from my life for a little while."

"You wanna go out somewhere?" he says and then seems

to grasp the meaning of his words 'cause he shakes his head. *It's night and the weekend. Downtown is hopping with clubs and parties…*"Right. Bad idea. Sorry."

"Maybe I could…?" I don't finish the sentence, but instead nod toward the unexposed crack in the doorway.

Nerves flicker across Brody's features. "Uh, yeah…I mean, I haven't really…I don't usually like…have people over." Without any further explanation, he opens the door all the way, allowing me to walk inside. The living room is dark, the blinds and curtains shut tight like maybe he'd been napping.

"Were you sleeping? 'Cause I can totally go somewhere else. I just thought—"

"It's fine."

But it doesn't sound fine. Have I interrupted something? *Jesus, I should have never come here. What the hell was I thinking?* He finds a light switch on the wall beside the door and turns it on, revealing the depths of what I'd anticipated would be a swanky, womanizing man cave.

All that sits in the living room is a metal futon with a worn-out black cushion, and several red milk crates flipped upside down and pressed together with a piece of plywood on top creating a makeshift coffee table. I turn in a half circle, spotting a card table and two chairs in the dining room. The kitchen looks pretty bare—a cheap white microwave is the only item on the countertops. Nothing is silver and shiny. No stereos with remote controls. No mood lighting. Not even a single floor lamp anywhere.

There's no way he brings models or actresses back here. Maybe he checks into hotels with his dates and orders expensive room service, like champagne and strawberries.

"Sorry," Brody says after watching me assess the contents of his home. He scratches the back of his head like he's embarrassed. "I haven't entertained guests or, like, had anyone over at all."

"It's nice. I like it."

He smiles, seeing through my bullshit answer, then he's all concerned again. "What's going on, Annie?"

I stare at the microwave. "It's just…I mean—"

My voice is cut off by the tears spilling down my cheeks. I hadn't even felt them coming on or I would have put a stop to it. I wipe my face quickly with both hands.

"What's going on?" Brody repeats.

"My mom's here," I say before he starts getting ideas about this being a heartbroken love crisis. "And she's staying for a while. Too long. My dad promised he wouldn't tell her where we are now. I don't know what to do—"

Suddenly, I'm pulled into Brody's arms, my cheek resting against his bare skin. One of his hands moves over my hair and the other arm wraps tight around me.

After a minute or two, I've gotten the tears completely shut off, and I extricate myself from his arms. He sits on the edge of the homemade coffee table, waiting patiently for me to vent or whatever.

My face is hot with embarrassment. This isn't like last night where he initiated the ride home and even though I hugged him first, he's the one that made it longer than friend-code allows. Today, I brought myself here for no other reason than the fact that I needed him and there's no way to conceal that.

On top of that, I've clearly made him uncomfortable by entering his empty apartment. "I'm sorry. I should leave."

I turn around and head for the door, but Brody steps in front of me, resting his hands on my shoulders. "Not so fast…" He leans down, his eyes meeting mine, searching for sanity or something. "What's going through that head of yours?"

My cheeks and neck flame up even hotter. "I just didn't think before I drove over here."

He turns me around by my shoulders and nudges me toward the couch/futon. "Come sit down. You're not leaving yet. I've made the decision for you."

I let him guide me over to the couch and take a seat at the very end, turning myself to face him and leaning my back against the metal armrest. "This is annoying, isn't it? Your only day off in, like, two weeks, and you've just had the game of your life, and as a consolation prize you get a whiny high school girl showing up to interrupt your nap."

"You're not annoying," he says right away. "And it was time for me to wake up anyway."

I examine my nails. "So what's the word? Johnson's not actually going to send you back to Triple-A after playing so well in Minnesota, right?"

He tries to hide his excitement, but I can clearly see it dancing in his eyes. "I'm getting a new contract next week. My agent's negotiating right now."

I smile at him, finally abandoning my nail inspection. "That's great. You deserve to be here."

He studies me carefully. "Why do you still look afraid that I might be hiding dead bodies in my closet or something?"

"Maybe it's your talent for getting four different girls alone in your hotel room during a three game series." The words are out of my mouth before I can stop them.

Brody leans back. "It's not as exciting as it sounds in the articles."

"Why?" I ask, honestly curious. "Do all the girls have fake boobs and C-section scars?"

He laughs really hard. "I have no idea."

"What? Like you're too into hooking up that you don't pay attention?" I can't get rid of the annoyance in my voice. He hasn't betrayed me, Dad has. Brody owes me nothing. And he's trying to be nice right now. It's not his fault that I have feelings for him.

"You heard what Savannah said awhile back, about expectations for single players under twenty-five?" His forehead wrinkles like he's debating something. "All of that stuff is just for publicity… I guess I thought maybe you knew that already or at least knew it to some extent. Nobody plays as many games as baseball players do and then has time to go on all those dates for real. I'd be dead on my feet. Almost all of my so-called dates are literally five minutes long with a photographer tipped off in advance. Like that night at the club…and the premiere of that movie I never watched."

So that's why Savannah had said she already knew why Brody and the photographers were there.

"So the articles are fake, too? You haven't really had four girls in your hotel room in three days?"

He scratches his head again. "Well, technically that part is true, but not like *that*. You know?"

My whole illusion of Brody's social life is shattering, and I have no idea what to think. "Then what do you do with them while they're in your room?"

He shrugs. "Sign autographs, offer them a drink. Then I make an excuse about needing to get ready to go somewhere, and they leave."

I stare at him in disbelief. "That's it?"

"Pretty much."

I narrow my eyes at him. "I find that hard to believe. You have so many opportunities to hook up, unlike me, who knows about two guys around here even remotely close to my age. Anyone in your situation would need a big reason to say no to every single girl."

"A big reason? Like STDs? Being drugged and having naked photos of me taken and posted everywhere," he recites. "And then there's undercover reporters who write detailed accounts of your…um, skills."

I crack a smile despite my mood. "No way! Who does that?"

He smiles. "I'm not kidding. Savannah gave me this list with detailed accounts of these things happening to other players and the protocol for each one, how the media will handle it and ways to cover it up. Scared the shit out of me. I don't get close in that way to anyone anymore. It's just not worth it."

"But Lenny told me her dad sleeps with—"

"He does," Brody says. "But it's not groupies or random girls in bars. He limits himself to other people's wives, doctors who have worked on him, maybe a dental hygienist or two."

"Gross." I shake my head in disgust. "Why can't Dad be like that every once in a while? Hook up with some other woman so he can forget about my mom?"

"I don't think it works like that," he says. "If you love someone, even the best one-night stand isn't going to erase that."

"Guess I'm too much of a kid to understand something so complex."

Brody shakes his head and scoots closer to me. "You are not a kid, Annie. I don't think of you that way. I've told you that before."

Yeah, he told me that in the car after laughing at my tight dress and red lipstick.

Tears spring to my eyes again, but this time I keep them from falling. "Yeah, that's a great memory."

He lets out a frustrated groan and leans his head back against the couch. His hands lift to cover his face. "This is impossible."

Okay, this was a terrible idea.

"I'm sorry. I should go," I repeat again and stand up and brush past him. One hand drops from his face and hooks around my waist, pulling me back down on the couch, so I'm practically seated on his lap. My heart takes off and my voice hitches in my throat.

He holds me tightly in place and leans in closer. "Just so you know, if I had the crisis you're having today, you're the first person I'd want to see. You're the only person I'd want to talk to."

Our eyes meet and my heart beats like a wild animal locked in a tiny cage. My lips part, but no words fall out. Brody's fingers move through my hair and my skin heats up, my thoughts jumbling and losing their grasp on reality.

"I'm sorry for not doing this sooner, and I'm sorry for doing it all," he says.

My eyes widen as he closes the gap between us, his lips hovering a millimeter from mine. His bare chest presses against me, and I feel the *thud, thud, thud* of his heart when his mouth touches mine.

chapter 18

This isn't real. It can't be real. I must have fallen asleep at the wheel and crashed my car.

But I'm the opposite of drowsy. My senses have never been more alert in my entire life. Brody's mouth is soft against mine, and his hands slide across my cheeks, resting on the sides of my neck. Unlike that night in his car, when his lips part, instead of pulling away he deepens the kiss. My eyes finally close and my mind is beautifully blank, endorphins flowing freely through my veins as my heart pumps at double speed.

I lift my hands and wrap them around his back, gliding my fingers up and down his bare skin, moving over his shoulders. How many times have I stared at him shirtless in the training room and been envious of old men touching and prodding him, wishing I had an excuse to do this? How many nights have I fallen asleep thinking up a moment just like this one?

His mouth breaks away from mine, arms wrapping around my back, sliding up my T-shirt. A shiver runs along my spine as we stretch out across the futon. We're completely pressed together. His heart thuds against my chest again, and his lips drift down to my neck.

When he raises his head, our eyes meet for a split second, both of us breathing heavily, hearts pounding. Then I reach for his dark hair, combing my fingers through it, pulling his mouth back to mine.

He brushes his fingers against my bra strap and then his mouth is traveling the length of my neck. I tilt my head back slightly, my chest arching into him.

"This is much better in real life," he whispers against my skin. "So much better than the fantasy."

My hands freeze in his hair. "You have fantasies about kissing me?"

He lifts his head from my neck and touches his forehead to mine. "Yes."

"Since when?"

There's the slightest bit of color creeping up to his cheeks. He laughs softly and drops his head again, resting it on my shoulder. "Probably since you told me that I couldn't choose to be a house elf because they're an enslaved race."

My jaw drops open. "But...But...you said—"

His mouth captures mine again, giving me another long lingering kiss before pulling away again. "I just wanted to do the right thing. For once in my life, I wanted to make the right choice."

"And that's not me?"

He rests a hand on my cheek. "Only because I respect your dad, and I know he doesn't want *this*."

I swallow the lump still in my throat from earlier. I don't really care what Dad wants. He promised me something, and then he broke that promise.

His arms go around me again. Brody's fingers on my bare

skin is the most amazing feeling ever. I lean my ear on his shoulder and touch my lips to his neck. He tries to speak evenly, but his voice keeps catching with every kiss. It makes me feel powerful.

"I've never seen anything like you and your dad together, Annie," he manages to say finally. "And he treats me with respect, like I'm not a screwup and like maybe I can do something with my life. And I know you're pissed at him right now, but you're the most important person in his life. I already feel guilty for having my hand up your shirt."

I laugh. I can't help it. "So guilty it took you about twenty seconds to dive in?"

"Yeah, but you're not counting the hundreds of other times I've wanted to touch you and didn't." He laughs and kisses me again. "I really want to take your bra off, too, and I haven't so I've still got a couple ounces of self-control left."

My emotions can hardly keep up with this huge turn of events, and I shift from swoon-happy to frustrated. I grip his face in my hands, our gazes locked. "Why did you make me feel like such an idiot for kissing you after we left the club that night? I've never been so humiliated in my entire life."

He closes his eyes and draws in a deep breath. "I'm so sorry. I just didn't know what to do. I never imagined you'd make the first move. I thought it would be about me not bringing you over to the dark side. I had no idea you were already there."

"I'm more of a dark side poser," I say. "For example, I'm still not sure this is really happening. That I'm laying horizontally on your couch with you, and your tongue was just in my mouth."

He kisses me once, twice, three times before speaking again. "I felt like such a dick for shooting you down like that. I was going to tell you how I felt but not…not this. I didn't mean to—"

"Well, you did." I wrap a leg around him and draw him closer until our bodies are practically glued together. "You can't take it back now."

"You're right. Guess I'm not as much of a good guy as I'd like to be." He tucks my hair behind my ears and looks me over carefully.

"You're horrible," I say. "I'm completely ruined. Morally corrupt, destined for prostitution and credit card fraud."

"After all the trouble I've been in, worrying about this probably seems pretty lame," he explains. "But you know how there are some people who can criticize you over and over and their lashing will barely even penetrate the surface? And then there are other people who can say nothing more than, 'I'm disappointed in you' and it feels like a kick in the nuts? You can't just shake it off?"

Unfortunately, I know exactly what he means. And it's the same exact person who's had that effect on me almost my entire life.

Dad.

I bury my face in Brody's chest again, pressing myself tight against him. His hand moves over my hair. "This is insane," I say. "Not that I haven't wanted to be in this exact position for weeks and weeks, but think about it? My dad aside, I can't just be…be your—"

"Girlfriend?" he finishes.

I lift my eyes to meet his. "I wasn't going to go there, but I'm just thinking of the bigger picture. It doesn't matter that you're not even two years older than me—you're a professional baseball player and I'm a girl in high school. You can't fool around with high school girls, right? I imagine that's not just Savannah's rule."

His forehead is creased with lines of worry. "You're right. You're completely right. I don't know, Annie... Do you want to stop right now? Just because I like you doesn't mean you have to be with me. I'm still here in whatever form you want me."

The look on his face, the tone of his voice—confused and fearful—he's not some grown man taking advantage of a teen-age girl. He's just Brody. Vulnerable and impulsive and young. Brody who lives in this practically empty apartment and goes on five minute long fake dates then returns here or to his hotel room on the road, completely alone. Brody who has never met his own dad and has no contact with his mother anymore, no other family to my knowledge. Brody whose position on the team creates jealousy and rivalry way more than it does friendships.

He should be allowed to have someone real in his life. No one deserves to be alone at nineteen.

But really he does have someone—Dad. And if he finds out about this, well that could be it for their bond.

I press my palm against his forehead, trying to rub out the wrinkles. "You know what? It's none of anyone's business what you and I think of each other. You don't have another girlfriend or a wife and a few kids or anything, right?"

He laughs and his face finally relaxes. "Nope." He cups my face and kisses me again, and I know that I don't care how much work it will be to hide this so long as I don't have to stop.

"Let me get this straight," Brody says, lifting another slice from the box of pizza we had delivered for dinner. "I text you what I want posted, and then you post it for me and fix my mistakes?"

"Yep," I say after relaying Savannah's social media plan to him. "And since I'm her official intern, you have a legit reason to be sending me text messages. Like all the time, if you want."

A grin slowing spreads across his face. "Clever, Annie."

He leans in to kiss me, but I put up a hand to stop him. "I just ate pizza." That doesn't deter him at all. He grips the back of my neck and gently brings our lips together before pulling away and going back to his slice of pizza.

After Brody finishes his dinner, he turns all serious again. "You're ignoring your phone, aren't you? You know you can't stay here all night."

I sink further into the couch cushion. "I can't go home. I don't want to look at her. I don't want to hear his excuses, his plea for me to understand his perspective, because you know what? There's not one fucking thing that I can comprehend, let alone accept, when it comes to him and Mom."

Brody stares at me for a long moment and then pulls out his phone to text someone. I wait in silence, avoiding asking if he's texting Dad. I'd like to think he knows better than to do that. He finally sets the phone on the coffee table beside the nearly empty pizza box. "Savannah said you could stay over there tonight. She'll let your dad know."

I glance at the clock on the cable box. It's almost ten. Lily's already asleep, and I'd hate to make Savannah wait up for me. I don't want to leave this apartment. I'm half expecting a spell to break once I step out the front door and this whole Brody being into me thing will be over. Or maybe it won't have even happened?

As if sensing my concerns, Brody squeezes my knee, leaving his hand on my leg. "There's nothing I want more than to keep you here all night, but we're too smart and conniving to get caught on the first day, right?"

I lean my head against his shoulder and close my eyes. "Yeah, I guess."

He's silent for a couple minutes and then finally exhales. "Before you go, I have, like, two or three more things to say."

I tilt my head up to see his face. "Okay?"

His eyes stay forward, focused on the door. "When I told you about dismissing all the chicks that trampled into my room, well, there was one girl who—" He speeds up, trying to spit everything out quickly. "Went all dominatrix on me and had me up against a wall for a good five minutes and I'll be completely honest and admit that it was pretty hot until I started envisioning what would come next—whips, chains, floggers—this chick seemed like the type to bypass handcuffs. And she was strong as hell. It took me awhile to get her off me and then I had to call security—"

He stops talking after noticing that I'm shaking with laughter. I'd started the second he said the word *dominatrix*. I can't picture some curvy, big-breasted girl in five-inch heels being able to physically overtake Brody with his six foot stature and athlete's strength.

"It wasn't funny," he says, but the corners of his mouth are twitching. "She had a really big purse, too. Who knows what was in that thing?"

"Floggers and chains, right?" I wrap an arm around my midsection, trying to rub away the cramp I've just given myself from laughing so hard with a stomach full of root beer and extra cheese pizza. "Okay, what's the second confession?"

He lifts his arm around my shoulders, pulling me in closer. "I used to use a fake ID a lot, drink a lot, occasional one-night stands. The day I got to Kansas City, there was this girl I met at a bar I went to with Jake London. I brought her back to the guesthouse…"

My entire body stiffens even though I'm screaming at it not to react. "Brody, seriously, we don't need to play confession. In fact, I'm totally cool with being oblivious to any of that."

He rests his chin on top of my head and sighs. "This isn't going to work if you try and stay away from rumors and information that gets leaked out. It's impossible to avoid and you're always going to wonder if there's truth in it. So, I'm telling you now that you'll hear everything from me—the good, the bad, and the really ugly—whether you want to or not. That's how I roll."

I'm temporarily stunned. It sounds like a terrible idea and yet I don't see a better way for us to trust each other. "You can't help the fact that girls are constantly coming up to you and asking you to sign their boobs—"

"I haven't signed any boobs," he interrupts.

"Boobs, belly buttons—same thing."

He straightens up and lifts my chin before planting a kiss on my forehead. "No secrets, I promise. That's about the only thing I can promise right this second."

"Can you promise not to like my mom no matter how hard she tries to wrap you around her finger?" I ask. "She has a way with men."

"I promise. Consider my ballot already cast. Can't change sides now."

Reluctantly, I stand up, grab my keys from the coffee table, and both of us head toward the front door. Before I open it, Brody turns me around, pressing himself against me and giving me another long kiss good-bye. I lift my hands above my head in surrender. "Take me to your red room of pain."

He laughs and gently brings my hands back down to my

sides. "I should have never told you that story."

"I guess I'll see you when you get back from California." Three days seems like forever and this constant in and out of town is a regular occurrence for Brody and Dad.

His entire body presses against mine, heat spreading from one area to another until I'm hot all over and contemplating telling Savannah that I'm not staying with her tonight. When he pulls away, the whoosh of cold, air-conditioned air flows between us, reminding me of my life outside of kissing this boy.

"I'll miss you," he says, light as a whisper when he leans down one last time to kiss my cheek.

I finally stumble out the door, down the elevator, and back to my car. I'm already wishing for more. For next time. Wishing I'd taken off my shirt too and felt our bare skin pressing together. A shiver runs up my spine as I pull out of the parking garage and head toward Savannah's neighborhood.

chapter 19

'm so used to Savannah in her business dressy attire, heels included, that I hardly recognize her when she opens her apartment door wearing sweats, her long reddish-brown hair pulled back in a messy bun and glasses in place of her contacts.

"Sorry, I know it's late," I say.

She shakes her head and swings the door open wider. "No worries. I was up getting some work done."

I step inside, taking in the living room/dining room/kitchen combo. There's a pink and purple Lego house and extra pieces strewn all over the coffee table. Neatly folded laundry covers the dining room table, and a basket of unfolded clothes sits on the floor beside the table. But the furniture and decorations are all nice and homey—warm. Nothing like Brody's lonely place.

Savannah catches me examining her place, and she tosses a sheepish grin at me before moving quickly to stack up the laundry into more condensed piles. "Life of a single mom. Can't possibly keep everything in order."

"Believe me, I know all about not being able to keep things in order." I take a seat on the floor in front of the couch and study the Lego project.

She shuffles down the hall and returns with two pillows and a blanket. "Are you okay with sleeping on the couch?"

"Totally," I say. "Thanks for letting me stay."

She sits down on the sofa, her hands now wrapped around a mug of tea. "I called your dad. He's really worried about you, but I told him it was too late to come over here and start a family feud."

I swallow back my anger and tears, putting the excess energy into snapping Lego pieces together. "Does Lily see her dad?"

Savannah's eyebrows go up, indicating that I may have crossed the line and asked too personal of a question, but she answers me anyway, "Yes, she does. Not as often as she'd like. She's not exactly a priority for him, unfortunately."

"What made you want to get divorced, like officially? Is it so you or he could get married again?"

She stares over the top of my head and releases a breath. "I guess my reasons all revolved around him not being a very trustworthy person. I needed everything on paper—child support, visitation."

I add more pieces to the sidewall of Lily's house, keeping my eyes focused on the coffee table. "How did you meet him?"

"College," she says with a sigh, relaxing back into the couch. "I got pregnant when I was twenty. We decided getting married was the best idea ever. I finished school by the time Lily was two and already it wasn't working. We bought a house in another suburb not too far from here after I started working. By the time Lily was three, I knew it was over."

"Did you just pack up and move one day?"

"Pretty much." She takes a sip of her tea. "Once I made the decision to leave, I wanted it to happen fast. My parents came down from Chicago and helped me move here and helped me get a lawyer, and then it was done."

"Do you ever regret it?"

"Which part?" She laughs. "Getting married or getting divorced?"

I finally get brave enough to peel my eyes from the toys. "Both."

"I don't regret meeting Lily's dad because then I wouldn't have her, and she's amazing," she says. "But I suppose I didn't have to get married. And no, I don't regret the divorce." She narrows her eyes at me. "Now tell me what this feud with your dad is about. Obviously it's not another PR issue or else we'd all have our noses in it, right?"

My focus is back on the Lego house, which I've decided is supposed to be a beauty shop. "My mom's here." I take a deep breath. "I came home from my community service and there she was, lounging on the couch with Dad and Grams like she belonged."

Confusion fills Savannah's face. "They're not divorced?"

"Nope." I pound my fist into a stubborn piece, forcing it to mold together. I explain to her about the show she's auditioned for and been granted a part in and through a bit more prodding Savannah gets me to spill almost as many details to her as I told to Brody about Mom.

"Do you think she wants a second chance? Maybe things aren't going well with her pursuit for fame."

I laugh bitterly. "Second chance? Try five hundredth chance. And she's only here because she knows about my dad's job now. She probably caught a game on TV or had an old friend call her up to tell her, but that would only provide her with a city. He had to have told her where we live, and he promised me he wouldn't do that."

"Have you ever really tried with her?" Savannah asks. "Tried to understand your mom's perspective or at least confronted her about why she keeps leaving?"

I shrug. "When I was younger, probably. I always wanted her to stay because it made Dad happy but never for me. I don't think she's ever known what to do with a kid besides dress them up for other people to admire. I was always in her way. Always bugging her and asking questions she didn't want to answer. Everything to do with taking care of me was too hard and too messy. Nothing like her idealistic version of motherhood, which probably included my dad signing multimillion dollar contracts with the Yankees and her hiring five nannys to take care of the kid she never wanted to have." I sniffle and discreetly wipe away a couple tears from my cheeks.

"I'm sorry, Annie," Savannah says. "But honestly, you're doing fine without her so if you want to write her off, go for it. And maybe if your dad doesn't, let him make his choice?"

"I'd do that," I say. "I totally would, but you haven't seen him after she takes off. He's a wreck, and I'm left to deal with it. And you heard Frank last month. Dad's got a lot on the line right now. He can't afford a breakdown."

Savannah pats my shoulder. "Well, you don't have to handle it alone anymore. A big part of my job is to deal with my players' and coaches' breakdowns and scandals. I do whatever I have to to get them in proper working order again."

A tiny smidge of relief washes over me. From my time spent around this woman, I've quickly learned that she gets things done, even when it seems impossible. And based on that list Brody referenced of all the actual past scandals, maybe she's cleaned up bigger messes than Dad after a visit from Mom.

"Why do you think he can't let go?" I ask. "It's not like she's the only option for him. He's a good-looking guy, right? He's not super old and he's fit and still has all his hair, and he has that Kevin Costner, brooding silence thing going on. Women would probably go crazy over that."

Color has crept up to Savannah's cheeks, and she smiles down at her mug. "He's not a hopeless cause, if that's what you're asking. And I can't tell you why he won't let her go, but that doesn't change how he feels about you. He's the one shouldering the responsibility of raising you, and I can tell you from experience, keeping a little girl out of trouble and preparing her for the world is no easy feat and Lily isn't even seven yet. I think it's all uphill from here."

I lean against the couch, resting my head on the cushion. "I'm so scared of being like him and at the same time I'm petrified of being like her. The way I see it, I'm doomed when it comes to relationships. I'm destined to end up like one of them, right?"

"Maybe not." Savannah smiles at me and pats my leg before standing up. "I better get some sleep. Lily's got to be at art camp at seven thirty."

I lie on the couch for nearly an hour, unable to fall asleep. I finally reach for my phone and turn it back on. Ignoring the texts and missed calls from Dad, I read the message Brody's sent since I left his place.

BRODY: Can you post this on FB for me? "if u r lucky enough to get a pretty girl alone in ur apartment, don't be stupid and make her leave."

ME: You really want me to post that?

BRODY: Its good advice. I want to have a positive impact on others.

ME: What about pretty girls with big bags of equipment? Should you warn people about them?

BRODY: Shouldve kept that story to myself. btw my couch smells like u. Can't get myself to stop sniffing the cushion. Is that weird?

ME: last night after you hugged me, I kept sniffing my shirt all the way home

BRODY: well I did reek of booze. And I'm pretty sure u hugged me

ME: but you were the one who lingered past the allotted friend time limit

BRODY: Yes I did

ME: Can I ask you something? You probably don't even remember what you said, but I'm wondering about that random Spanish…

BRODY: The tornado warning?

ME: Yes. That. I couldn't recall it well enough to translate later. Do you remember what you said?

BRODY: Yes.

ME: ????

BRODY: How bad do u want to know?

ME: Really bad now that I know you're trying to keep it from me!!

BRODY: You make me happy

ME: I like that

BRODY: I want to tell you all my secrets

ME: Like this secret?

BRODY: Yeah, like this. I'll tell you the rest in Spanish next time and you can figure it out. Tutoring at its best

ME: I can live with that

I'm grinning at my phone like an idiot. Yes, I could definitely become attached to Jason Brody in a dangerous way.

After being woken up at seven in the morning by Lily, who offered up several words of praise about last night's Lego building efforts, I headed home to face Dad and probably Mom, too. I wanted to put it off longer, but decided that Savannah had enough to deal with without having me and my drama hanging around her apartment all morning.

Dad's car is already gone, and I find Grams walking in circles around the yard. "Ginny," she says when she sees me. "Where have you been? I couldn't get that damn stove to work."

My heart plummets down to my stomach. I reach for Grams and guide her by her yellow nightgown back onto the porch and force her to sit in the swing. I race into the house. My tennis shoes, wet from morning dew on the grass, squeak across the tile floor. Sure enough, smoke is filling the kitchen, the detector beeping like crazy. I yank the frying pan from the burner, toss it into the sink and hit the lever, allowing a stream of cold water to land on top of the blackened egg in the center of the pan.

I jump back when the water hits the heated pan and sizzles loudly, producing flying bits of hot and cold water and more smoke and steam. I yank a chair under the smoke detector and climb on top, shutting the thing off by pulling out the battery. Once I get the kitchen windows open and about 10 percent of the smoke drifts outside, I take in the demolished kitchen.

A carton of eggs lies open on the counter and several cracked eggs and shells are dripping down the dark wood cabinets and onto the floor. An open bag of flour on the stove is tipped over, white powder scattered everywhere. A lump of raw ground sausage is plopped in the center of another frying pan, though luckily that burner hasn't been turned on. I gasp when I see the sharp knife and the plastic casing the sausage came in lying beside the frying pan.

What the hell was Dad thinking leaving her alone?

But there's no time to ponder this poor decision or even to be pissed off. I ignore the mess and the dripping eggs for now and get a pot to make Grams' oatmeal. It takes until the water starts boiling for my heart to finally slow down. A few minutes later, I bring Grams into the kitchen and set the bowl of oatmeal in front of her and then begin to tackle the train-wreck kitchen.

I'm scooping runny eggs and shells into the garbage disposal when Grams starts banging her spoon against the table. Her face is twisted with anger. "What is this shit? I made sausage gravy and biscuits!"

"Remember what your doctor said?" Who am I kidding? She doesn't remember my name. There's zero chance of her recalling the results of her yearly cholesterol screening. "You can't eat eggs or gravy and biscuits. They make your cholesterol too high."

"Horse shit!" She pelts the glass bowl at the wall. It shatters, spraying oatmeal and brown sugar everywhere. And unlike Dad, I added extra *extra* brown sugar to make it taste better. "There's not a damn thing wrong with my cholesterol." She points a finger at me, tipping her chair backward and walking in my direction, her wild gray hair sticking out in every direction. "You little liar. You've always been up to no good."

The front door opens just as Grams jabs me in the chest with her finger. My hands are shaking. I've never seen her this angry and even though I'm pissed as hell at Dad I want him here to help. I'm not sure I can handle this.

But it's not Dad who walks through the door, it's Caroline, Grams' babysitter. The sixty-five-year-old Hispanic lady glances around at the kitchen and at Grams, then gives me a tiny smile. "Rough morning?"

I let out a shaky breath, making sure my voice will come out steady. "I got home from…from a sleepover and Dad was gone. Grams was cooking, and now she won't eat the oatmeal—"

"You're goddamn right I won't," Grams snaps. "I'll fix my own damn breakfast you conniving little—"

"Annie?" a new voice comes from the other side of the screen door. Before I can check to see who it is, Savannah walks in, her eyes sweeping the kitchen and Grams' angry face. "I just wanted to stop by after I dropped Lily off to see if everything was okay?"

"What happened to your mother?" Caroline asks, her voice heavy with concern and her accent. "Your father said she would be here this morning, and I could wait until nine to come in. I'm sorry, honey."

"No freakin' way." I squeeze my hands into tight fists and stalk down the hall toward Dad's room. The curtains are drawn tightly closed but even in the dark, a long lump under the covers is clearly visible. I flip on the light switch and even then it takes Mom several seconds to raise her head and look around. Her gaze lands on the clock beside the bed. "It's early, Annie…give me a little longer to wake up. I've got rehearsal until midnight tonight."

"How could you sleep through the smoke alarm?" I demand, not making any attempt to turn off the light or lower my voice. "Grams almost burned the whole house down, and she could have sliced her finger off using a fucking knife!"

Mom sits up, rolls her eyes, and tosses the covers aside revealing an extremely skimpy piece of lingerie. "I didn't know Mom was awake. How am I supposed to know? It's not like she came in here and asked me for help."

I make a mental note of the fact that she doesn't point the blame at Dad or ask where he is. Which probably means that she knows he went to work and she may have even accepted the responsibility of keeping an eye on Grams during the two-hour gap of him leaving and Caroline arriving.

"God, you are completely incapable of doing anything for anyone!" I turn around and head back down the hall. Mom is quick at my heels, tying Dad's long blue robe around her waist.

"Watch your mouth, young lady," Mom says. "Being a bitch will get you nowhere fast."

She stops when she sees that we aren't alone. Her gaze freezes on Savannah, sizing her up from head to toe, taking in her usual black pencil skirt, blazer, and heels. Her conservatively styled auburn hair and natural makeup.

"Don't tell me you're a social worker?" Mom snaps at Savannah then she turns to me. "What did you do? Who did you call?"

Savannah's and Caroline's eyes are both wide, but Caroline stays focused on her job of taking care of Grams and she gets her to sit back down. "Evelyn, I'll whip up some sausage gravy and biscuits for you right now, okay? Let's just relax."

Savannah extends a hand to Mom. "I'm Savannah Dawson,

Jim's assistant and a Royals' PR rep."

Mom's eyebrows shoot way up. She flips her blond hair over her shoulder, straightens her back, then reaches out to shake Savannah's hand. "Ginny Lucas…a pleasure to meet you. Sorry about the commotion this morning. I'm a bit jet-lagged and missed my cue to wake up and help Mom."

Jet-lagged? Doesn't that require a jet?

I release a much too loud frustrated groan. But Savannah just flashes Mom a polite smile. "Nice to finally meet you, too. I should head into work now. Looks like you've got everything under control."

Yeah, right.

But I don't blame Savannah for choosing the fastest way to exit and not get involved in her boss's family drama. Even though she claims to clean up these kinds of messes all the time, she is the one who hired Caroline and made sure Grams had twenty-four-hour supervision. She's done her duties already in the crazy mother-in-law of the boss department.

She glances over her shoulder at me before stepping outside. "See you in the office at noon, Annie?"

"Yeah, I'll be there right after cross-country practice." After she's out the door, I ignore Mom and walk over to the stove where Caroline is making what looks like sausage gravy and biscuits. I lean in close to whisper, too afraid of causing another outburst from Grams. "My dad told you about her cholesterol problem, right?"

"Yes, he did." Caroline continues to stir the white liquid in the pan without pause.

"I don't mean to be bossy or anything," I say. "But it's just that I've been feeling so guilty for getting her ice cream and milk shakes all the time."

"No worries," she says, flashing me a smile. "I make this with turkey sausage and skim milk…no grease. It's a perfect compromise."

I lower my voice even more. "She won't know?"

"I fool her all the time," Caroline says proudly. "Tomorrow if you're around, I'll show you how to make the healthy milk shake, all right?"

I smile with relief. "Thanks. You're a genius."

Grams is digging through a basket in the center of the table now. I walk behind her and put my arms around her shoulder, giving her a squeeze. "I'm sorry, Gramsie. You're right. Your cholesterol is fine."

She places a hand on my arm and gives it a little pat. "Enough hanging on me, Annie. Now help me find my needlepoint."

I almost tear up again for like the fifth time in less than twenty-four hours. I give her one more squeeze and bury my face in her shoulder. I can't remember the last time Grams called me Annie. After I locate her needlepoint, I hurry into my room and change for cross-country practice and pack a bag for work later.

When I return to the kitchen, Grams is happily enjoying her not-so-unhealthy sausage gravy and biscuits. And Mom is seated right beside her, allowing Caroline to serve her a plate of food along with coffee and juice. My mouth hangs open, but I wait until Caroline shuffles down the hall to get clothes for Grams before speaking.

"She's not a maid," I hiss at Mom. "She gets paid to take care of Grams, not to cook you breakfast."

Mom shrugs and takes a dainty bite of scrambled eggs. "She offered, Annie. It would be rude to say no."

I toss my gym bag onto the table and fling the dishwasher open, loading each dish with an unnecessary amount of force.

By the time Caroline returns, I've got the dishes done and the counters cleaned.

"Sweetie, you go and do your running practice," Caroline says. "Let me clean up."

"It's fine. I'm almost done."

Mom sits there watching this exchange with mild interest. "This gravy is just fabulous. I'd love the recipe."

I roll my eyes but keep my back to them while I quickly butter a piece of toast, grab two bottles of Gatorade and a few granola bars for lunch. While the toast is hanging from my mouth and my hands are busy stuffing items in my bag, Mom finally takes a second to look me over.

"You're not going out like that, are you? No makeup? Shorts and gym shoes? Daddy's making enough money now to get you a little better wardrobe, right?" Her face lights up and she reaches out and grabs my wrist. "I know! Let's go shopping. Get you something nice and have some time to talk, just us. We never get to spend time together."

"And whose fault is that?" I yank the zipper on my bag closed and toss it over my shoulder. "I can't go shopping. I have cross-country practice."

I'm so looking forward to a nice long run, pounding my feet into the ground over and over again. Maybe I'll imagine Mom's face underneath my shoe.

Lenny London: *It's been brought to my attention that I'm not emotionally secure enough to date an intellectual superior. You know what? Screw you. And btw, you are so not smarter than me.*
2 hours ago

Jason Brody Royals Pitcher: *Less than 5 hours until my first trip to LA. What's on the must-see/must-do list?*
30 minutes ago

Annie Lucas: *Should eat more than a piece of toast before a 12-mile run. Starving. Craving hot dogs and fried mozzarella.*
5 minutes ago

'm texting Brody while walking through the stadium toward Savannah's office. My hair is wet from showering after practice, and I'm carting a bag full of sweaty, smelly clothes over my shoulder.

ME: where are you?

BRODY: in the stadium

ME: I know that, dork. But where exactly?

BRODY: telling you could put you in danger. Where are you?

ME: down the hall from Savannah's office

BRODY: don't move

I stop and glance around for less than a minute before Brody comes walking down the hall toward me. The second I catch sight of his stylishly messy dark hair and the suit and tie he's required to wear for team travel, my heart takes off and the memories of being tangled together on his couch yesterday come flooding back. To avoid showing him my flaming cheeks, I take my time bending over and tucking my phone back into my bag.

When I return to standing, Brody's leaning one shoulder against the wall, so I do the same and watch as he slides closer.

"Hey."

There are so many words loaded inside that one *hey,* and the weight of where we were and where we are now hits me in one quick punch.

"Hey," I say back then notice the hot dog in his hand. "Don't let Frank catch you with that. Ten thousand dollar fine."

He laughs and holds it out to me. "He did catch me and when I told him it was for you, I had to listen to a really long story about why he knows that you like ketchup on one side, mustard on the other and a pickle laying across the mustard side."

I drop my gaze to the hot dog and the memory I'd tucked carefully away for years comes back to me in an instant. I'm not in the mood to dredge up the past, so I ask Brody, "What did he tell you?"

His eyes meet mine, an amused smile tugging at his mouth. "Just that he took you to a Rangers game when you were like six or seven, and he bought you a hot dog with ketchup and you told him he made it wrong. While he was helping you carefully dress a new hot dog to your liking, he missed one of the greatest game-changing plays in major league baseball history."

The game-changing moment isn't anywhere in my memories, but Frank and me alone at the game is. Where was Dad?

And then I remember the relapse he'd had. There was another surgery, something that needed to be removed...a tumor, maybe? Then more radiation. He was sick most of second grade. And Mom stayed away the whole time. My teachers forgave the missed homework and reading time, my constant mess of tangled hair and worn-out clothes, not to mention my consistent lack of lunch money.

"You okay?" Brody asks.

I meet his gaze and force a smile before taking the hot dog from his hands. "Yeah, just thinking. I forget sometimes how long Frank has been hanging around my dad."

"Frank's a good guy." He leaves the statement open like a question, waiting for me to elaborate. I'm not going there today. He's right, Frank is a good guy, but every memory I have proving that comes with some pretty bad memories.

I brush my fingers down his blue striped tie. I barely notice him shuffling his feet closer to mine, but I feel the heat building in the space between us. I meet his gaze again. "Thanks for bringing me lunch."

His eyes dart around the hall and then fall back on mine. He leans down and touches his mouth to mine. My stomach flutters and without even realizing what I'm doing, my hands grip tightly around his tie, pulling him closer.

Brody breaks off the kiss just before my hot dog gets smashed between us. "Not here, okay? We're more covert than that." His fingers lace through mine, and he smiles again. "I'll call you tonight when I get to LA." He raises our hands to his lips, kissing my knuckles before releasing me.

I stand on my tiptoes and plant one more kiss on his mouth before turning around. "See you in three days."

I'm walking down the hall, smiling at my hot dog (it's almost too perfect to eat) when I hear Savannah's raised voice coming from her office around the corner. I almost head right in, assuming she's on the phone speaking sternly to some tabloid writer, but then I hear a second voice that causes me to stop and eavesdrop.

"Consider me informed," Dad says. "Evelyn won't be left alone with Ginny again, I swear."

And yeah, Brody's so right about us not getting touchy-feely in the stadium hallway. How close were we to getting caught by Dad?

"I just don't get it," Savannah says. "What are you possibly gaining from keeping her around?"

"I don't know," Dad says, his voice fading. "It's not something I can explain to you."

"Well, humor me," she snaps. "I'd love to be further educated on the workings of the insecure male mind."

Holy shit, she's pissed.

"She's still my wife. Ginny's known me almost my entire life. We grew up together."

"Then you should be able to see her for what she is better than anyone else—selfish and cold."

Oh boy…

"You spent thirty seconds with her." Dad's voice elevates, gaining strength and flipping into defensive mode. "You have no idea what you're talking about. She's the only woman who doesn't look at me like I'm an invalid."

"That's not true," Savannah says firm and eerie.

"How would you know?" Dad counters. "There's not exactly a plethora of women waiting to meet a thirty-six-year-old one-legged man with a teenage daughter and a mother-in-law with Alzheimer's to take care of."

I figure the conversation will be done after that because how can Savannah counter an answer like that? I glance around looking for something to dive behind so Dad doesn't think I've been listening in, but Savannah isn't finished.

"That's bullshit," she says. "I bet you haven't even tried to put yourself out there again. You assume that's what people see. Are you really insecure enough to believe she's the best you can get? Ask Annie what she thinks. Ask her how she feels about her mother constantly jerking both of you around."

"Don't act like you know my daughter better than I do just because she spent the night in your apartment complaining about her parents. I appreciate you helping and telling me about the Evelyn situation this morning, but I'm done discussing my personal life with you."

The door slams shut, vibrating through the hall. I dive behind a shelf full of white towels and wait for the thud of Dad's non-leg to fade away.

I can't believe Savannah laid into him like that. Especially after her being so neutral and see-the-bigger-picture last night. She seemed genuinely furious with him, and it had nothing to do with her at all. The endorphins built during cross-country practice must have done miracles for my mood because I'm actually feeling a tad bit sorry for Dad.

I munch on my hot dog while taking the long way around the stadium to Dad's office. The fight with Savannah distracted me enough to forget that I'd stormed out of the house yesterday pissed off at him. So when I walk inside his office and give a casual, "Hey, Dad," his mouth falls open and he's momentarily speechless.

"I'm sorry about leaving Grams this morning," he says finally. "And just so you know, I didn't tell Mom where we were. She found out on her own after seeing a game on TV."

"Okay," I say, slowly releasing a breath and leaning against the doorframe. "But now what?"

His face speaks a dozen words all at once. He's tired. He's afraid of what's going to happen with his coaching job. He's shaken by his fight with Savannah.

Dad sighs. "Do you think…would it be possible for you to put up with her for three days until I get back from California? Caroline's going to stay in the guest room the whole time and take care of Grams. You can have a three-day sleepover with Lenny if you want."

He's so desperate for a quick resolution, I'm half expecting him to offer me money next. And then I do what most girls my age would do and let my mind wander to places it shouldn't be. Ideas for using his guilt to my advantage. An opportunity to drop some sketchy info and not get hit with a retaliation of a million questions.

"Fine," I say.

His face sinks into his hands. "Thank you, Ann."

"I'm late already so I better get going to help Savannah," I say. "Have a good trip."

Dad stands up from his desk and walks around, pulling me into a hug before I can escape. "We'll figure something out when I get back, okay? I've got some thinking to do."

"Good." I pull away and then casually add, "Also…I've been helping Brody with his GED studying, just a little bit. And he passed one section of a practice test the other day. If I have time after you guys get back, I'm gonna try and help him study for the next part."

You know, alone in his apartment…

He leans in, kisses the top of my head, and gives me a winning Dad smile. "That community service is really carving a hole into your steel heart, huh?"

I roll my eyes. "Not a chance. I just know I'm going to end up editing all his social media stuff if he doesn't educate himself on the finer points of grammar and spelling."

"You don't fool me, Annie Marie." He gives me one more big hug. "I love you. Be good while I'm gone?"

"I love you, too, Dad," I say. "And I'll be a perfect angel while you're playing the Angels."

But when you get back, that's when I'll start taking cues from the little devil seated on my other shoulder.

chapter 20

Jason Brody Royals Pitcher: *L.A., you move way too fast, even for this Chicago boy.*
3 hours ago

Annie Lucas: *has played out the remainder of her day inside her head during hot, sticky cross-country practice run and is still anticipating the outcome. Correction—I'm anticipating being in the moment more so than seeing the end.*
27 minutes ago

It takes me an unnatural length of time to gain the courage to actually knock on Brody's door after days of anticipating this moment. We've spent so much more time as friends and hardly any time like *this*. And *this* caused me to chew a few fingernails and feel my stomach churn before facing him. I mean, it is a confusing situation with our roles shifting so suddenly. Do we hug? Do we kiss right away? Do we swing our arms awkwardly and not make eye contact for several uncomfortable minutes before someone says, "So…?" followed by the other person saying, "So…?"

But lucky for me, Brody has a plan of his own.

The second he opens the door to his apartment, I'm tugged inside before I even have a chance to get a good look at him. He shuts the door quickly and presses me against it.

"Did you really have to run past my window in that hot-pink sports bra three times this morning?" he asks, leaning down, his mouth hovering close to mine.

My heart is sprinting despite the fact that my legs are completely void of any energy. You wouldn't think three days apart would feel like an eternity, but they really did. "Coach picked the route. I just followed it."

He pulls back a little, his gaze meeting mine. "Are you hungry? Do you want to get lunch?"

I can tell food is the last thing on his mind, but he's trying to be polite. I drop my gym bag on the floor and lift my arms around his neck, pressing my fingers into it until our lips finally meet. My head spins, my vision blurring, my entire body tingling and completely at his mercy.

I barely take notice of his arms tightening around me, and then my feet are off the ground. I wrap my legs around his waist, and he carries me into the kitchen, setting me down on the counter beside the stove. Releasing my hold on his neck, I glance around, dazed and confused.

"This isn't exactly where I thought you were taking me." My eyes betray me and flit in the direction of his bedroom.

Brody leans back and laughs. "We're going to be very good today, Annie. Got it?"

I eye him skeptically. "What's your definition of good?"

He turns around and opens the fridge. "Making you lunch, kissing, studying, more kissing, avoiding my bedroom or the couch," he rattles off like he's rehearsed it.

And even though I've spent my fair share of time rounding

the bases—well, three of them, anyway—a small amount of pressure lifts from my shoulders hearing that his intentions for the afternoon aren't even R-rated. But there's no way I'm going to let him know about any of this apprehension. Not when I'm trying to shake the high-school-girl image from his brain.

I wrap my hands around the edge of the countertop for balance. "If that was your plan, why did you practically assault me the second you opened the door?"

He's sifting through half a dozen neatly stacked blue containers. "Only to keep you from biting your nails and turning bright red after seeing me."

I smile down at my lap, my face heating up again. Isn't that exactly what I did before he opened the door? "What's with the fridge full of GladWare?" I ask, changing the subject.

"The trainer hired this nutritionist who delivers precooked, organic, healthy, full-of-vegetables-I-didn't-know-existed meals." He drops a stack of three containers into my lap and sets three of his own onto the stove in front of him. "Guess she came while I was gone. You inspect those, and I'll try and identify these."

I feel under my ass for the paper I remembered Brody sitting me on top of a minute ago. "There's a cheat sheet." I take a minute to read it over. "I've got chicken parm with asparagus, blackened catfish with apple stuffing, and roasted crab cakes with lobster sauce."

He lifts the lid on the chicken dish on top of my stack and leans in, sniffing. "That doesn't sound terrible."

"I'm claiming the crab cakes." I glance at the paper again for the reheating instructions. "I bet this fancy meal-delivery service costs a fortune."

"I know," he agrees. "Can't believe they footed the bill. Beats buying groceries."

"Wow, so you're just gonna jump right from poor minor league player to not even doing your own grocery shopping and letting a fancy service cook for you?" Nobody except hired help cooks at Lenny's house, and it's just really weird.

Brody rolls his eyes. "I went to the grocery store. Several times. I even put things in my cart, but then I'd go to check out and I couldn't bring myself to spend the money. I ended up putting almost everything back. Except the ramen noodles, pizza rolls, and ketchup."

"No wonder you're always eating at my house."

I feel lips graze my ear, and it gives me instant goose bumps. "Right. That's why I'm always at your house."

My stomach flips over, anxiety bubbling. It's one thing for him to have this impulsive urge to kiss me, this attraction between us. But it's a completely different thing to hear that he simply likes being around me. It's too much.

Too much like love.

But I'm enjoying this too much to let that thought stick around for more than a few seconds. I hand over the middle container of the three on my lap. "You can have the catfish dinner. It's got the lowest calories, which is good, since you've spent two games sitting on the bench."

"I wasn't benched." He grabs onto the side of the crab cake dinner. "It's called the pitching rotation. It wasn't my turn."

"Regardless…" I yank the crab cakes from him and pat his stomach, feeling nothing but rock-hard abs. "Wouldn't want you to get flabby while you're on the lazy part of the rotation."

He narrows his eyes playfully. "I'm pitching tomorrow, but whatever. Eat my crab cakes."

I hop down from the counter and flash him another smile. "Thanks."

"Why can't we sit on the couch?" I beg. "I know you haven't exercised your legs recently, but mine are screaming at me."

Brody finally sighs and snatches the thick GED study book, then pulls me up by my hand in one swift motion. We've been at his kitchen table for two hours now, and it took us less than twenty minutes to eat.

I skip my way over to the couch and flop onto my back, making a big show of leaving room for Brody. The way he's acting all panicked today, I wouldn't put it past him to sit on the floor instead of beside me. Luckily, he sinks into the empty spot, places the book on my stomach, and brings my feet onto his lap.

"So…why is it so hard for you to buy groceries? Aren't they paying you enough?" I ask, wanting to take advantage of the GED break to drill him with more personal questions.

"Yeah, they're paying me enough." He glances at me and then at the ceiling. "My agent says people like me will either struggle to spend money once they have it or spend it all and go bankrupt every month. It's a big change, you know?"

I guess maybe I do know. Sort of. Dad's salary change was pretty big, but we went from lower class to middle class. Brody's gone from lower class to rich. And he's just one person. Dad is supporting three people. Four if we're counting Mom now.

My stomach twists into knots of frustration and anger. *Don't think about that now.*

"I hate putting money in the bank, too," Brody admits. "I want to keep it all in front of me where I can see it and make sure it doesn't disappear. I don't trust banks."

"Please tell me you don't have stacks of hundreds piled inside a briefcase somewhere in this apartment."

He leans in close to me, causing a shiver to run down my

spine. "Just don't look under the cushion you're sitting on."

My eyes widen, and my hand immediately fumbles around, reaching under my ass. All I feel is a cold metal bar.

Brody busts out laughing. "That was too easy. And I said I didn't like banks, not that I refused to conform." He removes his wallet from his pocket and spreads it open for me to see inside. "Less than a hundred in cash, plus I've got these…"

I watch as he drops a Visa debit card onto the coffee table, followed by an American Express card and a platinum Master-Card. "Whoa, look at you. You really sold out."

"I know, right?" He tucks everything neatly back in but leaves the wallet resting on the table. "Now if I could just get myself to use one of these cards."

My gaze sweeps the near-empty room. "Maybe buy some furniture."

"Such a big commitment…" He smacks my knee playfully. "Are we studying or what?"

I raise the book and flip to the page in the social studies section where we'd left off. "Okay, number ten. If a drought severely reduces the amount of corn available to consumers, what would we expect to happen?"

He takes one of my bare feet in his hands and begins massaging it, completely distracting me from reading the rest of the question.

"The price of corn goes up," he says before hearing the answer options.

I know nothing about corn, so I flip to the back and look up number ten. "Correct. What type of government does the United States have?"

His eyes are focused on rubbing my feet. "Democracy."

"Uh-huh." His hand creeps up to my calf, and my heart

takes off again. "Which government official is appointed and not elected by the U.S. citizens?"

"Supreme court judge," he says right away.

"It's multiple choice," I remind him. "Are you going to let me read the choices?"

"Sure." He shrugs. "If I don't know the answer."

I rest the book on my stomach again. "I don't think you can call me a tutor. I keep having to look up answers. I'd probably flunk this test if I had to take it."

His fingers drift over my other calf. I close my eyes and enjoy the feeling. "I'm older. I'm supposed to know more than you."

"Not really. I'm the one still in high school. No one actually uses this stuff after graduating, so a year out and you've forgotten everything. I have no excuse for not acing it."

He returns to massaging my feet, his eyes locked on my toes. "My mom's a teacher's aid," he says. I freeze and try not to shake him from this potential sharing session. He's said so little about his mom. "She went to college for two years, got a scholarship to Eastern Illinois University. She was the first person in her family to even graduate high school, let alone go to college."

"So why didn't she finish?" I ask, but the answer comes to me right away. "She got pregnant?"

He nods. "But she still got a pretty good job with her associate degree. She helped with a lot of special-needs kids who the school district had integrated into the regular classroom. She devoted every spare minute studying with me, reading to me, making sure my teachers all understood my disability and tested me properly. She knew every benefit the public school system was obligated to offer me and she got it."

"Then why did you drop out? Why don't you talk to her anymore?"

"Because I'm an unappreciative asshole." He leans his head against the back of the couch, staring up at the ceiling. "I got sick of being her project. I guess to me, dyslexia has always been embarrassing, something I'd rather not discuss, and it was all my mom wanted to talk about."

"How long since you've seen her?"

He shakes his head. "About three years. I was really messed up then, and it freaked her out. I have a younger brother and sister, too, and a stepdad. He told me not to go near my mom unless I cleaned up my act."

I set the book on the floor and sit up. "What did you do that was so bad? You said you would tell me everything, remember? The good, the bad, and the ugly…"

He turns his head and looks at me. "I did say that, didn't I?" I nod and wait for him to continue. "You name it, Annie, and I did it—drugs, drinking, stealing, breaking and entering."

My eyes widen, but I use all my power to hold back any shocked reactions. "Murder? Identity theft? Robbing a bank? Did you do all that, too? Is that why you don't trust banks?"

"No." He lets out a nervous laugh. "Guess I got caught before working my way through the whole list."

"How did you get from *that* to baseball?"

"Well, first off, juvie sucks. I spent six months there and, after turning eighteen and getting out, I had no desire to see how much worse real prison is."

"Wait a minute…" I say. "So Johnson has been totally exaggerating all this time. You're not an ex-convict. You're a…a…?"

"Former juvenile ex-convict?" Brody suggests. "What did you think? That I went to real prison and that somehow didn't make it into any of the papers or stories about me? Juvenile records aren't public information, Annie."

"Huh," I say. "I probably should have asked you that a long time ago. Okay, back to your answer…Juvie to baseball, how'd it happen?"

"I'm glad you didn't ask me those questions sooner." Brody flashes me a smile so I know he's not angry or upset with me for thinking he's an ex-convict. "It's cool how your dad and you just took me at face value—no past interfering with your judgment. And I got to play baseball in juvie. That's where Frank Steadman found me."

"They have baseball teams in juvie?" I ask, working hard to keep up. "And Frank trolls juvenile detention centers looking for recruits? Seriously? Does Johnson know this? He'd have a shit fit."

He laughs again. "Some have baseball programs, and re-cruiting kids from juvie isn't a regular thing for Frank. But he can't ignore a seventeen-year-old with a ninety-mile-an-hour fastball. Speed overlooks all kinds of indiscretions. Frank never said anything when he came to see me. But after I got out, he sent a bus ticket to a minor league tryout. He put me on the Royals' farm team last summer, then invited me to spring train-ing this year. And now here I am."

"Here you are," I repeat, my head spinning from this overload of Jason Brody info. "Don't you think your mom would be proud of you? Look at everything you've accomplished. And what about your brother and sister; how old are they?"

"Twelve and nine," he says. "And which part would make her proud? Me taking the easy way out and using a God-given ability to avoid education and actual work? And then there's my secret flings with high school girls. She'd be so proud of that."

"Flings?" I shove him in the shoulder. "There better not be flings."

His hand slides up my leg, almost reaching the hem of my very short jean shorts. "I'm kidding. It's just you." He reaches for my waist, and then tugs me gently until I'm one step away from straddling his lap.

The newly acquired knowledge and the emotion wrapped around Brody finally telling me about his past causes me to forget my earlier apprehension, and I quickly swing a leg over him, molding us together. I have this strong desire to touch everything—his smoothly shaved cheeks, the curly hair at the nape of his neck, the muscles on his back that bulge when his arms lift up to wrap around me. My fingers curl around the bottom of his T-shirt, gently raising it up and over his head, tossing it right on top of the GED book.

And that concludes today's study session.

I hold still as he lifts up my hair, piling it on top of my head, and plants kisses from below my ear to my collarbone. I'm doing everything I can to breathe normally, to not let him hear the nerves and desire, to not let him feel the throbbing between my legs because it's embarrassing and I know I'm not ready to do anything about it. But after his mouth connects with mine, his own desire becomes lodged between us. Before I can stop myself, my entire body stiffens.

I don't even know why I freeze up. It's not like I'm afraid of Jason. Not exactly. It just seems so real all of a sudden. In my head, I imagine guys like Brody kiss a girl, get hard, then get off, and that's that. Whereas in my world—in my experience—the boys (yes, boys) get boners all the time, and there's no built-in pretense as to what is done about said boners.

Why does this relationship feel so complicated at the worst times imaginable?

Brody must sense my momentary reaction to his...um...*reaction* because he leans back, his eyebrows pulled together. "Too much?"

I swing my leg back over him and plant myself on the cushion beside Brody, my eyes zoomed in on the coffee table, my face hot and hands twisting in my lap. "I'm not…I mean…I don't know," I say, and that long awkward silence that I'd been so afraid of before when knocking on the door falls between us.

Brody leans forward, resting his head in his hands, possibly in an attempt to cover up his lap. "I have to meet the trainer in half an hour—"

I spring up from my seat on the couch and hunt down my shoes. "No problem. I have to help Savannah in an hour."

He lifts his head, draws in a deep breath, and reaches for his T-shirt on the floor. "I was going to say, if you had let me finish…" His eyes meet mine. "Maybe we should talk about stuff like *this*."

I wiggle one foot at a time into my shoes, already shaking my head in protest of his plan. "I think talking about it is a bad idea."

He tugs his head through the hole in his shirt. "Communicating is a bad idea? Since when?"

I fold my arms across my chest, turning to face him, attempting confidence. "I see this going one of two ways. Option one—we both spill our past experiences and conclude what I already know, that high school is a very different world than after high school. Or option two—you give me some dignified, noble speech about how you're afraid of stealing my innocence and you're willing to walk around with blue balls until, like, forever if that's what I need."

He mimics my crossed-arm position and returns my stare. "Or option three—I tell you how I'm very aware of the fact that you suddenly got super uncomfortable, and even though I'm not at all willing to walk around forever with blue balls, I'm also not going to enjoy something that you're clearly not enjoying."

I let out a defeated sigh. "This is impossible, right? I'm me and you're…well, you—"

Brody strides across the room, reaches for my hand, and pulls me against him. "It's not impossible. I really wish you'd stop saying that. You know me, not the baseball player from the tabloids and newspapers. That's more than any other girl can say right now, and it's really going to piss me off if you decide to start seeing me as the public me, okay?"

"Okay," I whisper.

He releases a breath. "Ride with me to the stadium? We can talk in the car."

Brody hoists his own gym bag onto his shoulder, picks up my bag, and slips on his flip-flops, then holds the door open for me, giving me no other option but to follow him into the hall.

He's very careful to take the residents-only elevator into the parking garage, making sure no one spots us together before we're in the confines of his black SUV with the conveniently tinted windows.

"So here's the truth, Annie Lucas," he says, flashing me a sideways grin. "Sometimes, when a dude has his tongue in an attractive girl's mouth, blood travels from his brain to his—"

I snort back a laugh and smack his shoulder. "I know how it works."

His dark eyebrows pop up. "Then you know that this reaction can occur at virtually any moment and honestly, nothing is expected from the girl who's allowed the dude access to her mouth."

I peel my gaze from his. "I guess I know it works like that for me in my world, but it's different for you, right?"

The sarcasm and teasing drops from his voice. "Hypothetically, if I were to take a fangirl or any random girl from a club or bar home with me for the night, that's exactly what would be expected for the most part—and I'm not going to lie and say that I've never done something like that before. I've already told you about the one incident. But last year, I had a girlfriend for a significant amount of time—at least it was for me—and we did things the normal way, kissing on the first date and nothing more, so I went home with a pair of blue balls."

I glance down at my lap. "Significant amount of time?"

"About three months," he says.

"So what happened?" I spilled all about my gay ex, like, forever ago, so he totally owes me this answer.

"Jessie's in college, and she waits tables part-time," he says. "Dating her was something brand new for me. Before that, I had flings and nothing more."

"So what happened?"

He shrugs. "I'm not sure it was one specific thing. She had a high school boyfriend who I think she was still hung up on. She didn't understand the athlete's life. The fact that I couldn't blow off practice or stay out all night and expect to be able to pitch the next day. To her, it was a game and not a real job. Which would basically be true had I not moved up—it's pretty hard to live off the minor league salary without any other work on top of playing ball. It wasn't a big dramatic breakup or anything. We're still friends."

"You didn't love her?"

Brody pulls out of the garage and stops at a traffic light, allowing him to glance my way. "I don't think so. We didn't really toss that word around."

"Really? After three months?"

"Is that bad?" he asks. "Did you tell your ex you loved him? And when? After getting off the phone or in text messages?"

"Yes to all of those," I say. "Probably two months, though I don't really think we were in love like you should be, but at the time it was the most in love I was aware of."

"Is it cliché to say that I have trouble with that word?" He rests a hand on my knee and hits the gas when the light turns green. "I've heard both you and your dad on the phone, and it seems so easy for you to tell him you love him and the other way around. That's all really weird to me."

I laugh and throw a couple sideways glances his way to see if he's being serious. Judging by the color creeping into his cheeks, I assume he is. "It's not so hard once you get used to using the word. Maybe if you practice a little. Find an excuse to use the dreaded L-word."

"What, like now?" he asks.

I shrug. "Why not? Say something you love, but it can't be food related. That's too easy."

It takes Brody nearly the rest of the three-block drive to the stadium to reply, "Okay, I love…"

"What?" I prompt. "The smell of new shoes? The feeling you get after running ten miles and then taking a shower and putting on clean clothes? Fireworks? Summer holidays? Sleeping babies in those little front pouch things?" I suggest.

"I love…" he continues, shooting a sideways glance in my direction. "The sound of your voice when you read math and social studies facts."

My breath catches in my throat, but I try to sound cool when I say, "Really?"

"I got addicted to it after listening to sixteen hours of the recordings you made me," he admits. "I'm starting to wonder if that was your plan all along."

I look away quickly. "Yeah, right." My gaze drifts back to his. "What else do you love?"

"Hmm…" We've reached the stadium now, and Brody pulls into his assigned parking space in the exclusive player lot. He hops out of the car and grabs both our bags from the back. When I get out of the car and follow him to the door, he pauses in front of it, not yet swiping his access badge. He moves close enough for me to feel the heat radiating off his body. "I love how you smell like sunscreen all the time, and I love how your eyes can change from bright blue to gray-blue depending on what you're wearing." He pauses to look me square in the eyes, one eyebrow raised. "And I love how you hate to lose, but you threw your two-mile race at state to let Jackie win—"

"I didn't—" I protest, but Brody lifts his index finger to my lips, causing that whole blood-shifting-from-the-brain-down-lower reaction he so expertly described earlier to happen.

"Yes, you did," he says. "But it's our secret. I'll take it to the grave. I love how you worry about your dad and Grams and even me. And I love your legs in those short running shorts. Makes me want to hold you in place and run my fingers up and down them."

Oh my God.

And yeah, I have virtually nothing to say, because I started this game and clearly I've lost.

He flashes me his best arrogant smirk. "And I love how flustered you are right now. It's adorable, and even more so because you absolutely refuse to admit that you're off your game and trying so hard to prove how mature you are." He leans in, and my stomach flip-flops. Goose bumps crawl up my arms. "Despite the fact that I've never told you I thought otherwise."

His lips touch mine at the same moment his hand lands on my cheek. This kiss is better than all the other ones combined, and even though I hate to admit it, it's obvious Brody was right about us needing to have this chat.

He pulls away after only a short time, probably due to the fact that we're technically inside the stadium and not doing such a good job of keeping this thing between us a secret. He rests his forehead against mine. "This is where I'm drawing the line for now, and when you want that to change, all you have to do is tell me. Sound good?"

"What about your blue balls?" I ask, half joking, half concerned.

He nods, all serious. "Let's just hope medical science finds a cure soon."

I shove him back, laughing before swiping my own access card that came with my internship. "I'll donate to the research foundation." I wait until he opens the door before casually adding, "And just so you know, I'm not exactly inexperienced."

He stops and stares at me. "No?"

"No," I say firmly. "I've done everything at least once."

And while I'm watching his expression go from curious to surprised, I convince myself that's the only lie I'm going to tell Brody.

chapter 21

Lenny London: *is wondering if Annie Lucas ate my chocolate stash late last night? Make me brownies and you're forgiven.*
13 minutes ago

Annie Lucas: *is in fact guilty of eating Lenny London's gourmet chocolate and will be baking tonight.*
11 minutes ago

Jason Brody Royals Pitcher: *In the rotation tomorrow! Like this status if you'll be at Kauffman Stadium tomorrow afternoon.*
5 minutes ago

Dad asks me to ride home with him after work, even though my car is parked at the school a few blocks away. I have a feeling he wants to talk. Considering the way we left things hanging before California and the fact that I selfishly went straight to Brody's after practice today instead of going to see Dad at work, it's probably a task that needs to be dealt with.

"I just got out of a meeting with Johnson," he says when we're pulling out of the stadium parking area.

My stomach sinks. "Is it good news or bad news?" I blurt out.

Dad glances at me, smiles, then pats my leg. "It's good news. The club is happy with the progress I've made with three of their pitchers, and they're going to give me a contract for the rest of the season and for the off months so I can help with recruiting."

"Are you serious?" I squeal.

Dad's grin widens. "Completely serious."

My brain spins and flips, turning all the negatives around in my head. "So they can't come up with an excuse to fire you or anything like that? We can breathe easy?"

The smile fades a little. "We can absolutely breathe easy, but there's always a way to let a coach go, Ann. I can't prevent every scenario. And next season is up in the air still."

I exhale and nod. "Okay, I can accept that. It's better than living game-to-game."

We're both quiet for a few minutes while Dad maneuvers through freeway traffic.

"Did you enjoy your three-day vacation at Lenny's?" he asks, sarcasm dripping from every word. He's still not a fan of First Base and his family, though he tolerates Lenny.

"Hey, it was your idea for me to stay there," I protest. "Besides, Mom is probably gone now, and I can stay home—" He's staring straight ahead, no longer making occasional eye contact with me. "Don't tell me she's still there?"

"You heard what she said. Her show's going to last a few months." He's still not looking at me.

And oh God, a few months? "You aren't seriously going to let her stay a few months? Really?"

Dad's jaw tightens, and his fingers grip the steering wheel more firmly. "You know what? I'm not asking your permission. I've never been very hard on you. I've never made you do something you didn't want to, but Mom being here and you staying at home more often than not aren't negotiable."

I'm fighting the urge to yell so hard I can barely think straight. "This is insane. She's awful, Dad. You can't even see it!"

"Enough!" he shouts, and I clamp my mouth shut. "The world doesn't revolve around you, Annie. This is something you're going to have to deal with, and I really don't need to hear you constantly whining and complaining like a five-year-old."

I sink farther in my seat. A lump forms in my throat, and my eyes burn with tears, preventing me from responding.

When we pull into the garage at home, Dad yanks the keys from the ignition but doesn't unlock the doors right away. "Your mom's cooking dinner, and Frank and some of the guys on the team are coming over."

"What's the occasion?" I make no effort to conceal my own sarcasm.

"We're celebrating the fact that I still have a job," he says, returning to his calm tone. "And no, you can't stay at Lenny's tonight."

I get out, slam the car door, and head straight to my room, texting Lenny along the way. I'd finally confided in her about Mom on the third night at her house. She would only take my weak excuses for staying over for so long before pushing me to tell her the truth.

ME: she's still here

LENNY: seriously? why?

ME: the gold digger possibilities have intrigued her enough to stick around longer than 48 hours

LENNY: Maybe there's a way to run her off again. Thinking…give me some time

I close my bedroom door, lock it, and blast music as loud as it will go. I need to cool off before facing anyone else at this celebratory dinner we're hosting. I ignore the random knocks on my door that happen over the next hour while I lie on my bed staring at the ceiling. I don't notice the knob being jiggled or the door creaking open, so when Brody's voice floats over the music, I jump and reach for the speaker, cranking it down.

"Are you decent?" he asks before opening the door all the way.

I sit up and cross my legs. My heart is already speeding up just knowing he's in my house. Or more specifically—in my bedroom. "What are you doing here?"

He opens the door but stays leaning against the frame. "Having dinner. Your dad invited me. Good news about his season contract, huh?"

"Yeah, sure." I roll my eyes and finally let myself look at Brody. He's all hotness and muscle in his jeans and white and navy baseball tee. He gives me a smile like we're about to pick up where we left off earlier today.

"Oh boy, this should be a fun meal." I slide off my bed and brush past him. "How did you get in my room, anyway?"

"Picked the lock," he says. "Your dad sent me to get you, and you didn't open the door. I'm not big on failed missions."

"Lovely." I shake my head, trying not to be amused by his breaking-and-entering skills. "Who else is at this shindig?"

"Frank," he says, and then lists the names of two other pitchers, both of whom have taken a recent liking to Dad and his coaching ways. Both of whom are young, too, like Brody. Though not teens, more early- to mid-twenties. It's obvious Dad's wisdom is absorbed only by the young players. The veterans are too full of themselves to be open to trying new things and correction.

Brody and I walk into the kitchen, where Mom is dumping some store-bought pasta salads into fancy bowls that I'm pretty sure we didn't own three days ago. Which means she went shopping after all. Did Dad give her a credit card? God, I hope not.

Mom sees me before I have a chance to sneak past her and head into the backyard, where it looks like Dad is grilling something and Frank, Grams, and the other two pitchers are sitting around drinking beer. Well, Grams isn't drinking beer.

Mom's gaze travels from my feet to my head, and she reaches for my shoulders, spins me around, and points me back toward the hallway. "Go put on something nicer and fix your hair, and put on some makeup."

I step right out of her grip, leaving her hands hanging in midair, before turning around to face her. "I'm not going to change just so I can have dinner in the backyard."

Mom notices Brody standing beside me, and her judgmental expression turns to sweet and syrupy. "Just a little lip gloss, maybe some mascara." She takes me by the arm and tugs me in the direction of my bedroom again. "I'll help."

In one quick motion, Brody hooks an arm around my waist and pulls me in front of him, glaring at Mom. "I think she looks fine."

"See?" I give her my best fake smile. "I look fine."

When I open the back door to let both of us outside, I hear Brody release a frustrated sigh, but he doesn't say anything. At least he's keeping his promise to not join the Mom fan club.

After saying a quick hello to the other guys, Brody tosses me Dad's glove and produces his own glove and a baseball. "Want to play catch?"

My eyebrows shoot up. "With you? No freaking way. You'll kill me."

He laughs and heads out farther into the yard, even though I turned down the offer. "Come on, Annie, you're not afraid of the ball, are you?"

"When it's traveling ninety-eight miles an hour? Yes, yes I am."

Frank and the other guys laugh, but Brody still nods for me to join him. "I'll go easy on you, I promise."

Maybe he's just trying to keep Mom from luring me inside for a new outfit. And maybe if he knocks me out, Dad will feel sorry for me and apologize for calling me selfish and whatever else he said on the way home. Besides, it's a good way to force some distance between us and keep me from accidentally bumping legs with Brody or sneaking a kiss or two.

I slip Dad's old, worn glove over my left hand and tentatively hold it out to the side of my body. I cover my face with the other arm. "Okay, fire away."

Brody laughs at me but throws the ball anyway. It lands perfectly in the pocket of Dad's glove without me having to move a single muscle or even uncover my face. And it was more like a toss than a real pitch.

And yeah, I've played plenty of catch in my lifetime, but never with a pitcher whose fastball could kill me. I suppose Dad would have fit in that category back in the day, but never when I'd been on the receiving end of his throw.

I return the ball with a good amount of force, and Brody isn't as easy on me the next time around. Thirty minutes into our game, he's got me diving in the grass to catch ground balls, getting grass stains all over my white tank top. I'm starting to wonder if baseball is Brody's form of anger management, because tossing my body onto the ground and throwing an object at someone with as much force as I can muster is way more effective at cooling me off than loud music and studying my bedroom ceiling.

"All right," I say eventually. "I'm ready for the heat. Give me a fastball. I want to see if I can catch it."

Brody winds up like he's going to do it. Dad glances over his shoulder, the grill smoking in front of him. "Don't even think about it."

Brody stares at him, surprised. "Of course I'm not thinking about it."

And while my eyes are bouncing between them, he throws the ball to my right, trying to catch me off guard. My reaction is a couple seconds too late, so I have to really dive for it, reaching out my left-gloved hand as far as possible before my side makes contact with the ground. The ball just barely lands in my glove. I roll over on my back, groaning and laughing at the same time.

I wave my hand up in surrender. "That's it, I'm retiring."

Brody walks across the yard and stands over me. "Never take your head out of the game, Annie."

"Been watching *High School Musical* on your days off?" I say, and both the other pitchers laugh. I follow it up by singing a few lines from the HSM song "Get Your Head in the Game."

"I was going to help you up, but now I think I'll just leave you here." Brody drops his arms to his sides for a full five seconds, then eventually reaches out a hand. But of course he drops it as soon as I'm securely on my feet.

Mom has now placed all the store-bought food in dishes to look like we've made it ourselves, and everyone's heading to the patio table to sit down for dinner. Mom rushes over to me, dusting the grass off my back.

"At least go wash your hands before you eat," she says, hissing the words into my ear.

I let the screen door slam a little too hard when I head inside to wash up at the kitchen sink. After I return, I have nowhere to sit but right between Mom and Brody. I slide my chair closer to Brody and keep myself busy piling large portions of everything onto my plate. Mom opens her mouth a few times like she wants to advise me on taking dainty womanly portions, but my glare shuts her up.

That is, until the clueless number five mid-relief pitcher tries to make casual conversation. "It's amazing how much your daughter looks like you, Mrs. Lucas."

Mom grins at him. "Call me Ginny, please. And I know, she's just a miniature me. It's surreal."

I shovel potato salad into my mouth, scowling down at my plate.

"I bet you have all the boys following you around like little lost puppies," the other pitcher says, like he's Frank's age and he's trying to tease Dad, but since he's under thirty, the comment doesn't go over too well.

Brody and Dad both shoot identical glares at said pitcher. This entire meal is going to be nothing but people glaring and chewing. Frank coughs loudly, as if to give the clueless guy a signal, but Mom interrupts, oblivious to the tension. "She did have a boyfriend back in Arizona. What a cutie…" She turns to me with that stupid smile again. "Whatever happened to him, honey?"

I set down my fork, take a big gulp of Dad's beer that happens to be very close to my glass of water, and before he can protest, I turn to Mom and say, "He's gay."

"Gay?" she says, like she's never heard the term before, and

Dad simultaneously says, "What?"

"Gay," I repeat. "Homosexual. He likes boys. More specifically, one boy he met at church."

Awkward silence falls over the dinner table. I pretend to be like Grams, like I have no clue what's going on in the world, and continue eating and stealing occasional drinks of Dad's beer, even though I hate beer. It just feels like something I can control. I mean, how many things can he possibly reprimand me for in one day? I figure there's got to be a cap-off point, and I've probably hit it already.

After dinner, Brody finds me in the kitchen washing dishes and leans close to whisper, "Can you sneak out with me for a little while?"

My face heats up. He's on the other side of the room before I can even respond. I dry my hands and open the back door, calling outside to Dad, "I'm going to Lenny's."

"Annie," he says. "You're staying home tonight, remember?"

"I know that," I snap. "I'm just going to return a shirt I borrowed. I'll be back to tuck myself into my own bed tonight."

His eyes narrow, giving me that you're-pushing-it look, but I turn around and head out the front door before he can argue. I walk a couple blocks, and Brody eventually pulls up beside me. I check to see if any neighbors are watching, and then I open the passenger door and hop inside.

"You want to get ice cream or something?" he asks. "We can go through a drive-through, and no one will see us."

I hold my stomach and groan. "No, thanks. I ate way too much for dinner."

He laughs. "You might want to explore new techniques in self-control, or you'll give yourself heartburn from potato salad overload."

Brody drives out of our neighborhood and down a dirt road that Savannah once told me leads to a lake. The sun has already set, but it's still warm and clear outside. When Brody parks a good distance from the water, we can still see the path clearly thanks to the lack of clouds and the nearly full moon. I text Lenny as I walk beside Brody, through a dirt path leading to the grassy area in front of the water, where I assume we're going to sit.

ME: If anyone asks, I'm at your house right now.

LENNY: ok. No problem. Yep…there you are. Apparently you've locked yourself in the bathroom. What are you doing in there? Dyeing your hair black in an act of rebellion?

ME: I'm with Brody.

LENNY: I sense a secret…

ME: later?

LENNY: uh huh

I tuck my phone away before Brody can read the exchange. I'll have to tell Lenny about what's going on. It was practically torture keeping it from her these past few days, but I doubt Brody would approve of her knowing.

"Is this your favorite makeout spot?" I tease. "You bring all the girls here, right?"

He wraps his arms around my waist from behind and pulls me closer until his mouth can reach my ear. A shiver runs down my back. "I have to tell you something very important."

"Yeah?" I say. "The L-word, right? All that practice earlier made you fall in love with me. I knew it would work."

He laughs against my skin. "You look...not only hot tonight, but also like many girls between the age of fifteen and twenty-two, so please don't let your mom get you to start smearing crazy red lipstick all over yourself or gobs of eyeliner."

I lean back into his arms. "That's exactly what I'm going to do. Smear a tube of red lipstick all over my entire body. Like *everywhere...*"

"Well, if you do that, I'd be interested in seeing the finished product." He slides a hand up my leg and rubs my right hip. "You're gonna have a bruise here from that last dive in the grass."

"Probably." Feeling extra bold, I tilt my head to look at his face. "Can we swim in this lake? 'Cause I really want to."

"I saw a bunch of people swimming last month, but I don't think—"

I escape his hold before he finishes. I wiggle out of my jean shorts, bravely showing off a pair of black panties. I walk down the rocks leading to the water in just my tank top and underwear. I glance over my shoulder at Brody. He looks relieved that I haven't completely stripped naked. Seriously? Like I'm bold enough to actually skinny-dip with him.

The water's a little cold, but it feels good against my skin. I had gotten sweaty earlier playing catch, and it would have made Mom too happy if I'd gone inside and showered and changed. I get out to waist-deep water before waving at him. "Come on. Get in."

He stands there not moving, so I prod him some more. "Are you a boxers or a briefs guy? If you're sporting some tighty whities, then I totally get your apprehension. I can close my eyes if that makes you feel more comfortable."

Even in the dark, I can see him roll his eyes before grinning.

He removes a shoe and then another, followed by his jeans, revealing his black boxer briefs. I duck underwater after getting a quick glimpse of the Jason Brody package. When I resurface, he's wading toward me, his abs flexing in response to the cold temperature.

"This water should help you with that problem you had earlier today."

Brody launches himself toward me, pushing my head back under. We come up laughing, and he says, "You're such a pain."

I smile at him in the dark. The lack of light seems to be giving me confidence. "A pain? Like a little sister?"

He shakes his head, protesting this analogy. My tank top has bunched up under my boobs, and I feel fingers brushing against my bare midsection. Brody gently guides me closer until his mouth can reach mine. Our lips part and his tongue mingles with mine, my hands resting on his face and water dripping from his eyelashes onto my cheeks. I open my eyes in the middle of the kiss, taking in the glow of the moon against his tan skin. The nerves and apprehension I had in his apartment this afternoon vanish.

I break the kiss and move back just enough to pull my tank top over my head. I bunch it up into a ball and toss it toward the grassy area beside Brody's jeans and shirt.

"Okay, this just got a lot more entertaining," Brody says, his voice rising an octave.

"You sound nervous." I step closer, trying to avoid the pointy rocks on the bottom of the lake. My fingers graze his stomach and then his sides. "Are you nervous?"

He shakes his head, his eyes focused downward on the water between us. His hands travel from my hipbones slowly up and over my stomach. Another shiver moves down my spine. His thumbs brush the bottom of my bra and stop there.

I close my eyes and bite back the too-revealing sigh that's about to escape my lips. I take Brody's fingers and tug them around my back until they land on the clasp of my bra. He gets the hint and, with one hand, unfastens it, causing the white satin material to float up to the surface. My eyes had been focused on Brody's chest, but he places a finger under my chin and lifts it until our eyes meet. I suck in a breath and hold it while he slips the straps down my arms until my boobs are half exposed, half underwater. The bra gets pushed to the side to float away. It's one of my favorites, but I couldn't care less.

He's still got his gaze locked with mine, probably using his gifted intuition to read my mood. To make sure I'm not uncomfortable.

Brody places a hand on my lower back and gently guides our bodies together until my chest is pressed against his warmth. Then he dips his head and kisses up and down my neck, one hand drifting lower over my black panties. The water starts to feel so much warmer, and I'm completely lost in the moment, my cheek now resting against his chest, my own fingers toying with the elastic waistband of his boxer briefs.

I'm about to dip my hand inside but chicken out at the last minute and instead, I tentatively move my fingers over the front of his underwear, feeling him through the material. The inquisition of this act, of applying what I'm feeling between my fingers to guess what it might look like temporarily distracts me from noticing anything else—like Brody's heart rate doubling against my cheek or even his fingers brushing along my inner thigh.

I lift my head from his chest and look up at him. "It's not quite as intimidating as I imagined. Private parts of public figures…"

His forehead touches mine, and he laughs lightly despite his now uneven breathing. He finds my free hand underwater and laces his fingers through mine. "I love…" he says, dragging out the words in dramatic fashion. "Your hands. And your boobs. They're perfect."

I'm almost laughing too hard to kiss him, but then he pulls my mouth to his and cuts me off. My hand explores him with a little more courage, pressing firmly against the front of his underwear until he's breathing too rapidly to keep his lips glued to mine.

Brody gets just as lost as I do in this adventure, and suddenly his hand is touching me, moving in gentle but firm motions over my panties. My forehead rests near his shoulder and it only takes a minute or two for him to finish me and another thirty seconds for me to reciprocate. And once he's caught his breath, we're kissing again, our half-naked bodies pressed together, and I'm waiting for the spell to wear off, for me to start freaking out because holy shit I just gave Jason Brody a hand job. Well, technically I haven't *handled* him, and I guess technically he didn't *handle* me.

But seriously, he totally handled me. Like a pro.

After a few minutes of some more awesome kissing, my teeth start chattering. Brody holds onto me with one hand and reaches through the water to retrieve my bra with the other. My gaze stays focused on his while I fasten it back on. I keep thinking, the second I look away, it's going to get awkward again.

We make our way back to the grassy area, and Brody pulls his shirt over my head. The sleeves go past my elbows and it hangs down to the back of my thighs. We both stretch out in the grass to dry off, and after a couple minutes of comfortable silence, Brody says, "I did not plan on that happening."

I rest my hands behind my head and stare up at the sky, laughing. "Me neither."

He leans on one elbow, facing me. "Totally not complaining. In fact, I think we should come here every single night. And mornings, too. Maybe an occasional lunch."

My whole body shakes from laughing. I reach up and bring his face closer so I can kiss his cheek. "You are intimidatingly handsome. I'm just now getting used to looking at you."

Brody smiles and kisses my lips. "And you are intimidatingly pretty."

I wrinkle my nose. "I wish I didn't look like her."

"I don't see any resemblance." He lifts the borrowed T-shirt and slides down and kisses the exposed skin right between my boobs, then he lays his ear against my chest. I immediately set my fingers into his dark hair and comb them through it.

"Can I ask you a personal question?" I say, waiting for him to stiffen or look serious again, but he's like a relaxed rag doll lying half on top of me.

"Ask me anything you want, Annie," he mumbles.

"I'm wondering if," I say, biting back any hesitation, "you've had a girl handle your parts and totally do it wrong? Like the worst hand job ever?"

"Not possible." He lifts his head just enough to kiss my neck and then rest it on me again. "I mean, we're not talking about violent acts or anything, are we? Because I guess that could happen, hypothetically."

"I was thinking more along the lines of accidental failures, not intentional."

"Nope, not possible," he repeats.

"Well, I've definitely had my own episode of fingers gone wrong," I admit.

"Douchebag boys," he mumbles against my skin. "Just stick with me; you'll be fine."

Warmth that has nothing to do with the air temperature spreads all over me. It's such a simple statement. I don't want to read too much into it, but I can't help feeling so many things all at once.

Maybe even the L-word.

chapter 22

"Holy shit," Lenny says, pulling her eyes away from the road to study my face, probably making sure I'm not messing with her. "You and Brody? Seriously?"

We're both still in our community service clothing—old T-shirts, gym shoes, and jean shorts all speckled with blue and white paint. Today was our final six hours of community service, so of course Johnson sent his camera crew. The car ride to the stadium for the game today is the first chance I've had to fill Lenny in on my recent life's drama.

And she wanted to go home and change first, which would have made us late to the game, but I convinced her that showing up in these clothes would piss off both our moms. She couldn't resist that temptation. And yes, Mom is attending the game today, and she's sitting with us. I'm super excited about that.

I swallow hard, already feeling anxious having this secret in the hands of one other person. Especially given my lack of experience in sharing secrets with girlfriends. "You seriously can't tell anyone, Len. Promise?"

"Of course," she says. "I'm just shocked by the fact that I got it all wrong."

I sigh and rest my head on the back of the seat. Being away from Brody for several hours or days causes that I-don't-care-about-my-fears-or-the-complications feeling to wear off and the anxiety to creep in. Things like worrying about what the hell we're doing and what it's going to do to me if it's a long-term thing or, worse, if it's not. "I'm just as shocked as you are, if that helps any."

Lenny releases a breath, revealing a level of tension and concern I hadn't anticipated from her. I figured we'd dive right in to the kiss-and-tell stories.

"He'll get raked over the coals if this gets out," she says.

My heart sinks. "Yeah, I know."

"And you'll be painted the teenage victim of a sexual deviant ball player who likes to use his power and fame to prey on innocent young girls."

I squeeze my eyes shut and rub my throbbing temples in a clockwise motion. "He's still a sexual deviant, even if there hasn't been any sex involved in this story?"

Lenny glances at me again, her eyebrows lifted way up. "There hasn't been any sex *yet*. And no one cares what actually happened. It's perceived under the 'relations' umbrella."

Relations. We've definitely had relations. My mind instantly drifts to last night in the lake, and I can feel Brody's hands on me all over again—the warmth of his fingers in contrast to the cold water, the tentative way he approached me, hesitating before sliding my bra straps down my arms. And then the moment when we both shifted to that abandoned freedom when my hands drifted south. I rub my arms, pressing the goose bumps back into my skin. I'd do it all over again right now if I could. But this time I'd probably be brave enough to actually put my hand inside his underwear instead of leaving it outside. Or I'd just strip the boxer briefs off of him. Now I can't stop picturing his Calvin Kleins floating in the lake water beside my white bra.

Just as quickly as the memory came on, the feeling I had lying beside Brody in the grass replaces the other image.

Nausea hits hard. I can't be in this deep, this quick, can I? I rub the tightness from my chest. Now all I can think about is Dad. Dad after he's been run over by Mom—him sitting on the couch among a sea of newspapers and dishes, staring at the TV, eyes glazed over. Those memories go almost as far back as I can remember.

I can't turn into that.

I shoot upright in my seat and turn to Lenny. "I'm gonna break things off with him. He'll understand…I mean, Jesus, he's Jason freaking Brody; plenty of women will be willing to swim around in a lake with him and give him hand jobs, right?"

Lenny lifts an eyebrow as if to say, *yeah, I'm not answering that question.* "So you're just going to tell him what? That it's too risky?"

I blow out a breath, my heart already breaking but my head filling with resolve. "Yes, it's too risky, and I still want to be friends."

"Friends?"

"Friends," I say, sounding more determined than I feel. "If anybody can stay friends after…well, after what we did together, it's us."

She shakes her head. "Good luck."

We pull up to the valet guy who parks cars for the players and families on game days. We both hop out, and Lenny hands over her keys to the guy. It's ninety degrees outside, so I'm grateful for the air-conditioned suites we get to sit in and watch the game, but still both of us take our time walking inside, knowing the moms are waiting.

"So what's your plan?" she asks me. "Just don't tell anyone after you break things off? Not even your dad?"

For a few seconds, I let myself fantasize about telling Dad that I have a new boyfriend and his name is Jason Brody and it's probably best that we don't tell anyone outside of the family. And Dad's affection for Brody would make this so easy and keep him from worrying about me being with some asshole guy he doesn't know very well. But deep down, I know the truth. Dad hasn't ever considered the possibility of the two of us being together, or else he wouldn't have let Brody hang out with me or give me rides. He would have had some negative reaction when I mentioned studying together last week. Telling him would be like yanking a big giant rug out from underneath him.

Yet another reason to end it.

"And when are you going to tell Brody?" Lenny drills. "After the game?"

"Actually, I'm gonna put it on the Jumbotron," I snap, and then quickly apologize. "Sorry."

"There you are, honey!" Mom rushes over to me and gives me one of her big annoying hugs. She pulls back just enough to see my face. "Isn't this exciting!"

Lenny's completely fascinated by the idea of Mom from my descriptions. She sticks a hand out to introduce herself, and I dart around them, ignoring the free food. I'll be starving to death when Lenny and I leave later, but now I can't even fathom eating a bite of food. God, why did I let this happen? And why did I have to like it so much?

While I'm standing nearly pressed against the glass window, pretending to watch the game closely, I catch bits and pieces of

Lenny using her Lenny London charm to press my mom for specifics on this sketchy play she's supposedly been cast in.

"So it's like *Mamma Mia*?"

"Well, I suppose that could be a good comparison, but a few less songs. It's very cutting edge. A really young, talented writer and director."

During the first two innings, Brody is in the bullpen warming up with Dad. But at the start of the third inning, he jogs out to the field with the rest of the team. This is the first home game I can stare at him shamelessly and think inappropriate thoughts. Before, I was always afraid he'd make eye contact with me again like he had that first game.

Except now that I've decided that we shouldn't do inappropriate things together anymore, I can't really enjoy this freedom.

The chatter around me dissolves when Brody faces the first batter. I zoom in on number eleven. He uses the sleeve of his jersey to wipe sweat from his forehead. They all must be dying out there. It's still late afternoon, and the sun is relentlessly beating down on the players.

Brody strikes out the first two batters with six straight fastballs, then Dad gives him a new signal. Brody's face tenses, and he shakes off whatever pitch the catcher has just suggested. He throws another fastball.

98 mph.

The Angels' batter manages to tip it, but it's a foul ball. Brody throws another strike.

99 mph.

Brody shakes off the next pitch, prepping with his usual stance. Our catcher keeps shifting around like someone is changing the plan on him. Brody throws another pitch, and the Angels' batter swings way too late.

100 mph.

The crowd gets on their feet to cheer, but I'm not sure which is causing more excitement—the fact that we've gotten three outs and we're up to bat now or that Brody just threw a freaking hundred-mile-an-hour pitch.

My gaze follows Brody as he jogs into the dugout. I shouldn't stare at his ass in those white pants, but I can't help myself. His head drops the second he gets near Dad. There's no clap on the back for cranking out a hundred-mile-an-hour pitch, not to mention three outs in a row.

Oh no…please don't tell me we've been outed.

Frank does give Brody's shoulder a squeeze, and he says something that looks like *good job* from up here. But Dad doesn't even make eye contact. My heart is flying when he leaves Brody on the bench and heads to the bullpen to instruct some of the other guys. For the first time that I've witnessed, Dad has three relief pitchers actually stopping and looking at him while he offers instruction, using words I can't hear and hand motions and body movements that mean nothing to me.

Obviously he's only ticked at one person. *Oh boy, this is bad. Very bad.*

Brody's got a wet towel over his head, a fan blowing hard on him. He looks like someone who just struck out, not a pitcher who banged out nine strikes in a row.

If only I could sit down there with him and ask him what's wrong. I lift my hand to the glass, pressing my thumb against the surface. It's only a little bit smaller than Brody's head from all the way up here. I close my eyes and sigh, knowing I've just been defeated by my own self.

There's no way I'm ending this thing with Brody today. I'll never get the words out without wanting to touch him, kiss him…*yeah, it's not happening.*

Maybe I'll get lucky and he'll dump me first. Seems fitting, considering I'm the one who is in the deepest.

Or if Dad has somehow managed to find out about us, then it'll be over for sure.

The noise level in the suites skyrockets. I peel my eyes from the dugout and realize that First Base just hit a homerun and there's now finally a score to be put onto the scoreboard. I glance at Lenny over my shoulder. She sees me and rolls her eyes.

By the ninth inning, Brody's still throwing fastballs, though more in the mid-nineties and less near a hundred miles per hour, but he still looks tense and Dad doesn't appear to be any more enthusiastic with him. He's also still shaking off pitches.

I'm glued to this last inning, dying to figure out what the hell is going on behind the scenes, when Mom approaches me with one of the publicists I've met a couple times while helping Savannah.

"Come on, Annie," she says, steering me away from the window. "Daddy wants us down on the field after the game's over."

I open my mouth to protest going anywhere with Mom, but the publicist beside her nods to me, as if to say that it's a legit request and now we both have to put up with Mom. Amy, the publicist, hands me a Royals Jersey, ironically with Brody's number eleven, and a matching hat. "Just put this over your, um…*shirt*," she says, eyeing my old, paint-speckled T-shirt.

Since I have on a sports bra, I decide to discard the old T-shirt while walking behind Mom and Amy. The jersey is one of the expensive replica ones, and it smells like golf balls. I pull it over my head and then realize Lenny and her mom are also behind us. Lenny's sporting the Royals' blue and white now, too, only hers is number twenty-four, First Base.

"What are we doing?" I whisper to Lenny.

She glances at me and wrinkles her nose. "Showing our love and support for our dear fathers, of course."

"We've never had to do this before."

Lenny leans in close to me, lowering her voice. "Thanks to your Latin lover boyfriend, we're in a pennant race now. Well, soon-to-be ex-boyfriend, I guess."

"I can't do it," I rush out under my breath.

"Show support for your family?" Lenny says. "Yeah, I know the feeling."

"Not that." I shake my head furiously. Who am I furious with? Lenny? No, me. For being a chicken shit.

"Big surprise there." Lenny flashes me a half smile, showing her support for my bad decisions. At least I have someone to cry to when this goes all wrong.

The game is over now and the field is full of players, cameras, and crewmembers trying to preserve the field. Mom is way ahead of us, moving straight for Dad, who's standing outside the dugout talking to Frank. She throws her arms around Dad's neck in dramatic fashion. I stop and Lenny halts beside me, her gaze traveling to where mine has landed. From the corner of my eye, I see Savannah ushering a local news crew toward the dugout. I didn't even know she was here today. Usually she sits with us. I can't help but wonder, after hearing her tell Dad exactly what she thought of Mom, whether maybe she didn't want to be in there with her.

I refocus on Mom and her show. Lenny squeezes my elbow. "That woman is something else. And I'm pretty sure that show is some kind of porn exhibition. I need to do some Googling later on."

I rub my face with both hands, attempting to shake off the

visual. Dad's face is tight, and he reaches behind his head, extracting Mom's hands from his neck. He drops her arms and takes a big step back, shaking his head. Lenny turns to me, a puzzled look on her face.

There's no time for Lenny and me to psychoanalyze Dad's behavior, because he's heading toward me, leaving Mom looking frustrated but not confused like Lenny and I are. My heart speeds up, processing the most likely theory—not the theory I had earlier where Dad has found out about Brody and me— she's leaving and she told him before the game. But that doesn't explain his behavior toward Brody.

I accept Dad's hug and take the opportunity to whisper to him, "What's going on? She's leaving, isn't she?"

Okay, now I'm nearly positive that he doesn't know about Brody and me.

He pulls back, his gaze darting to one side and then the other before focusing on my face again. "We'll talk later. Not here."

My eyes are glued to his. Already my chest is physically aching for him. I hate that she's here even though I said I wanted her to leave. What I really meant was that I never wanted her to come in the first place. Because he's going to break into pieces again and probably believe everything he told Savannah last week about not being able to find someone else.

A few months ago, I thought it was enough that he had me, but even while daydreaming about hooking up with Brody, I'd already started to understand the different kinds of people we need in our lives to love us. As much as I want to be enough for him and vice versa, I know it's not the same.

I give Dad another squeeze around the middle, pressing my cheek against his sweaty uniform shirt. "I'm sorry."

"Coach Lucas," a man says, standing in front of us with a

camera crew and a microphone. "Mind if we do some post-game interview questions?"

Savannah magically appears behind the cameraman and nods. I let go of Dad and start to step away, but the interviewer says to the cameraman, "Let's get the daughter, too?"

"Um…okay, s-sure," Dad stutters. "If it's okay with Annie?"

I can feel Mom's glare as she stands off to the side, arms folded over her chest. Does she expect Dad to invite her into this interview as his wife if she's taking off again? She's mental.

Savannah gives me a thumbs-up, and then she rushes forward, cutting among the crewmembers. She grabs the hat that's been hanging limply in my hand, arranges my hair over one shoulder, and places it on my head. Then she vanishes out of the picture, a quiet observer behind the cameraman.

I look up at Dad for help. Too much is going through my head right now to even think about plastering on a happy face for the cameras. Dad pulls me in front of him, his six-two body towering over my five-foot-five height. One of his arms wraps around my shoulders, holding me in place, like I might run. He leans down close to my ear. "Please no phony smiles like the London family."

The interviewer guy is busy untangling his microphone. "Are you okay?" I whisper back.

There's an obvious note of pain in his expression, but I'm not sure if that's because of Mom or he's actually in pain. Wouldn't surprise me after standing for this many hours. He's probably got some swelling in his leg, too.

"Just a little sore," he says, shifting some of his weight onto me. "But I'm okay, I promise. About everything."

I grip his arm and give him a squeeze just before the camera guy clips a microphone on both my shirt and Dad's. I know he can't be okay, but that's so like him to make sure that I don't worry.

"This isn't live," the cameraman tells us. "No need to be nervous."

Both Dad and I tense up instantly.

"Coach Lucas," he says. "Are you enjoying major league coaching so far? Is it strange to be back in this world after such a long absence?"

"It's been a great season so far," Dad says. "I never imagined I'd find my way back to baseball, but it's like an old friend—you take some time to catch up, and then it's like you were never separated."

"What do you predict for the Royals this season?"

I lean into Dad and angle my head upward so I can see him. He seems so much like himself. I figured there'd be a false front for the cameras or a pre-transcribed media answer.

"I think the young guys are hungry and it's giving everyone a boost," he says. "It's rejuvenating. Frank Steadman has put together a great team this season. He's focused on technique, using our strengths, and developing younger players. There's potential to snag a division championship, maybe even taking the American League title."

"And let's be honest," the interviewer guy says. "By young and hungry, you're talking about Jason Brody, right?" He looks down at me. "And I see you've got his number on today, Annie. Have you joined the Jason Brody fan club?"

Hell yes.

Luckily the heat is making everyone a little red in the face. "I make a point to join the fan club of any player who records a hundred-mile-an-hour pitch," I say.

Dad laughs, and Savannah gives me two thumbs up for that answer. *Phew.*

"We're mixing this clip with footage of your community service project in a one-hour special on major league players and their families for *Dateline* next month," the interviewer says. "Can you tell me a little about your experience with helping a family build a house?"

So Savannah got that *Dateline* story after all.

Am I supposed to talk about why we're doing that community service in the first place? Underage drinking and having two guys grope me at once in a nightclub isn't something I want to mention on camera. But Savannah's signaling from behind the interviewer guy for me to answer the question.

"Um…well." I look down at my paint-splattered jean shorts and then lift my eyes again. "Today was our last day at the building site—we came right from there to the game, actually—and Lenny and I got to walk the family through the house. The four kids have always been crammed into one bedroom, and now three of them have their own space. They have closets and dressers, and they even picked out the paint colors. The organization made sure they had a table where all six people in their family could sit. The first thing they did when they walked inside the kitchen was sit at that table together. It was pretty awesome to see the results. I'm ready to do it again, and I know Lenny is, too."

"What do you think of your dad's new job?"

I smile up at Dad and then back to the camera. "It's awesome. I'm so proud of him. Not that I wasn't proud of him before; he's always worked hard at whatever job he had, but this is where he belongs. He knows this game so well, and he's still got a lot more to contribute to the team."

Take that, Larry Johnson. Let's see that next-season contract.

"Did you put her up to that?" the guy jokes with Dad.

"Absolutely," Dad says. "We've been rehearsing that answer for weeks." He lets out a short laugh and then turns serious again. "Honestly, Annie's the reason I'm here. She talked me into accepting Frank's job offer. As much as I hate to admit it, she's in charge most of the time. Very bossy girl."

"Hey!" I give Dad a shove, and then reach out to grip his arm again after remembering that his leg is sore.

Savannah produces a director's chair and places it behind Dad. "We're going to do some solo questions, too, right?"

The camera light shuts off and the interviewer lowers his microphone. "Thanks, Annie," he says to me. "This will be a nice addition to our special."

Savannah removes my tiny microphone and hands it back before steering me away, leaving Dad alone to answer more questions. At least he's got a chair now.

"Great job," Savannah whispers. "I about died when he asked about the community service. Sorry I couldn't prep you for that."

I laugh, relieved it's over. "Yeah, I was so not wanting to discuss our newspaper fame."

"Johnson had us negotiate this TV special, and we're not supposed to have any mention of the community service being a punishment. He said that we made the statement during the press release in May and that would be the only mention of it ever." She rolls her eyes. "Of course, we'll have plenty of footage of Carl London in Brazil at the children's home. Don't even ask me how much work we had to do to make that look authentic. At least you and Lenny actually got your hands dirty and did the work."

I pull out a strand of hair speckled with paint to prove that the dirt extended even beyond our hands. Savannah gives me another grin, and then I move off to the side, giving her room to work.

I'd planned to stand and listen to the rest of Dad's interview, but something catches my attention in the bullpen. Brody still in uniform pitching to a stand, just like he's done so many times in my front yard. I walk in that direction but keep my distance. Something's going on with him, and I haven't figured out what yet.

At least I know it isn't Dad finding out about us.

A few of the Royals players walk past Brody. I hear one of the guys say, not nearly low enough, "Show off much, kid?" and another adds, "I don't know, haven't seen him on the cover of *People* yet…"

"I'm just counting the days until his arm goes out," a third player says—a relief pitcher for Christ's sake! Have some respect, dude! It could be your arm going out just as easily.

I'm about to flip them off behind their backs, but I spot too many cameras nearby, ready to catch me in the act. But seriously, they deserve it. *Assholes.*

A group of little boys hangs from the railing and asks Brody for an autograph. He saunters over, tucks away the melancholy face, and climbs up to their level, signing balls, gloves, hats, and T-shirts. His smile looks genuine as he asks their names and what positions they play, but the second the moms usher the boys away, he's on the ground again, throwing more pitches and ignoring the commotion around us.

I keep an eye on him and another eye on Lenny, who's retreating further into her own shadow with each passing minute. Her dad is alive with excitement after hitting two homeruns today. I want to talk to Brody, but there's no way I'd risk one of the many cameras turning our way and catching us standing too close.

After about ten minutes, Dad appears and heads straight for the bullpen. A noticeable limp—well, more noticeable than usual—plagues him. He watches Brody throw a few pitches without saying anything, his back against the fence. I inch closer but still stay a good distance away.

"Frank told me to come over here and apologize," Dad says. "He thinks I was too hard on you."

Really? Did he tell him he needed to record a hundred-mile-an-hour pitch?

I glance around and see that the field is quickly clearing out. Brody's drenched in sweat, his blue hat pulled low over his forehead to block out the sun. Dust from the mound is all over his white pants.

"You weren't too hard on me," Brody says. "I choked."

Choked? How? He was amazing.

"Wipe the slate clean," Dad says. "Next game, get it right."

Brody squeezes the ball in his hand and turns to Dad. "Sometimes I get out there ready to throw, and I can't get myself to deviate from my fastball. I'm comfortable with it. It's gonna do exactly what I want it to."

Oh, maybe he was supposed to do a different kind of pitch?

Dad bends over to pick up a loose ball from the dirt and tosses it to Brody. "You're a rookie. You can throw some bad pitches and be forgiven. But the second your arm starts to give out, they'll get scared and dump you. And if you throw hundred-mile-an-hour pitches for long enough, you're done by thirty. Maybe even sooner."

Brody takes his stance again and pelts another baseball at the stand. "It's hard to think about being thirty when I'm up there trying not to screw up *this game*. Hard to think about anything except right now."

"Then cut off your leg, so to speak." Dad laughs darkly at his very bad joke. "Convince yourself that you've got nothing but your change-up or slider, whichever applies."

Brody nods but looks unconvinced. I decide it's safe to approach them and quit eavesdropping. I've made a bad habit of it lately.

"Game's over, you know?" I say, getting both of their attention. "We won."

Brody gives me a half smile. "Nice shirt."

I return the smile, trying to converse silently with him. "Publicity made me wear it." Seconds later, I'm pulled away by Dad and Lenny, and all I can do is give Brody the we'll-talk-later look before walking away.

Maybe he's planning on dumping me? Why does that scare me so much? It shouldn't.

chapter 23

Lenny London: *is seriously considering studying abroad senior year. I see many advantages to getting away from my life. Worked out well for* **Carl London**.
20 minutes ago

Jason Brody Royals Pitcher: *Extremely proud to be part of a record-breaking Royals season! We are on a roll, so watch out, American League, Kansas City is climbing to the top!*
5 minutes ago

When Lenny drops me off at home, I'm surprised to see Dad's SUV in the driveway. I figured he'd have more interviews and post-game work to do. The sound of raised voices causes me to stop in the yard, my stomach already doing flip-flops.

Mom kicks open the screen door, her big pink suitcase rolling behind her. I exhale and close my eyes. Here we go again.

I charge up the porch steps and stand in front of her, blocking her way out. "Why do you keep doing this to him? Just divorce him or something. Let him go."

Her eyes meet mine, and I'm grateful for the fact that hers are brown and mine are blue like Dad's. "You can look at me like I'm terrible all you want, Annie, but let me tell you something about your daddy."

"What are you doing, Ginny?" Dad shoves open the screen door and steps outside.

Mom's gaze bounces between the two of us and finally rests on me. "You know, he didn't even want you. He tried to get me to have an abortion. Even drove me to the clinic, but I refused. Jimmy only cared about me and baseball. You didn't even make his priority list back then."

I can't breathe. It's like she kicked me with her high heels right in the gut. There're no words forming in my head, let alone falling from my tongue.

Dad grabs her arm, forcing her to spin around and face him. "You're pissed at me? Fine. Do *not* take this out on Annie."

Mom jerks her arm away. "I'll take it out on whomever I goddamn want. And she deserves to know the truth about her perfect father."

Both of us stand there watching her walk away and toss her suitcase into the back of the beat-up blue truck. After another minute, she drives off. The sting of her words clings to my skin like a permanent scar.

"Annie," Dad says finally, his voice full of a dozen different emotions.

I swallow the lump in my throat and lift my eyes to meet his. He takes two tentative steps in my direction, then rests his hands on my shoulders. "Listen to me, okay?"

His eyes are swimming with tears. I have no memory of my dad ever crying. I've seen him drunk and depressed. I've seen him pissed off. But I've never seen him cry.

"I wish I could tell you that I was just young and scared," he says. "And believe me, I *was* petrified, but also very self-centered. I didn't want anything to get in the way of my goals. I wanted your mom by my side and I wanted to be a star—not a father. Remember when you asked me if I was anything like Jason Brody when I played ball?"

My head moves up and down, answering Dad's question. It feels like years ago when I stomped into the house, pissed off at Brody, thinking he was nothing but an arrogant pig-headed rookie.

"I was bigger than life then. No one knew better than I did, and I didn't answer to anyone—not coaches or trainers. I threw the pitches I wanted to throw—" He stops, shakes his head, and then starts talking again, "I can't change the past or take back what I said or did, but I'm so glad that I have you."

The reason behind his concerns finally clicks into place. "Is that what you're worried about? That I'm going to feel rejected because you…" I can't use the words Mom said out loud. "Because you considered other options when Mom got pregnant?"

Some of the fear in his expression shifts to confusion. "Don't you?" he asks. "You're feeling something, I can see it on your face."

I wiggle out of his grip and sit down on the porch swing. This seems to be the spot where important things are revealed. "How old were you?"

He shuffles sideways and wraps a hand around the chain on the swing for balance. "Eighteen."

And yes, I knew this already. Math is a concept I've managed to grasp just fine, but I needed to hear him say it. "I'll be eighteen in October, and if I got pregnant, if I couldn't go to college or run track…" I shake my head. I don't want to open the door for safe-sex lectures. "Almost everybody in your situation would at least consider other options."

"Then why—?"

"Because she said it to hurt you," I interrupt, not able to keep the waver out of my voice. "She just threw those words at me without any hesitation. I mean, it's not like I didn't know that her priorities don't include me, but..." I draw in a shaky breath. "But that's the first time I've been presented with such concrete evidence."

"Annie." Dad falls into the spot beside me and lifts an arm around my shoulders.

I quickly wipe away the two or three tears that fell without permission and attempt to laugh. "Guess I know who she'd offer up to the Nazis if they made her choose between me and you."

Dad gives me a blank stare. "Huh?"

I laugh again. "*Sophie's Choice*..." Dad's face is still blank. "It's on my summer reading list for senior lit."

He narrows his eyes at me. "I haven't seen you with a book all summer."

My head rests comfortably against his arm. "That's because I watched the movie."

"Cheater." Dad plants a kiss on the top of my head. "And you're allowed to be angry with me, Ann."

"I'm not angry." I look up at him and exhale before saying, "I just want you to let her go."

He gives my shoulders a squeeze. "I did."

I lift my head and turn to face him. "Wait, did you tell her—"

"To leave," he finishes, carefully concealing a small trace of pain on his face. "Yes, I did."

I'm fighting a strong urge to throw my arms around his neck and then leap up to perform a celebratory dance, but I know better than to believe it's really over for good. "You deserve more," I say carefully, thinking through each word.

He gives me a sad smile. "Yeah, I've been hearing that a lot. Maybe it's time I let it sink in, right?"

Savannah. She told him that. If I hadn't been eavesdropping during that conversation, I'd call her up right now and thank her.

"So, like, you're gonna get divorce papers and all that?" The words are out of my mouth before I can stop them. I should have held that question off for tomorrow.

He scrubs his hands over his face and then finally says, "Yeah, I'm going to get the ball rolling this week."

I stare at him in disbelief. Is this the same man who yelled at me a few days ago and basically called me a selfish brat for wanting her to leave? Maybe shouting those words at me, speaking them out loud, showed him the situation from a different perspective.

We both relax again and sit in comfortable silence for a few minutes.

"I thought she'd come around eventually," Dad says. "I hoped at least that she'd appreciate having you and being part of our family despite everything that she went through with me. And Annie, I'm not going to lie, your mom held it together for a while and me…I put her through hell after my surgery."

The idea of Dad being selfish and wallowing in pity is pretty much unfathomable to me. I reach over and squeeze his hand. "I think you've made up for it by now."

He nods, staring straight ahead. "Maybe I have."

I sigh. "I can't help thinking that this is how it is for Lenny, except it's both of her parents. They care about her as much as Mom cares about me."

His silence confirms my theory. Instead of Mom's abrupt departure being on my mind tonight, Lenny and the way she disappeared into the shadows of her life after the game today is what sits with me as I get ready for bed and crawl under the covers. Which is ironic, because the second my eyes close, she sends me a text.

LENNY: Hanging out in pool with your bf. Want to come over?

"I climbed out my window."

Brody and Lenny both laugh, taking in my pajama shorts and tank top. The lights in the London house are dimmed, but the backyard is illuminated, the pool glowing blue and yellow. They're sitting beside each other in the full-length pool chairs, both in swimsuits dripping wet. I bite back the tiniest hint of jealousy at the idea of Brody and Lenny swimming together late at night. But if they wanted to hook up, I doubt they'd invite me to join them.

I'm still on an emotional roller coaster myself, but I haven't forgotten the mood shifts both of them had earlier, so I tentatively take the seat beside Brody. Lenny gives us a sly smile and then hops up from her chair, wrapping a towel around her waist. "Be right back. I'm getting drinks."

I watch Lenny disappear into the guesthouse, then spit out the truth. "She knows."

Brody's eyes widen, water dripping from his forehead and chin. "How?"

"I told her," I admit, looking down at my hands. "She would have guessed anyway, and I needed her to cover for me last night."

Last night…boy, could I use a repeat of that right now.

Brody exhales and then nods. "Yeah, okay, I get it. It's just that rich kids make me nervous."

"You know Lenny isn't like that."

After a few seconds, his face relaxes, and he slides his chair over, pressing it up against mine. I stretch out on my chair, resting my head against the back, and breathe in the chlorine and perfect Jason Brody scent wafting into my air space.

"Thanks for posting exciting exclamation point statements for me on Facebook tonight." He reaches for my hand, flipping it palm up and drawing circles against my skin with his thumb.

Heat drifts from my hand up my arm. "I figured you weren't feeling the exclamation points, but I thought your fans might be."

Brody keeps his eyes focused on our hands. "That's why it has to be you." He lifts his head, meeting my gaze again. "You know, for the Facebook page."

A grin slides across his face, and I feel my own smile forming. "Right. For Facebook."

Lenny returns, handing both of us some fancy red drinks garnished with a pineapple slice and a little umbrella. Brody lifts the drink and looks it over like he's just been handed an infant with a dirty diaper. "Are we celebrating something?"

"Yep." She takes her seat again and holds up her own glass. "To me, deciding to run away to Spain in October and avoid suffering through the off-season with the birth parents being around all the time. You'd think baseball season would be worse, but if I have to see my dad, I prefer to do it with an entire stadium between us."

I give Brody a weary glance, but we both raise our glasses anyway. "To Spain," I say. "An awesome excuse to run away."

Lenny turns to me and smiles. "I'm so glad you feel that way, Annie, 'cause I'm totally planning on convincing you to come with me."

I choke on the red syrupy drink I'd just gulped that went down the wrong pipe. I cough until I can speak again. "What? I can't go to Spain. You know my Spanish is terrible."

"Emersion is the only way to truly grasp a foreign language," Lenny says. "And I need a roommate, or else I'll get stuck with some crazy girl…or worse, a baseball fan. It's only four months."

My apprehension betrays me, and my eyes flit in Brody's direction. The off-season is something I've secretly been looking forward to because Brody will be in Kansas City all the time, no more on the road five days a week or whatever. "I have track… and my dad a-and Grams," I stutter.

"We'll leave after cross country and before track starts," Lenny argues.

I don't get a chance to counter that because the back door swings open. Brody's back straightens, and he looks at Lenny, alarmed. "You said nobody was home."

First Base strides out onto the patio, heading straight for the steps leading into the pool. All three of us sit frozen, waiting for him to notice us or for an escape route to materialize. My heart is pounding, but for a split second it looks like he's about to dunk his head underwater and we might have a second to hide.

No such luck.

He angles his body in our direction and finally lifts his gaze. His eyebrows shoot up immediately. "Well, well, can't say I didn't call this one months ago."

I hold my breath as he emerges back up the pool steps, grabs a towel, and stands in front of us. Brody's hands clench around the towel beneath him. We'd let go of our hands the second the door opened, but now I've slid toward the far side of my chair. Lenny's eyes bounce between the two of us, probably taking in the panic on both our faces. Then she launches herself into Brody's lap.

He's obviously startled but doesn't move or push her away. First Base stops, his mouth falling open, the smirk dissolving from his face. I pull my knees to my chest and hug them tight.

"You and…" First Base points between Brody and Lenny, tangled in a tight, wet, half-naked embrace.

Lenny rolls her eyes. "Relax, Dad. We're just fooling around. No big deal."

Several different emotions cross his face until he finally says, "If this shows up in the media, I'll kick your ass back to triple-A."

"Got it," Brody says, clearly pissed off at the threat, but not enough to tell the truth.

"And if you knock her up," he adds, "I'll hire someone to kill you."

Those are probably words my dad would use if he knew about Brody and me, but the reason behind them would have nothing to do with public image. The hurt on Lenny's face is clear even in the dim lighting.

First Base must have decided against the swim, because he shakes his head and goes back inside. Lenny moves back to her chair and gathers up her phone and other items. I plant my feet back on the ground, scrambling to think of something to say. "Thank you…"

"It's fine," she says, bending over to grab something under her chair.

"Len?" I ask. "You okay?"

She swallows hard and nods, forcing a tense smile. "Yeah,

just tired. I'm heading inside."

I stand up and reach for her arm. "Want me to stay over tonight?"

She shakes off my grip. "I'm fine, Annie," she snaps.

I open my mouth to argue, but Brody shakes his head. After she's inside, he stands up and takes my hand. "Let her go. I'll walk you home, okay?"

We take a minute to clean up the towels and return the drinks back to the guesthouse kitchen. When we're two houses away, I release all the tension in one long exhale. "I can't believe she did that."

Can't believe she knew with such sureness that her dad wouldn't give a shit who she hooked up with. My heart sinks down to my stomach.

Brody rubs his eyes, looking even more stressed than I am. "Girl's got some balls, that's for sure. I feel like an ass for being relieved."

I reach for his hand and lace our fingers together. "I'm sure he'll catch another tabloid photo of you with some groupie girls and forget about you and Lenny." I try to sound casual, like I'm super cool with all this, but it's hard to be in the background, knowing the truth but being shown something different.

Brody stops in the middle of the sidewalk, wrapping his arms around me from behind. His lips are on my neck so fast, planting kisses against my skin. I close my eyes and pretend we're naked in the lake again. His mouth pauses just below my ear, sending a shiver up my spine. "I'm always thinking about you. No matter what."

His kisses travel across my cheek until I turn my head just enough for our lips to meet. I can feel his worry about today's game, about living up to expectations, about being with me. It's like he's channeling all his feelings into kissing me like he does on the pitcher's mound. And knowing that I'm up there on his priority list with baseball makes my heart swell and scares the crap out of me at the same time.

I spin around, and he takes my face in his hands, smiling against my lips. "I think if I could've taken a couple breaks to do this during the game, I might have pulled off the pitches I should've thrown."

My face heats up. "Yeah right." I glide my fingers up under his shirt, feeling his abs flex in response.

"After last night at the lake," Brody says, planting more kisses on my neck, "I didn't think I'd be able to look your dad in the eye again. Wasn't even sure if I could look at *you*, either."

I shove him back. "What happened to never treating me like a kid?"

He lifts his head, his expression going from amused to solemn. He nods toward his car parked across the street. "I feel too exposed right now. All the suburban families with sleeping kids. Let's sit in the car."

We walk over, and I climb into the passenger side, leaving my seat belt unbuckled. Brody gets in, drives to a more secluded spot a few blocks away, and quickly returns to his earlier train of thought. "I didn't mean that I regret watching you strip your clothes off and swimming almost naked with you," he says, causing my heart to skip a few beats. "But it meant a lot more to me than what it would look like to anyone else. That's the problem. I see your dad or Savannah or even Frank, and suddenly I picture being with you from their eyes and yeah…"

I'd had the same problem earlier today. The longer I'm away from him, the more complicated everything seems. But right now, my objectives are very simple and clear.

Brody reaches for me, pulling me across the center console, onto his lap. His mouth is hungry against mine, hands drifting under my shirt, lifting it over my head, tossing it aside. The swim trunks he's wearing do little to hide anything, and I'm already debating touching him for real this time. He leans forward, helping me to remove his T-shirt. The sweet, gentle expression he often wears around me is gone and there's this intensity in his eyes.

He reaches under my arms, lifting me a few inches, kissing me everywhere. Just the warmth of his mouth against my sensitive skin almost makes me lose myself, but I force it away, afraid he'll be able to tell how much he affects me. I don't know why it matters, but something about losing control is embarrassing, like admitting to touching myself or something.

His lips slide over, landing between my boobs, and he holds them there, resting his forehead against my chest and hugging me tight. His back rises and falls rapidly, keeping up with his speeding heart. "Tell me something."

I tangle my fingers in his hair, and rest my mouth on the top of his head. "Tell you what?"

He kisses all the way up to my collarbone, pulling me lower until our foreheads meet. "Something you've never told anyone."

"Why?" I kiss his lips, lingering there and forgetting every bit of drama my day held.

"It makes me sure that you and I are real." There's a trace of doubt in his voice, vulnerability that I've never heard before. And I remind myself that he doesn't have anyone. Just an empty apartment and the memory of his mom kicking him out years ago. "I like keeping your secrets."

I squeeze my eyes shut and take a deep breath. "You know what happened at the lake yesterday? I'm kind of easy that way." Brody's body tightens in alarm, and I quickly realize my mistake. "Not that kind of easy! *Jesus Christ.*"

He laughs, relieved. "What kind of easy, then, Annie?"

I love the way he says my name, like the word is part of his breath, his lips, his tongue. There are undertones to it that I don't hear when he says Lenny's or Savannah's or anyone else's names. I'm being hypnotized into spilling my guts. Maybe I should open a window? "I don't have any trouble…you know… *enjoying myself.*" I close my eyes again, my cheeks flaming hot. "I've heard enough girl gossip to know that often it just…it just doesn't happen."

"*Orgasm* is a difficult word for you to say, huh?" he teases. "And you're right, it was very easy to get you there last night. I didn't even touch you."

I open my eyes, my eyebrows lifting up. "You did too touch me. And I was totally faking it. Besides, you were just as easy."

The famous Jason-Brody-raised-eyebrow is back. "You weren't faking. And you're right, I was easy, too. But I've had months of day dreaming about you and it all built up." He leans in, nibbling my ear lobe, then stops suddenly and starts laughing, like really hard, his face pressed into my shoulder.

Self-conscious isn't a strong enough word to describe my current feelings. "What's so funny?"

He shakes his head back and forth, practically doubled over while I'm straddling his lap. "It makes sense…holy shit."

Annoyed, I lift my leg to climb off of him and retrieve my shirt, but he holds me firmly in place. "It's always about that finish line with you, isn't it? You gotta get there and get there first."

I smack his shoulder, but I'm laughing now, too. Who knows? He could be right. "That's the last secret I'll ever tell you."

His smile fades, and that hot intensity returns, giving me

instant goose bumps. "Can I try again?"

I reach down, feeling for the waistband of his shorts, but he catches my wrist and pulls it to his mouth. "I didn't mean me, just you."

My heart is flying. What the hell am I supposed to say to that? *No, don't give me an orgasm because it's embarrassing if you don't have one, too.*

His fingers glide down my stomach, my hips, pausing on my inner thighs. I bite back a gasp and force myself to shake my head. "Not now…I mean, not here."

Eventually, he kisses my bare shoulder lightly, and then removes his hands from my thighs, brings his hands to my face, pulling us into a deep kiss that lasts for minutes or hours. I'm not sure. Eventually, Brody returns me to my seat. I grab the discarded shirt and pull it over my head inside out. We're both breathing hard and getting sweaty, so he starts the car and gets the AC blasting before we head home.

I watch him drum his fingers against the steering wheel, thinking. "Does what I just asked to do to you make you uncomfortable?"

Yes. But I shrug and attempt a cool attitude. "In my previous experience, things just kind of happened and we didn't talk about it much. So that part's weird…maybe even a little embarrassing," I admit.

He turns all fake serious. "Huh…okay, I guess I'll just have to embarrass myself then."

I roll my eyes. "Like that's possible."

He angles himself to face me. "We've already gone over the normal male reaction to being turned on, so maybe I should spell out exactly how that problem is often dealt with when I'm alone."

I clap a hand over his mouth. "No! I do *not* need those details."

He winks, not looking even a little bit embarrassed, then removes my hand from his mouth. "I wasn't planning on describing the act, just the fact that I do it, and lately that's been because I've been around you and left before any finish lines were crossed."

My hands instinctively go over my face, hiding the blush and the fact that I can't stop laughing. Brody's kind of adorable when he goes all *I'm older than you, therefore I will be giving regular sex ed lessons.* "Except for last night."

"True," he says., "But when I got home, I kept replaying it and then several times today as well, so it kind of made things worse."

I drop my hands and stare at him. "Then I'll refrain from doing that again."

He grabs my hand and holds it to his heart. "It's worth all the trouble. Seriously. As much as I enjoy thinking about you touching yourself, I figure I'd rather leave you satisfied than hanging if possible." He gets all fake-serious. "It's how I was raised, Annie. Respect women and their wishes."

I grin. "God, you're, like, the corniest nineteen- year- old in the history of nineteen- year- olds. I plan on being way cooler when I'm your age."

He glares at me, then opens his car door. "Time for you to go home."

Instead of driving closer, we walk the rest of the way to my house in silence, our hands swinging at our sides, the word *yes* and then *yes again* ready to spill from my lips, yet stuck there at the same time. As soon as I am standing beside my open bedroom window, Brody spins me around, pressing my back against the house. His lips are at my ear, whispering in a low, sexy voice, "*Me persigues en mis sueños. Nunca puedo tener suficiente de ti.*"

I don't know what he said, but I turn all self-conscious and spit out the first words to form on my lips. "Can you come back tomorrow?"

Brody laughs, and the warmth of his mouth presses into mine. "I'll be in Toronto, remember?"

I reach out and take his face in my hands. "Then I'll just have to ask you to quit for me. No more road trips. No more baseball. Just this. You and me, a few too many mosquitoes, and the moon."

"If I didn't know better, I'd think you were drunk." He kisses me again, long and slow.. Then he pulls back, like he's yanking himself away. "I need to leave."

Now it's my turn to laugh. "I know what you're going to do when you get home."

"It will be a long drive," he says into my ear, causing me to blush again when a mental image forms in my head of him—

Yeah, um…time to go inside.

"Good luck at the game tomorrow."

His gaze darts toward Dad's bedroom window and then back to me. "You know what? If I can stand this close to Jim Lucas's window while talking about getting off, I figure I've got the balls to try some new pitches tomorrow."

I shake my head. "That's what I'm here for. Moral support and all."

He gives me one more quick kiss on the mouth before backing away. I lift myself through window and, after landing safely onto my bedroom carpet, I watch Brody jog down the sidewalk toward where his car is parked between my house and Lenny's.

Both excitement and anxiety swirl around inside my stomach. I'm getting so attached to this boy it's not even funny. And the lie is doubling in size every day. I know it can't go on forever, and when the haziness of our amazing evening wears off, fear takes over, just as I'm drifting off to sleep.

post
SEASON

chapter 24

Lenny London: *Wishes Lisa Frank folders were still cool. Fu*k it. I'm sporting some pink glittery kitty cat folders today. Deal with it.*
12 hours ago

Annie Lucas: *SUUUUUMMMMEEER. Why did you dump me? Why? Are we never ever ever getting back together?*
11 hours ago

Annie Lucas: *Just learned that kangaroos aren't in the bible but unicorns are? I'm confused. How is this not mythology?*
55 minutes ago

Jason Brody Royals Pitcher: *Who's got the top division spot? Yep, that's right. We do.*
2 minutes ago

BRODY: My place again tonite?

ME: Yep. For studying.

BRODY: Rite. Studying. You're cute.

ME: Stop staring at me! Lift your damn weights.

BRODY: I can see up ur skrt 🙂

ME: Oh. My. God. Please tell me you delete these texts?

BRODY: Why? Not like I hve parents snoopin around my phone.

ME: You haven't deleted any?? Seriously? We do this like every day, how many inappropriate texts do you have to/ from me?

BRODY: Hundreds. Lite blue panties, huh? 🙂

ME: This would be way more fun if you were shirtless

BRODY: done 🙂

ME: Wait! The new trainer is coming to see me in 5. Put it back on!

BRODY: No 🙂

ME: would you stop with the damn smiley faces!

BRODY: you know you love them 🙂

ME: maybe a little 🙂

"Word of advice, Annie. When your knee hurts and suddenly looks larger than the other one, don't run four more miles."

"Really?" I roll my eyes. "Who knew?"

Kevin, the new Royals' assistant trainer, leans down, brushing his fingers over my bare knee. I grip the hem of my pleated red skirt, holding it down tight, leaving him nothing to view underneath. From the corner of my eye, I catch Brody holding a set of dumbbells mid-lift, shooting a glare at Kevin.

It took ten minutes of this close-up exam for Brody to go from amused to…well, to *this*.

I narrow my eyes at Brody, and he resumes lifting weights, but the glare doesn't fade. Luckily, Dad breezes in before Brody can throw a punch. He sees me on the table, my knee being examined, and his eyes go wide. "What happened, Ann?"

"Did you feel a pop or anything give out on you?" Kevin asks.

I shake my head. "It's just sore and a little swollen. No big deal."

"Is it her ACL?"

Kevin proceeds to find more ways to put his hands on my skin by pointing out various ligaments and tendons. After a couple minutes, weights slam to the floor, making all of us jump. And then Brody's sticking his arm between Kevin and my leg. A bag of ice lands on my knee.

"Gotta get that swelling down, right?" Brody stands beside me, arms folded over his chest as if he plans on physically watching the swelling reduce.

Cut it out, I say with my eyes.

He might as well makeout with me in front of Dad.

But Dad's too worried about me to pay attention to his star

pitcher. "Think she needs an MRI, just in case?"

Kevin laughs like he's an overly concerned father, which he is, but he does know a thing or two about athletic injuries. "It's just a little fluid buildup from overuse. No need to bring on the fancy expensive tests."

Dad's concern doesn't fade. I rest a hand on his arm. "I'll sit out the meets tomorrow and Saturday. It'll be fine."

I like to do well, but I'm only running cross country to stay in shape for track. Especially this year, when I've got scholarships on the line. I need to be in top form next spring.

Kevin's eyes bounce from me to Dad. "That's an excellent plan. Five days rest, and then I'll take a look and see if she needs some rehab or, if there's still swelling, maybe an MRI."

Dad accepts this plan, and Kevin finally packs up his stuff and leaves, allowing Brody to fully concentrate on his workout again.

"Are you heading home now?" Dad asks me.

I'm careful to only nod toward Brody without actually making eye contact. "We're gonna study."

"Great." Dad's focused on the dozen pink slips that he had in his hand when he walked in the training room. Messages Savannah just handed him, most likely. "What are you two studying tonight?"

Brody chokes on the big swig of water he just took, spraying drops all over one of the treadmills. I fling open a textbook, duck my head, and hope my hair covers the redness on my face. "Equations. Lots of equations," I mumble.

"Well, better you than me." Dad smiles and gives my uninjured leg a pat, then he holds up the pink slips of paper. "I've got some calls to return. I'll be in my office."

The second he exits, leaving Brody and me alone, I lean

back against the wall, close my eyes, and let out a huge breath. "Jason Brody, are you trying to give me an anxiety attack?" I say in a low voice.

He walks over and adjusts the bag of ice on my knee. "Come on, that dude's a creeper. Tell me you were not creeped out?"

I shrug. "He likes to invade personal space, but I'm sure he's harmless. Plus, he's old."

Brody glides one hand down my skirt, his fingers slowly walking in and out of each pleat. "I've been looking forward to peeling one of these skirts off of you all day," he whispers.

Despite our hundreds of slightly dirty texts messages, we hardly ever get any time alone. All the baseball-related travel plus the fact that Jason Brody, Royals' pitcher, is in contention for Rookie of the Year puts a damper on our secret makeout sessions. And if I'm being completely honest, I haven't seen Dad much lately, either. When Brody is traveling, he's traveling, too. Both of them returned from a five-day trip this afternoon while I was finishing up my first day of senior year.

I catch Brody's hand and move it away from my skirt before someone walks in. He's all post-workout sweaty, and I'm so ready to peel off his layers, too. I'm just not as free with admitting these things as Brody is.

"You owe me a practice test." I hold out my hand and wait for him to retrieve the papers from his gym bag. After he does, Brody sits at the end of the training table. It only takes a few minutes for me to check his answers with the code in the back of the GED book. I scribble a big 96 percent on the page and slide it in front of him. "Seventy is passing. You've never gotten below an eighty-five. I think it's time for you to take the damn test for real."

Brody frowns, then nods like he's done the other two times I gave the exact same argument. I know what the problem is.

We both know. He doesn't want to contact his mom and get the paperwork that proves his dyslexia so he can have an oral exam. Not to mention the fact that we'd have no excuse to study together if he got his GED.

I'm very close to asking Savannah *again* about surprising players by inviting family members to games. I know she has her rules, but Jesus, he's obviously done his time, and all he needs is an ounce of support from his own mother and copies of some paperwork so he can add high school graduate to his résumé. This is not something Brody should have to stress over.

"I'll do it soon," he says, placing a note of finality on the topic. He wraps his fingers around my ankle and then looks up at me with his brain-melting smile. "Let's practice Spanish. I'd hate for you to get behind."

Oh God, if only we could right now…

I take a deep breath and inhale the scent of cheese and pepperoni. "Do you smell pizza?"

I'm off the table, carting my bag of ice and heading toward the locker room before he can answer. My nose didn't fail me. Savannah is directing a dude with a huge stack of pizza boxes. A few players and most of the publicity team are milling around. Lily is trailing behind Savannah, her red hair in two braids, hands stuffed in the pockets of her green plaid jumper.

Her face lights up when she sees Brody and me, and within seconds, she runs right into his arms, demanding to be lifted on his shoulders.

"What's with the pizza?" I ask Savannah.

Her heels are clinking around the locker, helping to set up tables and giving orders. "The *Dateline* special starts in a couple minutes."

Oh right, the corny promo about players and their families.

"I'm recording it at home."

Dad's emerged from his office and is already fishing through pizza boxes.

Savannah opens a cooler full of soda and beer. "Well, my people and I decided it might be fun to watch it live from the locker room. Especially considering the number of people I had to sleep with to make this happen."

"You went to a slumber party?" Lily asks from her seat on top of Brody's shoulders.

Savannah has that oops-forgot-the-kid-was-in-the-room look. "Nope, no slumber parties. I was just kidding." Dad and I are both staring at her, and she finally rolls her eyes and adds, "I'm really kidding. But I did slay a few dragons, metaphorically speaking, and that entitles me to an extra thousand calories today and a pizza party on the Royals' tab."

One of the interns flips on the big-screen TV, and everyone starts grabbing plates and pizza slices.

"I would like just cheese, please," Lily says, pointing Brody toward the table. He hands her a slice, and already the cheese is dangling in his hair.

I snort back a laugh, and Savannah reaches up and grabs her daughter, bringing her back to ground level. Dad's drifting in the direction of his office, balancing a beer and a plate of pizza in his hands.

"Where are you going?" Savannah nods at the TV. "The show's about to start."

Dad turns around to face the room again. "I think I'm gonna go home and make that dentist appointment I've been putting off."

"You'd rather take care of dental matters than watch your interview on national television?" Savannah asks.

"Absolutely," he says without hesitation.

I make a move to stop him and drag him back, but Savannah shakes her head. She's smiling at Dad's retreating form. "He's infuriately stubborn, isn't he?" Savannah asks, though she doesn't sound even a little bit angry.

My eyebrows have lifted up, lots of theories spinning through my head. I catch Brody's eye from a few feet away and see that he's thinking it, too. Put today's little nuances together with the conversation I eavesdropped on, hearing Savannah chew Dad out about letting Mom back in our lives…But now Mom is out of the picture. The divorce papers are signed.

Butterflies flap in my stomach. I can't quite grasp how I feel about this newfound insight. Yeah, I planned on trying to find Dad a new woman, but sometimes those concepts are so much easier in hypothetical form than in reality.

And Savannah is awesome. And beautiful. Dad would have to be an idiot not to see that, and he's not an idiot. Which means…

I'm about to grab my school bag and take off so I can pester him until he gives me some answers, but I can tell the publicity team is excited to have some players around to join the party and at least one family member. I swipe two slices of pepperoni pizza and a bottle of water, then take a seat beside Brody on a locker room bench.

Brody leans in close to me and whispers, "She totally wants your dad."

I stare at the big screen, leaving my pizza neglected in my lap. "Can't believe I didn't see it before."

When I first heard about this *Dateline* program, I figured it would be about many players and their families. I figured the interview Dad and I did together would get ten seconds or maybe thirty if the Royals were still winning games. Never in a million years did I expect the program to open with video footage of Dad on the pitcher's mound in a Yankees uniform. Dad as young as Brody is right now.

Dad with two legs.

Tom Brokaw's voice-over narration fills the locker room, surround-sound speakers kicking in all around us. *"Jim Lucas became a New York Yankee before he even started college. Scouts got wind of not only his fastball but a slider that held up with the best of the best. They used every tactic aside from camping out on his parents' front lawn to try and sign the high school boy. And the future star embraced his role without hesitation, turning down offer after offer until his price nearly broke records for major league baseball rookies."*

I set my plate on the bench beside me and leaned forward, glued to the screen, watching Dad throw pitch after pitch. He looked like a star.

The program cuts to an interview of young Dad, still in uniform, following a preseason game, seated in one of those fancy director's chairs. *"You can't be afraid to ask for what you think you deserve. If I'm the best, I want the biggest number. That doesn't mean I don't love baseball. That I'm only in it for the money. Status is status, and I plan on breaking some season records, and I'd like to be paid accordingly. Nothing wrong with that."*

Holy shit. Who is that man? Did aliens abduct my real dad, and I've been living with a body snatcher all my life?

"But Jim Lucas didn't break any records. In fact, his pitching career ended abruptly after one regular season game."

The footage of Dad at practice sessions and preseason games continues along with more voice-over explaining his cancer diagnosis and the immediate surgery that followed. I glance around. The room is completely still, everyone entranced. Brody has also ditched his pizza and is now leaning forward, elbows resting on his knees, his face intense.

I hear another publicist mumble to Savannah, "Where did they get this footage?"

Savannah just shrugs, her eyes never leaving the screen.

And then Dad's leg is gone. Just like that. He's in the middle of a fancy physical therapy room. He's much thinner, and wires are hooked up to his chest while he attempts to walk on a treadmill with his new prosthetic leg.

"While Jim Lucas's wife grew distant and his daughter went from infant to rambunctious two-year-old, great medical minds at places like Johns Hopkins University worked day and night, all racing to be the one to put an amputee in major league baseball."

The younger Dad in the training room stops the treadmill, a doctor unhooks the wire, and he grabs a towel, turning to face the cameras. *"It's harder than I thought."*

The camera shifts, and suddenly there's Mom. She looks so beautiful and young. It takes me a second to process the fact that the blond toddler in a pink dress with pigtails and ribbons is me. I watch my younger self squirm and twist in Mom's arms, and then Dad reaches out and takes her from Mom's hold.

"I'm sure your daughter would be proud to see her dad pitch in the major league again someday," a voice from behind the camera says.

Dad looks down at me, his eyes noticeably avoiding the cameras. *"I'll be glad just to be able to chase this one around. She's destined to run off a cliff or stick her finger in an outlet."*

The younger me rests her head on Dad's chest, stuffing a thumb in her mouth. I glance down at my thumb in my lap. Thank God I broke that habit before elementary school.

"So are you saying that you won't be the first player with a prosthetic limb in professional baseball?"

"I know I won't," he says. *"Bert Shepard pitched one game in 1945 after losing a leg in World War Two."*

"Will you be the first in modern baseball?" the interviewer presses.

"I don't know." Dad shakes his head. *"I just don't know."*

The camera moves to Mom, shock and disappointment written all over her face. Instead of moving closer to comfort Dad, she slides back a step.

"Four years after losing his leg to cancer, Jim Lucas's support well had run dry. He declined further interviews and endorsements, claiming that he wasn't a ballplayer anymore and it was time for him to accept that. And for Jim, accepting that fact meant no college degree and a string of dead-end manual labor jobs so that he could feed and support his family."

A present-day Frank is leaning against the dugout in his manager uniform. *"There's something about Jimmy Lucas that I couldn't shake after all those years. Don't get me wrong, he was an arrogant son-of-a-bitch in his glory days, and I practically had to wrestle lions to get him to sign with the Yankees. But I always knew he had the potential to be a game-changer no matter what role he's in—player or coach."*

Tom Brokaw's voice returns, alongside a montage of major league players and their wives and kids. *"Dateline spent hours upon hours with players in their homes, around the family dinner table, and what we often found was a media front that we couldn't penetrate enough to give you a true inside look. Except when it came to Jim Lucas and his daughter, Annie. That feisty toddler you saw in video clips moments ago is now seventeen years old."*

The program cuts to the post-game interview Dad and I

did weeks ago. Me with my Jason Brody jersey and Royals hat and Dad in his sweaty uniform. They play the part where I talk about how proud I am of him and that he belongs in baseball. And then we hear Dad saying that I'm the reason he took the job.

Then it's just Dad sitting in the chair Savannah had brought him. I never heard this part of the interview because I was watching Brody practice.

"Do you wish Annie would have grown up around baseball? Or maybe seen you pitch a game with the Yankees?"

Dad seems to sit on this question for several seconds. *"I think everything turned out how it was supposed to. She was born right before my first spring training started. And all through the preseason and my opening day with the Yankees, she was this little thing that someone else dealt with. Her mom or the nanny she hired. After my surgery, the looks of pity got old real fast, and there was so much anger I had to deal with. And that's the thing about babies—they don't care how you feel or what you've been through. They demand and you serve."* He laughs and then turns serious again. *"But at the same time, as Annie got older and I could really talk to her, I realized that she just wanted me to be her dad. She never cared if I played baseball or worked in a factory."*

I swallow the lump in my throat and discreetly wipe away a tear that escapes.

"She copied everything I did. Even went through a phase where she hopped around on one leg or pretended to take her fake leg off at night. She'd tell me, 'I think I'm gonna save up my money for a pink leg. This silver one is ugly.'" Dad laughs again. *"She became the reason I got up in the morning and the reason I went to work. Sometimes I wonder whether, if I hadn't gotten sick,*

would she still be this small part of my life like she'd been during that first season? Would someone else know her like I know her? I can't imagine living in that world."

"Tell me about your pitching lineup. Let's start with baseball's hottest topic, Jason Brody."

Dad nods and fidgets with the armrests on the chair. *"I think we could be witnessing the rookie season of a future Hall of Famer. Of course, I know better than anyone that life doesn't always cooperate, but Jason Brody works harder than any player I've seen. He's smart enough to keep his ears open, to not let his head explode. God knows he's got some distractions at his age and being on the road, not to mention the pressure of being a hyped pitcher. But I genuinely believe good things happen to good people. His head and his heart are in the game, and when you add phenomenal talent to the mix…Yes, he's gonna go far. I'm honored just to be able to take part in the beginning of his career. He's a pleasure to work with."*

"So we shouldn't believe everything we read online about his wild side?"

Dad laughs and shakes his head. *"He's a good kid. That's all I need to know. I have a teenage daughter, so I'm already drowning in TMI moments, as Annie calls them. Don't need my players adding to it."*

I'm watching Brody now, trying to read something in the impassive expression he's wearing. His jaw is tense, and I can tell he's intentionally not looking at me.

The interviewer names a couple more pitchers, and Dad gives some positive feedback. With a few, it's obvious he's rattling off stats and not commenting on anything personal because I doubt he works with them at all. By the time he's done talking about players, we're fifteen minutes into the program and finally it's someone else's turn to be under scrutiny. Brody stands up and nods toward the door out of the locker room. I grab my bag, say a quiet good-bye to Savannah, and follow Brody.

"Still want to come over for a little while?" he asks when we've walked out of the stadium doors.

"Yeah, okay."

The car ride to Brody's apartment is free of smiles and innuendos about removing my skirt. His silence is nerve-racking. The bad vibe continues as he opens the door to his apartment and quietly tells me he's going to take a shower and to get whatever I want from the kitchen, since neither of us touched our pizza.

He hasn't touched me or made any comments about jumping in the shower with him or laid down rules about us being good while alone in his apartment. The only thing I can bring myself to eat is a banana I find on the counter. I pace back and forth, making paths with my feet and the patterned kitchen tiles until Brody returns wearing only gym shorts, his black hair dripping. I freeze and hold my breath, the half-eaten banana hanging limply in my hand.

"What's wrong?" I manage to say.

He looks so sad and defeated, I'm sure he's about to dump me. I don't understand why, and yet it kind of feels like the inevitable conclusion, considering everything.

It will be easier this way. I'm so far gone, I've lost control of my own heart.

He walks slowly toward me, takes the banana from my hand, sets it on the counter, and leads me to his bedroom. Is this the breakup room? I've never been in his room. It has to be bad news. We could easily make out on the couch; it's not like we haven't already done that.

The bed is unmade, and clothes are strewn all over the floor, mostly T-shirts and different Royals merchandise with tags still on them. With a bedside table and a lamp, this is the most furnished room in the entire apartment.

Long, dark curtains cover almost an entire wall. Looking for a distraction from the bad news, I drop his hand and cross the room, shifting the dark blue curtains aside. On the other side is a sliding glass door and a beautiful balcony overlooking the stadium with its famous crown.

"Wow," I say, hoping to divert his attention. "How did I not know this was here?" I open the door and step outside, heading straight for the railing. I lean against the metal, keeping my gaze focused on the stadium and the city lights. I'm literally digging for excuses, for ways to wipe that sad expression off his face.

The warmth of Brody's body invades my personal space. He leans against me, his cheek touching mine, his hands drifting down my arms.

"This view's amazing," I say, trying to conceal my nerves.

He turns his head just enough so his nose brushes my cheek. "Best spot in the whole apartment."

I take a deep breath and focus on the beautiful lights. "Brody—"

His lips brush against my neck, cutting off my words. *Okay, not breakup moves.* "We should go in," he whispers.

My heart is sprinting, and I shuffle my feet backward as I'm pulled through the door, curtains closing behind us. And this isn't the mad rush to touch as much skin as possible like we did in the car last time. He's looking me over carefully, still wearing those sad eyes, while his fingers glide at a snail's pace under my school polo. My heart is aching already, a physical pain spreading across my chest.

When did we get like this? When did it stop being about having fun and sneaking around?

Who am I kidding? It's never been about that. Exactly why I'm so scared right now.

My shirt is slowly raised over my head, landing lightly on the floor. Since Brody's philosophy of openness has worked well in the past, I attempt to start up a discussion regarding his shift in mood. "Do you think we should talk about—"

He shakes his head and pulls me against him, skin-to-skin. I open my mouth to speak again, but he cuts me off with a kiss so gentle and so intense at the same time that I can tell he needs something from me words can't offer. And I think I need this, too. I know I do.

His skilled fingers find the button and the zipper on my skirt, and soon it's landing at my feet, leaving me standing in my underwear and bra. I tug the waist of his gym shorts until they, too, fall around his ankles, giving me a view of his black Calvin Klein boxer briefs. Our eyes lock again, and just to be sure we take things further than last time, I tug my panties down until they're on top of my skirt. Brody shuffles back a step, draws in a breath, and then *his* underwear are on the floor and he's laying me across the bed.

And even though we're both nearly naked, I'm not thinking about sex. Not specifically. I just want him to touch me—with his hands, with his mouth—and I want to touch him.

I nudge him gently until he rolls all the way on his back. The lamp beside the bed is on, casting a dim light over us. I muster up the courage to let my gaze travel south, taking in his very erect…*yeah.*

I move my hand down his chest, pausing to feel his pounding heart, then down over his abs and eventually, *lower*. His breath quickens just from that small touch, and an instant surge of power comes over me. I want to drive him crazy. I want him to keep thinking about this for hours, maybe days, after I leave.

I take hold of him, but loosely enough to make this more of an examination and less of a hand job. The skin is stretched tight, and I can feel a pulse beating against my hand.

Warm fingers are gliding up my back, fiddling with my bra clasp. Cool air brushes against my skin, and Brody tugs the straps down my arms, forcing me to let go for a second. My gaze lowers, and I'm thinking about going for it, but I've only done this one time before and it wasn't the most pleasant experience.

I can't stop my mind from calculating this, being relieved that he's fresh out of the shower and everything is squeaky clean. It's not the most romantic thoughts a person could have in this situation, but I can't help it.

Brody touches my cheek. He seems so calm, not in that urgent kiss-me-or-I'll-die mode, but he's obviously turned on and into this. I can see *that* with my own eyes. "Annie…what's going through that head of yours?"

"You ask me that a lot." I return my hand to its previous location, enjoying the feel of his smooth skin. "It's usually a girl question, you know?"

He rolls his eyes. "Just tell me what you're thinking about."

"I'm thinking about putting my mouth where my hand is right now."

His eyebrows shoot up, but he says nothing. Maybe he's afraid to encourage me. His fingers trace gentle circles down my arm. His patience, the lack of pressure, relaxes me enough to share my concerns.

"This one time — well, the only time I've done that…" *Breathe in. Breathe out.* "I didn't get any warning before — you know — and I'm not sure I'm ready for that. Maybe you can warn me —"

"Okay," he says so quickly I know he wants me to do this. I lower my head and slide him into my mouth before I can change my mind. I expect some kind of bad taste or at least an odd one, but I only get a hint of water from the shower and maybe a little bit of soap.

Within seconds he's completely tensed up, breathing irregularly, both hands tangled in my hair. I stop after only thirty seconds, feeling a little guilty for starting something that I'm not willing to finish. But Brody doesn't seem frustrated. His eyes are wide, his chest rising and falling quickly. I lay my head beside him and allow him to shower me with dozens of kisses landing in nearly all the spaces between my neck and my waist. His fingers dance around the inside of my thighs for a while before he finally makes his move.

Without giving it a second thought, my hand is reaching out, wrapping around him, stroking up and down, until we both tip over the edge at almost the same time.

We lay there for several moments, slowly climbing back down to reality. Then Brody grabs a tissue and cleans himself off before pulling me into his arms.

My cheek sticks to his sweaty chest, but I love hearing his heart drumming against my ear, trying to slow down. He pushes the hair off my face and kisses my forehead, leaving his mouth against my skin. I sigh and fall deeper into this sleepy, relaxed haze, all the bad from earlier washed away.

Best. Not sex. Ever.

"Annie?"

"Uh-huh," I mumble, closing my eyes.

"I have to tell your dad."

My eyes fly open, and my heart jumps to my throat. "What? Why?"

He pulls up to a sitting position, and I do the same. "It's the right thing to do. Watching that show today, hearing the way he talked about me…I feel like I'm living a lie, and it's starting to eat at me."

I'm breathing hard, thinking of a way out, some magic words to fix this. He can't tell Dad. He just can't. I feel like I'm trying to talk a suicidal man off a ledge. Stall.

It would almost be easier if he just dumped me now. And Dad would never have to know.

"Okay," I say, nodding. "Maybe you're right. But not right now, when the season is hitting its peak. We could wait until October when everything's over."

"There's no we." He shakes his head. "I'm taking the hit for this one. I have to. But you're right, I can wait until the end of the season and then flee the country until spring training if he decides to kills me."

Now I get the reason for the sad eyes. He thinks telling Dad will be the end of it, but who's deciding that? Him or Dad? Obviously my dad's not going to give his blessing, so that must be enough for Brody to take off and be done with us? And why does this freak me out? Isn't this what I want? *No, I don't think it's what I want.*

My stomach churns and tears threaten to form. I can't push for these details now because he's agreed to wait. I can't start a fight about how it's my choice, too. He's not going to see it that way.

I've got time to come up with a new plan. "After the last game, then you'll talk to him."

He leans forward and kisses me on the mouth. "I'm sorry to dump it on you like this. That show, hearing that someone in my life thinks of me as a respectable person, a good person, even… That's not something I've been told in a long time, and I don't want to lose that part of me."

"I think you're a good person," I say quietly, before slipping off the bed to retrieve my clothes.

He exhales, and his eyes meet mine. "All I know is that I want to be the person you and your dad think I am. Maybe even more than I want to be a great pitcher."

I take a deep breath, pulling my skirt back on. Stopping him from telling Dad is going to be a much more difficult task than I'd anticipated.

division
CHAMPIONSHIPS

chapter 25

Annie Lucas: *Looking forward to a weekend in the Windy City but hoping late September doesn't mean cold weather?*
8 hours ago

Jason Brody Royals Pitcher: *Still can't believe we're in the running for division champions! The White Sox are a great club, will be a tough match, but I know we can win!*
4 hours ago

Lenny London: *Annie Lucas has yet to shop with Lenny London. She's about to get her mind blown. Magnificent Mile, here we come.*
20 minutes ago

"What kind of activity could possibly be better than shopping in Chicago?" Lenny says, turning to face me in the car that's taken us from O'Hare airport to Michigan Avenue. "Please tell me this is not a secret boyfriend meet-up?"

Lenny's still a bit sensitive about the Jason-Brody-is-my-boyfriend issue since her dad caught us in the backyard, but luckily he's never brought it up to her again and Brody says he doesn't treat him any differently. I think Lenny is hurt more by the fact that he didn't get upset or want more details or at least threaten Brody.

I wring my hands in my lap. I've been planning this adventure for a few weeks (and it's involved lots of sneaking into Savannah's desk and file folders and other James Bond–like missions), but I'm still petrified and afraid I'm gonna chicken out.

"It's a boyfriend-related activity," I say. "But he's not actually involved in it."

Lenny manages to lift her eyebrows, revealing her curiosity, and lets out a frustrated sigh at the same time. "Please tell me you aren't going to a free clinic for birth control or something, because I can totally hook you up with a doctor who won't give details to Daddy if that's what you need."

I stare at her face for an entire minute, trying to decide if I can really explain my mission. I finally conclude that the free clinic theory is worse than the truth. "There's something I need to get from Brody's mom, and she lives in the suburbs."

Surprise fills her face. "Did he ask you to do this?"

I shake my head. "He doesn't talk to her. She's kind of shunned him."

"Oh boy." Lenny sinks back into her seat. "Okay, fuck it. Let's do your activity. This should be interesting, at least."

It's raining when we reach Brody's mom's apartment in Evanston. I know from what he's told me that they used to live in Chicago, so she's moved since he left home. I don't know why or how Savannah had her address, and since I snagged it without permission, I couldn't exactly ask.

Lenny and I are both soaked through to our tennis shoes, having walked four blocks after getting off the El train. Her teeth are chattering as I hit the buzzer on the outside of the building door. "She better be here, or I'm going to be extremely pissed at you," she says.

"Yes?" a female voice says through the intercom.

Before I can answer, a man pushes past us and holds the door open. Lenny takes it and nods for me to walk through. I hesitate but eventually follow her, because I'm not exactly sure what to say to the woman on the other side of the intercom to get her to let us into the building.

We take the stairs, traveling up to the third floor, and knock on apartment 3-B. A few seconds later, the door opens a couple inches and a woman slightly older than my dad, with dark Hispanic features and long beautiful hair, peeks through the space.

"Hi," I say, and then freeze until Lenny elbows me in the side. "Are you Jason Brody's mother?"

I hear her gasp from behind the door, and then she opens it all the way, her eyes fluttering shut. "He's dead, isn't he? I knew this day would come—"

"What the hell," Lenny mutters under her breath.

"We're not cops or whatever." I shake my head, trying to keep up with this odd turn of events. "We're in high school."

"But we know your son," Lenny adds.

"If he needs money, I'm not helping him," she says firmly, her fingers curled around the edge of the door, ready to close it. "I can't help him. I have two other children who haven't screwed up their lives. He's on his own now."

Already my anger is hitting a boiling point. Obviously, she has no idea who her son is and what he's been doing for the past months. Or years, maybe? "He doesn't need money. And now I see why he hasn't called you to ask for this information himself."

With great reluctance, the responsible teacher's aid in her winning out, I'm sure, she opens the door even more, allowing us to step inside the apartment. It's full of worn furniture, but everything looks nice and neat. There's a definite scent in the air of home-cooked meals and freshly laundered clothes—things I'm sure Brody misses, especially knowing the state of his bare apartment and fridge full of meals cooked in someone else's kitchen.

Lenny and I stand in the living room, watching her close the door and turn to face us, foot tapping like she's got somewhere better to be. It breaks my heart. How awful of a son could he have been and still turn into the kind person I know?

"Brody—I mean Jason," I say, "wants to take his GED, but he needs proof of his dyslexia diagnosis so he can take an oral exam."

"And now it makes sense why he didn't want to ask you for it," Lenny concludes, stealing the words straight from my head.

She folds her arms across her chest, but she's not fooling me. I can see this request has surprised her. "That's all?"

I blow air out of my cheeks. "That's all."

She spins around and takes off down the hallway. Literally sixty seconds later, she returns holding out a manila folder full of white papers labeled: JASON'S SCHOOL RECORDS. She moves toward the door, opens it a couple inches, and waits. Lenny heads for the exit, but I stay put. "Don't you want to know where he is? Or what he's doing? You don't care?"

Her mouth forms a thin line. "I can't care about him at the detriment of my other children. When your oldest child brings gangbangers into your home, steals from you, and leaves you in fear for your family's lives so much that you have to move and disconnect from everyone you knew before, get a new job...It changes my ability to forgive."

Lenny looks at me and mouths, *Gangbangers?* I shrug because I've really not heard anything about that part. Brody never said anything about being in a gang. I think she's exaggerating, but either way, he didn't try to intentionally hurt anyone, so some part of her has to be worried about him.

"And I'm too afraid to even ask why, at nineteen years old, he's associated with high school girls," she adds with a shake of her head.

I'm so pissed off I can't bite my tongue and leave like I know I should. "My dad is a pitching coach for the Kansas City Royals. He coaches your son. And Lenny"—I nod in her direction—"is the daughter of the Royals' first baseman. Brody's a pitcher. A major league baseball pitcher. Possibly Rookie of the Year. Do you not read the papers ever? Or turn on ESPN?"

Her mouth falls open and, after a lengthy hesitation, she nods. "He's playing baseball. I guess that makes sense."

I scowl at her, remembering how Brody said she'd look down on it, like he'd taken the easy road. "Yeah, he's playing baseball. He's also an incredibly selfless, hard-working person who has a very hard time believing that people might actually think highly of him."

"I wonder why that is?" Lenny says.

We make an awesome tag team.

I reach in my purse and hand her a white envelope. "Tickets to the game tomorrow. We're playing the White Sox for the division championships. Your son is pitching."

There's really nothing left to say, so we both head out the door and run the entire four blocks back to the El train. It's not until we're sitting down that Lenny says, "That was a very purposeful activity."

"And successful." I pat my stomach where I've stuffed the folder under my shirt and jacket to keep it from getting ruined in the rain. "I can't decide if I want her to show up at the game or not. Maybe she doesn't deserve to see him."

"Do you think he was really in a gang?" Lenny asks.

I shake my head. "No way. He had rough friends and his mom probably called them gangbangers, but I don't think he'd be able to get away from them so easily, right?" As if I actually know how gangs work.

After Lenny and I get checked in at the front desk of our hotel, we head up to our room that she booked for us, and I nearly faint when I see the fancy two-bedroom suite. "Wow, are you really that much of an attention seeker, Len? Trying to piss off Mom and Dad?"

She laughs and tosses her suitcase on the bed in one of the bedrooms. "I think you're under the impression that my parents pay any attention to what I charge on my credit card and that my mother could ever fathom the idea of not booking a luxury suite when staying in a hotel."

After I'd begged to see the playoffs in Chicago, it had actually been Dad's idea for me to invite Lenny. Lenny agreed to let him pay for the flight if she could pick up the hotel tab. Of course, we fly for free on the team's chartered flight.

I text Brody and give him the room number, telling him I have a surprise for him. I'd been afraid to tell him about my mission but hadn't thought it'd be a problem once I'd already done the task.

Lenny lets him in and, after whistling at the size of our suite, he takes in our soaked clothes. He laughs and reaches over to squeeze water from the ends of my hair. "Guess the shopping didn't go to well?"

"Actually…" I pick up the folder from the coffee table and hand it over to him. "We didn't go shopping."

He doesn't even open it, just sees the label on the side and his jaw tenses. "Where did you get this?"

I suck in a breath and step back. This isn't the happy kind of surprise. Lenny throws me a wary glance and heads for the bedroom she's already picked out, closing the door behind her.

"I…uh…I went to see your mom. I knew you didn't want to call her, and I just wanted you to be able to take your test."

His glare is like pain shooting right into my heart. He throws the folder back onto the table. "You had no right to do that, Annie. Why wouldn't you ask me first?"

I had a pretty sucky time walking in the rain to find his mom, so I'm not exactly excited about being yelled at. "Because you would have said no and honestly, you're being completely stupid, letting her keep you from living your life! One of us had to do something."

"You're right, I would have said no." He lowers his voice, making him sound more cold and angry.

I lift up my hands. "Well, I've already done it, so the only thing you really can do is move on and take the damn test. And just so you know, I gave her tickets to the game tomorrow, too."

He steps farther away from me, shaking his head. "You don't get it, do you? If you told me not to butt into your life, I'd never go behind your back. I trust you."

"If you trust me, then what's the problem? I did what I thought was best for you."

"I trust you to ask me for help when you need it. To accept it when I offer, to understand that I'll do the same if I need your input," he says, disappointment and frustration filling each word. "I'm serious about us, and now I can see that you don't feel the same way."

I groan and try to move closer, but he holds up a hand to stop me. "Of course I feel the same way; don't be crazy."

"I've never treated you like a kid, Annie, but it's fucking hard not to when you keep acting like one. Like you don't care how your actions affect other people. You just take off in a sprint and don't look back. That shit scares me." He shakes his head. "That was my life before this—impulsive and destructive. I can't be that person anymore. I won't."

I stand there stunned, watching him walk out the door and slam it shut. I sink down onto the couch and try to figure out what the hell just happened. Lenny opens her bedroom door and slowly reenters the room.

"Are you okay?"

My hands are shaking, but it's more anger than anything else. How could he think that I don't care? That I'm not constantly trying to make his life better? I look up at Lenny, my eyes wide. "Did we just break up?"

chapter 26

"Where's Brody?" Savannah turns around and glances back into the hotel lobby. "I thought he was coming to dinner with us?"

I bite back an angry and completely invalid response and plop down on the steps in front of the circle drive, not caring if my dress gets dirty. Dad joins Savannah in looking around for Brody while one of the other pitchers in our group starts laughing.

"I think he's busy picking up chicks in the bar on the top floor."

Lenny glances warily at me, then snaps at the pitcher, "How do you know that?"

"Some girl just tweeted a picture," he says, shaking a finger in front of Lenny's face.

She pulls out her phone immediately, but I tuck my hands underneath me, forcing myself to steer clear of Twitter pictures of my maybe-ex-boyfriend who's pissed at me for helping him with something he didn't have the balls to do himself. Screw that.

"He's not coming," I shout at Dad and Savannah. "Can we

go already? I'm starving."

Both of them spin around to face me, and Dad says, "What's with you?"

I'm scowling at no one in particular, so Lenny hooks her arm through mine, pulling me to my feet. "She's not cut out for shopping with me, that's all. I wouldn't let her stop for ice cream or Cinnabon."

"Yeah, it was just one disappointment after another," I say.

I don't think I fooled anyone, but they decide to leave me alone for now. Lenny sits next to me in the car on the way to the restaurant.

All through dinner, Dad and Savannah keep bringing up Jason Brody and how awesome he is, how impressed Larry Johnson is with the endorsements he's been getting and his potential for being awarded Rookie of the Year. I just sit there stabbing my steak and stuffing so much food in my mouth, I won't be expected to chime in.

It's not that I'm not hurt and fighting the urge to cry over a tub of ice cream and charge chick flicks from the hotel room TV to Lenny's parents' credit card—I am. But it's easier to let anger dominate. Anger I can deal with. A broken heart is something I haven't experienced yet. Besides, what are my options? Apologize? I'm not sorry for helping him. I'm not sorry for caring, for defending him to his mom. That's fucking stupid.

"Oh, look," Third Base says during dinner, holding his phone out to Lenny and me. "He's getting mobbed in the lobby. Maybe we shouldn't have left him alone?"

"I doubt he's alone." I poke my steak again. *Stab, stab, stab.* "And I'm sure he'll be fine."

wasn't even going to go to the game. And now that Brody is finally entering during the sixth inning, I'm really wishing I had listened to my angry girlfriend voice.

Lenny elbows me in the side. "You should probably wipe that scowl off your face before the camera swivels in our direction."

My cheeks relax, but I'm still cursing Brody inside my head. Why did he have to throw the one insult at me that I can't handle—calling me a child? It's what I've been afraid of since we first became friends. Maybe ever since I dropped my notebook in the locker room and got his attention.

"That's better." Lenny passes a giant bag of popcorn from her lap to mine.

I busy myself stuffing handful after handful into my mouth while Brody warms up. He's fumbling the ball like I've never seen him do before. The popcorn lodges in my throat, my fingers freezing inside the bag—something's wrong.

This is worse than his warm-up on opening day. But we're up by three runs. That's a small cushion for error, at least.

Seven pitches later, Brody has walked the White Sox batter, and Dad is now pacing in the dugout. What the hell? Dad never paces. His nervous position is always the motionless statue Dad. Is he angry? Worried?

Jesus Christ. Can't I just get one day to be pissed off at my boyfriend and not have to worry about Brody's or Dad's jobs? Is that too much to ask?

Brody's gaze is locked on the field. He's not even attempting to glance toward the stands where Lenny and I are seated near the third base line. And he's definitely not looking toward the empty seats that would belong to his mother, had she decided to come and see her son play.

No, don't go feeling sorry for him. You're pissed, remember?

Brody's next pitch is straight over the plate but not fast enough. The crack of the bat against the ball causes my stomach to sink. The ball soars way out toward center. Seconds later, Brody ends up with the ball again and the job of stopping the runner he walked earlier from advancing to third. He completely overthrows and sends Third Base scrambling for the ball behind him.

The error gives just enough room for the White Sox runner to take off for home plate. Brody darts forward to help the catcher cover home plate, but it's too late.

The White Sox score, and they've got a runner on second base.

I stare at the giant stadium screen, my mouth hanging open in shock while Brody's shitty throw to third is replayed over and over, along with the White Sox runner's slide into home plate.

Oh God, what did I do? I rattled him. This is my fault. I know it's my fault.

I toss the popcorn back at Lenny so I can wring my hands in my lap.

Brody takes the mound again, the cheers in the stadium erupting to an ear-damaging level. They stop replaying Brody's error, and the camera zooms in on his face. There are hints of fear and panic on Brody's face that I haven't seen from him before.

He draws in a breath, gripping the ball in his right hand. I run my palms over my jeans, wiping off the sweat. Brody's next pitch is a bad attempt at a curveball. Frank throws his hands up in the air and Dad finally stops pacing.

Oh God. I just screwed over the team. They're gonna lose this game and then the White Sox are going to advance to the next round...

Brody shakes off the call from the catcher twice before pitching. It's right down the strike zone and a little too slow for the batter to miss. He sends a line drive toward the mound. I gasp, my hand flying up to cover my mouth as the ball smacks Brody right in the chest.

My heart pounds, and panic floods through my veins.

Brody reacts immediately, obvious pain on his face, but he scoops up the ball and makes the throw to first before dropping to his knees.

I jump to my feet, looking around for a way down to the field. Lenny pulls me back to reality, grabbing my shirt and tugging until I'm in my seat again.

"You can't go down there," she says in a low voice and with a level of concern that surprises me.

The umpire calls a time-out, while Dad, Frank, several players, and the team doctor gather around the mound. Brody is rubbing his chest, still kneeling but attempting to stand. Dad presses on his shoulders to keep him in place.

Oh God, oh God, oh God. "This is my fault," I mumble, not meaning to speak out loud.

"No, Annie," Lenny says right away. "Stop it."

But no matter what logic I come up with, I can't untie the huge knot of guilt forming in my stomach.

Finally, after what feels like hours, Brody gets to his feet, and Frank calls another pitcher in from the bullpen. I sigh with relief when Brody manages to walk unassisted to the dugout, and my eyes never leave him the rest of the game. He keeps his head down, and his hand continues to periodically rub his chest where the ball hit him. I don't even know the final score until Lenny and I are walking up the steps to exit the stadium. I glance over my shoulder and look while the scoreboard is still in view.

We won. The Royals are officially in a pennant race.

Later on, when we're back at the hotel, I still don't know for sure if we broke up or not. I'm still pissed at him. I don't understand his argument, and I truly believe it's pride and embarrassment that caused him to lash out, but that doesn't stop me from jumping to my feet and heading out the door when he texts me again an hour later.

BRODY: I'm in room 518 if u want to talk.

chapter 27

The door to Brody's room swings open, and yes, I feel super guilty still about rattling him for the game today, but I'm ready to argue again. I'm ready to make him see my side of it. To make sure he knows that I'd do a lot more for him than go behind his back and contact his mom for information. I'd make a lot of sacrifices for this boy, and that should mean something to him. He said I wasn't taking us seriously, but maybe I'm the one who's in too deep?

Brody leans against the doorframe, his expression unreadable. "Savannah sends her money every month," he says quietly.

All the words and sentences I'd rehearsed in the elevator fall away. "Who? Your mom? What for?"

He nods and then opens the door to let me in. I shuffle in behind him, and after we're in the privacy of his room, he answers my questions. "Last year, my stepdad and my sister were in a car accident. They're okay, but they've been through a lot of surgeries and rehab. Since the accident was his fault, there wasn't much insurance coverage. I tried to go home and visit after I found out about the car crash, but she told me to stay away, that she'd just moved and was finally free of my bad connections. When I signed my official contract with the Royals, I told Savannah that I wanted to help but knew my mom would never let me. Savannah made up an organization that offered financial help to public school employees who have overwhelming medical bills."

I'm stunned to silence and finally croak out a couple words. "So she doesn't know where the money comes from?" *Obviously. He's said that twice already.*

"I'm guessing she probably does now." He looks down at his hands. My heart is pounding, knowing I might have really screwed up. "But I know your heart was in the right place. It's just frustrating not to be able to help like I can. I have money now. Way more than I need."

I stand near the end of the bed, my legs turning to jelly. How could something be so clear one minute and then present a completely different picture the next? "You think she won't take the money anymore?"

He laughs bitterly. "If I know my mom well enough, she's probably going to attempt to return the money I've already sent."

My face must reflect the horror I feel because Brody moves closer and touches my hair. "This wouldn't have happened if I'd told you more, so stop looking like you've just murdered a dozen kittens."

"Maybe," I say, trying to free myself of the guilt. But in truth, telling me something like this would have been risky. I don't need to know what he does with his money. Unless he wants me to know, and I have to assume that he'll say something if this is the case— *Oh God...*

An overwhelming sense of dread hits me, accompanying the

truth of what I've done. And then my eyes latch onto a huge gift basket placed in the center of his king-size bed. Right on top of the candy and snacks only young bachelors would enjoy is a big box of condoms. My eyes widen, my heart speeding up, my mouth falling open, but no words exit.

Brody follows my gaze and tenses immediately. "Those are not— I mean, they're a gift; I didn't buy them, and if I had, it would be for us, not anyone else."

A hundred emotions hit me all at once, and I sit down on the edge of the bed, covering my face with my hands. *Oh God. Condoms...*

Brody squats down in front of me, prying my hands from my face. "Hey, what's wrong?"

"I lied to you." I can't meet his gaze. "You trusted me. You got me to talk about stuff and be upfront and I lied. I told you I've done everything at least once, and I haven't."

He stiffens, but I can tell he's trying not to show any signs of shock. "Sex...we're talking about sex, right?"

"Yeah." I chance a glimpse into his now very wide brown eyes as he exhales and inhales a couple times.

He stands up and takes a seat beside me on the bed. "Let me get this straight—you're a virgin?" I nod and hold back the long speech I delivered to Lenny regarding my opinions on this definition. He grips the footboard with both hands. "Okay, I did not see that one coming. I mean, I was surprised when you told me you weren't, but since then—"

"I'm sorry." I don't know why, but I suddenly feel like crying. "I'm just really scared right now," I say as a feeble attempt to explain the tears.

Brody turns me to face him. "Scared of what, Annie? I'd never rush you into something you're not comfortable with.

Please tell me you know that by now? I think I'd hate myself if you were this upset over having to say no."

I hear the frustration he's biting back, probably because I'm so visibly upset. "I'm not scared of that. I'm scared that you aren't going to believe me if I say I'm ready. That you're always going to wonder if I'm lying or if I'm acting out of impulse and not thinking things through." I meet his eyes again. "I'm scared that I ruined everything, that I'm too young for you, and that if I tell you I love you, there's no way it will mean what it does when you say it to me."

He draws in a quick breath after I spill that last part. I can't believe I said it out loud. Brody stares at me for the length of two heartbeats, and then he moves closer and wraps his arms around me. I'm trying to catch my breath and stop crying, but for some reason my cheek against his chest brings the full-on sobs.

"Annie," he whispers into my hair. "If you weren't ready to be with me, then you wouldn't be this upset about lying. Or about what happened with my mom."

I turn my head, pushing my face against his shirt. "You're right. We have to tell my dad." That's what people who are serious about their relationships do.

"Yeah, we do." He tightens his hold on me, planting a kiss on the side of my face. "This is really hard for you, isn't it? You're afraid of ending up like him, not being able to let go?"

I answer by wiping more tears onto his shirt.

"I know I'm quite a catch, but you'd never stay hung up on me forever." He laughs against my hair. "Probably not even half of forever. Controlling everything isn't going to make it easier to let go. That's what you're doing, you know? Keeping the ball in your court."

My arms go around his neck, and I give him a tight squeeze before standing up. I lift the bottom of my Royals T-shirt and wipe my face with it one last time. "I don't want to be that way anymore. I'm trying, I promise."

"Okay." He gives me a half smile and lifts my palm to his lips. "That's good enough for me."

I sniff again, laughing a little. "Why am I always crying? I never used to cry."

He pushes up to his feet. "Do you want me to cry, too? Will that help? And where are you going?"

I've taken a few steps toward the door, and I'm reaching for the handle now. "Back to my room. I figured you'd want me to leave, since…" *I don't know what I'm saying now. I'm confused. Did we break up? Are we back together? Does he not want me now that he knows I'm a virgin?*

He leans against the door, preventing me from exiting. "What are you really scared of? I'll give you this one free-access pass. I'll believe whatever you tell me, but think before you speak."

I take a deep breath. "I love you. I really think it's true, but I'm afraid you'll never see me as anything but the reckless kid who ruined things with your mom. That I'll never be an adult in your eyes."

Brody slides closer, leaving very little space between us. "I said those things because I got scared and then angry, Annie. I didn't mean them." He picks up a strand of my hair, twirling it around his finger. "I promise…I don't think of you as a kid right now."

I swallow back my nerves. I need to show him I'm old enough to know what I want. "I want this…you and me…together."

Brody keeps his eyes locked with mine and raises a hand,

sliding the chain over the lock. Then he tugs me by the waist until we're pressed together. My heart thuds so loudly the second his mouth meets mine.

The kiss is slow at first, and then it's deep and I'm being lifted off the ground. I wrap my legs around Brody's waist, and his hands are sliding under my shirt. He pauses, breathing hard, gripping me tightly, lips on my neck. "You can change your mind anytime. I won't be upset, I promise. I'll only be upset if you change your mind and don't tell me."

I answer him by bringing my mouth to his again, tangling my fingers in his hair. He drops me onto the bed, shoving the gift basket to the floor. Our clothes fall on top of it, one article at a time. When I finally get a good look at Brody's chest, I gently trace the red welt where the baseball hit him. It's already bruising. "I nearly had a heart attack at the game…"

Brody surprises me by smiling. "Yeah, my head went somewhere else. I need to work on that."

I touch my lips to his. "Or we can just never fight again so you have nothing to distract you or throw you off."

The smile fades from his face, and he presses our foreheads together, closing his eyes. "We're going to be adults about this and tell your dad tomorrow, okay? No more sneaking around."

This time, I don't try to stall or manipulate him out of this plan. I nod and swallow back a gallon of fear. "No more sneaking around," I agree.

Brody grins. "After tonight."

"After tonight…"

This isn't like last month in his apartment when he laid back and let me lead the expedition. It's obvious who's in charge, and maybe this is his way of testing me, knowing I need to practice handing over control.

Brody pauses after spending several minutes kissing my neck. He lifts his head and hovers over me, our foreheads almost touching. "Stop thinking so much. I can hear your brain turning in circles."

I reach up and take his face in my hands. "I'm sorry. I'm just a little…"

"Nervous?" he finishes. I bite my lip, afraid he's going to stop this activity, and I don't want that, either. "You trust me, right?"

I take several seconds to think over what that really means. I trust him to do what? Hold my wallet without stealing anything? Throw a baseball at me without giving me a concussion? Love me and never stop loving me? There are so many levels of trust—I can't commit to the word as a whole.

"I trust you with some things, just not everything…yet," I add.

"Good answer." He smiles and leans down to kiss my lips. "Trust me to make sure you enjoy this, okay? That's my job, but you have to let me have it. It's like handing over the remote control and trusting me to pick a show you like."

I give a nervous laugh. "I hate the History channel. And it's your favorite."

He's back to working his mouth down my neck and over my collarbone. "I have a feeling we'll have no problem finding mutual ground tonight."

I run my hands through his hair, combing through it and anticipating whatever he has planned next. I'm not going to think. Just feel.

He slides down to my body, kissing me in all the right places, causing me to breathe more loudly than I'd like. And then his hands join his mouth in exploring my body.

My hands grow tingly, my toes going numb. I let go of Brody's hair and grip the sheets, my eyelids falling. His lips drift down my stomach and eventually touch the inside of my thigh. I didn't really anticipate his mouth going *there*. But I'm too caught up in the feeling, the intensity, to worry.

My entire body is hot and buzzing. I'm trying to hold off, to not be as easy to carry across the finish line, but a minute later, I'm balling the sheets in my hands and clamping my jaw shut to prevent making any embarrassing sounds as I race to the finish.

Colors light up behind my eyes—possibly from lack of oxygen—and my limbs turn to jelly. I feel like I've taken Vicodin or drank a few glasses of wine—relaxed and fuzzy.

Brody takes a condom from the box and rolls it over himself.

Before I can even think about what's happening or tense up and make it a difficult task, he slides carefully inside me. I feel some pulling and stretching, but it's not painful like I've heard from other people. Brody holds my face with one hand, trying to get my attention. He smiles at me. "You're still in there, right?"

I return the smile and wrap my arms around him, pulling his mouth to mine. He's moving slowly, probably not wanting to hurt me, and I'm so filled with emotion, it's like I can't turn it off. But this isn't the life-changing moment like people always say. For us, I think our big moment happened at the lake that night and then in his car and his bedroom…

The more I love him, the better all the physical stuff gets.

Later on, in the bathroom, I clean up and snatch the white terry cloth hotel robe from the back of the bathroom door and wrap it around me.

Brody's lying across the bed, wearing his usual black boxer

briefs. He smiles and tugs my hand, pulling me down next to him.

"You look really happy for someone who had an off game and got hit with a hundred-and-thirty-mile-per-hour baseball," I say.

"It sucked," he admits. "But mostly because I didn't feel like you were there with me, you know? And if I have that, then I can handle all the other stuff."

Okay, so he hasn't said he loves me even though I said it to him, but *that*…that's kinda better. It's real. "And if you manage to throw a little faster next time…" I tease.

His eyebrows shoot up, and he flips me over onto my back, pinning my arms above my head. My heartbeat speeds up, my breath quickening. "Faster, huh? Just like that?"

"Isn't that what they pay you to do?" It feels great to get back to being us. At least until tomorrow when we talk to Dad. That's gonna be…Yeah, I'm not thinking about it yet.

Brody puts his full weight on top of me, kissing me hard, flinging the sides of the hotel robe open so our skin can touch.

The phone in the hotel room rings, startling both of us. Brody glances at it, then returns his focus to my face.

"Don't you need to answer that?" I ask. "Even though you practically got knocked out today, we did still win, and we're going to the playoffs. I bet everyone wants to celebrate with you and interview you."

He leans down and kisses me again. "It can wait until morning. And I *am* celebrating, aren't you?"

I laugh and nod at the same time. "Totally."

And yeah, everything else can wait until morning.

My eyes open at eight the next morning. I'm still in the white robe in Brody's bed, the blankets covering half my body. I feel him beside me, but he's not lying down. He's sitting up, looking freshly showered, wearing gym shorts and listening to his iPhone.

He runs a hand over my hair. "Hey…"

"Hey." I shift over so my head is resting on his legs. "Please tell me you have Diet Coke hiding somewhere in this room. I'm going to die if I don't get one in the next two minutes."

He laughs and picks up the phone beside him. "Don't worry. I've been assigned a personal assistant to fetch me whatever I need." I wait while he punches in a number and requests Diet Coke for his room and then hangs up. "He said five minutes. Is that gonna be too late?"

"I'll try to make it. No promises." I sit up, straddling his lap and wrapping my arms around his neck. My hands explore his chest and my lips head straight for his neck, preventing any morning-breath exposure. Four minutes later, I slide off the bed and head toward the bathroom. When I exit sixty seconds later, the Diet Coke guy is knocking at the door.

I glance at Brody and grin. "He's good. You should tip him well."

Brody leaps off the bed and heads for his wallet on the table beside the door. While he's digging for cash, I unlatch the chain, staying half behind the door when I open it.

"Hey, Brody, we were just…" Savannah's voice trails off.

Oh shit, oh shit. My heart takes off in a sprint, but my entire body freezes up. Brody's standing in front of the door, the ten dollar bill hanging limply in one hand.

"I told you it was too early," I hear Dad say.

Omigod, omigod. Say something, Brody! Tell them you're

busy.

"Just wanted to check in with you after the game," Dad continues. "You know it happens—"

He stops midsentence, and the silence that follows is so long and eerie I almost pass out from stress and holding my breath. But before that happens, I realize way too late that my foot is in plain sight. My silver ankle bracelet Dad gave me for my thirteenth birthday is also in plain sight.

"Annie?"

chapter 28

The door swings toward me—Brody's fingers have no chance of keeping their grip against that force, and I have no choice but to dive out of the way, leaving me standing in front of Dad and Savannah.

Oh shit, oh shit.

I'm in a half-opened robe. Brody's wearing only gym shorts, and we both have the appearance of two people who've recently woken up. Together.

My heart jumps up to my throat, my airway suddenly constricted like something's lodged in it. Brody exhales and swears in Spanish under his breath. And now the uniformed hotel employee has appeared with two bottles of Diet Coke. Savannah is front and center, her eyes huge, her mouth hanging open. I don't think I've ever seen her look less composed.

I can't look at Dad. I can't even move a muscle, but I see Savannah shoving him from behind.

Savannah's eyes sweep the room. I start breathing fast, anxious breaths. My clothes are scattered everywhere. My bra is lying over a chair out in the open. Finally, my gaze lifts up to

Dad. I've never seen him so shocked, like a rug has been yanked out from under him and his non-leg has been swiped in a matter of seconds.

We all watch as Dad slowly raises his hands up in front of him, shaking his head. His focus zooms in on Brody, who looks absolutely petrified. "How could you? I trusted you. Anything else…anything at all could be forgivable, but this—"

"Listen, just let me explain—" Brody pleads.

"Don't talk to me right now! I'm trying very hard not to kill you, and I suggest you don't give me another reason to add onto this pile." Dad turns to me, his features sharp. "Get your clothes, Ann."

I'm still frozen in place, my gaze bouncing between Dad and Brody. But when Dad raises his voice and adds, "Now!" I move quickly, snatching my jeans and my Royals T-shirt from the floor. Savannah tucks my bra and panties into the pile in my arms and steers me toward the door.

"We were gonna tell you," Brody starts, even though Dad told him not to say anything.

"Tell me what?" Dad booms. "That you're playing games with my daughter?"

"You didn't have a problem with me hanging out with her before," Brody argues.

"That's because I never thought you'd cross that line with her!" Dad is turning a light shade of purple. I sink back against Savannah, not sure what to do. I want to say something, but I don't want to make things worse. "I've spent practically her whole life keeping her away from guys like you."

"Guys like me?" Brody repeats, hurt and disgust rolling around with the words. "You mean a former juvenile delinquent from the wrong side of the tracks? Right. I get it."

"It's true. That's what you are. What the hell do you want me to say? That I'm okay with all that?" Dad's voice shakes. "I thought you were better than what they say about you, but you're not. You're not the man I thought you were."

The pain on Brody's face is so obvious, it's almost too hard to look at him. It hurts too much.

"Jim…" Savannah says, stepping around me to grip the back of Dad's shirt. "That's enough."

Dad shrugs off her grip but turns, heading for the door. His hands land on my shoulders, and he pushes me out in front of him. He doesn't let go of me until we're safely in the confines of my and Lenny's suit.

I turn to face him. I need to tell him it's my fault, not Brody's. "Dad—"

He stops me, his hands balling up at his sides. "Not now, Ann. Not now."

"But Dad," I say, my clothes still in my arms, "it's not Brody's fault."

I move closer, and he backs away. Tears tumble down my cheeks. I hate this wall between us. We've never had a wall before. "Please, Dad, just listen to me. This isn't a one-time thing. We've been together—like a real couple—for a while."

"Is that supposed to help me understand what the hell is going on in my own daughter's life? Is that supposed to make me feel better about you screwing a nineteen-year-old ballplayer?" He shakes his head. "I don't even know you right now."

The knot full of guilt that I had in my stomach yesterday over Brody's game is nothing compared to the one I have now. For lying to Dad. For hiding this from him. I never want to see him so disappointed, so shocked, so lonely again.

I drop the clothes from my arms and tighten the borrowed

robe. "Dad, tell me what to do to fix this. Please, I'll do anything…" I choke up on the last word, swallowing back more tears.

Some of the anger drops from Dad's face, and he finally
meets my gaze. "Anything?"

I exhale, close my eyes, and nod.

"Stay away from him," Dad says, his voice quiet but dead
serious. "No calling, no texting, no running together, no ball-
games."

The lump in my throat grows, and several more tears spill
down my cheeks, but I wipe them away quickly. I want to tell
him that I can't give up Brody, but I know if I do, things will
never be good between him and Brody again. And I can't do
that to Brody. He needs my dad, in some ways more than he'll
ever need me. I wrap my arms around my waist and manage to
say, "Okay."

Relief washes over Dad's features, and he moves closer,
both hands landing gently on my arms. He lowers his head until
we're at eye level. "Look at me, Ann." I draw in a breath and
nod. "I know his type. I know that down the road, this will be the
best decision you'll ever make. Trust me, okay?"

The door to Lenny's bedroom opens, and she emerges
wearing pajama pants and a confused expression. A knock on
the hotel room door followed by Savannah alerting us that
it's her on the other side—where was that warning earlier in
Brody's room?—causes Dad to release me and let Savannah in.

"Did I miss something?" Lenny whispers to me.

I just shake my head and wipe away a few more tears that
escape.

Dad and Savannah have this silent showdown. I don't know
what it's about, but he turns his head, looking pissed off all over
again. His hand is on the door, ready to leave, but before he does,

he turns to Lenny and me. "Do not leave this room, understand?"

Savannah touches his shoulder. "Jim, you can't go back to—"

"I'm just going for a damn walk," Dad snaps, and then he's on the other side of the door.

I sink onto the couch, finally feeling the impact of what has just happened. What I've just agreed to.

My hands are shaking and I'm crying again when Savannah stands in front of me and asks, calm professional face planted on, "How long has this been going on?"

I wipe my face and take a breath. "Since summer…end of June, I think."

She looks at Lenny. "I take it you knew?"

Lenny's eyes widen. She looks from Savannah to me and finally nods, probably realizing what has happened this morning while she slept in.

Savannah sighs. "You should have told me, Annie. It goes beyond you and your dad. Brody's reputation is on the line. Do you know what this could do to him? You know better than anyone how hard he's worked to overcome all these obstacles, to be respected."

"It's not my fault people are so judgmental and won't see us as anything but Brody hooking up with a high school girl," I say with some trace of defiance. I need to argue with someone about this. Dad was too hurt to have this fight with him.

"No," Savannah says, returning the defiance and anger. "That's what they'll think if you sneak around and get caught. If someone else is the one to break the story."

"I'm sorry," I say.

But Savannah isn't finished. "Sneaking around is what impulsive, immature teenagers do, Annie. If you want the relationship to be taken seriously, if you want to be treated like an adult, then you should have been honest and upfront about it. I could have worked with this. I could have spun it into a story that people would root for rather than look down on. But that's a little hard to do when there's evidence of Brody at red carpet premieres and big fund-raisers with girls who aren't you."

The knot of guilt doubles in size. I should have listened to Brody a month ago when he wanted to tell Dad. All I could think about was myself and how I didn't want to confront Dad about it. How hard it would be for me. Never once, even last night, did I really see myself telling Dad, standing up to him and asking for him to accept us. And we just punched him right in the gut with it instead of easing him into the idea. In Dad's mind, Brody and I went from friends to naked in a hotel room together. Overnight.

The tears come down at a nonstop pace, and Lenny takes a seat beside me, her body stiff with nerves. I shake my head and finally say, "It doesn't matter now. It's over."

chapter 29

BRODY: You ok?

BRODY: Annie, come on. talk to me…

BRODY: your dad won't even stand in the same dugout as me. I can't have both of you ignoring me

BRODY: ok. I get it now. You picked him. I would probably do the same. So yeah, I get it

"No cell phones, Annie," Coach K reminds me.

I glance over Brody's messages one last time—text messages that stopped more than a week ago—before dropping the phone into my gym bag. One of my teammates has my race number and safety pins in her hands, ready to help me.

I've read those texts from Brody at least a hundred times, and every time, this sinking feeling that I'm doing something wrong by not replying gets heavier. But it's the opposite. Replying would be wrong. I promised Dad. I shouldn't have even read Brody's words.

Another part of me argues, *What if it was an emergency? What if Brody needed something? Who else would he contact?* No one. He has no one else. But he might have my dad again if I stay away.

"You ready, Ann?"

I shake out of my haze and glance up to see Dad standing beside Coach K under our cross-country team's tent.

"Did you hear the news?" Dad says. "The Dartmouth track coach is here, recruiting distance runners."

I force a smile. After my teammate Kennedy has finished pinning on my number, I busy myself helping her with hers.

"Could be a big day for you," Dad says.

I attempt to joke. "With my grades?"

"You have a three point oh."

Technically this is true, but that's because an occasional A balances out an occasional C. I doubt Dartmouth lets in students with Cs. Athlete or not, they're still Ivy League. And this recruiter is not even watching my best events—the mile and two mile, on a track, not up and down muddy hills like this cross-country race. Which is three miles. A distance that seems especially daunting today.

Just when I'm about to fake an ankle sprain so I can go home and lie on my bed and stare at the ceiling, the varsity runners are called to the starting line. Dad gives me a hug and plants a kiss on top of my head, wishing me luck. I try to look fired up, but I'm not.

Not even a little bit.

All I can think about when the gun fires, signaling the start of the race, or when I'm barely making my way to the middle of the pack, is how much I miss my runs with Brody. I miss thinking about him during a race. I miss thinking about him thinking about me.

With every runner that breezes past me, the voice in my head grows louder, telling me that I'm tired, that it hurts too much, that I can't. I just can't.

My chest aches, and my stomach, too. My arms and legs feel heavy, like dead weight. I rub my palm against my chest.

So this is what a broken heart feels like.

"Are you hurt? Sick?" Dad asks on the ride home from the meet.

Yes. I'm hurt and sick. Even on my worst day, my times are never terrible, so it wasn't a total flop. But I definitely didn't give Dartmouth any reason to overlook my non-spectacular grades.

I shrug and stare out the passenger window. Dad pats my leg and smiles. "Dartmouth is probably full of east coast snobs anyway."

I glance at him for a second, attempting a smile, and then clutch my phone tightly in one hand. I can't read Brody's messages again like I want to, but I can feel them through my fingers. He understands why I'm doing what I'm doing. Why I'm choosing Dad. That should make this easier, but it only makes me worry about Brody more.

Dad pulls into our driveway but doesn't move to get out of the car. "I've got to get to the stadium. We started batting practice at ten, so I'm already late."

"Right." The pennant race. Game one. This afternoon. Yankees. I grip the door handle, preparing to exit. "Thanks for coming to my race, Dad. You're allowed to miss one every once in a while, you know?"

He grins. "Not a chance."

"Even if I suck, like today?"

The smile drops from his face. "You didn't suck, Ann. You qualified for state. Nothing sucky about that."

I exhale and nod, the heaviness returning to my legs and chest.

"Get some rest, okay? Load up on carbs." Dad reaches for my hand and gives it a squeeze. "I love you."

"Love you, too, Dad." Tears are brimming in my eyes, so I exit quickly and head for the front door before he can see any fall down my face. I can't even explain the emotional outbursts that keep hitting me when I least expect it. It's been this way for well over a week. It's more than breakup aftermath. Something is wrong, something I need to fix or undo. I can't shake it. Nothing I do to please Dad is helping. And I thought it would. I thought Dad's forgiveness was the answer.

After dismissing Caroline, I curl up with Grams on the couch while she watches the Game Show Network. I try to hide the fact that I'm crying even though Grams isn't going to tell Dad or anyone, but she still notices.

She shakes her head at me. "Always so dramatic, Ginny." But then she lifts a hand, reaches over, and rubs my back until I fall asleep. I try to pretend it's the real Grams with me, the one who knows me as Annie. It helps a little.

When I wake up nearly two hours later, Grams is still beside me—thank God—but she's no longer watching Game Show Network.

She's turned on the ballgame. Even though I vowed not to watch it, even though it's probably going to kill me to see Brody on the pitcher's mound, I sit up, eyeing the remote control lying on the couch between Grams and me.

And I leave it right where it is.

chapter 30

"*R*ookie of the Year or not, Jason Brody should come out *of this game.*"

And that's how I find out that Brody was voted Rookie of the Year. Not from him, not from Dad or even Savannah, not from the internet or newspapers, because I've steered clear of those. The source of this big piece of news comes from an offhand comment the game announcers make during the seventh inning.

Over the course of the game, I've drifted from the couch, to the living room carpet, to sitting a foot from the TV like maybe if I get close enough I can teleport to the game.

"*He's struggling, Bob. Frank Steadman might have claimed this flu wouldn't affect his pitching, but obviously it has.*"

Flu? Is Brody sick?

"*And this is not the kind of game you want to play at less than a hundred percent.*"

I snatch my phone from the coffee table and quickly type in: Jason Brody flu. While I'm waiting for results, I watch Grams's head fall to the side. Her trademark snoring rises above the announcers' voices.

The headlines pop up on my phone, all stating the same thing: Royals pitcher and Rookie of the Year is down and out with a nasty flu bug during the biggest game series of his life.

My own grim feelings get pushed aside, while I lean in closer to the TV, studying Brody. He looks pale. The camera zooms in on his face as he winds up, showing the dark purple lines beneath his eyes. He looks miserable.

Brody walks another Yankee batter, and Frank calls a time-out. Frank walks toward Dad first, but Dad turns his back and heads to the bullpen. To an outsider, it probably looks like they made a decision about who to put in Brody's place and Dad has gone to let the pitcher know, but I'm not sure that's what happened. I think Frank tried to ask for Dad's input, and he refused.

Because Brody is involved.

Now who's being immature?

Frank joins Brody on the mound, claps him on the shoulder, and they duck their heads, exchanging words. The station goes to commercial for three minutes and when they return, Brody is in the dugout, now wearing a jacket zipped all the way up. His head is resting against the wall of the dugout like he's not strong enough to hold it up.

I snatch the remote and crank the volume up so I can hear the announcers over Grams's snoring.

"What most people don't realize is the toll dehydration can take on your body. Especially when you're playing a game this big. There's no room for weakness."

"Let's just hope Brody gets the rest and hydration he needs before it's his turn in the lineup again. The Royals owe much of their record-breaking season to this rookie."

"Absolutely, Bob. Also, Frank Steadman and Jim Lucas have

really done a great job turning this team around."

There is about five seats' worth of space between Brody and the other players on the bench. One of the trainers squats down in front of him, exchanging words we can't hear. Brody shakes his head, accepts the wet towel the trainer hands him, and then closes his eyes.

Dad is far away, in the bullpen. Frank is near the other end of the bench watching the game with a careful eye. And Brody is alone.

Miserable and alone.

I sink back onto my butt, putting some distance between the TV and me. Now that the shock of that morning in Brody's Chicago hotel room has worn off, I'm able to process the words Dad said to him.

"I've spent practically her whole life keeping her away from guys like you."

It's what Brody feared more than anything. What had he said to me only a month ago when he first wanted to tell Dad about us?

"All I know is that I want to be the person you and your dad think I am. Maybe even more than I want to be a great pitcher."

If I had just let him talk to Dad right then. If we had marched straight over to my house and confessed to everything, maybe Brody would still be that good person in Dad's eyes. Maybe he wouldn't be sitting by himself on the bench, sick and miserable.

I reach for my phone, ready to text him, but I stop myself. No, that's impulsive and immature. I promised Dad. I need to go about this the right way this time.

I have energy flowing through my veins for the first time in forever. And the problem—the feeling I've been carrying around for days that something was wrong—is suddenly clear.

Choosing Dad had seemed like the responsible choice, but really, all it accomplished was to shut Brody out. Because no matter what, I'm always gonna be there for Dad. He always has me. And I have him.

I just need to convince him of this. And if he refuses to let me talk to Brody, then I need to convince him that he has to. Someone has to.

t's late evening by the time Dad gets home. The game was tied after the ninth inning, and it took three more innings for the Yankees to score another run and take the win. I've showered and cooked Dad's favorite pasta for dinner. The table is set.

"It smells good in here," Dad says after walking into the kitchen. He smiles at me, but he looks exhausted. Shutting people out of your life who you have to see or hear about every day is exhausting.

"Thanks." I wait until we're both seated and have our plates full of food before beginning the grown-up chat I have planned. "So...how's Brody doing? He looked really sick during the game."

Dad keeps his eyes on the plate in front of him and shrugs. "The flu is going around the team. Lots of the pitchers are coming down with it."

"Yeah, but none of them had to play today." When he doesn't respond to that, I shift topics. "How come you didn't mention that Brody got Rookie of the Year?"

He finally looks at me, one eyebrow lifting. "I think you know why."

"Yeah, I do." I set down my fork. "You know how you said

that I would be really happy down the road if I decided not to…
be with Brody?"

"Annie," Dad warns. "I'm not changing my mind, so if moping around and then turning into Suzie Homemaker is part of your plot to get me to rethink this, I can assure you that my opinions aren't going to change."

"I haven't been moping around!" I exhale and calm myself down. Yelling is a little too teenage girl, and I'm trying to not be that. In a week, I'll be eighteen. A real adult. So it's time to practice. "I'm not asking you to change your mind about that." *Not yet, anyway.* "But I do think that what you're doing to Brody is wrong. Have you even talked to him? Have you checked to see if he's doing okay?"

Dad rolls his eyes. "He'll be fine in a few days."

"I'm glad *you're* so sure of that." I stare at him, hoping to catch a glimpse of guilt or remorse on his face, but he's stone cold.

"Is this some kind of teenage rebellion?" Dad challenges. "It's that why you were so off in the race this morning? Are you really planning on ruining your future over a boy who probably would have run all over you?"

"Dad, stop." I close my eyes, fighting off the hurt. Why does he think I'm so impossible to love? Or Brody so incapable of loving? I know Brody never said he loved me, but we were right there hovering around it. It wasn't meaningless. "You are not listening to me."

Dad gestures with one hand, giving me permission to continue, but I can tell he'd rather I didn't.

"I met his mom in Chicago—did you know that? She's horrible. She won't even acknowledge that her son might be a decent person. I gave her tickets to the game, but she didn't come.

He hasn't seen her in years. He's never seen his father…"

"What's your point, Annie?" The words are sharp, but it's obvious some of this information has surprised Dad.

"He hates everything about his past; he's ashamed of it. And you were the only person who accepted him. He respected you. He needs you. I know you don't really hate him, Dad."

He pushes away from the table and stands up so abruptly that I jump. "I'm done with this conversation. Brody is work. It's none of your concern."

I look him right in the eyes. "It's still Brody, Dad. He's the same person he was when you first met him. And he doesn't have anyone else but us."

For a second, I catch a flicker of guilt in Dad's eyes, but then he shakes his head. "I'm not choosing him over my own damn daughter, Annie."

"Who says you have to choose?" But he's already down the hall, walking toward his bedroom, slamming the door behind him.

I lean my head against the table, my hands shaking from the built-up emotion. But I do feel a sense of resolve. Maybe I didn't come right out and say this to Dad, but he has to know that if he's not planning on being there for Brody, I'm sure as hell not going to leave him alone.

chapter 31

"You shouldn't be here."

My stomach sinks. Brody looks even worse than he did on TV this afternoon. His useful shirtless-in-doors look has been replaced with baggy sweatpants and a long-sleeve Royals T-shirt.

And oh my God, how have I gone this many days without seeing him in person? I'm hit with a tidal wave of emotions—panic, excitement, fear…It's all there and relevant.

I ignore his suggestion and hold up the shopping bags in my hands. "These are really heavy. Maybe I can come in and set them down somewhere…?"

I'm trying to be all cool and casual, but as I look at his face a little longer, I'm thinking about the last time we were together and about all the things I said to Dad earlier…And before I can stop myself, I'm dropping the bags in the hallway and pulling him closer, pressing my cheek against his shirt.

Brody leans into me and sighs, his strong arms squeezing me like bands of steel, like he wanted to lock me in place and never let me go. "Does your dad know you're here?"

"Not exactly," I admit, and then reluctantly pull away, snatching my bags off the floor. He's sick enough to be a little slow today, and I duck under his arm and enter the apartment before he can stop me. "I'm not *intentionally* going behind his back."

"Really? 'Cause that's what it sounds like." Brody closes the door behind him and locks the deadbolt.

"I gave him a proper warning. He won't be surprised to find me here."

Brody walks across the apartment and then seems to get dizzy, because he stops and leans against the wall right beside his bedroom door. "I wish I could stand here and chat with you, but I'm not really up for it. And you should go, Annie. You're going to get sick."

I carry the bags over to him and nudge him from behind until he starts walking toward his bed. "They have these things called flu shots. It's this really advanced medical breakthrough…"

He sits down on the side of his bed and flashes me a half-hearted smile. "I missed this. You pissing me off." He holds my gaze. "I miss *you*."

My heart is breaking and piecing back together all at the same time. I want to go to him, hold him, reassure him that he's not lost me forever, but I need to stick to my plan. First, get him well again so he can kick ass in the series… "I brought Gatorade and soup and Jell-O…and cold medicine."

After I place all the supplies on the nightstand beside Brody, he stretches out across the bed, pulling the thick blanket up to his neck. I sit beside him and try not to think about kissing him again. My head turns in his direction, but I keep a good two feet between our mouths. "Did I forget anything? Do you need anything else?"

He fumbles around underneath the covers, finally pulling

out his hand and lacing his fingers through mine. "Just you. This sucks. Everything sucks right now."

"I'm only staying a few minutes," I blurt out before I change my mind. I'd forgotten how warm his hands are, how well they cover mine. "Give me some time. I'm gonna try and fix at least some of this mess, okay?"

Brody closes his eyes, like they won't stay open any longer. "He's right. Jim is right. I'm not the kind of guy someone would want with his daughter. What kind of guy sneaks around and…" His voice fades away, but we both know the end of that sentence.

The lump returns to my throat. I hate that Dad said that to him. "No. No way. He's wrong. He knows he's wrong. It's just me— He doesn't want *me* with anyone. And the way he found out…"

Brody flinches. "God, I was such an idiot."

"We both kind of were. But I should have listened to you. We should have told him sooner. If we did it your way, we would have." I rest my free hand on his forehead. It's burning up. "You should get some rest."

Brody lays his fingers against my cheek. "If I text you, will you answer?"

I grip his fingers, keeping them on my skin. "Yeah, I will. I mean, I don't really have a choice. If my dad isn't going to talk to you, then it's got to be me. You're in a pennant race— you need moral support."

He smiles with his eyes closed. "You are absolutely right. I need moral support. And emoticons. Lots of them."

I lean forward and kiss his forehead. "Promise you'll stay hydrated and call Savannah if you get worse? She's a mom. She knows all kinds of sick-people things, probably way more than me."

I only hang around about fifteen more minutes before Brody is fast asleep. Even with him out cold, it's hard to leave. *I love him.* That's not something I can turn off just because Dad asked me to. And it isn't just him I love, it's his scent—something this apartment is engulfed in—his being around me, the texting, knowing that he'd come over if I were sick. Probably even during a pennant race *without* a flu shot. But none of those are the real reasons I came over tonight. I came because he needed someone. Even if he wasn't willing to ask for help, he needed someone. That's why I don't care if Dad knows.

I creep quietly out of Brody's apartment, leaving the lamp on and locking the door behind me. I need to talk to Savannah now. And I can get her to check on Brody. Or Frank, maybe. I want Dad to trust me, so I *do* need to limit the home-nurse visits myself. Especially considering the fact that it took nearly all my self-control to *not* crawl under the covers with him.

"Annie," Savannah says after opening the door to her apartment. "What's wrong?"

I spot Lily at the dining room table in her pajamas with a full cup of hot chocolate. I look back at Savannah and keep my voice low. "Remember how you said you could have spun the Annie/Brody story to be positive…?"

I'm literally wringing my hands, anticipating the rare, stern, yelling Savannah's return. And really, it's justified. I should have told her. She would have been professional about it on her end.

She rests a hand on her hip, swinging the door open for me. "Just couldn't stay away from each other, huh?"

She's trying to be sarcastic, I can tell, but I don't miss the amusement in her voice. Maybe she knew all along we'd be back in this place. Maybe she's just doing her job and dealing with what's handed to her.

She settles Lily down in front of the TV, warning her three times not to spill the hot chocolate, and then we both sit at her dining table.

"This isn't about dating," I explain, and her eyebrows lift. "Not only about dating, anyway. My dad won't even talk to Brody, won't look at him. I went over to his apartment to check on him, and Dad should have done that."

She covers her face and groans. "Seriously, Annie?"

"I only stayed a few minutes, and he was barely coherent."

She drops her hands. "He looked terrible during the game today. I felt so bad for him. It's an off day tomorrow, so I'll stop by and check on him."

"Good." I nod. "So what should we do? You know my dad doesn't really hate him. Should we force them into a room together until he comes to this conclusion himself?"

Savannah stares at me for a long moment. "You two really are...you know, serious? It's not just a temporary crush?"

"I think so." My cheeks warm, and I drop my gaze to my hands. "I know *I'm* serious, but I can only speak for myself. You can ask Brody what he is."

"You didn't give Jim much of an opportunity to ease into the idea," Savannah points out. "Maybe you tell your dad that dating is off the table right now." I open my mouth to protest but she waves a hand for me to stop. "For now. And you give him some time, at least until the series is over, to get used to you talking to Brody again. And maybe he'll follow suit. In the meantime, I'll work on the story. Who knows, you might have him warmed to the idea before the season is over."

I doubt that, but whatever. I'll take it. It's way better having this plan than feeling all helpless and depressed like I was this morning.

I stand up, preparing to leave, and another idea pops into my head. "Can Lenny and I go to New York with you and Lily next week?"

"Oh," Savannah says, mocking me. "You mean game four of the series when Brody will pitch again?"

"Please," I beg. "We'll watch Lily for you, and you can go see the Empire State Building or whatever. We'll sit with you and all that. Adult supervision. And we'll do whatever you say... Well, I will. I can't speak for Lenny."

She laughs and glances at Lily, who has a mouth full of cocoa but gives her mom two thumbs up.

"It's my birthday next week..."

"Your eighteenth birthday," she concedes. "Guess I can't really say no. And we do have two doubles in our hotel room..." She narrows her eyes. "But you have to break the news to your dad."

"Got it." I head for the door for real this time. "Thanks, Savannah."

She waves away the thank-you, saying, "Any time."

When I get home a few minutes later, I bust right into Dad's room, flipping on the light. He must have been asleep because he sits up, looking confused.

"I went to Brody's apartment to drop off some soup. Nothing happened," I blurt out. Dad's mouth falls open, but I don't let him get a word in. "I'm going to go along with your wishes partially, and I'm not going to date him. But you can't keep me from talking to him. Or watching the games. He's my friend, and I'm his. And I think he used to be your friend. So if you're going to keep ignoring him, then I can't do the same. I'm turning eighteen next week, in case you forgot, so it's time you start thinking of me as an adult—capable of making adult decisions about my own life and who I love."

Dad scrubs his hands over his face. "Annie—"

I hold up a hand to stop him again. "I don't need to hear your thoughts again. I'm doing the right thing, and you know it."

I flip off the light switch, leaving him in the dark. "Also, I'm going to New York with Savannah next week to watch Brody play."

I'm out of his room fast and behind the safety of my locked bedroom door before he can protest. I might be bolder today, but I'm still shaking and not wanting to continue the confrontation.

And I'm so not willing to be "just friends" with Brody indefinitely. We're more than that. We will always be more than that. But all I can do is cross my fingers that Savannah is right. That Dad needs time to digest it slowly, in bits, with all clothing intact.

chapter 32

ME: Feeling better?

BRODY: Much

ME: Good 🙂

BRODY: Great, actually 🙂

ME: Guess what?

BRODY: You're secretly twenty-one and we can elope in the off-season?

ME: Ha! I'm coming to watch your game.

BRODY: What game?! Tonight? In New York?

ME: yep. I'm in NYC right now with Len and Savannah/Lily

BRODY: 🙂 🙂 🙂 *thanks, Annie. This is a pretty awesome surprise*

ME: You're welcome. Make it worth my time, all right?

BRODY: whatever you want

ME: good luck 😊

BRODY: Oh and Annie? Happy birthday. 😊

"If you want to get excited and squeal to everyone that's your boyfriend, I won't make fun of you," Lenny says, elbowing me in the side.

For only the second time in his career, Brody played starting pitcher today.

Right before the game, our top starter dislocated his elbow. Unfortunately, I had to witness this and nearly puked when I got a glimpse of the out-of-place joint. The other starter was coming off four days in a row of pitching and Brody was fresher and more ready, so his name got pulled from the roster. To start in a championship game to decide if they go to the World Freaking Series...

I thought my heart was going to stop when I saw him take the mound for the first time, but now it's the top of the eighth inning and Jason Brody, rookie pitcher of the year, is currently in the midst of a perfect game.

The Yankees have managed to hit two of his pitches, but both were caught in the outfield. The Royals haven't let anyone on base. And the score is 1-0.

I hug Lily tighter on my lap, trying to keep both of us warm. Who knew October could be so damn cold?

"Why is he doing this to us?" I whine to Savannah, seated beside me. "I can't take this."

"I know. Me neither," Savannah says, and Lenny nods her

agreement from my other side.

"I like when the umpire yells, 'Strike!'" Lily says, mimicking the deep, firm voice. She repeats this a few more times while Brody gets ready on the mound to throw a real strike. *Hopefully.* "Look! I see ten and eleven innings on the scoreboard."

"Yep, but it's the eighth inning now," I remind her.

Lily hops up and down on my lap. "Let's have ten! That's way better than nine, right, Annie?"

"No!" Savannah and I both say together.

The Royals have already gone further this season than they have in decades. But the further you get, the more you want. And I know the team, including Brody and Dad, and probably everyone in Kansas City, want that World Series spot.

And now, we all want the perfect game. Thanks to Brody dangling it in front of our faces for this many innings.

We're right behind home plate, not more than ten or twelve rows up from the field. I've got a clear view of Brody adjusting the ball in his hand, breathing smoke from the cold air. Dad shifts his weight from his foot to his non-leg in the dugout. He hasn't been home much since I chewed him out last Saturday, so I don't know if he's pissed off. He's been texting updates and letting me know when he arrives places, but he still isn't talking to Brody. And I know *that* for a fact because I *am*.

"Come on, Brody," Savannah whispers beside me, but I catch her looking at Dad, too, and not the pitcher.

I lean in close to her, away from Lily. "You know he is legally divorced now…"

She shoots me a look, and I laugh but shut my mouth. It's only the hundredth time I've said those same words to her since we left Kansas City. I figure a hundred more and maybe she'll be the brave one and ask him out. Brody says single moms are extremely careful with who they date because the guys will be around their kids. But Dad and Lily already get along just fine. Plus, he did raise me pretty much on his own. That has to count for something.

"Strike!" Lily says, along with the umpire. Oh God. Only one more inning separates Brody from a perfect game. He must be so excited. And scared.

"Are we done yet?" Lily asks, pointing to the Royals leaving the field to file into the dugout.

Brody pauses briefly in front of Dad but moves into the dugout when it's obvious he's not going to say anything. Instead, Frank and Dad converse privately, their heads close together.

"No, sweetie," I say, rubbing my hands together. "We get one more at bat, and then the other team gets another shot at the bat. And if they don't score? Brody will be famous." I'm not sure how I feel about that last statement. Excited for Brody, obviously. But also a little nervous about *us*.

"You look cold." Lily hops off my lap and places her blue earmuffs on my head. Then she wanders down the row of seats, stopping to visiting with some of the other players' wives and kids seated in this section.

"I did ask him out," Savannah tells me a few minutes later, keeping her eyes on the field.

My frozen hands and toes are quickly forgotten, along with the game hanging by a thread. "Wait…what?"

She looks like she might be blushing, but we're all red-faced from the temperature. "He said he had to talk to you first."

I spin around to face her and feel Lenny leaning in, eavesdropping and probably soon joining in on our conversation. "Why would he say that? Seriously? He's such a wimp!"

"You did throw quite a few fits about your mom," Lenny

reminds me. "Maybe he doesn't want to deal with your tantrums."

I elbow her in the side but laugh. She's got a point. "How did he sound when he said, *'I'll have to ask Annie first'*?"

"Did he say anything before that?" Lenny adds.

Savannah glances at us for a second, then back at the field. "It wasn't the cop-out answer you're making it into. It was a grown-up discussion."

I roll my eyes when she says *grown-up*. "I'm eighteen today, remember?"

Lenny and I sit there waiting for Savannah to tell us more details while Third Base hits a ground ball toward the shortstop and gets the second out for the Royals at the bottom of the eighth inning.

"I'm not gonna sit here and gossip about your dad, if that's what you think," Savannah finally says after noticing Lenny and me still staring at her.

I face forward again, folding my arms over my chest. "Fine. I'll get him to tell me, then."

She fights a smile. "You do that, Annie."

Maybe it's a selfish thought, but it seems like if Dad dated Savannah, maybe it would be easier for him to accept Brody and me. Because I'm going insane right now from lack of Jason Brody kisses and lack of in-person contact at all. This is the closest we've been since I brought him soup last Saturday. And there is a hell of a lot of space between us right now. Literal and metaphorical.

"I bet they hooked up and haven't gone on a real date," Lenny whispers to me.

"Stop." I shake the image from my head. I'm perfectly happy living under the delusion that my dad and Savannah will have a G-rated relationship if they do end up dating.

We both shut up quickly when Lenny's dad comes to the plate. If anyone is going to hit a homer today, it's First Base. He's due for one. And that would lift the pressure off Brody next inning.

First Base connects with the very first pitch, and our entire row pulls in a deep breath. The ball soars way out into center field.

But before it can cross over the wall, the Yankees outfielder leaps up to an inhuman height and snatches the ball right out of the cold air. The stadium erupts with cheers, while our section remains seated.

In the dugout, Brody scrubs his hands over his face, shakes out his arms, then grabs his glove before heading to the field.

He wanted that home run. It would have taken so much pressure off of him. One tiny run from the Yankees and this game is tied. And Brody's arm has got to feel like a wet noodle by now...

Lily skips her way back to her open seat on Savannah's other side, blocking my view of Brody's first pitch, but I hear the bat connect with the ball. I nudge Lily out of the way in time to see Brody dive through the air and catch an infield grounder, throwing it carefully to first base.

"Oh my God, this is awful," I shout.

The Yankees fans seated in the row in front of us turn around to give me bewildered looks, and I smile sheepishly. "I meant the weather."

Two more outs. Two more outs.

I rub my hands together, no longer feeling the cold. The entire Royals' dugout is on its feet, leaning against the fence.

Brody attempts a few of his newer pitches—a slider and a curveball—gaining the batter two balls and zero strikes.

"What if he walks someone?" Lenny asks.

I shake my head, indicating that it would end the perfect game. "He could still get a no-hitter with a walk. But for a perfect game, we can't let anyone on base."

Brody throws a decent curveball this time, surprising the Yankee batter, and earns a strike. Boos erupt as the fans protest the call, but the strike was perfectly clear from our seats behind home plate.

The booing and the roller coaster of emotions oozing from the fans seem to have rattled Brody. He takes an uncharacteristically long time pulling his cleats through the dirt, adjusting his hat, and rolling the ball around his right hand before finally making the throw.

Brody throws a fastball that registered at only 86 mph. Not his fastest. The batter connects with the ball, and I almost cover my eyes, my stomach turning dozens of cartwheels. But Short Stop sweeps up the ball from the ground and makes a perfect long throw to first, and Lenny's dad makes the catch seconds before the batter tags the base.

"Oh my God! I just had a heart attack," I say.

Holy shit. We have two outs.

"This is insane," I say.

"He's getting tired, isn't he?" Lenny says. "That last pitch was slow."

I exhale and nod. "Slow for him."

Savannah opens her mouth to respond but is distracted by Frank calling a timeout. Well, not so much the timeout, but more that Dad—Dad!—is the one walking out to the pitcher's mound.

Oh my God, is the first thing he says to Brody in nearly two weeks going to be, *You're out of the game*? He's not that angry, is he?

"What's he doing?" I ask Savannah. "Are they pulling Brody out?"

"Why would they do that when he's throwing a perfect game?" Lenny protests.

"It still counts if you switch pitchers."

"Oh no, what are you doing, Jim?" Savannah mumbles, but she's not watching Dad, she's staring at her phone, shaking her head. "This is not going to work."

"What? What's he doing?" I grasp Savannah's shoulder, but she brushes me off. She's not explaining.

Brody looks up, clearly surprised to see Dad in front of him. He adjusts his hat again, keeping his head down while listening to Dad. Even from our seats, I see his body stiffen, his eyes lift to meet Dad's, his mouth hanging open.

What the hell is he saying to him? I have to know! Is he pulling him out of the game or what?

Dad turns abruptly and hobbles off the field like this wasn't a huge mega event in the world of Jason Brody and Jim Lucas. Brody's still standing there like he's in shock. Savannah covers her face with both hands and groans. "I don't know if this is a good idea…"

She chances a glance in my direction and then refocuses on the field.

"What?" I demand.

But both of us are glued to Brody now as he drags his cleats through the dirt. Adjusts his hat. Pulls at his collar and rolls his shoulders. And then he gazes straight down home plate.

He winds up, a look of pure determination on his face. The pitch is a fastball.

I don't even need to hear the umpire or Lily yell "Strike" to know that he hit the mark. I do glance up at the scoreboard to see the speed: 99 mph.

Come on, Brody. Come on.

I squeeze my eyes shut after the next throw, listening for the sound of the ball hitting the pocket of our catcher's glove.

"Strike two!"

100 mph.

I grip the seat in front of me, leaning in to see Brody catch the ball and accept the signal from the catcher. He pauses and lifts his eyes upward until he's looking right into our section. It's dark out and the stadium lights are bright. I don't know if he can see me, but I stare hard enough for both us.

One more strike. Just one more.

The game moves in slow motion, Brody inching his way through his pre-pitch rituals, and I'm thinking about Grams and wishing she were here even if she wouldn't know what was going on. And I wish Brody's mom were here watching. Maybe she's watching on TV somewhere, but I wish she were here in person. Witnessing her kid out there looking more like a grown man. One who is kind and selfless and hard-working. Someone she should be proud to call hers. Why is it so hard for people to accept what's right in front of them? Like Dad with Brody.

Brody tosses one more glance in Dad's direction and draws in a deep breath, nodding at the catcher. He winds up and releases the ball. I squeeze my eyes shut and listen to the sound of the perfect pitch smacking the catcher's glove.

101 mph.

chapter 33

The field is a zoo of TV cameras, reporters, players, and family. I push through several clusters of people, glancing over shoulders, trying to find Dad.

I spot him and Frank about three yards away, but before I can get to them, I spot Brody and I can't move anywhere else. I mean, I literally can't with all these people on the field.

An ABC News reporter shoves a microphone into Brody's face. "A perfect game *and* the Royals are going to the World Series. Bet that feels great." Brody laughs because, well, *duh*. "You looked like you were wiped out on the field before Coach Lucas came out in that last inning. What did he say to you on the mound?" the reporter guy asks. "What did he say to pull those hundred-mile-an-hour pitches out of you?"

Brody's eyes search the crowd until they land on me. A grin spreads across his face, and he turns to the reporter and says, "He said if I was good enough to throw a perfect game, I'd be good enough to date his daughter."

If I wasn't frozen in shock before, I am now. My mouth falls open and then before I can process, Brody is abandoning his interview and parting the crowd, reaching for me.

I'm swept off my feet so fast I almost scream. For about half a second, when my eyes are first meeting Brody's, I forget about the rest of the world and about internet and newspapers and Twitter and Facebook. My arms go around his neck, squeezing him tight. He returns my feet to the ground but pulls me in closer. Before I can protest, Jason Brody is kissing me like we're alone in his apartment. The euphoria of witnessing his series-winning, perfect-game-achieving pitch returns and I'm kissing him back, more tears sliding down my cheeks.

He pulls his mouth from mine after way too many seconds have passed and wraps me up in another feet-lifting hug. "*Eres la persona más maravillosa que he conocido. Te amo, Annie.*" His voice is rough with emotion.

"I know what you just said," I say, unable to hold back my grin. "I'm not *that* bad at Spanish. And it counts, by the way. No matter what language you say those words in."

"I love you," he says in English this time, proving he knows it, too. "And FYI, we're going out with your dad tonight."

This is a good sign. A very good sign. "Maybe he was pulling your leg with that 'permission to date his daughter' deal. Plus, that's not a real date if my dad is there."

Brody leans in and kisses me again. "It is now that I get to hold your hand and call you my girlfriend if anyone asks."

"Really?" I squeal. He nods, and I throw my arms around his neck again. "So my dad said we could date and other people are allowed to know about it?"

"He did."

"And we can sneak away from everyone later and—"

Brody laughs. "Well, he didn't give me permission for that, but we're doing it anyway."

I pull away and look up at him. "Promise?"

"Promise."

My phone buzzes in my pocket, and from where we're standing, I can see Dad was texting. I glance at the message, not surprised that it's from Dad.

DAD: Happy Birthday 🙂

I smile and catch his eye before Brody tugs me in the direction of the Royals' publicity team, where I know he'll be asked a million and one questions about each inning of tonight's game. Our fingers are laced together in plain sight for anyone to photograph. Brody stops and turns to me before reaching the next reporter. "You *are* wearing my number under that jacket, right?"

After a long, dramatic pause, I slowly pull the zipper of my coat down until the number eleven jersey is revealed. "Of course, although Short Stop was looking pretty good out there tonight."

"Brat."

Epilogue

BRODY: can you post this on FB for me? "I am no longer dating a high school girl"

ME: what happened? Underage girls not your type anymore?

BRODY: not if they aren't you

ME: and I'm not in high school anymore. I get it 😊

BRODY: see you at Lenny's in 5

"Why is my name on that cake?" Brody's forehead wrinkles as he stares at the giant graduation cap–shaped cake the Londons splurged for after convincing Dad the combo Annie/Lenny party would be so much fun.

"It was Lenny's idea," I say quickly.

Lenny shakes her head. "No way. Savannah did this."

"Did what?" Dad and Savannah say from behind us.

Before we can point blame elsewhere, Jake London stands in front of the huge party-guest turnout (98 percent Lenny London guests) and raises his glass of champagne.

"Oh my God," Lenny mutters, "he's giving a speech. Why the hell is he giving a speech? Who does that at a graduation party?"

"Wishing you could go back to Spain?" I joke even though I know she missed her parents. A little.

Lenny grins. "You know me, I love drama."

At least nobody is throwing a punch.

Jake London and Dad seem to tolerate each other these days. Which is a far cry from this time last year. Brody and Jake London…that relationship is even better than Dad and Jake's.

Teammates becoming unlikely World Series Champions makes it way easier to put personal differences aside and bond.

"I would just like to thank my teammates for coming out here to celebrate two of the smartest and most athletic Royals' kids," Jake says. Lenny looks at me and rolls her eyes, but I can tell she's surprised by the compliment. She always says her parents rarely mention the fact that she's a straight-A honor student. "We've got a National Honor Society member and a two-time record-holding state champion in the one-mile run—"

"And the two mile!" Brody shouts.

I elbow him in the side, but I don't hate that he brought that up. After handing over the two-mile race to Jackie last year, I wasn't sure if I'd be able to get myself back up to the top. I did, and I even shaved a couple seconds from my time.

"And the two mile," Jake says, nodding in Brody's direction.

Brody's arm snakes around my waist, and he tugs me closer. He was probably more excited about my state win than I was. He even made sure the pitching rotation allowed him to watch my meet.

And then there were negotiations with the head coach from University of Kansas—who offered me a full ride. The way Brody and Dad attacked that woman… Let's just say I will never run out of clean towels in the locker room. And they have my favorite Gatorade flavors listed on letterhead.

"So why is my name on the cake?" Brody whispers into my ear while Jake London continues talking.

"I can't tell you." My face heats up, mostly from Brody's mouth on my neck, but also because I'm now terrible at keeping secrets from him.

"Is it a couple's thing? Or future planning? You know, if we were married, technically you'd be Annie Brody…"

Lenny overhears him and spins around to face us, pointing a finger. "If you propose at my graduation party, I'll kill you."

"You'd have to beat me to the job," Dad chimes in.

Ignoring them, I glance over my shoulder at Brody and smile. "You would sound way better with my last name than the other way around. Don't you think?"

Dad puts an arm around both of our shoulders, clapping his hands over Brody's and my mouths. "Enough of this marriage talk. I need to get through sending Annie away to college first."

"It's forty minutes away, Dad."

He shrugs, and we both return to listening to Jake London's lengthy speech. "In addition to my Harvard-bound daughter and Jim's daughter getting a full ride to University of Kansas, a top women's track and field school…we have one more academic achievement to acknowledge."

Mrs. London rushes forward and hands Jake the envelope Savannah must have given them earlier.

"My teammate and last season's Rookie of the Year, probably

the main reason we made it all the way to the World Series for the first time in decades, Jason Brody"—Jake holds up the certificate for everyone to see—"is now a high school graduate. And he completed his diploma while playing his first season in the major leagues. That's quite an accomplishment. I don't think many of us could have done both of those at once."

I back away from Brody so I can see his face—he's blushing, which is a rare thing for Brody, but he looks ecstatic. I reach out and squeeze his hand. Dad is the first to clap him on the back. But several of his teammates follow. My heart squeezes at how far he's come in a year—from the kid no one would give the time of day to, to having players treat him like a valued member of the team. One of them.

A few minutes later, Jake is finally done with his speech and Brody is standing beside me, staring at his GED. I lean in close to get a look.

"Pretty cool, huh?" he says.

I take the certificate from him and set it on the table beside us before reaching up to bring his face closer to mine so I can kiss him. "It would be even cooler with my last name," I say.

Brody laughs, but when his eyes meet mine, I can tell this idea isn't so much of a joke to him—well, the name part is, because what would people do with all those Jason Brody Rookie of the Year cards?—but us being together forever…he's pretty serious about that.

And so am I.

I glance over at Dad and catch him reaching for Savannah's hand. I shake my head, hardly able to believe they've gone there. Life is funny sometimes…the worst possible things can get you to the best possible places.

If you just enjoy the game.

acknowledgments

'd like to thank my superstar agent, Nicole Resciniti, for being the first to listen to this book idea and keeping me sane while I worked through the editorial phase. My Entangled editorial team: Heather Howland, Kari Olson, and Liz Pelletier for all the time and passion put into this story. Mark Perini and Gaby Navarro for helping with the Spanish translations.

My family, for their continued support, and all the readers who have stuck by me.

Don't miss these other romantic reads from Julie Cross:

For Tate and Claire, hockey isn't just a game. And they both might not survive a body check to the heart.

At Holden Prep, the rich and powerful rule the school...and they'll do just about anything to keep their dirty little secrets hidden.

Check out more of Entangled Teen's hottest reads...

REMEMBER ME FOREVER

by Sara Wolf

Isis Blake hasn't fallen in love in three years, forty-three weeks, and two days. Or so she thinks. The boy she maybe-sort-of-definitely loved and sort-of-maybe-definitely hated has dropped off the face of the planet, leaving a Jack Hunter–shaped hole. Determined to be happy, Isis fills it in with lies and puts on a brave smile for her new life at Ohio State University. But the smile lasts only until he shows up. The threat from her past, her darkest moment…Nameless, attending OSU right alongside her. Whispering that he has something Isis wants—something she needs to see to move forward. To move on.

Isis is good at pretending everything is okay, at putting herself back together. But Jack Hunter is better.

OTHER BREAKABLE THINGS

by Kelley York and Rowan Altwood

Luc Argent has always been intimately acquainted with death. After a car crash got him a second chance at life—via someone else's transplanted heart—he tried to embrace it. He truly did. But he always knew death could be right around the corner again. And now it is. Luc is ready to let his failing heart give out, ready to give up. A road trip to Oregon—where death with dignity is legal—is his answer. But along for the ride is his best friend, Evelyn. And she's not giving up so easily.

WHY I LOATHE STERLING LANE

by Ingrid Paulson

537 rules hold Harper's world together, until spoiled, seditious, self-righteous Sterling Lane corrupts her brother. Worst of all, Sterling has perfected the role of a charming, misguided student trying to make amends for his past transgressions, and only Harper sees him for the troublemaker he absolutely is. As Harper breaks Rule after precious Rule in her battle of wits against Sterling and tension between them hits a boiling point, she's horrified to discover that perhaps the two of them aren't as different as she thought, and MAYBE she doesn't entirely hate him after all. Teaming up with Sterling to save her brother might be the only way to keep from breaking the most important rule—protecting Cole.

VIOLET GRENADE

by Victoria Scott

DOMINO (def.): A girl with blue hair and a demon in her mind.
CAIN (def.): A stone giant on the brink of exploding.
MADAM KARINA (def.): A woman who demands obedience.
WILSON (def.): The one who will destroy them all.

When Madam Karina discovers Domino in an alleyway, she offers her a position inside her home for entertainers in secluded West Texas. Left with few alternatives and an agenda of her own, Domino accepts. It isn't long before she is fighting her way up the ranks to gain the madam's approval. But after suffering weeks of bullying and unearthing the madam's secrets, Domino decides to leave. It'll be harder than she thinks, though, because the madam doesn't like to lose inventory. But then, Madam Karina doesn't know about the person living inside Domino's mind. Madam Karina doesn't know about Wilson.